House My Father Built

by
Anna Kudro

DORRANCE PUBLISHING CO
EST. 1920
PITTSBURGH, PENNSYLVANIA 15238

The contents of this work, including, but not limited to, the accuracy of events, people, and places depicted; opinions expressed; permission to use previously published materials included; and any advice given or actions advocated are solely the responsibility of the author, who assumes all liability for said work and indemnifies the publisher against any claims stemming from publication of the work.

All Rights Reserved
Copyright © 2023 by Anna Kudro

No part of this book may be reproduced or transmitted, downloaded, distributed, reverse engineered, or stored in or introduced into any information storage and retrieval system, in any form or by any means, including photocopying and recording, whether electronic or mechanical, now known or hereinafter invented without permission in writing from the publisher.

Dorrance Publishing Co
585 Alpha Drive
Suite 103
Pittsburgh, PA 15238
Visit our website at *www.dorrancebookstore.com*

ISBN: 979-8-88925-077-7
eISBN: 979-8-88925-577-2

★ ★ ★

In gratitude for Josef and Emmi

★ ★ ★

*If history is a guide what happened in Czechoslovakia
can happen here in America if the Socialists have their way!*

*We don't want the Ukraine to become another Sudetenland…
Angela Merkel, German Chancellor*

*During the period of European migration German Tribes named the Boii
farmed a region they called Bohemia (Latin: hemia for home)
Over a thousand years until…*

*Around the year 700 a Russian clansmen named Czech brought his tribe
from Russia to Bohemia and named it Czech. As the Czech population
increased the German tribes were pushed into the surrounding mountains.
After WWI the Armistice Agreement gave birth to a new country
Czechoslovakia to be ruled by "Democratic Principles" as demanded by
President Woodrow Wilson*

*Germans living in the Sudeta mountain regions surrounding the newly
created country were given a new name "Sudeten Germans"*

*When evil replaced evil and ether dripped into veins slowly No one noticed
what was happening until it was too late and a diabolical frenzy for power
and control lead the world into a deadly abyss*

They once had it all…they had love…they had dreams…and a lot of Pain…

What was left

…LOVE…

Prologue

It was a warm October morning when the ship SS Berlin passed the Statue of Liberty and the looming canyons of skyscrapers. I had arrived dressed in a sable trimmed designer coat my father had bought, so I would not arrive as one of the "hungry and huddled masses" in a world he saw as one of glitz and glamour. I knew that the man I had adored and feared much of my eighteen years, had loved me after all. He had loved me so much, once he knew nothing could dissuade me from boarding the train that would take me to the seaport from which there was no return, he had made sure his little girl would arrive in style.

Unbeknown to me, my father had cleaned out the savings account he and my mother had scraped together over many years. My parents had hoped to build a real house at a future date. One morning my father dressed in his best suit, told my mother he would take me shopping and said to her. "You stay home because you'll spend hours turning over every price tag, looking for a bargain." I followed him to the tram and rode into the shopping center where he strode ahead to the most expensive fashion boutique in Kings Plaza. Never looking at a price tag he assembled an assortment of clothes fit for a queen. His gift of love was a sable fur trimmed coat that would deliver me to an uncertain fate.

A gift, I was forced to hock after my arrival in order to survive. Potential employers would take one look at my coat and I believed I could read their minds.

"With a coat like this...you don't look like you need a job." What an arduous journey it had been since my arrival, I dared not tell anyone. They would all tell me. "I told you so."

I leaned against the glass facade of the restaurant Windows of the World in the World Trade Center, and gazed dreamily at the broad stretch of lights across the Verrazano Bridge over the New York harbor. I was lost in memories of the day I had looked in awe upon the famous Lady Liberty upon my arrival as an 18-year-old immigrant.

I was awed and alone, blonde and blue-eyed. I could neither dance nor sing outside a choir stall. I was naïve about a world that was built upon competition. I had one dollar pinned to my ample bra and no marketable skills or talents with which I could earn a living. It was not hard to remember my history and what had driven me to leave home for an uncertain future to begin with? I remember stepping on my father's shoes with my bare feet when I was five and how he waltzed me around a room until my feet slid off his shoes. I stumbled and the magic ended in laughter. I remember how he played Saint Nickolas when I was six. I remember riding on his shoulders for a long piggy back ride home after school when another kid had thrown a rock at my head.

I was determined that I would escape the shacks of my childhood against my parents' lamenting protestations. "You'll wind up in the gutters of New York… your American dream will become a nightmare."My father had said it so often it had become a daily litany. I had arrived without a clue on how to earn a living. It never occurred to me that I would someday stand on a podium lecturing a spellbound audience on how women should take charge of family finance and talk about mergers, acquisitions and capital markets. I smiled to myself, somewhat pleased at my small accomplishments.

I never told anyone what it took to get to this level of living the American dream that could just as easily have turned into a nightmare. Grudgingly, I had to admit just how right my father had been. I remember when I was eight months pregnant, the moment when self-awareness awakened in me and I realized that the man I had married decided that living in a shack was good enough. I knew then I had to take charge of my life and the lives of those who depended on me to put a roof over their heads, food on the table and clothes on their backs.

Many years, I had to work three jobs, smile all day and wait on tables serving breakfast, lunch and dinner. After getting home, cram into the wee hours and get up at five a.m. to catch the 6:09 to Grand Central Station. I looked down from the 'Windows on the World' and gasped at the height of the twin towers and the little yellow cabs crawling like ants around the New York City canyons. I smiled to myself, feeling a little smug as I draped my elegant black Glama mink around my shoulders. 'I can't believe I have made it to this height despite my fathers' dire predictions that I would end up in the gutters of New York. I thought to myself and smiled. 'If only he could see me now.'

The House My Father Built

"Yet, here I was, holding seminars on the top floor of the World Trade Center for women in banking. I was exhausted from watching the Dow Jones numbers stream across banners that stirred up hype and stress around the world. Just when my soul needed a break from Wall Street stress, dark clouds were forming on my Wall Street horizon and I bailed out before the first lightning strike lit up the sky knowing thunder was sure to follow. Black Friday signaled a market crash that would become a spiral downward and no amount of number crunching could stop its natural flow. This seminar would be my last hurrah for some time before the market would recover. Now was a good time to go home! But where was home?

I felt disheartened, knowing he never would see me standing here. The soft fur teased my neck and chin, reminding me of the reality of the day. My fathers' pleading words had echoed in my ears all these years. Unfortunately, the more he had pleaded with me not to cross the pond, the greater my wall of defiance built inside me. I was determined to go and leave the past behind.

Memories continued to haunt me, especially the memory of the day, my father bought an expensive coat so I would not arrive in America looking like a pauper. Knowing he would ask me about the coat he had bought for me, I rushed to a store and bought one just as luxurious, I certainly did not want to come home looking like a pauper. I wanted to reassure my father that I had done well for myself and he need not have worried about me. I hoped he would not remember what the original coat looked like.

Now it was time to pay back a debt, a debt of gratitude to a man I had feared much of my childhood, loved him nonetheless, even though he remained a frightening enigma to me. I fingered the letter in my pocket, unfolded it and read one line over and over as my eyes filled with tears. "Please come home. He is longing to see you. If you don't have the money, I'll repay you for your flight. I fear that this will be his last Christmas! All my Love, MOM."

I had always known my mom loved me, loved me so much, she had worked her fingers to the bone cleaning the latrines in a grimy steel factory. I shuddered at the thought and wondered how my mother could stomach this kind of work. She had looked at me sadly, and said with gentle admonition. "I do this so that you will never have to." Those were the words that haunted me for years. Such was my mothers' love for me that she never missed a day of grueling work to pay for my tuition at an international business school. She had done all within her capacity, to ease the pain of growing up as a dirt-poor refugee child from a Soviet labor camp.

I had a closet full of bad and good memories, although I often bemoaned the bad memories; I had never thanked my mother for any of the good. I remember a shack I hated to call home and a time when I was hiding from my father's drunken stupor and uncontrolled fury under my bed.

I had escaped the shack but not its memories. Amidst its squalor filled with hand-me-downs, I remember a silver framed black and white photo of a beautiful mansion, with a glistening copper roof and rounded veranda. It was a majestic building surrounded by fruitful gardens with delicate cherry trees in full bloom in front of the dining room alcove. In memory of this building my mother lit a votive candle every Sunday beside this photo as if in mourning of a beloved someone, saying. "This is the house your father had built brick by brick with meticulous attention to detail. He had planted rows of white birches that surrounded the property. The garden was filled with apple, pear and plum trees, but his favorite was a cherry tree to which he paid special attention. He had planted the cherry tree in front of the dining room alcove with the explanation.

"I want to stretch out my hand and pluck a bowl full of cherries right from my window."

Despite my mothers' fanciful stories of an ancestral home, I had no memory of a stately home and its history. My mother never tired of telling me stories of our family history. She showed me wedding photos of grandmas and grandpas, aunts and uncles, communion photos of cousins who all lived in noble houses that once had belonged to a large family dynasty. I had never met and never would I meet any of those who had once enjoyed great name recognition and prominence. I only knew life in a shack and often spouted off. "I am not staying in this shack …this is not a home with lights and bathtubs, water, electricity, radio and television. It's a shack with four walls and a roof."

I dismissed the image of a home in a gilded frame on my mother's armoire as a mirage. I did not want to spend the rest of my life fantasizing or wishing for a better fairytale ending. My childhood home was not a place into which my mother could welcome high browed friends or nosey neighbors. I remember being ashamed and afraid of my fathers' drunken rants. But one day a nosey classmate followed me home and found out that I had three older brothers, who had grown into handsome young men, one who greased his hair like Elvis Presley and played a guitar and an accordion.

My lanky brothers played soccer with their friends in skimpy shorts across lush green meadows, showing off muscular calves with superbly aimed powerful kicks to the roaring sound of GOOOOAL! My mother never invited anyone for the same reason that I dared not invite any of my classmates to our shack, because we were ashamed to let them see how we lived as pitiful refugees and paupers who had fled brutal repression of Soviet domination. I remember the many winter mornings when I was too young to be left home alone, and my mother had to wake me at four a.m. to wait in endless breadlines until the store opened at eight. I remember my mother sitting on a folding chair and I was sitting on my mothers' lap for warmth.

I remember how my mother clutched ration cards for flour, sugar and margarine, only to find out that the shelves were bare, the noodle boxes were for show only, and the slab of butter was rancid margarin. Now at last we had a bountiful vegetable garden and soup on the stove.

My memories were tucked in the corners of my mind, based on black and white photos and the stories my mother had portrayed for me as proof that the family had once been a prominent family of great ancestry and great wealth.

The house of my birth had been labeled the Villa Staffa, a grand home of which I had no recollection. I had often felt pangs of envy as my classmates talked glowingly about grandmas and grandpas or aunts and uncles. How I wished I had at least one grandma who baked cookies or sprinkled sugar on a slice of buttered bread, or a grandpa who would give me an apple from his garden or bounce me on his knee. Instead, my mother held black and white faces on photographs under my nose when she leafed through an aged cigar box looking for stored treasures and retold their life stories that had held me spellbound for years. I lingered in memories and fascination of people I had never seen in the flesh and would never see in my life face to face. All I remembered was life in a shack in a nameless existence of a forgotten people…a face of nameless refugees.

To me, home had been any place where I could lay my head. I remember crawling behind my mother picking potatoes and biting into them dirt and all and riding on my fathers' shoulders to freedom only to spend weeks in a refugee tent until we were allowed to go and we were free to fend for ourselves within the ruins of a landscape ravaged by war.

Anna Kudro

We settled in a town where gardens were available for citizens to grow their own fruits and vegetables. Within these lush gardens my father found a vacant lot where he built a small shack in defiance of city ordinance. These garden sheds were allowed to hold garden tools but not allowed for human habitation.

Years earlier my father had defied the terror of National Socialism followed by years of Communist oppression! Now he had to defy low level overzealous bureaucrats within the Socialist Democratic System.

I remember waiting alone in a garden shack while my mother worked day and night in a factory, cleaning latrines and my father stoked the fires of an iron smelter at bare minimum wages, while my brothers dug for scrap metals in the bomb craters that surrounded the garden shack. Every morning my brothers had to lug buckets of water from the nearby utilities company for cooking. When their chores were done, they played soccer with other boys in the neighborhood in war scared fields. I often watched their games and having no one to play with and getting bored I ran out on the field and kicked the ball in the opposite direction just to annoy my rothers' and they would chase me off their turf with a shout of "skedaddle, go home play, with your dolls." Paper dolls, no less which I had drawn on colored paper and dressed in cut out paper clothes. It kept my mind occupied until I discovered books in which I could bury my soul within the romantic lives of imagined heroines.

My brothers were hunks to girls wearing stilettos, wide hooped petticoats, poodle skirts and bright red lipsticks. I was surprised when these classmates suddenly treated me as if we were best friends and invited themselves to our shack. It became very obvious to me that these all too eager girls feigned their friendly overtures because they had carnal interests in my brothers, and used friendly encounters as a pathway to their attention. My brothers ignored their blatant flirtations because they wanted no appendage to hold them back, because one by one they had set their sights already on the brighter shores of America.

I remember coming home from school one day as my brother Otto was packing his scarce belongings. My father merely shook his hand and said good-bye as Otto hoisted his knapsack over his back and lugged his most prized possession, the Hohner accordion with which he hoped to earn a few dollars and cents on US street corners. I surmised then that I would never see my brother again.

I was a young teenager when my brothers left home and a new world had opened up for me. I buried my face in books. If I wasn't in a library reading Gone with the Wind or A Tree grows in Brooklyn where my image of America was formed in the books I had read in English and German, and where I was moved to tears in the same passages as when Rhett Butler told Scarlett, *"frankly my dear I don't give a damn,"* and disappeared into the foggy night, I wanted to yell, No! A fairytale can't end like this. You have to go back and live happily ever after. Other days, I could be found in a movie theater watching a Doris Day and Rock Hudson movie.

The heroines of books and movies became my role models. How much worse could life be in glorious America? While my image of a home was that of Tara, I remember my fathers' sober pleas. "Stay home or you'll wind up in the gutters of New York …across the big pond they have nothing but cowboys and Indians, gangsters and charlatans." Your image of America is a mirage. To which my mother would chime in. "Stay home my little sparrow, stay home or we have nothing left. Americans know nothing about Beethoven's music. Americans only listen to bellyache music. Stick Buddy Jamboree music gives me a bellyache. To me it sounds like the singers have a bellyache."

My mother always concurred with my father's sober assessments of world events and all dire predictions, "That someday the Russian tanks will roll across the Rhine River."

In sullen rejection of a scary fate that might befall me, if my father's predictions were to come true, I determined, if my brothers were able to get jobs so would I.

How proud my parents were to learn that Otto became a layout man in the manufacture of nuclear reactors on which his initials OS are stamped before being shipped around the world. It was his job to transfer precise blueprint measurements to metal sheets, and mark the spot where a welder had to fuse the plates together. Otto had found his lifelong vocation.

His workmanship was known for precision and accuracy and earned him laud from his superiors and countless wall plaques. We had no idea how a soulful boy, who played a guitar and an accordion for our entertainment in a garden shed, could do so well for himself in America.

I had no idea what I would be good at and enjoy doing, good enough to earn a living? I was still trying to figure it out. No matter how often I watched my mother cook and bake, I was never able to match her skills around a stove. I tried to remember how she managed to put meals on the table without a recipe book, with such ease like a child at play in a sandbox, as she chopped and stirred and added finishing touches of parsley or chives to a meal and I knew cooking was not my vocation.

Envelopes with red, white and blue borders started to arrive at regular intervals. Tucked inside were crisp dollar bills and a few coins were taped to a piece of cardboard which my mother handed to me. "Here, this is for you, buy yourself a movie ticket." I gleefully spent 50 cents on a Rock Hudson and Doris Day movie.

I discovered what an amazing magician my mother was. Not only was she a fantastic cook, who could cook soup from stones. But she was also an amazing seamstress, who three days after I had described dresses of Hollywood divas to my mother, she would say to me after I got home from school. "Take a look inside your armoire."

To my surprise there would be a new dress for me to wear to the envy of my classmates, who soon called me Miss Hollywood, due to the fact that my mother could dress me like Coco Chanel.

I watched in wonder how she could sew my clothes from patterns drawn with chalk on day-old newspapers; then she transferred the pattern to fabric cut from old clothes which she had found in a Catholic charities thrift shop. She separated the parts of a coat or dress by the seams, cut away frayed edges. She washed and ironed them and cut out the patterns to fit me with such perfection to make me feel like Sandra Dee.

My mother fooled them all. She knew not only how to dress me so I never looked like an impoverished refugee but she fixed up the shack to look like a doll house prompting an occasional visitor to proclaim in wonder. "But you live in paradise"

I questioned the idea of paradise? To an opinionated teenager it was a shack in which the living room was wallpapered with forget-me-not blue floral wall paper. From a distance there was a faint hint of paradise to our dismal abode in the surrounding floral splendor when my mother planted friendly looking pansies near the front door and watered flowers that came up effortlessly every year in ever greater profusion of colorful silver and purple bearded irises, magenta peonies and blue delphiniums.

I had owed it to my mother to come home, thinking, I have no more excuses and I will go home no matter the cost. I will spend this one last Christmas with the one man to whom I owe my life and a legacy I could not understand. I planned to spend hours, days or months by my fathers' bedside, hold his hands and thank him, but for what? I had overcome the past and defied the odds stacked against me from the accident of my birth at the end of a devastating war that left nothing but a brutal history to ponder.

I was who I was because of lessons learned in the hardships my parents had endured and had shielded me from the worst. I remembered how my parents dealt with the many difficulties they had to face in more horrid times. Whenever I had to face a difficult situation I looked back and asked myself one question. "What would my mother have done?"

The circumstances of my new life were so different from that of my parents. Living under such repressive Socialist regimes, my parents had no choice and made the best of bad circumstances. I was free to make choices. I remembered only a garden shack nestled deep into the woods, where city dwellers worked fruit and vegetable gardens.

My father had built a shack at night working tirelessly after a hard day's work stoking an iron smelter in brutal heat, so hot his body had to be hosed down by his co-workers to cool him down. Every evening he came home dragging a handcart laden with bricks which he had scraped from the ruins of a war-ravaged country.

Then he labored into the night. I had watched his agile fingers string the outlines of the foundation of a house. His calloused hands dug out the dirt for the foundation with a shovel.

I watched as he slapped the mortar between bricks, row by row until we had a secure roof over our heads under which he hoped to rebuild our shattered lives.

My father had defied the strangle hold of socialist bureaucracies and built a shack without a permit so deep into the woods it could not be seen from the road. Only a narrow footpath through thick weeds led to the shack. History had taught my father to mistrust all government agencies and labeled lifelong career politicians of any party as "nothing but crooks". Our existence was not to be known to bureaucrats thus we could not connect the shack to any city services for electricity, sewer and water. I had to hide my indignities in the bushes since there was no toilet and no running water, no radio or telephone or television.

I remember sneaking out from under the blanket which was spread on a straw covered concrete floor next to my mother. My stomach would often growl in the middle of the night and I was prowling for a slice of bread only to stumble upon a brother who was also prowling for food in the dark. My father was too proud to ask for help from Catholic charities in a time when every day was a fight for survival.

My father preferred spending his days and nights in anonymous poverty eking out a meager sustenance in demeaning and back braking labor to asking anyone for help. Instead, he prepared the soil of the surrounding property with an ample vegetable and fruitful garden surrounding our shack, and a chicken coop in the back. My mother was not too proud to accept charity and furnished the shack with meager hand-me-downs given to us by some nameless benefactor.

She had hauled one priceless piece of machinery across the border. The night before we defected across the Iron Curtain she disassembled the Singer sewing machine and packed side panels into each of my brothers' knapsacks, the head of the old cast iron machine, she stashed into her own knapsack and lugged it on her back across the border. She kept it humming with her agile fingers, sewing not just clothes, but ruffled white curtains, pillows and down comforters.

Room by room a certain creature comfort settled over our shack. On my way home from school there was always the anticipation of something good to eat. No longer did we sneak around at night looking for a dried slice of bread or look into an empty pot. The aroma wafting from our kitchen window signaled to me that the worst of times were behind us.

Now that the roof over our heads was secure there was nothing more for my father to do after work. I often found him spending the evening hours cursing our miserable existence and spending more time in the adjacent chicken coop emptying beer bottles until he was in a drunken stupor, while my brothers played Chess and I played Checkers with my mother.

We ignored my father as he staggered to his bedroom screaming and cursing God and the world of politicians. We knew nothing of what he had suffered as a German soldier at the Russian front in the most bitterly fought battle over Stalingrad. We children thought of him only as a drunk, we knew nothing about posttraumatic stress.

We were relieved when he was too drunk to stand up straight and went to bed to snore away his memories of a life of plenty and a splendid house on a hill known to all as the Villa Staffa.

Isolated thus from the world, books from the nearby America House, the American library in the center of town wherein American idealism was promoted with noble literary works, whose heroes became my childhood friends, and all my knowledge of an idealistic and grandiose world was gleaned from them. As far back as I could remember the characters of library books filled my daydreams and fanciful imaginations of another world, like the lost world that was immortalized in "Gone with the Wind."

Book characters were my only companions, I had no one else to relate to, commiserate and laugh with. I would have loved to know what it was like to have a loving grandparent, a gift bearing aunt or uncle, a cousin to play with, or a mother or father I could talk to after school.

Long ago, I had stopped sitting on my father's lap to be bounced on his knees, no longer did I step on his feet to learn dance steps and no longer ran down the garden path to welcome him home. Instead, I tiptoed around him, even avoided any conversation for fear of a confrontation with him. I had learned to fear my father whether drunk or sober, even as he lay in bed. He only stopped screaming and cursing at crooked politicians and everyone under heaven, when exhausted from his tirades he fell into bed and a thick featherbed covered his emaciated body.

Peace settled over the shack and everyone sighed with relief, especially my mother who, with stoic determination to make life bearable for all of us kids, stood by my father, wringing her hands, listening to the turmoil of his tortured soul with sadness and dismay in her eyes, as she vainly tried to explain his miserable condition and what had brought him down so low.

After another drunken episode I blurted out the one question that had never been uttered in our Catholic home. "Why don't you divorce him?" Divorce had never been a part of Catholic vocabulary. But I had heard it often whispered by a classmate who was growing up with "uncles" instead of fathers. I asked my mother. "Why don't you leave him?"

She looked horrified and meekly shook her head, mumbling. "I could never leave him.

You don't know the kind of man he was before the politics of the time changed the life we knew.

You can't imagine how he suffered and what he endured all his life."

Emmi looked dreamily into space. "He was such a fine man in his youth and I was proud to walk beside him. When he courted me, I could not stop looking at him from the side. I will never forget his waxen fine skin and forget-me-not blue eyes. Even from a great distance I recognized him by his great smile and pearly white teeth."

My mother giggled like a little girl, describing how he groomed his hair when they were first dating. "He had a little tuft of hair that curled down over his forehead and he had his sister Marie use her curling iron to turn the tuft into a curl. During the many years of war, while we were apart he was always on my mind. I could never forget him. How could I?" She looked dreamily into space as she reminisced on their youthful days.

"He was the love of my life from the time we were seventeen. We were young and naïve with no idea of what the world had in store for us. He was a hard worker with a head full of ideas. He was a student at a German engineering school. Every day he rode his BMW bike past my parents' house on his way to school. I could hear him gun the engine to signal me that he was around. He often stopped at my mothers' Gasthaus for Schnitzel and Sauerbraten and Bohemian dumplings, and of course… me, after our eyes met one day across my mother's billiard table, I was smitten when he said…'someday I'll marry the prettiest girl in Klein Borowitz." She continued her musings.

"That Spring his father was murdered by his Czech employees after he had paid their wages and a generous round of beer. They pulled him into the icy waters of a brook that flows into the Elbe River. Authorities claimed it was a drunken accident. The murder of his father signaled the changes to come to our lives and the lives of the people of our homeland. He was the youngest of six sons, yet his father's last will and testament declared him to be the worthiest of his children to inherit the Staffa lumber business.

But with this inheritance he inherited the scorn of his siblings. He was scorned by family members, who faulted his mother for giving him the name Josef. A first son who had died in infancy was also named Josef. Anna had nicknamed him in the Czech language Pepiczek. It was as if his mother Anna had replaced one child with another. .Anna had ensured that one of her sons would bear the Josef Staffa family name and become heir to the Josef Staffa enterprises.

While young Josef was growing up, he worked tirelessly alongside his father and learned to love the land, but he also heard his father heap scorn upon his uncle Stefan and oldest son Adolf for their wasteful drinking. Josef understood why both were left with nothing in the will. Yet, young Josef tried to keep the peace in the family and worked to appease his kin and worked out equitable splits of the properties among them. But nothing was enough.

He gave everybody a share in the management of the business, with titles and healthy salaries and a monthly stipend to his two sisters. He renovated and repainted the old buildings, repaired wood saws and proudly engraved the family name Josef Staffa above the factory portal as a permanent reminder of the family's standing in the community.

"We were married on January 30, 1932, and thought we had a well-planned future ahead." She went on explaining. "Josef wanted a home abuzz with children. He loved children and we bought six chairs for our dining room. We planned to fill the chairs with four children. From the day of their birth, he opened bank accounts for each child. Our lives revolved around family. We never paid attention to world events.

Only one year to the date of our wedding a man came to power in Berlin with unforeseen consequences five years later. Berlin was too remote from our concerns and nothing could have prepared us for what was to come. Josef had built a beautiful house he had designed. It was the grandest villa and visible for miles around because he had built it on a bluff overlooking the entire area. He planted rows upon rows of white birches and fruit trees and berry bushes. His favorite was a cherry tree which he planted in front of the dining room alcove. He always said with a chuckle. "I just want to reach out and pluck the cherries through the window before the birds get to them."

His desk was full of blueprints and his head full of ideas for the entire region. The trucks that hauled lumber needed gas, he had planned to build a network of stations across Czech boundaries into Slovakia. But the rug was pulled out from under him in unforeseen world events. He lost it all and suffered a lot. We all suffered … all we had left, is our love. The world wants to forget that we ever existed." She said with a sigh and looked up with sad eyes and whispered. "We suffered too. We had the misfortune of living in Hitler's time."

I had stopped listening to her stories of the past, stories of a lost war, lost wealth and how the world had re-designed their lives in their quest for world peace and democratic nation building. Nobody I knew wanted to hear anything about the loss of a beloved homeland anymore. My brothers had grown tired of listening to my mothers' ceaseless prayers for a return home. They had fled the cramped poverty of the shack as soon as they could spread their wings and before they even saw in their little sister as anything more than another mouth to feed.

Competition for food had been an everyday conquest since the family's defection to what they thought would be a better world. They fled the chicken coop existence and escaped the wars' abyss and horrid aftermath. I had sought out friends who lived in newly built homes out of the ruins the war had left behind, classmates who lived in homes with electricity, running water, gleaming white bathtubs, and oh yes… telephones and televisions.

These new friends became the representatives of a young generation of Germans determined to live in peace and prosperity fifteen years after a devastating war.

I had never thought of my mother as anything more than a great cook and seamstress taking all her goodness and grace for granted, but never had I thought of her as a scholarly historian. Knowing I was a history buff, she had compiled a booklet filled with historical facts and picture books before my departure from my homeland to the New World.

"I lay this on your heart. Don't forget from where you came…this is the history of your homeland. The world would rather forget that we ever existed… our forefathers gave us a thousand-year history buried in this soil…our soil…we were not invaders as the Czechs claim."

I thankfully tucked the booklet away as a keepsake. "I know you have other things on your mind right now, but some day you may want to read up on your heritage and family history. Maybe it will lend some understanding of what history had in store for us.

Like domino stones, war mongers eager to bloody one another's nose crashed into each other. But it all started with King Wenceslas."

I gave my mother a quizzical look and hummed a melody. "Good King Wenceslas went out on the feast of Stephen, "That King?" She nodded emphatically. "Yes. Our history goes back one thousand years, all the way back to

King Wenceslas who invited us. Our history was lost in the evil of the time into which we were born. After the Black Plague spread across Europe it was stopped by the Sudeten German people because we were a very pious and healthy flock, living in monogamous relationships for centuries. The Czech Nationalists' claim that Germans invaded this land…that's a lie. We were not invaders!"

She repeated these words over and over with great emphasis. Then she hugged me one last Time, turned on heels and never looked back to watch me board the SS Berlin. I did not want her to see me cry and she did not want me to see her cry.

I stashed the flipcharts and handouts into my briefcase, retrieved my suitcase from the locker, slung the black mink coat over my Chanel suited shoulders, and hurried to the express elevator. My tight skirt and Italian stiletto heels made running difficult, leaving only a clickety-click echo behind.

I was in a big hurry, having dreamed with longing for this day for many years. It had been twenty-five years in which I had neither the money nor the time to visit my parents. Either I did not have the money nor the time while I was busy putting my life on track in a country that glorified accomplishments in a fiercely competitive world in which I had secured the money for a solid roof over everyone's head, food on the table and sneakers and jeans times five. The thought of those, who had depended on my resolve to succeed in this topsy-turvy world, had kept me on the straight and narrow…the path of the American Dream … knowing just how easily the American Dream can turn into a nightmare on a dime. I wheeled my luggage to the curb and raised my arm against oncoming traffic. Instantly a taxi sped towards me and tires screeched to a halt. "Kennedy Airport! Lufthansa Terminal…Hurry!"

I felt the thrill of American expediency that had prompted me to accelerate my goals. I climbed unhindered into the backseat of the yellow cab, and slumped against the cushions that hugged my small frame. It had been a stressful day and I had a six-hour flight ahead, on which I could reminisce on my mother's stories of an alien heritage through my foggy memories. My mothers' stories of a time of plenty were the only link to the past that remained a surreal mystery.

As soon as the plane leveled at 30,000 feet in the air I pulled the little book from my carry-on, clutched the crumpled and worn pages of what looked more like a diary full of crib notes. I settled into my business class seat, closed my eyes and let my head roll against the cushioned seat …in the six-hour flight I had enough time to cram through pages of a thousand-year odyssey that had brought me to this point. I could not help but wonder what a thousand-year history had to do with my ancestry now? We are who we are because of the history gone before us, but a thousand years?'

My eyes scanned the pages wearily as my mind drifted off into the pages of a turbulent historical past…my ancestral history and that of a forgotten people…

The turbulent history of Bohemia ...

Seeking Peace and Plenty, around 480 B.C.E Celtic tribes began to migrate from mainland Europe across the North Sea Waters to get away from European wars. German tribes named the Boii migrated into the region and called it Boii hemia, latin for home. Bohemia was home to German tribes for more than a thousand years. After Christianity spread throughout Western Europe, German tribes held to one unifying faith, Roman Christianity.

In contrast around the year 700 a clansman named Czech migrated from Russia into Bohemia. The word Slavic is a Latin name meaning "slave of the devil," given to those who had not converted to Christianity. The Russians settled in the low lands of Bohemia and renamed it "Czech."

As the Czech population grew over the centuries they pushed the German people, who staunchly adhered to their Roman Christian faith, into the surrounding mountains. Over the centuries most Czechs maintained their Slavic identity, agrarian culture and assimilation with that of mother Russia.

In the tenth-century, Ludmilla, grandmother of the benevolent King Wenceslas, Duke of Bohemia, became a Christian. She raised the good King as a Christian, who heeded her counsel and earned his sainthood by going out among the poor peasants on the feast of Saint Stephens, and giving generous alms to them.

His country had been decimated by the Black Plague, which obliterated great portions of the Czech population. There was no one to work the ravaged land with which to fill royal coffers. He beckoned his German neighbors to inhabit the land.

Ludmilla sent Wenceslas to college in Budweis, over sixty miles from Prague. He was young when his father died. His mother, Drahomira, assumed the title of regent and seized control of the government. She had concealed her rage against Christians while her husband was alive. But now she let loose her full rage against them. Ludmilla, full of concern for her Christian faith, showed Wenceslas the necessity of taking the reign of government into his own hands. The young duke obeyed, and the Bohemians testified their approbation of his conduct. To prevent disputes between Wenceslas and his younger brother, Boleslav, the two divided the country between them. Wenceslas sought Ludmillas' advice, to promote the establishment of peace, justice and religion and chose able Christian administrators for his government.

Drahomira, the ambitious pagan, ceaselessly indulged in evil court intrigues, and looked upon her mother as the first counsel in favor of the Christian religion, and laid a plot to take away her life. The pious Ludmilla was laying in prayer before the altar of her chapel, where her assassins found her and strangled her with her veil.

King Wenceslas had encouraged the work of German missionary priests to come to Bohemia. They brought along their own skilled laborers to build churches, monasteries, girls' schools, religious orders and glass workshops. Vineyards and farms dotted the fertile landscape, wineries and breweries filled the cellars of the nobles, to the ire of Czech bureaucrats. The good king Wenceslas gave much of the harvest to the poor.

His generosity toward the peasantry greatly antagonized his mother, Drahomira, his brother, Boleslav, and the Czech nobles, who together conspired to murder the pious king.

On the feast of Saint Stephens, at midnight on September 28, 929 a.d. King Wenceslas went to offer his customary prayers in church. At the instigation of Drahomira, brother Boleslav followed him with his assassins. The assassins merely wounded Wenceslas. When Boleslav saw that his brother was still alive, he ran a lance through the good king. Wenceslas died in front of the church portals.

Reports of miracles occurring at Wenceslas' tomb frightened the murderous Boleslav. He had his brothers remains transferred to Saint Vitus Church in Prague, which became a great center of pilgrimage. The good King Wenceslas became Bohemia's patron saint, whose virtues have been praised in eternal songs at Christmas time around the world ever since.

German settlers and craftsmen, who had voted for King Wenceslas I, brought Austria into his dynasty. Over the centuries, although many Czechs and Germans became related through marriage, the Czech and German population remained as fiercely divided in pious faith and political fervor, just as Wenceslas and Boleslav had been.

The House My Father Built

In the eleventh-century, the first dynasty was the Prmysl Family of which Ottokar I married a German princess. Their son chose a German princess for his wife. In 1176, Count Sobeslav invited German craftsmen to "come and work the land." He decreed that the Germans were to be held in high esteem and live under his protection, and "imported" these skilled laborers, farmers, woodsmen, monks and missionaries to revitalize the uninhabited mountain regions. Their bountiful harvests and masterful crafts filled the gap left by the Czech peasants.

The period of European migration followed the Black Plague, which had swept across Europe. Eastern Europe was especially hard hit, when 37,000 of the Czech population died. The deadly spread was halted by healthy robust Germans, who lived off the land and in monogamous relationships.

In desperation, the Czech Royals called again on the German pioneering spirit, who heeded the call "to work the land," and Bohemia prospered once more. Villages and towns nestled into the northern mountain region bordering Poland. Its latin name, Sudeta, gave its inhabitants their name, Sudeten Germans, the Iron-Ore mountains bordering Germany and the Bohemian forests in the South bordering Austria.

These German settlers met the challenges of the mountains. German merchants and traders added considerable wealth to the land. German influence at the royal court caused a rich flowering of the arts, especially in literature, music, and architecture.

From 1310 to 1437 the country was ruled by kings of the House of Luxembourg of the Holy Roman Empire. Prague University was founded in 1348 by the German Emperor Karl IV, as the German Imperial Institution for Higher Education for the nation of Nemcis a Ceskis, Germans and Czechs. It was the first Central European University. The German architect, Peter Parler built the Prague Cathedral. The name of the famous Karl's Bridge was anglicized under Churchill's influence to Charles Bridge.

In the fifteenth century Europe was besieged by the Ottoman Empire under the Turkish Sultan Mustafa the Magnificent. It was his aim to bring Islam to the rest of Europe. Hungarian kings ruled Bohemia, who in 1444 lost the battles against the Ottoman Empires Turkish marauders.

Ferdinand I of Austria, of the Royal Habsburg Family was elected king of Austria and Bohemia. Under his reign the Turks were beaten back in the battle of Vienna under the command of Adolf von Schwarzenberg. As a reward Ferdinand I gave him the title of Imperial Count in honor and commemoration of the defeat of the Turks, and awarded him great properties and castles in Bohemia. Germans added great wealth among the Czech nobility, church men and merchants. The Czech royals were aware of the sacrifices and strenuous efforts Germans had made and rewarded these industrious people with promises of tax incentives for a secure future. Those who had chopped and tilled, planted and harvested, hammered and sawed, were the founders of world industries. They were given inalienable rights as landowners and patriarchs of a unique culture. Daring young woodsmen, farmers, and craftsmen were endowed with brain and brawn. They had not come as empty-handed beggars to their new land. They had brought with them "modern" farm equipment and techniques, livestock, plants, seeds and money, to help them weather the first unproductive years.

The ancestors of this German population had been handpicked for their loyalty to the Catholic faith by the early missionaries and their descendants remained just as devout. Even the tiniest of communities boasted two pubs, one for finer folks and one for ruffians. Neatly planted farms, factories and forests provided ample creature comfort in a perfect and complete infrastructure. There was a butcher, a baker, a general store to cover all their earthly needs. Even the smallest village boasted one gold-domed Roman Catholic Church, which provided a sanctuary for the soul, and a painters' focal point within the rolling landscape sprinkled with simple charm against mountain peaks.

In their love for nature the German settlers also discovered a vast reservoir of natural resources in these mountains. For centuries, world renowned coal and metal industries added prestige to the region. Mother lodes of iron ore and uranium, coal, gold and silver, precious garnet stones were mined by a hardworking labor force in 900 mines.

Eight thousand miners extracted 20 million tons of coal annually. The German region boasted the highest per capita income in Europe. Raw materials were always in abundant supply, along with the skilled craftsmen, who gladly taught the intricacies of a craft to willing apprentices, with a zeal for perfection.

The perfection of a craft was passed down through the generation. Poets found idyllic wellsprings of folklore and fairytales, and hideaways in which to polish their craft, surrounded by such romantic vision to charm a Roman. The Germans had built settlements in this region where red roof tiles crowned sturdy structures which survived the ravages of a thousand years and beautiful monuments to the accomplishments of simple people to charm artists and painters that marked the cornerstone of a flourishing tourist industry wherein European royals paid a mighty Thaler, who flocked for respite and good health to more than fifty luxurious health spas in Karlsbad, Marienbad, Franzisbad, Johannisbad, and Joachimsthal where Count von Schlick owned silver mines and in 1520 minted coins, which he named Thaler, anglicized to dollars, of such beauty and delicate filigrees to become the favorite currency around the world.

The land was so rich with natural resources, that Austrian Empress Maria Theresa and the Prussian King Fredrick the Great, contemporaries of George Washington, waged two wars over the regions that bordered Poland and Austria, forming an arrowhead into Germany.

Family-owned factories produced thousands of wood and wind instruments. Glass factories date back to the year 1366. Glasscutter Kaspar Schindler was mentioned as early as 1551 as a tax payer, Sebastian Schindler`s name was engraved on a church bell in 1592.

In 1918 the Germans living in these mountains were labeled Sudeten Germans. Two of them Oskar Schindler and Ferdinand Porsche will live on in perpetuity.

Four thousand German entrepreneurs preferred working in the quiet anonymity of family businesses, who concentrated their wealth in their own craftsmanship but employed thousands and claimed the largest private industry in the world per square mile, in which they felt comfort in their own culture and complete infrastructure.

In service of churches and schools, they built Franciscan monasteries. For women they built Ursuline cloisters and schools for girls. Young women were taught proper etiquette, haute couture, sewing, knitting, crocheting, and needle point and the fine arts of homemaking in preparation for well-planned marriages and a potential life at a royal court since 1597.

Linen and textile mills date to the sixteenth century. A Higher Institutes for Milliner Art, Trade and Technology was established in the mid-nineteenth century. Crocheted lace finery, hats, stockings, scarves and mittens were produced in the millions annually by twenty-thousand girlish fingers until old age stiffened their joints.

Since the nineteenth century, Bohemian crystal was a World Exhibit winner for its multi-colored, hand cut, prismatic, long-stemmed goblets, which delightfully catch the light inside a cabinet of many a proud Hausfrau and Christmas trees were decorated with hand blown glass ornaments and wood carved crèches and figurines the world over.

To this day beer lovers hail Pilsner and Budweiser beer as the finest brew in the world. Five hundred export firms sent these goods into the world, on 7000 ships floating north on the Elbe River. Despite their slight stature, these German pioneers had managed to extract such affluence from rocky soil, while the Czech peasant, who had retained the fruitful lowlands, abundant with meadows along the swollen Elbe and Moldau Rivers lived in abject poverty.

Jan Hus, a Czech protestant whose doctrines are acknowledged to be the root cause of a thirty-year war which devastated Europe. The first shot of that war was fired in Prague. Jan Hus needled the clergy from a modest chapel and demanded religious reforms, in which he sought to destroy Catholicism as he shouted. "Christ was poor, why are so you rich?"

In 1620, his followers called Hussites, stormed City Hall and tossed three Habsburg bureaucrats out a window. The three bureaucrats survived, but rich Germans were expelled.

The Hussite upheaval created trade barriers and stifled growth. Czechs ruled a land that now had a stagnant economy. The Imperial Habsburg forces crushed the Czech protesters, which marked the beginning of another glittering period of re-Catholicization. A building-boom in churches full of artistic creations in the baroque style of the seventeenth and eighteenth century filled with dynamism, discipline and emotion followed and Viennese culture radiated eastward.

Atheist Czechs and Catholic German communities bordered each other in a zigzag formation, each determined to maintain their isolating identity. With that isolation, the economic disparity between nationalities became more apparent. To appease Czechs and Germans even handedly Austrian Empress Maria Theresa introduced mandatory schooling in the language of a child's mother. Though well intentioned, the dual language system with a multitude of ethnic dialects had the opposite effect and resulted in even greater isolation between Czech and German speaking communities and destroyed any meaningful communication and unity between the varying ethnic groups.

The House My Father Built

To preserve and teach cultural values and technologies German schools trained German teachers, town halls and community centers installed German mayors. Institutions for higher education, science and technology, auditoriums for music and cultural events were established. Each community hunkered down within safe familiar enclaves as soccer clubs, volunteer fire and rescue squads, hikers, bikers and gym clubs were formed.

German enterprises contributed 75 percent of GNP to the Austro-Hungarian economy. The German communities had built a cohesive infrastructure and saw no reason to change their way of life, staunchly resisting any subversion of their cultural and religious values. While Czech peasants who lacked economic independence had a disdain for disciplined tasks, worked as farm hands, and often for a German boss, spawning greed among peasants at a time when greed became another driving force in the world. On the heels of the Industrial Revolution, which shaped Western Europe in the middle of the nineteenth century, a constant Slavic push for economic power ensued.

Next to the Austro-Hungary Monarchy was the Kingdom of Serbia who, like the Czechs were cousins to mother Russia. Serbia was long suspected by Austria's Habsburgs of fomenting Slavic nationalism and separatism. The Industrial Revolutions' demand for capital goods forced Western industrialists to import low-cost laborers from Eastern Europe, mainly from Hungary, Poland, Ukraine, Russia, and Slovakia because of the shortage of locals to fill low-cost jobs, which in turn created pockets of slums within the well-established German communities.

As European capitals were being transformed by grand construction projects, prosperity and poverty became neighbors. While the Habsburgs treated Prague as a provincial backwater, in which few public investments were made, Czechs maintained economic parity only with minorities. Many politicians eagerly exploited the economic disparity with these minorities. The ensuing tensions between the various ethnic groups and religious and the non-religious factions drove their ultimate goal for power. In countries related to mother Russia, nationalistic uprisings were started by the Serbs.

As each ethnic group demanded a greater share of economic power, they pitted themselves against one another. The Czechs never forgot the Hus doctrines which were embraced by those who hoped for another salvation in a growing political popularity sweeping the European continent like a plague in a quest for wealth distribution-Communism.

Posters filled with hateful diatribes advocating violence confronted these minorities, house by house and neighbor by neighbor. They turned against each other. Czechs turned against Germans, Slovaks against Czechs, Serbs against Bosnians and Croats, Hungarians against Rumanians. Economic disparity magnified cultural and religious differences and national identities all across Europe, and collided within the Austro-Hungarian Empire. Alliances of protection formed among them, only to be betrayed and broken until they all fell victim to their revolutionary zeal.

For many centuries worldly events had not affected these tiny hamlets where streets had no names and neighbors knew each other by their trade name or business. Within these mountain hamlets accessible only over narrow winding paths, lived a sharing and caring people, who knew each other's ills and needs. If prayers could not cure the ills, fate was remanded to a higher authority as a matter of faith. If crops failed one year, neighbor supported neighbor generously in their poverty and sustained each other with the simple faith of their mothers and fruits harvested from their father's land. These simple people whose wants were few and their dress home spun lived in rustic simplicity, united only in their abhorrence for politicians and those encroaching on their economic independence as a new political process advocated by politicians was an anti-German and anti-Catholic rhetoric billowed with ever increasing bluster and bravado, threatened violence from the venomous mouths of power grabbing politicians.

The disparity between ethnic groups provoked threats against those of the Roman Christian faith with stories and doctrines alien to the simple faith of pious people, who had little or no contact with the outside world, and sought none.

The vitriol spewed from mouths of overzealous politicians, aped from the mouths of neighbors, followed up with stone-hurled assaults with increasing voracity, until sticks and mallets and threats of "bloodying the white socks of Nemci (German) invaders" were acted out.

The region became a powder keg in a widely accepted slogan that Germans were INVADERS! Czech National Socialists, the Narodny Vybor, were political revolutionaries who were planted into the tiniest German communities to agitate against the "ruling" class. These simple mountain people lived in fear of vendettas being executed by vigilantes and tolerated by bureaucrats in support of systematically rooting out the German minority and break their economic power.

To facilitate this aim, they had to destroy Catholicism, in that Catholicism posed the greatest opposition to Communism.

Staunch resistance to Communism came from devout German Catholics who found their faith and robust economies pushed to the edge. Germans distanced themselves from their Czech neighbors out of fear of erosion of their faith and cultural values. They built theatres and opera houses, covered with dynamic emotional frescoes, religious roadside sculptures and gilded altars dazzled the faithful. Crucifixes adorned intersections and pilgrim chapels crowned hillsides and mountain trails to the summit that formed the border between Poland, Germany and Czechoslovakia.

The faithful flock held prayerful processions around village squares, worshipped at roadside altars in protestations of their steadfast faith. Their once-thriving businesses were sorely put to the test as higher taxes and regulations were imposed. Ethnic hatred spun out of control until bullets plunged the world into an abyss. Catholic Germans could not be persuaded to abandon the faith of their mothers and the land of their fathers as sanctioned by the spirit of the mountains…such was the history of one such tiny village that could not be found on a map, a hamlet called Mastig.

The Home Coming...

For years, I had crunched numbers, calculating ratios that measured a company's financial health as an analyst for quarterly and annual reports and watched world events unfold before my eyes through the curtains that covered my windows, knowing the market was a barometer of financial health of a country and the world with eyes glued to tickertapes. But no amount of number crunching could stop a market crash and its aftermath. It horrified me to read in the headlines that investors had jumped out of windows when the Stock Market crashed on a Black Friday in October and they knew they had lost everything. It saddened me to think, people saw no way out but a jump from a window.

I put my headset on, listened to my favorite music, Beethoven's Ninth Symphony, reasoning if Beethoven's music survived world war carnage over more than a century so would I and decided to go home instead.

When the captain announced the preparation for the landing, I closed the booklet and stashed it in my carry-on bag thinking of the history that had preceded my existence on a destructive path of which I could not change its outcome any more than I could change the market crash, I felt helpless to change world events that hit the global markets like an avalanche. I glanced out the window of the plane and my heart skipped a beat as the familiar German landscape became recognizable.

Moments before the landing I viewed the rolling landscape dotted with small villages, red tiled rooftops surrounding single church spires. I was as excited as a young girl at her first dance. The familiarity took my breath away, when I realized that not much had changed beyond the modern gleaming glass facades of the New World Frankfurt. The stucco and cross beamed farmhouses that had stood firmly through centuries and survived the pestilence of wars and stormy weather were monuments of an old-world culture. I could feel my heart beat faster and warmth settling around my chest as sweet melancholic tears flooded my eyes. I smiled feeling a peace within myself as a passenger said to me. This is Frankfurt, but we call it Main-hattan for the Manhattan like skyline."

I was awed at the Manhattan-like skyline of glass towers rising above the dark green soil and historic buildings with red tiled roofs blending beautifully along the Main River. When the plane touched down, I felt the bump and the slowing crawl to a stop and I realized that I was home at last!

I wanted to savor the slow train ride through the beautiful landscape to enjoy the familiarity of old farm houses with crossbeams and whitewashed stucco that date back a thousand years. Red geraniums and white lace curtains grace windows with simple charm. Behind each house were the vegetable gardens and barren fruit trees that had been plucked clean in the last harvest.

The train breezed through villages where church spires peered out from their centers. I smiled when I saw little boys playing soccer in the fields wearing shorts and lose t-shirts, without head gear and body armor.

As soon as the train arrived in the place I had thought of as my home town, I was Filled with anticipation to "be home." I could hardly wait to put my arms around my mother. But what else would I find? Would I find a home wherein the memory of the aroma of moms' cooking had welcomed me home after school? Or would I find a shack wherein my father's drunken terror had driven me across the big pond. I took a Mercedes taxi from the train station, to the new address of the apartment complex my parents had moved into five years after I had left home.

As I lifted my suitcase from the trunk and wheeled it toward the door, I could see my mother waving a white handkerchief as she leaned out the third-floor window. It looked as if she had waited anxiously all day for the sound of a taxi screeching to a halt in front of the house. I rang the bell and was buzzed in immediately. I entered a stately apartment building as if on hallowed ground. In her haste to ring the buzzer she had dropped a pot and spilled the beans. I called out as I had when I was a child coming home from school. "Anybody home?"

From the top floor a shrill soprano voice shouted in reply as she leaned over the banister and snickered. "Ya! I am here! I have waited all morning … listening for a taxi to pull up in the driveway and when it did, I dropped a pot of beans."

I heard her laughter while I dragged my suitcase up the stairs and she cleaned the floor. "Yoohoo! Mamimka, I am home." I could see her beaming face with eyes alit with joy. She watched me drag my luggage up the three flights of stairs.

"Leave it. Let one of our tenants bring it up when he gets home. I can't wait to wrap my arms around you."

I ran up the black marble stairs until we stretched out our arms and fell around each other. She squeezed the air out of my belfry in her exuberance. "My little sparrow! Now I will never let you fly away again." We hugged and cried on one another's shoulders.

My mother screeched so loud, I was afraid the neighbors would hear the commotion, and they did and came out of their apartments to greet me. Once we had recovered, and tears were dried, my mother could not help but admonish me as she playfully wagged a finger in my face. "But Mamimka is Czech. We are in Germany. Here we speak German." I chuckled. "Okay, mom!" knowing the implications of her gentle reprimand.

"Every day for as long as you are here, I will make your favorite dishes. I remember them all. For today I made powidl dumplings, tomorrow I will make wiener schnitzel." She listed my favorite entrees and desserts as my mouth began to water. I laughed out loud in surprise to hear how well she recalled my lip smacking favorites and as if she had read my mind she said. "Oh yes, surprise? I remember all your favorites, Schnitzel, Sauerbraten, Bohemian dumplings, red cabbage, Roulade, Plum cake, Beehive Cake. I have already baked a Rum Stollen for Christmas." "You forgot one, Cherry Perogies." I chimed in.

"Sorry to say, if you want Cherry Perogies you have to wait until cherries are in season next year in June or July." I felt my stomach growl and my mouth watering. "Mm, mom, you make me hungry for Perogies I always loved a plate full. But everything you cooked was best of the Bohemian traditional kitchen. Your kitchen always had this unmistakable blend of aromas, nutmeg, cardamon, cinnamon, ginger and butter. Everything tastes better with butter and nothing smells better than Mamas kitchen."

I sighed and whispered. "It is so good to be home again…you make me feel like a child again."

I looked around a dimly lit hallway as my mother pointed to a door. "This is your bedroom."

I dragged my luggage inside the tiny room and looked around. I felt as if I had stepped back in time, as if I had been here before. The room was as tiny as a jail cell, cold as a chicken coop. My eyes adjusted to the dim overhead light, I was surprised to see the room was identical to the bedroom of my childhood. A chicken coop had been transformed into my bedroom covered in twenty-year old wallpaper, with designs of a little girl swinging on a branch of an old apple tree, a plaster wall hanging of Hansel and Gretel lost in the woods. An old fairytale book lay on the bedside table.

I opened the dresser drawer and inside were my grammar school books and my first English book and on the armoire was a black and white photo of a stately villa. I felt the tears stinging in my eyes.

My mother had transported me back into my childhood as if the past twenty years had never been a time of separation. I was a child again. I finally mustered the courage to ask.

"Where is Papa?"

"He is in bed…he suffered a nervous breakdown after you had left for America. I had to call an ambulance to take him to the hospital, that's when doctors discovered that he is a diabetic, which explains his uncontrolled rages fueled by the horror of war memories. All his life he suffered so much trauma, he can't un-see what he has seen and forty-five years later he is still haunted by memories of the war at the Russian front. Getting wounded in the battle of Stalingrad probably saved your father's life. He was transported back and allowed to recover at home. You were born nine months later."

I knew my mother had hoped to find understanding for my father's angry outbursts. I did not know the root cause of his helplessness, hopelessness, and the frustration he felt at being at the mercy of a merciless world of politics he could not reconcile himself to.

I had never heard of post-traumatic-stress with which my mother tried to explain my father's abhorrent behavior. I did not respond to her explanations, because I wanted to enjoy this time with my mother without arguments about past world events. I just wanted to enjoy being home, feeling the safety of being mollycoddled like a little girl again and not dwell on the past. As a child, I had not understood why my father was so furious all the time and why my mother stood by him all these years, even as we begged her to leave him and live in America.

My brothers had established themselves comfortably and could have afforded our mother a comfortable home in retirement. They had begged her to leave him and live with them in America, to enjoy her cooking and housekeeping, but she turned them down every time. She always shook her head and replied. "After sixty-years togetherness, I can't just leave him. We were both seventeen years old when our eyes met across a billiard table. I knew from that moment on, he was the love of my life. You don't know the kind of man he was. Besides you don't transplant an old tree."

"That's what I would like to find out. Who my father was? What kind of a man was he?" The man I knew as my father was a man who had lost faith in humankind. He was suspicious of everyone. He trusted nobody whether they were relatives or neighbors, doctors or lawyers or God Himself. He had stopped going to church, never voted and never went to an assembly. He had no use for politicians, his special wrath was reserved for bureaucrats of any party. He avoided all human contact even an occasional visitor who stopped by the house to say hello to my mother was not welcomed. I asked my mother as I unpacked my clothes and organized them in the armoire. "How did you get him to go to the hospital?"

She replied sheepishly. "He did not go willingly. He fought the medical personnel tooth and nail, they had to put him in a straight-jacket and then they sedated him. He was in the hospital for six weeks, and screaming and insulting the doctors and nurses, calling them horse doctors." She paused a moment shaking her head and continued. "I was so embarrassed, but I understand, why he is such an angry man. He had the rug pulled out from under his whole life. He never got over losing everything, the factory and land on which he had planted every tree since his childhood alongside his father. The house he built was his pride and joy of achievement and roots of his life's work had found an anchor in the soil. This was his heritage where his name found recognition. He got a kick in the ass at every turn of his life. But the worst kick was when his children left one after the other never to return, but hardest was the kick when you left. He had lost his sons with a handshake…but when you left, he lost his mind, losing you was more than he could take."

I felt a lump in my throat of guilt and shame and I looked down on the floor not knowing what to say. I realized the pain I had caused my parents. My mother whispered without reproach, she wanted to talk with magnanimity in her voice. "I know and understand, why you all left home for an uncertain future at such a young age." I understand why you all left.

But you were his only daughter, the daughter he had longed and prayed for since we first met." She paused remembering. "From the first day of our marriage he said. "I want a little girl like Gitchen with little blond curls." His Sister Marie, had a little girl named Margit, she is your cousin. When you were born, he called you his favorite birthday present." He loved you so much he sobbed and sobbed non-stop when you left. He had a nervous breakdown. I was so frightened, I called the ambulance of Saint Elizabeth hospital." She stepped aside and pointed to a closed door.

"Now, go see if he is awake." I slowly pressed the door handle and entered the darkened room. I tip toed to my fathers' bedside, still wearing my fur coat I carefully sat down on the chair beside his bed. I did not want the rustle of my coat to wake him. I watched my father sleep as tears flooded my eyes seeing him look so small, frail and emaciated beneath billowing down comforters. Not knowing how he would react, I sat quietly, afraid to wake him because I did not want to startle him? Would he be shocked or angry? Would the sight of me stir up memories and irrational fits of rage? Or would he be glad to see me?

As I looked down on the sleeping face of the man I had loved and feared much of my life, I pressed back the tears as they welled up inside me and held fast not to burst open like a dam and let the tears flow at the sad and pathetic sight. I did not want my father to see me cry pitifully. I did not want mascara streaking down my face. I wanted him to see me looking happy and self-assured. I did not want him to see me looking like a sad little girl, like the last time he saw me leave the shack of my childhood.

I remember a joyous Christmas night when Saint Nicholas came to our house. What I didnot know at the time, my father had crossed the infamous Iron Curtain border at risk to his own life, dressed as Saint Nicholas, because he did not want me to miss out on Christmas Eve. Days later the many toys and dollhouse he had built himself, complete with furniture he had dragged across a dangerous guarded Iron Curtain that Christmas night, his gifts of love had to be left behind the night of our own escape. All that remained was a childhood fantasy of one glorious Christmas Eve.

Finally, my father stirred and opened his eyes. He looked as if he were seeing a mirage. He rubbed his eyes and softly whispered. "It's a miracle! You have come home… home for my funeral, Yes, you came…for my funeral." I could no longer contain the tears as I bent over to kiss him on the cheek. I sat silently, as he started to talk about the past and I listened as he talked and talked, telling me stories of the old days, which had not been good. I carefully turned on my little tape recorder, unnoticed, so as not to distract his train of thoughts. "Yes, your mother and I once had everything…we had love, we had dreams, we had plans for our children.

You see, I had inherited my fathers' business. I had plans to build on my inheritance like building blocks. I had a great base to start from and lots of ideas, which my father passed on to me, he always told me. "Never stretch your legs any further than the blanket that covers them. I had a big blanket." He chuckled and I smiled knowing exactly what he was talking about from my own Wall Street business experience. "That's good advice, Papa. It's best not to be exposed! Everyone should have a blanket big enough to cover his feet." He murmured during a long silence. "Oh yes, mmmh." He was thinking over my reply. "I saw my lumber business as a springboard from which I planned to build future enterprises. You see, my trucks hauled the lumber across the country and trucks need gasoline so I planned to build gas stations along trucking routes throughoutCzechoslovakia …I thought once the war is over the world would come to its senses and life would return to normal. I was wrong. Evil had dripped like ether into veins of unsuspecting people so slowly nobody knew what was happening until it was too late. Evil had replaced evil.

All was lost in the aftermath of war. We suffered too. We suffered until the bitter end and were left with nothing but recrimination and condemnation for the sins of others. I reached for my fathers' hand, and gently said. "I know Papa. The world has not been kind to you. You suffered a lot all your life. I came home to tell you that I owe you a thousand thank you's." He placed a finger over his mouth as if he had to mull my words over carefully. He whispered slowly," Thank me? Thank me for what?"

"For everything you have given me, my life! My life in freedom." I mumbled not knowing what more I could say. I could not talk anymore, lest the dam would break and I would burst into tears. While his eyes held my tearful gaze, I collected myself. "Your whole life was a fight for survival. You built a house you never even got to enjoy. You were pulled from one opposing political power to another. But because of you, I have a life worth living. You defied the National Socialist, dragged our mother and us four children out of a Soviet labor camp.

You risked your life to escape East-Germany, then came back to make sure I would enjoy a Christmas to remember. Were it not for you, mother would have died and we would have been enslaved in a Soviet labor camp, picking potatoes until we died."

He was thinking this over and said slowly. "We all would have died. The communists just work people to death and drop them in a hole without fanfare. You must understand, I did it for my children, for you. I wanted my children to have a chance for a better life. I did it for you!"

He mumbled meekly, and I replied. "That is why, I owe you a thousand times thank you…my brothers and I would never have had the chance to enjoy the life we have now. I know, how much you have suffered, but you gave us a life worth living. You could have given in to communists and make your peace with their Socialist ideology, but you did not cave. You were brave enough to risk it all for us." I cried softly and let the tears fall into my coat collar.

"All is well, little one, all is well." He murmured. "You see, one can never make peace with a communist. They lure you with utopian promises that cannot be fulfilled. It is not about me, because I won't be here much longer." His eyes glazed over as he gazed into space.

"I want to go home to the beloved land of my fathers, Czechoslovakia, but only in my dreams can I be where I belong, so I just hope to fall asleep and never wake up." He gazed upon a crucifix hanging on the opposite wall and said softly. "Every morning when I wake up, I ask. "Dear Lord Jesus Christ, was I such a bad man, that now you don't want me?" At that moment, it took every ounce of control not to burst into tears. I looked down on his emaciated face and held the gaze of his forget me not blue eyes.

He sat up and asked in a more direct manner. "But now I want to know how you have fared all these years. We could not tell much from the occasional greeting cards and the many different addresses." He reached for his glasses on the night stand and adjusted them and looked me squarely in the eyes. "Why did you move around so much? Your poor mother watched news coverage from New York to San Francisco, thinking she might catch a glimpse of her little sparrow flitting in the streets during news coverages. She still watches the American TV shows, Dallas and Denver and whatever news coverage television brings to Germany."

I had to laugh at the thought of my poor mother scanning for a glimpse of me among the millions walking the streets of New York and San Francisco. "Your mother thinks everybody gets rich as Rockefeller in America, but I don't think life was easy for you." His inquisitive words sounded like a sober assessment. I searched for a proper reply and smiled. "Papa, you were right all along! Nothing was easy. I had married the first guy, who asked me, because I wanted to put down roots and belong to the American way of life. By the time, I had five children, I had a rude awakening, when I realized, I am responsible for the lives of five people, some day I might have to fend for them and myself." He mumbled. "Aha, aha! But why did you move around so much?"

"In America you go, where the jobs are. I had married a man who would be contend to live in a bread truck with pie in the sky ideas that never materialized. I remember my husband saying."I want to give you the moon babe." Which prompted me to reply. "I don't want the moon, just a mortgage we can afford. We moved around a lot looking for that pie in the sky, for work, a paycheck and affordable housing. I realized, I could no longer allow myself to become a victim of circumstances and misfortunes. I finally decided to take the bull by the horn and take the reins of family responsibility into my hands. I had to take charge of my life and the lives of my children. I could not rely on anyone else least of all my husband." He mumbled. "Why didn't you write?"

"I did not want to worry you and mother with unpleasant truths while I was busy putting my life in order. I did not want to complain about just how miserable life could become without a good life partner, a home and family, without roots, without a sense of belonging.

You and mother weathered everything together to survive. But you could no longer help me and I did not want to worry you and hear you say. "We told you so. I worked three jobs to secure a house from foreclosure. I served breakfast at an Inn, dinner at a diner, steak and lobster at country clubs on weekends, where smiling sweetly pays for college tuition. Mine was in Finance.

That's how it works in America. You just have to look for help wanted signs, walk in, and avail yourself for work." I realized my father tried to comprehend, what I had said. "We moved around for work and because no house felt like a home. I felt no attachment to four walls. In the worst of days, I reminded myself how you and mom defied the odds stacked against you, being caught between the National Socialist and Communist period. How you survived now you have to deal with socialist democrats and overzealous bureaucrats. How much worse could my life be in America?" He looked deep in thought. "Don't forget, Socialists lure the proletarian masses with false promises of a utopian world order. Many German people have been lured away from Germany to America with promises of wealth thinking, wealth is safe there. Some have made it big in America, but many have not." I meekly replied. "I know Papa. People fall through the cracks but I think they would have fallen through the cracks anywhere. Life in America is a roller coaster ride. But you have to get up, dust yourself off and keep going. You suffered more than I ever will and you survived. Every day, I thought just how hard you had to fight all your life?" He murmured softly. "Aha mh."

Just then my mother entered the darkened room with gauze and medications and Ben-Gay.. My father looked about as if remembering something. "Where is your coat?" I knew he might ask me about the coat. I was glad, I had bought one almost as luxurious as the one he had bought for me years ago. Just to prove, I had not ended up in gutters of New York.

I clasped the fur collar and chimed. "Here it is! See?" By the look in my mother's eyes, I knew she knew, this could not be the same coat. I hoped my father would not recognize this was a coat from a different animal. "Papa, I am sorry I could not come home sooner, I was too busy earning a living. Now my children are married. I have an empty nest and the time and money to spend with you and mom."

He nodded and replied. "I can only imagine that life has not been easy for you with five children". My mother never said a word about the coat while she helped my father get out of bed and guided him into the wheelchair. When the pajama leg was pushed up above the knee I saw his amputated and bandaged knee stumps. I pressed back the tears and covered my mouth to suppress the look of horror as he whispered. "Look, little one, look, see what these horse doctors have done to me." My mother applied fresh ointment. across a purplish wound, covered the stumps with fresh gauze and with a smile on her lips kissed him on the cheek. I was amazed how calm and skilled my mother tended to my father's needs. She wheeled him into the kitchen and pushed the chair close to the table and fastened a bib around his neck, placed a tray of food on the table.

"Okay. Let's eat…we have plenty of time for storytelling." My father looked down on his food. He wanted to talk more than he wanted to eat. I was eager to capture every word. For my children's sake I resolved to preserve what I could of a heritage that the world would rather not remember, but my children should know the stories of their ancestry.

The House My Father Built

I was wondering what was going through his mind and said. "Papa, I am sorry because my children will never have the chance to get to know their grandfather."

As soon as he started talking again, I pressed the tape recorder button, so I could tell my children about their ancestry and where it all had started…

Schneekoppe vom Koppenplan
kol. Lithografie, Carl Mattis Schmiedeberg, um 1830

Mastig...

Nestled in the heart of the mountains that form the border between Poland and Czechoslovakia, which Germans named Giant Mountains and the Czechs named Krokonose lay tiny villages, one of them was Mastig, so tiny it could not be found on a map, much to the delight of the folks whose motto was, if they can't find us they won't bother us.

Mastig had no village square, no town hall, no police station, no theatre, and no form of entertainment, except church on Sunday. There was nothing to do except gather to gossip over a tilted stone mug, filled with frothy Pilsner brew in the Hample Pub, where chickens wandered freely about the yard until a patron ordered a chicken dinner and the cook had to wring its neck and pluck its feathers before being thrown in the frying pan. The Hample Pub provided respite to the hardworking grist millers, lumber jacks and field hands at the end of the day over a frothy brew on tap. While at the other end of Mastig, the pub of Gustav Gernert provided a friendly place to unwind for the more gentile folks.

Everyone's family name and identity was known by his business. The Linhart flour miller and the Haase grist miller propagated their wealth in well planned marriages.

Along its one thoroughfare, was the butcher shop of Gustav Gernerts' brother, the pub keeper and the Schubert baker, the Staffa shoemaker and the Staffa carpenter.

Along the main thoroughfare, the Josef Staffa farm, forest and lumber operation buttressed the sports field and took up most of the property at Mastig's only intersection across from Luschnitz's General store, which served the basic needs of the villagers.

Josef Staffa was a name borne of pride. An ancestry that had become well entrenched in archives and emblazoned on many public buildings. In baptismal records in a church and war memorial plaques in cemeteries in neighboring Ober-Prausnitz, the name Josef Staffa was recorded as early as the fifteenth century.

They fought in wars against the Turks and the French wars to become eternally entombed within the trenches in foreign lands.

Attesting to the family's great pride and ancient wealth were black marble grave plates, emblazoned with huge golden crosses and the names of the souls at rest of the wives of the fallen whose maiden names of five generations were Tauchmann, Kaufmann, Hartmann, Lorenz and Lauschmann. Marriage among cousins was a common means to propagate the Josef Staffa dynasty. So important was the continuity of the name "Josef" that, if a family lacked a male off spring, a girl was named Josepha. Therefore, Josepha Staffa married her cousin, Josef Staffa. They were born fourteen years and six house numbers apart. They had two sons, Josef and Stefan who started his own lumber business in nearby Königinhof.

Josef decided to sell a huge acreage of forest land when he decided to marry, and needed the money to establish his own lumber business in Mastig. He sold the land in 1898 to Adolf Mandl with his brothers, Josef, Eduard and Heinrich, who arrived with their wives and sons in splendid carriages to make the village of Mastig their home much to the open-mouthed amazement of the villagers.

The Mandls had bought the land that stretched from one end of the village to the other. They were a wealthy Jewish family from Vienna, who with their entourage brought Viennese haute couture and culture.

Adolf Mandl and Josef Staffa never met again after the land sale was signed and sealed. Adolf Mandl built a villa and a textile factory, that spanned the entire length of the village and buttressed the soccer and sports field. Judging by its size, it was accepted that the clan of Adolf Mandl had come to stay. The villagers scratched their heads wondering why such a wealthy family would come from Vienna to a place that could not be found on a map.

Adolf Mandl built a train station and railroad tracks into the factory complex and villa property. The villagers looked aghast as they compared the Mandl villa to the castle in Berlin, and shook their heads at such opulence in their tiny hamlet.

The villas proximity to the train station enabled Adolfs' family to slip in and out of their palace without being seen, which suited the Mandls' desire to remain an enigma.

Just one look at the ostentatious villa led to the Mandls' renown as the wealthiest men in the world. Adolf Mandls' presence in this backwater hamlet was viewed with great suspicion by the villagers of the region. As much as the villagers had cherished their anonymity the presence of the Mandl family had placed this tiny hamlet, Mastig on the industrial world map.

In swift succession, the parameters of the Mandl factory yard were surrounded by a chain link fence. Box-shaped cottages were slapped together to house the low-wage workers, their wives and children, which Adolf had to import from neighboring Slavic countries to operate his textile factory at a healthy profit. Quick to scrutinize such flimsy construction, the Germans called these ramshackle box shaped huts, made of light weight linear boards "Bretterbuden." Adolf Mandl had come as an enigma to this German community, yet his fame spread.

He knew how to appease these disgruntled villagers with ample generosity to make heads wag in astonishment. He made generous donations to Saint Joseph Catholic Church in nearby Klein-Borowitz, built new schools amidst this agrarian community, and financed the German Kindergarten and Elementary School in Mastig.

A great mystery revolved around red haired children born out of wedlock to blond Nemci (German) mothers, one of whom was rumored to be a baroness from Reichenberg, the strong hold of blond and blue-eyed, light-skinned Aryans. The handsomely dark children were scuttled off, and settled comfortably in elite German boarding schools, where light skin was the pride of the neighborhood. In the minds of these simple people, stories of endowment and endearment never warranted more than a wink of the eye and a shrug of the shoulders.

Adolf Mandl never bothered these simple folks and the appeased villagers never bothered him. Adolf and his clan were so elusive they were never heard nor seen by ordinary people, none ever saw them coming or going, thus Adolf Mandl remained an enigma.

In 1902, the wife of Josef Staffa, Maria Menzel died shortly after giving birth to a daughter at the tender age of twenty-seven. Her death left Josef a grieving widower with three small sons and an infant daughter to raise. Josef's widowed mother, fifty-seven-year old Josepha, served as surrogate as best she could. But within a few months Josepha prodded her son to find a new wife, when she felt her own strength failing to meet the demands of the lively brood. Josepha at last succeeded in persuading her son to attend a special May dance, sponsored annually by the Catholic Church to propagate the faith.

The festival was a welcomed reprieve from the harsh realities of the daily grind. Once a year, the medieval Holy Family church in Ober-Prausnitz, offered the most attractive setting for young men and women of marriageable age to meet at a dance from miles around. The church with its towers proudly peering above tree tops was visible as soon as one rounded a hillside. The young men wore their finest Sunday attire watching the young women arrive in their laciest Sunday dirndls and white stockings from every direction down the narrow cleft in the mountain side, on foot or on bicycles, or in brightly decorated hay wagons with hopes to capture someone's fancy as they twirled around a rainbow-colored May wreath.

The church was surrounded by a park and a duck pond behind the church rectory. The park was filled with ornately gilded statues of sanguinely smiling Saints who provided the perfect setting in which to propagate faith and family empires. The willow trees and wildflowers along the path around the pond in back of the church and rectory, filled a sojourner's soul with rare and exquisite vistas, where a young girl with a gentle peasant face dressed in rustic simplicity was sitting demurely beside the pond shaded by a huge willow.

At this moment in her life, she preferred the companionship of ducks to the giggling crowd inside the parish hall. The girl threw stale breadcrumbs into the water, and clacked her tongue. The ducks moved in close, as she called out to them and chatted with them in a peasant dialect, as if they were old friends.

It appeared that ducks would be her only companions that night, and all her efforts in adorning herself would be for naught. The girl had not a notion of how to meet the eyes of a man.

Her name was Anna Kudronovsky. She marked this day in her prayer book only with the initials A.K., to commemorate this special day to no one but herself, this—-her eighteenth birthday. Indeed, at eighteen years of age, A.K. had very little reason to smile, even on her birthday. Since the age of fourteen Anna had seen it her duty to support her widowed mother.

Her "Mamimka," as she tenderly called her mother in her Czech language, had found work in the grimy Mandl factory to support herself and her only child, whereas, Anna considered herself lucky to have found work as a servant girl in the wealthiest household in Mastig, that of Adolf Mandl.

Inside the posh Mandl villa, Anna washed and ironed her youth away and beat dirt and crumbs off Persian carpets slung across the metal bars outside the coal cellar. She likened the looks of this Jewish household to a palace in comparison to the plain peasant homes with peek-a-boo windows.

Being of marriageable age, the pious girl lacked suitors, and the neighboring villages lacked suitable prospects. With every birthday, she feared old age would creep up on her, and hope of being noticed by a bachelor male would have to be dashed. Her life would have remained routine enough to make even a devout Catholic as herself cringe with foreboding.

Anna spent her moments of reprieve immersed in her most luxurious possession, a prayer book covered with white leather, adorned with 24K gold leaved roses and a mother of pearl crucifix. Gently, she turned the delicate pages edged in gold and satin ribbons with which she marked her favorite passages. The beauty of the palm-sized book evoked a loving tenderness giving a clue to the lyrics and poetry of tender mercies. Anna had nothing to look back on with regret, nor anything to look forward to with relish. She was content to fulfill her rustic duties with a scythe or a scrub pail, and never thought of a task as demeaning.

In the fall, she went with field hands to pick potatoes, to fill the cellars of the Mandl potato cellar. Sometimes the lady of the house would allow her to take a few sacks of potatoes home to her Mamimka. In her humility, Anna considered it a generous reward.

Except to work as a maid, Anna had never ventured out of the "little nest" provided by her widowed and now ailing Mamimka. Shy and demure, Anna needed much prodding to attend any public function, especially a dance.

Her mother clasped her hands and pleaded with her child. "You must go out and meet young people. Or you'll have a lonely existence in old age." Anna grudgingly obliged. She brushed her crimped tresses and twisted them about her head, donned her finest dirndl and white stockings, draped a fringed shawl about her narrow shoulders, and with a final glance in the mirror, nodded encouragement to her image, as a blush was creeping over her exposed décolleté.She trekked the miles alone on foot, from Nieder-Prausnitz to Ober-Prausnitz, over the Switchin mountain top past the Inn at Mastig Bad until she could see the spires of the church of the Holy Family peering out from lush greenery.

Alongside the roadway, forget-me-nots bloomed in wild profusion. She picked a handful and wove them into the crown of her golden hair. She cringed at the thought of twirling around a Maypole, without an inkling of the joy and woebegone awaiting her in the arms of a man. On this, her eighteenth birthday she would not allow anything to discern her. Had a young widower not noticed her sitting by the pond, her special day would have passed uncelebrated.

Josef recognized Anna as the servant girl from the Mandl villa. His forget-me-not-blue eyes never left her face as he sat down beside her. Anna looked nervously flushed with excitement as she described her duties within the Mandl household. "I'm lucky …I don't have to work in the Mandl factory, a fate many widowed women in this area share, I fear such fate will befall me also." The young widower engaged Anna at once to set her heart on fire. Moments after their first dance had begun everyone knew that the prominent widower's attention was focused on A.K. exclusively.

She blushed with excitement as he gallantly helped her climb into the carriage for a slow ride home to Nieder-Prausnitz in plain view of quizzical glances. Anna knew she would be the target of whisperings around every village well between Mastig and Nieder-Prausnitz.

Indeed, Josef Staffa had seen in Anna the kind, motherly qualities his infant daughter and three young sons needed. Josef made no bones of his need for a wife who could tackle a large household as deftly as she could swing a pitchfork. Within days after the first kiss he made his "love interest" known, leaving no room to ponder, as to why someone like Josef Staffa would come at the end of every day to while away the evening hours, seated on a hard chair in her Mamimkas' dismally small kitchen with peek-a-boo windows.

At the mention of his famous name and sideways glances, her blush turned slowly crimson, creeping slowly from the base of her neck to charmingly cover her gentle face. But her initial embarrassment gave way to excitement. She yielded to his outstretched arms and with every kiss she knew that the cloak of youthful innocence would be torn to shreds.

Josef Staffa wasted no time in choosing Anna Kudronovsky for his bride. After four weeks of hectic courtship, he proposed marriage, offering her a home with wide windows that looked across blooming gardens as his gift of love. Unable to believe her good fortune, she stared at her reflection and adjusted her lace collar. She could see that she was no fair faced Nemci beauty. She was endowed with Ceski high-cheeks, a peasant femininity, filled with ripening sexual potential and a pure heart. "Peace is in knowing whom to thank for ones' good fortune." She glanced at the crucifix above her bed and crossed herself.

"Forgive me, dear Lord, I don't know for what, but I'll think of something." There was little for which Anna would need to be forgiven, she was a pure soul even after Josef Staffa had entered her life, she was without guile. She looked tired from her daily grind as she planned her wedding and sank into her goose down comforters late at night after she finished sewing her wedding gown, contended in the comfort of her first love.

Anna managed to scrape enough money together from her meager earnings to take the train to Prague, where she shopped for a gift befitting a man who had become the love of her life.

On the evening of their betrothal, Anna presented her betrothed a gold pocket watch covered with rich filigree, which she had engraved with "Eternal Love—-AK

While the baby girl gurgled with contentment in Anna's cradling arms, much to her dismay Josef's three sons Adolf, Franz and Emil wanted nothing to do with their father's new wife, and resented her for taking their mother's place. Anna tried to sweeten the new household ordinance with sugar sprinkled on thickly buttered bread. When the wedding plans were announced the three boys, stubbornly resisted even the kindest gestures of their new step-mother, especially Adolf, the oldest nudged his brothers into remembering that "Anna Kudronovsky is not our mother." When Anna tried to embrace Adolf, he wrestled free of her embrace and she muttered in colloquialism, "Jessesmarren." (Jesus and Mary)

Without fanfare, and unwilling to waste time on childish cockalorum, seeing it was good that Anna had been raised as a devout Catholic, two weeks after his proposal Josef Staffa married the young Czech girl on June 4, 1903, knowing Anna would be a devoted wife and mother, one who would fulfill her wifely duties without reservations and add her own offspring in due time to a teeming household.

The night before the wedding, Anna bathed the boys, and cherub faces emerged from beneath sweaty grime. On the morning of the simple wedding ceremony in the church in Oberprausnitz, six-year-old Adolf, flushed from crying his eyes out, stayed in bed feigning sickness. The boy looked feverish enough to cause alarm, but Anna knew his suffering was due to the turmoil of his grieving soul.

Anna could do nothing but remand his ailment to a purer heart. But as soon as the gaily decorated horse-drawn carriage left for the church in OberPrausnitz, a tormented child crawled out of bed. He scurried unnoticed along garden hedges a mere stones' throw from his house to St. Anna's cemetery.

While Anna gloried on her wedding day, knowing she looked lovely in a white silk gown, satin and lace bodice, and a lace veil that framed her small body from the top of her head and trailed ten feet behind her, as she walked down the aisle to meet her bridegroom. Josef could not take his forget-me-not blue eyes off her face. While a lonely boy huddled beside his mother's grave, which his father had adorned with an eternal flame. Weeping, he swore eternal love for the soul at rest and promised never to love that other woman.

Before their wedding day, Anna had seen her husband only in his work clothes, now she stood beside him and marveled at him for she had never seen him look more handsome, dressed in a black tuxedo, white bowtie and a sprig of carnations in his lapel. The chain of the pocket watch she had given him for their betrothal gleamed proudly from under his left lapel. Anna had never known another man. She burst with pride knowing this man would be her husband for the rest of her life. Her white gloved hand held her tiny white prayer book and she gave him her left hand in marriage as they said their vows. She could not imagine any other man in her life as he vowed to love her to the end of his life.

Like a Cinderella story it became village fodder, that a Czech scullery maid, who had worked for the wealthy Mandl family and now had married one of the richest men in the area. Josef Staffa was her husband now and Anna felt elevated as the wife of a rich man, second only to the rich Mandl clan from Vienna. Despite her new status as wife of the boss, Anna never put on airs and remained humble as she considered herself an equal to the field hands and servants.

She toiled hard alongside the field hands, matching every swing of a pitchfork and scythe, while her husband harvested tracts of timber which had been marked to be cut, and hauled away as logs or deadwood with chains to clear the woods for new seedlings to be planted. Healthy logs were cut into boards and roof shingles. He replanted swaths of forestland to secure rich harvests for future generations.

Among the village women, Anna earned the reputation of being the kindest mother a child could have. The children relished her sweet attention when she churned fresh butter and spread it on sliced home baked bread, then she sprinkled sugar and cinnamon on top. It was a treat as sweet as a piece of cake. But no amount of sugar could sweeten Adolf's heart. He closed himself off from his stepmother in a deep freeze. Cloaked in that solemn promise to his deceased mother, Adolf whiled away the lonely hours in his room or lingered around the unyielding cemetery. His heart wilted during his lonely childhood. While crying his heart out, he buried his tender soul beside the dearest soul he had ever known.

The one child that blossomed under Anna's care was the infant Maria, named after her deceased mother. The young woman cradled the child in her arms, clutching her to her breast as she murmured sweet assuagements. "I promised the soul of your beloved Mamimka, I hold you as tenderly in my heart, as I hold you in my arms. Anna looked in wonder as the infant curled tiny fingers around hers and clung to her for dear life. "How could I not love you, Marie? That's what I shall call you…Marie." Marie soaked up the tender affection lavished on her by the only mother she had known and loved, and blossomed into a happy, high-spirited, self-assured beauty.

Eleven months after the wedding, Anna gave birth to a daughter, and named her Anna Irena on March 9, 1904. A year later she gave birth to her first son whom she named "Pepiczek." The Czech name for Josef.

At regular intervals she added two more sons to Josef Staffa's burgeoning household named Karl and Alfred. Anna emerged with a sense of propriety as the wife of Josef Staffa, having given birth to an heir to the Josef Staffa Lumber dynasty. Anna took pains to exchange her initials AK on her linens for ASt. She was now referred to as the Chefin, wife of the boss. For Anna, life had become a worldly adventure in the marriage to a wealthy man.

But on June 19, 1906, Anna made her first mournful notation into her prayer book "Today, my precious and dearest Mamimka died." Still in mourning over the loss of her mother, two months later, on August 8, she filled the second page of the book with lamentations over the loss of her beloved firstborn son Pepiczek, dead of pneumonia before his first birthday. Dressed in black and heavily veiled, she followed the small coffin of her beloved son. Her face was shrouded by grief as she composed a requiem into her prayer book. "If the warmth of my love could restore you to my breast, cold earth would not be thy blanket of rest." From that day, Anna lived in perpetual mourning, painfully sighing at the mention of Pepiczek. Her heart was weighed down by grief. She yearned for another boy to fill the hole in her heart another boy like Pepiczek.

Anna Kudro

On October 10, 1910, the midwife beckoned Josef to welcome another son, whom Anna named Josef, not as replacement of the son she had lost four years earlier, but to perpetuate the name, Josef Staffa. Anna called him Pepi, his eight-year-old sister Marie called him Sef. Anna was pleased, for not only had she secured her position in the family, but her youngest son was the mirror image of his father. She afforded herself the luxury of a car. Anna became the first and only woman in the region to own a stately Dusenberg. She had learned to relish her new status and hired a young Czech named Pavel Koczian.

She allowed herself to be chauffeured about the regions business centers into Arnau, Reichenberg, Hohenelbe and on special occasions Prague. But her favorite outing was a trip into the splendid Giant mountains which formed the northern border to Poland. In the winter small communities hitched horse drawn sleds together, lit torches and the sleds wove trails through the idyllic winter landscape down the mountain paths.

As Josef grew up, Anna was pleased that her son was endowed with classic, finely chiseled features. An aquiline nose, blond hair and forget-me-not blue eyes like those of his German father. The fair-faced lad was Anna's sheer delight. His keen intelligence and delicate sense of humor combined in an exultant joy for life.

Anna showered him with adulation and hovered over him like the snarling Rottweiler who lazed in the sun beside the estates' garden gate. Anna would leap into action if anyone dared bend a hair on her sons' head. An unforeseen danger loomed for the boy from his uncle.

Uncle Stefan, brother of his father Josef, would become heir to the Staffa Lumber business, in case something happened to his brother. He was nonplussed to hear that his brother's second wife had given birth to another son, whom she named Josef in replacement of her first-born son, Pepiczek to insure that one of her sons would carry on the family name of Josef Staffa. Uncle Stefan was often overheard mumbling to himself, "Maybe a bullet in the head will get him."

The sensitive boy tended to befriend livestock, and called them by names. He refused to eat the meat of an animal he had known before its slaughter. Many chickens lived to a ripe old age long after they had stopped laying eggs, and died natural deaths. From the time he was able to stand up in his crib, he jumped up and down to the rhythm of the saw blades.

The House My Father Built

Every morning the boy eagerly followed his father around, showing a keen interest in all his fathers' labors. He joyously scampered behind him through the woodlands and helped him plant new seedlings.

He delighted in the wheezing of saw blades as the old trees were felled. His father proclaimed him a true Staffa and heir to his life's work much to the chagrin of his older sons, who had formed a wall of resistance between them and the children of his second wife, alliances of jealousy and anxiety over inheritance rights formed around the boy, dividing the household with the blind ambitions of love and hate.

Over the years, young Josef's half-brother Adolf had grown into a handsome young lad despite his alcoholic affliction, with which he alienated everyone around him. While mourning the loss of his mother had become a grotesque ritual, he had started a slow descent into his father's wine cellar before his daily walks to the cemetery. No one paid much heed to Adolf and his odd behavior, thus no one noticed his slow descent into alcoholism.

Adolf was clever enough to place the water-filled bottles beside those of the most recent wine bottles. His step-mother Anna had grown weary of the lads' stagger, believing him to be merely lazy. The lad's face portrayed a sulking frown whenever he looked at his stepmother. He was angry that she had borne yet another heir to his father's lumber business.

On June 28, 1914 the peaceful idyll in these mountain hamlets was brought to an end over more than family feuds. Sef was not yet four years old when a shot was fired in Sarajevo by a Serbian Nationalist that killed the Austrian heir to the throne, Franz Ferdinand and his wife, the Czech countess Chotek. Franz Ferdinand had countenanced many requests of the Czech people and had shown great benevolence toward them when he and his wife fell victim to Slavic separatism. In this remote mountain region nobody paid heed to the dark clouds forming on the far horizon. Sarajevo seemed too foreign and too far removed from the concerns of simple mountain people. Yet, it took only one bullet to plunge the entire world into the most divisive battle of the century, leaving pockmarks of battle on every nation for decades, which devastated many generations in the desolate areas of the Giant Mountains.

With jaunty jingoism and hateful jargons, European countries in a quest for economic power itched to bloody every ones' nose. Country after country collided like domino stones to be dragged into the bloodiest war in history. When Austria-Hungary threatened Serbia with retaliation for the murder of the heir to the Habsburg throne, Serbia appealed to their Russian cousins who declared war on Austria. Austria appealed to Germany for help.

Russia called on France for help and France declared war on Germany, Britain joined France and declared war on Germany and the United States sided with the British.

What was to be the war to end all wars was nothing more than a bloody family feud between European monarchs, who were all related through marriage to the royal House of Windsor. The mother of Britain's Queen Victoria was a German princess of Saxon-Coburg and Saalfeld. Victoria married her cousin German Prince Albert from Saxon Coburg and Gotha.

Victoria and Albert's marriage produced nine children, who also married into other European royal families. A family feud had erupted between the grandchildren of Queen Victoria and Prince Albert. Each sought to gain economic power over one another long before a shot was fired in Sarajevo. Russia's Czar, Nicholas II, the German Kaiser, Wilhelm I, and King Edward VII were cousins, who in their family feud plunged the world into the quagmire that killed millions on both sides. Russia's Czar Nicholas II had come to the aid of his Serbian cousins and he fell victim together with his family, to the Bolshevik Revolution in the aftermath and devastation the war had caused his Russian countrymen.

The slaughter that cost twelve million lives, officially ended November 11, 1918. Many memorial plaques had the name Josef Staffa listed as fallen husband and father who was lost in the quagmire of mud, lice and disease infested trenches in the war to end all wars..

Vae victis—
woe the vanquished—

Sef was eight years old when in the Armistice Agreement Germany was forced to accept responsibility for the war. The Austro-Hungary Empire was dissolved, and carved up. Czechoslovakia was born by decree of the victorious allies which American President Woodrow Wilson unveiled to the world as a newly created democratic country and hailed it as a role model for democratic nation building. Instead, Czechoslovakia was a farce from its birth when the German communities were ceded to Czechoslovakia. The area that forms an arrowhead into the motherland, Germany became another powder keg that evolved into another war that never ended.

While publicly hailing democracy as the Golden Calf, Czech President Eduard Benes forged a cultural sword aimed at more than three million Germans, who had become pawns in systematic terror and intimidation and labeled them invaders.

Eduard Benes ruled the country in total contradiction to the democratic principles advocated by Woodrow Wilson. In an eloquent speech Woodrow Wilson called for ethnic tolerance toward the Sudeten Germans and their right of self-determination in Czechoslovakia, when in effect his plans developed into a scheme of ethnic cleaning. To prevent Germans from gaining economic power their population was renamed Sudeten Germans.

At the time, the nation of Czechs and Slovaks ranked as the most densely populated region in Europe. "Der Volksbote," a weekly Catholic journal published a census which counted 7.4 million Czechs, 3.5 million Sudeten Germans who shared this region as the largest minority with 2.3 million Slovaks and a mix of one million Russians, Rumanians, Ukrainians, Poles, Hungarians, and Gypsies.

A process of persecution and deprivation followed, which affected future generations, a process that would end in colossal injustices and human suffering and pushed a peaceful people to the edge of an abyss.

Posters appeared everywhere proclaiming the ideology of Slavism, until it became a popular theory across the broadest Czech demography that the Germans were "colonists," whose acquired material goods belonged to the Czech people. A theory which the Czechs embraced readily. The German people had invaded their country and must lose their identity, their culture and their language or leave the country.

Czech bureaucrats wasted no time drafting new laws that would drive deeper wedges between the various ethnic groups. German town halls were closed and 33,000 German government employees were fired, and replaced with 41,000 Czech bureaucrats. The German sports and cultural clubs were banned. German merchants were ordered not to sell their products outside German territories, which put 525,000 Sudeten Germans out of work.

German women were still enamored by Viennese culture, music and dance. They had to look on in horror as Czech troops marched into German villages, tore down the pictures of the Austrian emperor and his wife Zita in public and private buildings.

Soldiers ransacked homes as women clutched the pictures of the empress Zita to their chests, pleading to be allowed keepsakes they had cherished in their homes for decades.

Without mercy the soldiers tore these "souvenirs" from trembling hands and burned them before their horrified eyes.

What love people once had for the Austrian emperor and his wife was replaced by winds of nationalistic fervor, for reasons the women did not understand. Terroristic measures of a hostile government were aimed to break down German resistance to the new Czech Government, and the destruction of German economic power. Czech National Socialists (Narodny Vybor) enforced the new Government decrees, carrying pistols and mallets. Saboteurs swung bullwhips to provoke a steady flood of terror and intimidation.

The Sudeten German people out of fear of losing their autonomy demanded the right to bring their case before the Allied powers and pressed for representation at a scheduled peace conference. The German representatives wanted to hear public announcements to enable them to make accurate assessments, but the Czech government denied their requests. Upon hearing of their exclusion, Sudeten Germans massed in the streets on March 4, 1919.

The House My Father Built

The Czech military opened fire and massacred fifty of the assembled representatives. March 4th became the National Day of Remembrance for the Sudeten German victims of that massacre. Their names were never forgotten and ever since before council meetings the names were read out loud followed by a moment of silence.

Fear and hatred boiled over, fanned by diabolical rhetoric, as new political reformers fought to wrest economic power from the German minority. Czech infiltrators and agitators were planted into German communities to create a constant state of anxiety as they sowed discord and unrest among people. Agitators would strut three abreast along narrow streets with cocksure brazenness, cracking whips and firing pistols into the air above the heads of very frightened people, who felt pressed to jump from sidewalks with every shattering noise or crack of a whip. Strangely disheveled, bushy, bearded young men, which no one had seen before moved into homes, whose previous owners had been forced to flee.

Anyone who refused to leave their home was shot and crimes against any German were not investigated, nor prosecuted even if caught red-handed or punished. Sniper fires could be heard at night and no one seemed to know where the gunshots came from.

The Czech authorities ignored complaints from German villagers, who shuttered their windows, and kept their children inside. Women ducked their heads at the slightest noise, as they scuttled between stores to secure basic needs at the bakery, butcher and general store.

Despite all these intimidations the German people banded together, determined to adhere to ancient customs. Blessings were counted in the abundance growing in a backyard, and stockpiles of preserved goods in the cellar. Neighbor helped neighbor, by handing fruits and vegetables over the fence to those in need, after the first fruits of the harvest had been brought tuthe altar from the fields, in which men and women labored from sunrise to sunset.

Children were oblivious of the devastation of war and its aftermath. They still played soccer in open fields wearing skimpy shorts. Still picked blueberries and mushrooms in the surrounding woodlands and only noticed when someone was missing in the empty church pew next to a weeping widow and when monuments for the fallen German soldiers who had fought under the Austro-Hungary banner were erected in village squares and wreaths were laid in their memory.

In 1918, oldest daughter, Annie celebrated her fifteenth-birthday, after which her mother allowed her to ride the train to Prague, where the young girl acquired a taste for haute couture. On rainy days Annie played the piano, dressed like a Bohemian princess and allowed herself to be chauffeured around in a stately Dusenberg to private girls' school, dance and piano lessons while her half-sister Marie, like Cinderella, uncomplaining performed the most tedious tasks and stayed at home to polish everyone's shoes. Despite that, Marie loved them all, yet she often found herself thrust into the middle of family disputes. More often she saw a need to protect her youngest brother from more than sibling rivalry as he got older. But beware the quiet girl, if anyone dared raise a hand against her beloved brother, Marie could pack a snowball and pelt them like a well-aiming javelin champion.

Sef knew Marie was his champion and always had his back, where the others would have rather seen him dead. If Marie was not at home Sef steered clear of his brothers and sauntered off into the solitude of the forest where he found mushrooms and a mossy bed for peaceful reflection and sweet sustenance in a handful of wild blueberries. He found a peaceful Shangri-la at the Fox Hollow Spring where he crouched beside the base of a fir tree from where crystal waters gushed out from under its thick roots that quenched his thirst as he heard a cuckoo in the distance. He tapped water into a bottle and when he held it to the light, he saw the water bubbling with natural carbonation.

From an early age, he scampered behind his father, between rows of white birches, lush green oak trees, evergreens and blueberry bushes which his father and grandfather had planted years ago. He felt peace and comfort of body and soul. Marie had taught him to love the land and its people. She was a born storyteller and her brother was an ardent listener. The ancient stories seemed to lie deeply rooted within the mother earth.

The telling of stories of good kings and evil queens, of virtuous princes and robber barons, mountain giants and cave dwelling dwarfs, witches and warlocks of German folklore, in which the good prevailed over evil, yielded an endless reservoir for books and musical fantasy the world over. All these tales had their sources and birth in these mountains.

Marie and Sef identified with this rich heritage, surrounded by gothic structures to support their pride. Their adventurous spirit led them to explore caves and tunnels dating back to medieval times, when robber barons waited for unsuspecting merchants traveling from East to West to market their wares. These robbers popped out of caves, holes and tunnels within these mountains overpowering their hapless victims only to disappear with the rich booty into the darkness of caverns and tunnels that led to their fortress on top of a hill, without leaving a trace.

Two statues over the village portal of Arnau told a tale of two giants, who terrorized the little people of this region for years, plundering and burning all their possessions. The bravery of the citizens of the regions shopping and banking district in Arnau, had grown tired of being victimized by these marauders. The people hatched a plan to bring an end to the terror. They posted sentries along mountain trails. As soon as the two giants were spotted the sentries released pigeons from a burlap sack. When the villagers saw the flock of birds ascend, they hoisted buckets of hot tar and a hundred sacks of goose feathers over the village gate.

As these giants passed under the gate, the rope was cut and hot tar poured over them like syrup over pancakes. Billowing white clouds of feathers filled the air so thick the giants couldn't see. Tarred and feathered, blindly screaming they ran off into the woods never to be seen again.

The little people of Arnau lived happily ever after. But the fairytale existence was short lived. The fate of blissful inhabitants of these mountains would never depend on simplistic solutions of little people, nor would a horror story end like that of a fairy tale.

Josef Staffa and his wife Anna were feeling the heat from a belligerent Czech government as tracts of land were confiscated from German landowners and given to Czech peasants. Josef paced off parcels of land before the government could claim it, and gave it to his most faithful field hands. He hitched up horses and hauled lumber for the construction of St. Anna's Church steeple before the government bureaucrats could confiscate more of his lumber.

Signs appeared at factory gates when trucks laden with lumber had been marked and the load could no longer be delivered outside German communities. Within a few months "Closed" signs hung outside the once productive enterprises.

Government agents seized properties, if not mismanaged they were laid to waste ever after. Many German businesses collapsed under newly enacted taxation, fees, penalties and repressive regulations.

The German school chancellor was fired and replaced with a Czech teacher. The German language was outlawed. Only Czech was allowed to be spoken. The Czech language is very difficult to master if not learned in early childhood. Vowels and consonants and rolling r's make a hissing sound that simply don't roll off a German tongue. Being fluent in both the Czech and German language the new laws had no effect on Anna and her children, yet even she voiced her strong objections and abhorrence of the ensuing confusion which the new laws caused when the German schools were closed.

Schools were scheduled to reopen after new textbooks were in place in the Czech language. German textbooks in metric math and science journals were never translated. Closing of German public schools caused unemployment among teachers, engineers and scientists, fueling more suspicions and hatred among those who could not afford to send their children to the few remaining private German schools across the border in Germany.

Unfortunately, many parents were too poor and had no options than to have their children struggle with a dismally inferior education system as the one offered in Czech schools. To avoid the political cockalorum Anna sent her children to private German schools. She was determined that her sons and daughters' education would not be hampered with teaching materials in the Czech language.

Anna was in agreement with a progressive society that promoted equality for women in education and the workplace. She refused to allow her daughters to be straddled in an inferior education system and end up as scullery maids, scrubbing floors, as she once had as long as there were options for them to learn skills that would give them a better life.

She sent Marie and Annie to an elite business school for girls in Reichenberg, dressed in slim, knee-length business skirts, white blouses, and smart looking neckties.

Next to Mastig was the tiny village of Klein-Borowitz. Within this dominant German community a few wealthy Czech families lived in peaceful coexistence with theirGerman neighbor, many of whom had intermarried. The spires of St. Joseph Catholic Church towered prominently over the valley. The church was built next to an elementary school. Both school and church were built with generous donations from Adolf Mandl, whose factory in neighboring Mastig needed more manpower and the women eagerly dropped their scythe and pitchforks to work the spools of yarn for Adolf Mandl.

The wealthy Borufka family of eight brothers and sisters had inter-married into the German community and married into wealth again. Karl Borufka married Maria Pfenninger, a daughter of a wealthy Swiss family, who owned a mustard factory in Eibau near Dresden close to the German border. Another Borufka brother owned a textile and lace factory in Rumburg. His wife took pride in exquisite taste, her whole house was adorned with Meissen porcelain and burgundy velvet sofas and lace doilies, draped across gilded rococo furniture in the "good" room, into which children were not allowed to enter. They were admonished to look but don't touch. Adults were told to take off their shoes.

Another Borufka brother manufactured leather goods, belts and purses. Their house reeked of lanolin, dyes, formaldehyde, pomades, medicines, Ben Gay and other pain-relievers. Occasional visitors held their noses on brief and rare visits. His barren wife wanted to adopt a child to fill the void in her life. But the thought of noisy children depriving her and her husband of well-deserved naptimes and the idea was dropped.

Another uncle, Dehnert or Dohnert, nobody could remember his name after his death, who went from riches to rags after he had made a shady deal with a Jewish business partner, when he refused to pay for his share of a business deal. He threatened instead to turn him in to the tax authorities after the uncle threatened to sue his partner for payment. He was the talk of the town and around the family dinner table. The ensuing scandal prompted the uncle to hang himself with his white scarf. His prideful wife lived in abject poverty ever after.

Another Borufka uncle owned community theatres in the far reaches of the Austro-Hungarian Empire in Vienna, Prague and Budapest. Others immigrated to America and were never heard from again.

Rather than living their lives as spinsters, two Borufka sisters married German pub owners. Pubs were on every street corner and so were thirsty patrons. The Cersovsky pub was preferred by the Czech peasants. Wenzel Lauschmann owned a butcher shop and a pub serving Bratwurst with Sauerkraut and frothy beer from a tap. Next door was the Scholz Pub with the favorite Pilsner beer on tap for the German crowds. Maria Borufka married the Scholz Pub owner with whom Maria had a son she named Bubi. Bubi Scholz grew up to become the mailman of the village. Her sister, Franziska Borufka married a poor but hardworking, handsomely tall and dark-haired Wenzel Lauschmann, whose lush mustache bobbed comically under his nose when he spoke and his large grey eyes twinkled with delight when he lovingly seduced a stern and unsmiling woman, he called Franny, to marry him in a simple civil ceremony. Franziska moved into Wenzel's house next door to her sister Maria's pub, above the butcher shop. The two sisters were happy to be supportive neighbors, and worked together in harmony to provide the people of this rural community with simple creature comfort around a green ceramic tiled wood stove. They had no radio or newspaper, but word got out from mouth to mouth, that Franciska served more than a bratwurst and beer.

She always had sizzling Bratwurst on the grill and sauerkraut curing in wooden barrels, while her sister Maria Scholz allowed the simple peasantry a place where they could let off steam and vent over political cockalorum around card tables.

Over time Franziska created a variety of meals of the hearty but simple Bohemian Cuisine. Every Sunday she served up many Bohemian dumplings with Sauerbraten and red cabbage smothered in rich gravy. Franziska became known for her best Sunday dinners and patrons came from miles around.

Within ten years Franny and Wenzel had three sons. Leopold, Otto, Rudi and in March 1910 they welcomed one pretty girl named Emilie. While Wenzel taught his sons the art of grinding out the best Bratwurst and curing cabbage into Sauerkraut, little Emmi learned the art of Bohemian cooking alongside her mother from an early age without looking at a recipe. Her mother taught her to measure with the tips of two fingers and a pinch of this and a pinch of that, seasoning to taste. Emmi enjoyed being the taste-tester of her mother's cooking. But sniffing the aromas filling the air was proof of her skills as it wafted around the kitchen and out the front door.

One day the calm coexistence of the region was broken when a bull horn sounded the start of World War I. Nineteen-year-old brother Leopold was drafted and sent to the Russian Front. His father Wenzel was ordered to deliver soups in canisters to soldiers at the Russian front and Hungary. Four years later all noise had ceased on Armistice Day and father Wenzel returned from lice infested trenches to the family he loved. He brought with him a steady nagging cough. Leopold returned with shrapnel in his head and was never the same again.

How much Wenzel suffered during the war was written all over his face and emaciated body. The horror of the Russian winter had taken its toll on a once healthy, strong, stately and vibrant man. The years of innocence were over. Problem solving no longer depended on ones' skills and steely determination.

One day the peace of the mountain panorama filled ones' heart, the next the Czech military set hearts racing with fear, as they charged into the Lauschmann Gasthaus. Czech Socialist Nationals tore down the pictures of the Austrian emperor and his wife, searched and confiscated valuables and brought the whole area and its perfect infrastructure into disarray.

Wenzel repaired what damage had been done to his Gasthaus by the Czech militia. He kept his head low and the hammer aimed at the nail head on the wall, out of harms' way of fierce local politicians who were only too eager to exploit the ensuing discord.

He worked feverishly to renovate and enlarge the Gasthaus, which had sustained the family during his absence. Franziska was busier than ever serving delicious meals in the finest Bohemian tradition to locals as well as to disheveled strangers who seemed to appear out of nowhere. Emmi was only nine years old, when she experienced her own humiliation when, in compliance with the new Czech laws, the German public schools were closed and her mother had to enroll her in the Czech "School for Minorities."

After the first day of school, Emmi ran home crying and complained bitterly to her mother. "The children called me Nemci Bes, (German Dog) don't make me go back there again." Franziska shook her head in dismay, knowing she had no options. They were too poor to send their children to the few private German schools, which were still allowed to remain open.

Emmi was ever more frightened to see her father work late into the night while a painful cough wracked his emaciated body. The joy of reunion was replaced by a looming fear that Wenzel's days were numbered.

Next to Marias pub was a small theater. Small productions were performed under the direction of Bruno Linhart, who led a small but very proficient group of actors and choristers.

The group performed many of Franz Lehar's whimsical operas. Emmi was a vivacious child with lofty ambitions and hoped to play a lead role in musicals under the direction of Bruno who was one of five sons of the flourmiller, Otto Linhart and his wife Franziska, whose family dynasty dated back to 1698.

At one end of the village between Klein-Borowitz and Mastig was the munitions factory and securely tucked behind these woods was the Linhart flour mill. Every morning Emmi tore open the windows of her tiny loft and filled the fresh mountain air with joyous songs. Taking two steps at a time, she ran outside to pump water from the well and splash her face. She wove ribbons into her long thick, golden-brown braids and sang all the way to school. Neighbors called her nightingale.

The popular girl with a feisty charm was welcomed to spend summer vacations at the homes of aunts and uncles on both her mother and her father's side in Budapest, Prague, Rumburg and Eibau, across the German border. Emmi knew the trails along the white waters of the Elbe River like the lines in the palm of her hands. She needed no roadmap, just good boots and a hiking stick, all the way to where the Elbe River has its spring. She enjoyed getting together with a multitude of cousins before sunrise, pack a plump knackwurst and slices of fresh bread into her knapsack and hike up to the summit of a mountain, where she stepped inside a hikers' chapel for solace in a prayer for her beloved father before the feet of white porcelain saints and angels.

She fit in easily with elite Czech and German societies and found it tantalizing to wine and dine at the Inn of Wenzel Lauer. She loved to ride the trains and walk the promenades in Karlsbad, Johannisbad or Vienna where she listened to gypsy minstrels, laugh at organ grinders with monkeys on their backs, and attend concerts in pavilions surrounded by splendid parks and the sound of Viennese Waltzes, which always set her feet in motion.

One place she avoided since childhood was the home of an aunt and uncle where she did not feel welcome. He was the richest uncle in the neighboring village of Nedarsch, whose wifes' lavish taste, sent out the message with a stern face. "Look, but don't touch," which contrasted sharply to the humble unadorned house of her mother. She avoided entering her uncles' house for all his wife's pomp and splendor. She liked lounging on the leather sofa beside her father who was grateful for every labored breath as he pounded another nail into wood beams. Emmi brewed chamomile tea, crushed chopped onions added honey and rum and spoon fed the mixture into her father's mouth. The precocious child helped him sip the tea slowly. "I put honey and rum in it…that should clear up the mucus." Emmi spent hours watching her father's skilled hands with great admiration, as he renovated the homestead and guest house.

He modernized the butcher shop next door, added a billiard room and a bar with comfortable leatherseating areas. He finished the stucco walls with cross beams. He was determined to leave the house in such condition to ensure that his wife had the means to sustain herself and the children with her expert cooking skills, if worse came to worse. One day after school, Emilie found her mother sitting behind the tiled wood burning stove, holding her head and weeping. Emmi sat down beside her and rubbed her back, to comfort her mother. "Mamimka, what's wrong?" Franziska looked weary, dark rings circled her brown eyes more deeply. The sound of children at play caused her blood pressure to rise threateningly, and to a bewildered nine-year old, her mother complained bitterly. "No sooner does he pull down his suspenders to hang his pants on the bedpost, I'm pregnant again." Sniveling, she pulled a starchy handkerchief from an apron pocket.

"At forty-six years I am too old, to have another child. I have given birth to four healthy children and suffered three miscarriages. I can't accept another child."

After the birth of Anna Maria, much to Franziska's relief, her husband, Wenzel and Emmi took turns caring for the baby. Emmi cooed to the baby delightedly whom she named.

"Anninka, my precious Anninka, you are my pretty dolly." That is how Emmi treated her baby sister, as her own dolly. She spent hours gussying up the child, gently brushing the child's silken fine curly locks, putting ribbons in her hair while cooing and crooning a lullaby and holding a mirror to the child's face. "See the pretty dolly? That's you in there, my pretty dolly."

She pushed her baby sister's pram up and down narrow winding dirt roads, closing the buggy's curtain so the sun would not shine into her "dolly's" eyes. Once the child began to toddle, Wenzel took the little girl for walks, to give his wife a reprieve from children's noise.

Emmi sang her heart out to dispel her fears over her father's steadily worsening cough, while he feverishly worked to finish the renovation of the Gasthaus. No sooner had Wenzel arduously pounded the last nail into the stucco wall, he turned as ashen as the mortar and whispered. "Franny, I don't feel well … I am going up to bed." He never made it up the first step.

With a heavy moan Wenzel fell flat on his back. By the time a frantically screaming Franny knelt over him, blood oozed from his mouth, his eyes rolled back into their sockets, and the last breath escaped with a slight rattle. He had choked on his own blood. Frannys' mournful wails summoned her oldest son Leopold from his butcher shop and screamed. "Poldi run to the school, and fetch the children…Papa just died." Poldi could not run. He limped painfully wheezing up the hill.

The Czech school chancellor summoned the Lauschmann children into his office. The boys wondered if they were brought in for a caning. With a casual sneer, the chancellor said.

"Well, you just got your wish…now you don't have to come to school anymore. Your father just died. Now you will have to work in the potato fields." The words of the chancellor plunged the youngsters into devastating anguish. They ran home as tears streamed down their faces. Never having to go back to the Czech school would have been a welcomed reprieve for any reason, except this one.

By the time the children entered the front room Leopold was pounding nails into his father's coffin, and placed his lifeless body inside. Five-year old Anninka cried. "Get up Papa. Why doesn't he get up?" The children looked down on a father never gentler, who had not so much as raised a hand in anger and touched his cold hands and face in a final farewell. The gentle soul, in life as in death, now lay in peaceful repose with his fingers curled around a rosary bead. The namesake of their patron Saint Wenceslas had lived up to his noble name Franny looked on dejectedly, filled with a seething rage, not only at her worn out belly, and her arthritic curved fingers, but at her husband's final surrender to the beckoning peace.

"He is at peace while I have to grovel for a living." Despite her own despair Emmi was able to prompt her relatives to lift their tear-streaked faces toward the choir loft. With a strong clear voice Emmi filled the church of St. Josef's in Klein-Borowitz with the haunting melody of Schubert's Ave Maria. It was a loving daughters' tender farewell. A voice of an angel filled the arched ceiling of the stone church.

Among the many uncles attending the funeral mass, was one who turned around to look at his niece in amazement as the sound of an angel's voice filled the nave.

The young girls' ability to control her emotions and perform with sublime tranquility this fragile piece of an angel's greeting left the uncle spellbound as the heavens opened the flood gate and pouring rain pelted the stain glass windows, providing a mythical accompaniment to the child's delicate tesa tora.

Black cloaked villagers stood with their heads bowed, as the coffin of a beloved husband and father, neighbor and friend was carried out of the church, down a narrow lane to the village cemetery. A throng of hundred mourners, with black umbrellas, followed the pall bearers across the village streets on foot to the gravesite. Emmi whispered as she wrapped her arms around her mother's thick waist. "It is befitting that angels are weeping for a good Papa."

Wenzel had taught his sons early on to accept responsibilities. Leopold knew how to manage the butcher shop, Rudi was a friendly man, who knew how to keep poor peasants happy with a frothy Pilsner beer from the tap. The tall dark and handsome Otto was a ladies' man and the women swarmed around him for company at the beer fountain with lively conversations. The poor peasants always found a warm welcome at the Lauschmann Gasthaus over a bratwurst and beer, or Sauerbraten with cabbage and Bohemian dumplings on Sundays.

Franny had divvied up the workload among her children before her husbands' body was cold, and gave the orders with a stern voice. "Emmi you have to take care of the child."

"The Child" was the name her mother had given little Anninka. Emmi was only too glad to be a surrogate mother even at such a tender age. Not a few Czech women in the neighborhood wondered about the cause for songs arising out of the laundry room, all of them knowing that Franziska was not well.

She was still in mourning over the loss of her husband and would be for a lifetime. Emmi was a strong willed thirteen-year-old now, who had to care for her mother and a little sister, with no time left for self-indulgence. While singing gave the impression of a child at play, Emmi was the one who hung out the family's hand laundered linens and undergarments on the clothesline.

Emmi feared if she would stop singing, she would surely die of despair over the loss of her gentle Papa, the loss of her carefree childhood and such arduous labor as pumping countless buckets of water from the well outside the house, with which she had to do the family laundry.

One day an uncle came from Budapest for an unexpected visit. With his portly frame, sporting an elegant handle-bar mustache, he filled the good room of the Lauschmann Gasthaus with his presence with grand dignity. His booming voice sucked the air out of the room and reverberated throughout the building, although the door was closed, Emmi could hear the uncle argue with her mother. She could hear her mother's repeated. "No...she can't. I need her here...I need help with the child."

With a disarming smile that lit up the room, the uncle replied. "Franny, she will only be away for a few weeks at a time. Uncle Gustav and Bertha always wanted to adopt a child. They can take care of Anninka for a few weeks in the meantime." Franny at last caved in, and the uncle emerged with a triumphant smile, and whistled the Radetzky March. His mustache twitched and his eyes danced with delight as he bowed before his favorite niece.

"May I have this dance? Tschapperl, I'll make an opera singer out of you yet…I'll arrange for singing, dancing and drama classes in Prague for you." Emmi could hardly contain her surprise when the uncle kissed her hand.

She curtsied with a low bow before him and a twirl of the dirndl, as a giggle escaped her throat. He twirled her around and she promptly fell in step to a robust Czardas, while her mother shook her head at such frivolity. Emmi noticed the displeasure on her mother's frowning face, and clasped her mouth. She wanted the chance to find solace for her tender soul and broaden her horizon. She had always wanted to see Vienna and Prague, a Slavic name which means "Threshold." Her budding womanhood was on that threshold, and she wanted to see what greater world lay beyond Klein-Borowitz.

This was her moment to seize the opportunity. From the day on which uncle Johann had heard his niece sing at her father's funeral, he knew, she would not disappoint him. He owned community theaters near Prague, Vienna and Budapest, and he knew he had found a diamond in the rough in his talented niece. Her vivacious spirit and high energy convinced him, that she was not only gifted in voice, but in spirit as well and endowed with an inner strength and determination to succeed. In Emmi the uncle saw an enormous potential beyond her tender years. He was determined to help her achieve a spot in the limelight.

For the next three years Emmi was consumed with tireless passion while lessons and rehearsals took up her time, her mother ceased caring for Anninka altogether. The little child was placed in foster care of the wealthy, childless and aging Aunt Bertha and Uncle Gustav in the neighboring village of Nedarsch. The aging couple had sought to adopt the child not out of love for Anninka, but sheer vanity. They liked parading a pretty little girl around the neighborhood like an obedient lap dog. But every afternoon, when Uncle Gustav and Aunt Bertha went to bed for their nap, the child was left to fend for herself. The lonely child quietly left the house. An alert neighbor found her wandering the streets in search of her mother's house, and brought her back to the disgruntled uncles' house.

The hawkeyed neighbor awakened a nonplussed Bertha und Gustav, who sought to curtail the child's wandering spirit and tied the child to the pedestal of the heavy dining room table to keep her from leaving the house before they went to bed for their nap. Another time Anninka got wind that her beloved sister Emmi, was visiting another aunt and uncle nearby. She yearned to be with her sister and skipped out of the house. The child was smart enough to find the house of the other aunt and uncle. They all wondered how this little girl figured out the difficult path to their house. Her escape antics caused a lot of laughter.

The laughter she had caused bolstered Anninka's determination to attempt more escapes. Aunt Bertha and Uncle Gustav were nonplussed and the ill-tempered uncle Gustav threw a loaf of bread against the wall in a fit of rage and tied the child's legs to the heavy oak table with a gauze band every afternoon. The tormented child quickly learned to loosen the noose around her thin limbs, slipped out the door and toddled off to her mother's house. But neighbors caught her again and after returning her to the aunt and uncle each time the noose was tied around the childs' legs ever tighter, even as the child whimpered. "I just want to go home."

Occasionally on weekends, to stop the child's torment, the exasperated aunt and uncle allowed the child to visit with her mother. Anninka spent the time complaining bitterly to her mother. "Uncle Gustav ties my legs to the table…so I can't run away." Franziska looked alarmed and refused to consider any further discussions about an adoption. But neither could she give the child the love and nurture she desperately sought and needed. Despite the child's desperate screams and pleas, the little girl was returned to the highbrowed Bertha and Gustav every time. The child lost her effervescent spirit. She held her eyes downcast and looked fearful at strangers as she glanced about herself.

She had lost the charm of an unperturbed childish innocence. The mischievous twinkle in her eyes with which she had charmed the world was dull, she no longer giggled with delight. Her shoulders hunched forward and she looked fearful at everyone from underneath her thin eyebrows.

Everyone thought that the child was a bit strange when they saw her sulk in a corner, purse her lips tightly, and never make a peep until Emmi walked through the door. Then the child opened like a flower, fling herself into her sisters' arms in a tight embrace and smothered her with kisses, screeching. "Now, I will never let you go!" Emmi was unaware of the devastating impact her frequent absence had caused in her little sisters' life every time she went on tour with the theatre ensemble. While she danced and sang her heart out until her feet were raw, and her throat scratchy, her little sister was devastated. Anninka withered like a daisy in the hot sun.

Emmi never tired of smiling broadly, charming the small-town folks in neighboring communities with portrayals of Franz Lehar's whimsical characters of a bygone era, in which she could transport her adoring audience to a world of romantic tenderness, to a time when a damsel could still find her Student Prince or Rosenkavalier and live happily ever after.

Emmi had won every lead role for three years. She was the favorite repertoire asset and glowed in the limelight, viewing the world around her through rosy colored glasses from center stage. Every time the curtains fell to thunderous applause, she crested with youthful, romantic visions of Vienna, Budapest and the National Theatre in Prague.

With a satisfied sigh, Emmi plunked herself into her favorite window seat in her loft above the Lauschmann Gasthaus. Here on the windowsill that overlooked Klein-Borowitz, she was free to muse about the quaint roles she loved to portray on stage that seemed so clearly befitting her dreamy-eyed, small-town innocence. With every new role, under the guidance of theater director, Bruno Linhart, the oldest of five sons of the well-endowed Linhart family.

She was more convinced than ever that acting was her chosen role in life. Emmi and Bruno were ideal stage partners, but when Bruno proposed marriage to her, her heart skipped a beat for a moment. Warmth spread through her chest. She was charmed and flattered thinking about this marvelous man who saw in her the ideal partner for his life. A gentle wave of ecstasy swept over her in surprise, but it did not sweep her off her feet.

She did not dare tell her mother about Bruno's proposal in earnest, instead she joked about it, knowing that her mother would prod her to accept the offer of such a fine man. Her mother did anyway as if she read her thoughts. "Now he is a man you should marry. He is strong and handsome. He comes from one of the finest families in our region. Their family has been well established here for centuries. If you marry a grist miller you'll never go hungry. Next to the flour mill thy have a well-stocked trout pond.

The House My Father Built

If you don't marry Bruno, Hilda Haase will. She has her sights set on that fine specimen of a strong and handsome man already. She is the daughter of the grist miller in Mastig. A marriage between them would suit both families. You know, money marries money. But a miller monopoly will make flour and bread more expensive. There won't be any competition for bread."

Emmi replied reflectively. "What happened to you, you came from money and married a poor man. I am too young to think of marriage, I am almost seventeen. I have not lived long enough to know what I want to do in my life. Bruno is ten years older. He is ready for marriage, I am not. Rudi is six years older than I am, he is strong and handsome but I wouldn't marry him even if he weren't my brother. every cup will find a saucer. Rudi will marry Paula. Poldi married Martha and Otto ran off to Germany with Hilda.

Life holds a lot of promises, but at the moment, I am not willing to give up the theatre for any man, just to sit at home, cook, bear children, and tend to a grindstone…and the Linharts' have a big grindstone. I am not ready to be a miller's wife and have a big millstone around my neck. Maybe after I have played the role of Verdi's Aida in Vienna."

Franny sneered at her daughter's fanciful musings as Emmi looked out the window and smiled in make-belief of the roles she hoped to play someday on a stage. Starring roles as in Die Fledermaus or The Merry Widow and The Bartered Bride." She felt as if her mother expected her daughter to be a bartered bride. She read her music notes Winzer Liesel, Du holde Kleine, am ganzen Rhein gibt's keine wie Du" She shook her head in disbelief, hummed the melody but could not remember the text. She dropped the music sheets, reached for her needlepoint and started stitching finely woven patterns.

A disturbing thought was interfering with images of future roles she hoped to play. Determinedly, she plunged the darning needle into her dainty petite point. The troubling pounding in her chest dislodged her from her clean needle point pattern more than the clearly envisioned path for her life. She mindlessly pulled the needle and thread through the wrong pattern, as the yarn got intangled she stopped pulling on the yarn, to gaze straight ahead, as if her eyes sought to wend around a mountain trail.

With a sigh, Emmi plunked herself into her favorite window seat in her loft above the Gasthaus. A steady din could be heard in the distance, echoing through the valley like through a bullhorn. Her heart started pounding in rhythm of a gunning engine. She turned on the radio to shut out the noise from outside, and the sublime chords of Beethoven's Ninth Symphony lifted her spirits. She flung the window wide open and thrust her voice up above the tree tops to filter into space, as a motorbike wound its way through the Sudeten Mountains at high speed.

Emmi lifted her voice to match the chorus playing over the radio, and the tiny loft vibrated with jubilation of a hundred voices. Freude schöner Götterfunken, Tochter aus Elysium…wir betreten feuertrunken…himmlische Dein Heiligtum… Deine Zauber binden wieder.

The meaning of the poetry was not clear to her, but she loved the magical message of Gods' love that binds mankind together. She was at peace with God and the world, and enjoyed life as it was right now. Despite her determination to forge ahead with life on a stage, after every performance, she realized her thoughts were drifting further and further from that goal, even as she was standing next to a man as self-assured as Bruno by her side. Emmi found herself at a fork in the road, as the push and pull of one love over another filled her with great anxiety whenever her thoughts of an immaculately groomed gallant young man distracted her from every endeavor.

She plunged the darning needle deep into the fabric, and thought. "I'll just have to keep my feelings in check…and keep that man at arms' length." Seconds later, she caught herself smiling as her thoughts wandered back to a moment when she first laid eyes on the polite man with the finely chiseled noble face, the funny little curl that managed to fall over his straight forehead, and the bluest forget me not eyes beneath heaven. "With Forget-me-not-blue eyes how can I forget him?" She mused. "How can I forget him? When I look inside the azure eyes and see only paradise. I forget Verdis' Aida."

As far back as Emmi could remember, the young man's family name had always been the cause of viscous gossip and tongue-wagging in every German and Czech village alike. Her fluency in both languages caused her ears to burn at the mention of the Staffa name inside her mothers' small Gasthaus.

His ancestry was the same as her own, German fathers and Czech mothers going back several generations. The Staffas' reputation was that of a cantankerous and drunken clan, who provided fodder every day for village gossip mongers. She tried to ignore the rumors and innuendos surrounding the drinking escapades of the Staffa brothers and the chichi nimbus of the women, who provided interesting news everywhere they batted their eyes, bedded down, or were at last laid to rest, as when the grand dame Josepha, died at the ripe old age of seventy-nine in 1924.

The villagers could always count on a great Staffa spectacle to bring the robust clan together. Overnight, much to her mother's chagrin, the Lauschmann Gasthaus had become a watering hole for thirsty and hungry travelers and local farmhands. Lately, it was a favorite hangout for the youngest "Staffa clique." With cocksure bravado their entourage swarmed into the tiny village with the sound of an air raid of bombers and locusts, leaving everyone standing agog in a cloud of BMW exhaust fumes.

Every week hence the mob was back, flaunting their fat wallets and thick exhaust fumes amid nonplussed peasant faces. Emmi quipped. "Once word reached all the way to Mastig, that Franziska Lauschmann serves the best Sauerbraten and Bohemian dumplings with red cabbage they came and have been back ever since. Her secret is the flavoring with a spoonful of currant jam to sweet-sour perfection. Gourmets go where the cooking is good. My Mamimka makes the best of the Bohemian cuisine."

Emmi leaned expertly across the billiard table and noticed through the thick smoke that filled the billiard room the white flashing teeth that were smiling for one girl only. Soon everyone knew and whispered about the die that had been cast for their favorite village daughter. Emmi giggled, thinking about that first encounter with the cocksure young man.

Suddenly an arm curled around her waist, his cheek pressed against hers, and his fingers caressed her arms trailing down to the fingertips as she aimed the cue stick at a ball.

"Can you teach me the game?" He whispered in her ear, and she froze as his fingers curled around hers. "I know nothing about this game. I will need a lot of lessons." He whispered in her ear.

She looked up into his eyes that glistened with delight as his arms, conveniently, yet somehow naturally, remained around her waist and his eyes never left her face. Out of the corner of her eyes Emmi glimpsed her mother's scornful look and furrowed forehead, heralding the brewing of a storm.

The pretty woman with the laughing eyes and happy disposition jabbed him with her elbow to keep him in line. He had noticed the slow response in her rebuke and the blush that crept over her lovely Madonna face. She freed herself from his embrace and said "For lessons you'll have to make an appointment." He straightened up to leave. "I'll be back tomorrow for my first lesson." He said as he headed for the door and went outside, got on his bike, gunned the engine and spun a few wheelies in front of the house.

He threw up a cloud of dust, as her smile and eyes told him she was amused, if not charmed by his antics on the motorbike, and he resolved to maintain a faithful schedule of billiard lessons. As she leaned out the window in the final adios for the evening, wisps of autumn-golden strands of hair softly veiled the exquisite contours of her face, the strands caught the light of the sun, and gusts of wind whipped her hair like spun gold. Her sudden smile burst forth like rays of sunshine through thick clouds and warmed his heart, as he noticed a front tooth glinting in the sun.

He heard Emmis mother snarl at her daughter. "Keep away from that guy. He is one of the rich Staffas. What does he want from a poor girl like you? They are all drinkers and womanizers, why does he court a poor girl like you." Her mother reached over her daughters' head and closed the window with a scornful look as she watched the young man leave with a roar back to his home turf in Mastig.

Nestled against the Swichin mountain ridge was Mastig Bad the spa-resort located on the road to Ober-Prausnitz, separated only by a dense forest teeming with wild game, rabbits, deer, wild boar and foxes. Rich and influential business people and bureaucrats from the tri-border region found stress relief on the tennis courts, bowling alleys, whirlpools and saunas. The hotels served up the finest of select menus of the Bohemian kitchen, at a hefty price. Thousands of hikers, bikers, hunters and skiers flocked here for annual sports events. Hunting parties were arranged by wealthy industrialists of such fame as the founder of Bosch Electric and Netherlands Reemtsma Cigarettes. Lately Mastig Bad was becoming a little Babel of sin when less desirable elements were attracted to a few gaming tables.

Down the road from Mastig Bad red tiled roofs of several imposing villas built solid enough to last a thousand years towered above the hamlet with sturdy confidence. To a casual observer, the buildings that arched up between the dark silhouettes of tree tops that shimmered in the light of a sickle-shaped moon, stood in stark contrast to the low-lying row houses with peek-a-boo windows that anchored the single thoroughfare.

The House My Father Built

Illuminated by the moon's silvery glow, the buildings were easily recognized as belonging to a prominent family. They were surrounded by thick fir trees and rows of white birches. The moonbeams cast eerie shadows across the buildings white stucco facades, and nearby barns, of similar, grandiose cross-beam and stucco design, were filled with neatly organized farm equipment, fastened along the barn walls. Hay protruded from the top windows of the steep rafters as proof of abundance, where livestock squawked and grunted contentedly in stalls until their slaughter, to become just another sumptuous family feast.

The property was cut in half by a gently flowing brook, weaving a path between the villas like a thin satin ribbon. Small wooden bridges allowed moonlight walks between these gentile neighbors surrounded by annuals and perennials and creeping phlox.

Looking in any direction, one could glimpse the steeply angled roof of yet another villa of similar design, the likeness of design designating them to one common ancestry.

Each property was bordered by thick hedges to prevent intrusion of prying eyes. Wooden garden benches beneath shady greenery allowed tired legs a few precious moments of elevation from the arduous labors of the day. Tired eyes could yield to temptation easily with an impromptu nodding off any time from morning to sunset, roll back into a peaceful repose within view of rose trellises waiting for spring to burst into blooming splendor.

Intricately designed lily ponds, amid rock gardens adorned with miniature replicas of castles from the surrounding landscape, gracing the rolling hills beyond the valley floor, gave off playful sounds as the water cascaded down between the terraces into the ponds to provide moments of respite for weary souls beckoning tired eyes to close.

In back of every villa were lush greenhouses. Vegetable gardens and fruit orchards held out promises of abundant yields for cool cellars and canning jars for periods of want. They were a frugal people whose lives routinely revolved around the motto of waste not want not mottos. The eyes followed the thin ribbon of water that flowed into natural ponds and a brook became a tributary to the Elbe River. Far beyond the thickly wooded land were several spring fed ponds. One was stocked with trout the other was deep enough to allow children the pleasure of a plunge into the frigid water on hot summer nights.

A chain link fence topped with a strand of barbed wire surrounded the entire complex, a padlock secured the gate, and a Rottweiler kept a watchful eye ready to pounce on any trespasser.

The only noise emitted in this sleepy village of about one thousand, in the heat of any day, was that of saw blades wheezing from sunrise to sunset. A rooster signaled the dawn of the day and crickets provided the only concert on warm summer nights. All noise had ceased except for the ceaseless fiddling and chirping of crickets. The meadows absorbed the heat of the day and slowly gave it back in misty, pulse-quickening fog.

The eerie silence was interrupted now and then by a rustle in the bushes along a creek, and by the intermittent ferocious barking of a dog. Faith of homesteaders rested in that assurance that a fearless Rottweiler, guardian of hearth and home, spared its inhabitants from marauding gypsies, and other such pesky intruders who dared tread upon their domain to make off with a plump chicken and disrupt their well-deserved sleep. The burly beast leaped to its feet with a guttural snarl and paced back and forth along the fence in highest agitation, the black stubbly hair on the back of the neck bristled with the dogs' emotion, as it lurched upward with great voracity, determined to break the chain that bound it to his turf.

Five small shadowy figures vainly dodged the glare of the moonlight as they slithered along the hedges. A moonbeam fell across their faces and, in its glow they looked swarthy, covered with sweaty grime. Their dark hair glistened with greasy sweat. Their raspy whispers, filled with heavy rolled r's of their Czech mother tongue, sounded as if they had to clear their throats laboriously.

The five boys crouched down beside the last barrier between them and the cool welcome of the mountain pond. Out of view from prying eyes, they waited until the dog stopped barking. Nothing would thwart their nightly swim, not even the fury of a chained Rottweiler. They would yell "Pritch! Pritch!" while they hastened to put chickens back into the coop.

Lock all the doors and windows. Everyone was afraid of the dark faced women, who with their fiery coal black eyes connived and bewildered many a befuddled villager. Who repeatedly relieved them of jewelry from their hands or sausages from their smoke chambers, all the while jovially distracting them with wild and irrational chatter. Tall tales were joked about the area that a gypsy woman had given birth in a barn without leaving a trace. A chicken might have gotten its neck wrung and the thief disappeared before dawn with a plucked chicken leaving behind only a section of umbilical cord.

They were nothing like the pesky Gypsy women, whom the Nemcis tried to scare away whenever they saw them ambling down the road toward their homes. Here they were children of the land, who, in sweltering heat, had endured the humiliation of sweaty labor in service of their Nemci bosses and landlords, tilling hay and pitching bales atop hay wagons, all the while they had suffered the laughter of children from behind hedged gardens, who were chauffeur driven to private schools, dance and piano lessons. These children were just looking for some fun. They had waited long enough for the night and a cooling respite from the daily grind, determined to enjoy at night what was forbidden to them during the day.

A lanky lad scaled the fence, dragging a raft behind him. "Ivanczek…wait." A moonbeam fell on the lad's face as he turned around revealing a coarsely angled, swarthy face, enhanced by a prominent nose, and bushy eyebrows too thick for his twelve years.

"Pavel…keep the damn thing steady…Vlad help him." Ivanczek blithely anchored himself atop the fence and snatched the rope held up to him. Pavel Shubrt clung to the fence with one hand and with the other he gave the raft another shove. "Pavel hold on …ease it down slowly… Otto, take the other side." The raft balanced on top of the fence for a moment, then crashed with a loud thud to the ground. "Damn, I told you to hold it steady…"

The dog barked immediately with increasing voracity and quickening the boys; pulse. The boys waited a few moments with baited breath for lights to flash, bells to ring, and sirens to wail. Nothing stirred inside the compound, because the owners were so used to the dogs barking at scurrying rats and squirrels. Finally, the dog quieted down and in the ensuing silence the children's raspy whispers seemed a more terrible noise. The youngest of the boys, Rudi Kostial cautiously grabbed the chain links to hoist himself up, hand over hand. The other boys swung their legs over the top of the eight-foot fence and jumped down into the dewy grass.

Ivanczek could feel the cloth of his pants rip away from the fence, and he let loose a salvo of curses as he dropped down. "Damn, my mother will beat my ass."

He ranted just as little Rudi reached the top wire, the barbs dug into his tender thigh, and he cried out.

"Ouch! I'm stuck. Wait for me." The older boys laughed and raced to the natural pond fed constantly with fresh mountain waters, as they dragged the raft behind them, and taunting Rudi. "Jump…we are not going to wait…you'll have to swim to the middle, so jump now. Nemci bes." Rudi tried to jump, he tore himself away from the spiked fence cutting his thigh. He heard a noise, and knew that his pants had ripped. "My pants are ripped in my crotch." Rudi cried. "Wait for me. I can't swim." Rudi's pants were impaled on top of the fence. The more he struggled to tear himself away from the spike, the more the pants ripped at the seam. The pants held firm as the other boys paddled out with the raft to the center of the pond and taunted Rudi. "Go to the trout pond catch a fish for your Mamimka. That will make her happy."

Rudi was envious when he heard the cajoling laughter of the boys as they plunged into the cold water and heard the rocking of the raft, the wild splashing of the water, as they jumped off only to climb back on top in rapid succession.

"You can't swim either. Maybe you will drown, you creeps!" He screamed and taunted his friends as they paddled to the center of the pond. Their frolicking noise only set his teeth on edge. He felt angry and abandoned by his pals, as he sat there stuck atop the fence. Rudi clenched his fist and cursed. "Damn you…I hope the Nemci bes hears you, and scream at you Pritch! Pritch!" But the big houses showed no signs of life, and the boys frolicked to exhaustion, sliding up and down the raft. The cooling night air was taking over and the boys felt a sudden chill. One boy after another climbed out of the water and unto the raft, clutching their chests as their bodies were shivering and teeth were chattering. Seeking each other's body warmth, they slid closer together, until the raft started to tilt like a seesaw from side to side.

With reckless abandon they rocked the raft even more. Suddenly the raft flipped over. The night air was filled with wild thrashing and screaming. The four boys clutched one another by their necks screaming for help. Rudi was still impaled atop the fence and he clung to the steel post thinking his pals were just clowning around. As he heard them scream for help, he was feeling gleeful with "Schaden Freude" a joyful feeling at someone else's misfortunes. "Serves them right!"

He watched in helplessness as a paralyzing fear crept over him. Then the barbed wire pierced his skin. He yanked his pant leg from the spike and fell backwards to the ground. He saw stars and lay there dazed for a moment then he picked himself off the ground and crept home.

Rudi went to bed without so much as a whisper to anyone, while his friends where thrashing in the pond clasping their fingers around each other's neck, clinging for dear life, until, one by one; they pulled each other beneath the surface of the water. Bubbles floated to the top for a few seconds until silence returned momentarily. Then the night air was filled again with nothing but crickets in concert, and the gentle splashing of the water against a raft floating upside down.

Before the rooster crowed the dawn of the day, screeching sirens blared through the small village of Mastig straight from hell. The usually quiet hamlet was thrown into an uproar, as Pani Shubrt came running from her hovel, wringing her hands, throwing them over her face and weeping loudly, peering into the dirty faces of children milling about.

Her neighbor Pani Push, cupped her mouth and called. "Ivan!" Vlad!"

Pani Push joined Pani Shubrt, until their voices became piercing screams echoing through the narrow, winding mountain paths. Beckoning other women to come running, as they raced from house to house, pounded on shuttered windows, rattled bolted doors, and screamed the names of their children at startled faces, while others milled around with quizzical looks on their faces, wondering what the commotion was all about.

Word spread that four or five children were missing and shrugged their shoulders, threw their arms up in despair crying, "Jessesmarren!"

Shaken and scared of his mother's wrath, Rudi feigned sleep as the rugged faced women peered through the window of his wooden shack. Moments later the furious women burst through the door. Rudis' mother rushed to his cot, grabbed him by the shoulder, and shook him out of his stupor. "What?" He cried rubbing his eyes in feigned surprise.

"Rudi Kostial! Wake up! Look at Mamimka. Where is your brother? Wake up!" she jostled him again. Rudi rubbed his eyes. "I donno."

His mother slapped his face. "Wake up! Look at me…you were seen with them." Her hand reached out again and he ducked his head and she grabbed him by the hair, slapped both sides with the front and back of her hand. In the mayhem, she twisted his ears until he was forced to look at her, and he cried out. "I don't know…I last saw them at the pond, I could not climb over the fence so I came home."

"Jessesmarren!" The women screeched in colloquial Czech and raced to the other end of the village, past the German villas, the grist mill and the Mandl Factory, up the road past the Gernert Garden café, and the Staffa factory, where timber was cut into building lumber. Someone must have summoned the fire and rescue trucks from surrounding villages. Sirens screeched from all around, ascending toward the mountain hamlet.

Czech and German villagers alike dropped what they were doing. They abandoned their work stations at the Mandl Factory, their morning brew at the Hample Pub, the breakfast coffee at the Gernert café. The baker forgot his bread in the oven, his wife Lydia forgot to diaper baby Lisa. The butcher dropped his meat cleaver and the Staffa carpenter dropped saws and levers. German families, Wanka, Sturm, Zippel, Maschka and Seidel joined the Czechs Czemetzky, Cersovsky, Hendrych, and followed the trucks that overran the lush Staffa estate.

Such ethnic mingling of men and women, who screamed obscenities at one another, in a mixture of Czech and German, happened only during natural disasters, like the flood in 1897 thirty years ago. The mob broke down the dainty wooden bridges, trampled pristine rose gardens and flower beds, pissed into the brook and vegetable gardens. They beat their breasts and each other, raised fists toward heaven, and belatedly crossed themselves.

The mob reached the natural pond, long before the rescue vehicles could wind their way through the mountain cleft. The women saw the fence and recognized the threads of cloth atop the fence, dropped to their knees, and looked on in dismay at the abandoned raft in the center of the pond. One man was already hooking up a pump and worked feverishly at the lever. The man's methodical movements appeared calm and measured, belying a roiling sickness within the pit of his stomach. Sweat of fear was pouring down his solemn face. He wearily cast sideways glances at the approaching mob, carrying rakes and shovels. The sun caught his piercing blue eyes as they darted nervously about the lowering surface of the water, like a flash of a diamond held to the light. Without a word the man continued his somber task fearing the worst and without another glimpse at angry faces, coming threateningly close to surround him he could smell their stinking breath.

The House My Father Built

As the water level sank in both the trout pond and the swimming pond, the trout started to pile up flopping frantically in their fight for survival. The quiet man of slight stature leaned his head on the handle of the pump, wiped the cold sweat from his brow, and closed his eyes. He knew the eyes of the villagers were on him filled with great expectations as if he could fix an inevitable outcome.

He could not perform a miracle, and if the boys had drowned in the pond, all his efforts would be for naught no matter how fast he worked the pumps. Yet, he felt their animosity at the seeming slowness of the operation. He winced imperceptibly at the thought of what they might find. But nothing had prepared him for the cruel sight that lay before him. He felt a sickness in his gut. His greatest fear had come true. He turned away and pushed through the gawking, forward pushing crowd in total silence. The crowd massed around the emptied pond screaming, yet eager to gawk in horror at the white and bloated bodies of four children, whose arms and legs were tangled around one another, their grips frozen in rigor mortis so tight, they could not be separated in death. As much as each grieving mother yearned to clutch her own child to her breast once more, they could not be parted without a hacksaw. The man walked slowly back to his lumber yard, and brought back a flatbed truck with lumber boards and chains.

The villagers raised their fists relentlessly toward the man and his worldly goods and swore eternal damnation on him and his offspring, whose wealth had thrust these poor peasants to the depths of hell. The women's wailing lamentations rose to highest heaven, they cursed and spat at the man, waved their fists under his nose and screamed "Nemci bes," (German dog) as he, without rebuke jammed the boards and chains underneath the children's lifeless bodies and slowly hoisted them from their watery grave. The man walked away, his head was tucked low between his shoulder blades. His eyes looked sunken beneath his high cheek bones and the crystal blueness no longer flashed like diamonds.

He looked dark and beaten down. Anna watched the events unfold from her front door stoop. Her heart went out to her husband not daring to mingle with the gathering of an ever more furious crowd. She did not want to add oil to the fire in the face of this tragedy. She waited for her husband of more than twenty years on the front door from where she could see how a shroud masked his revulsion and his dull sorrow. He looked haggardly grey and helplessly shrugged his shoulders. He saw his wife, Anna walked toward him, with wringing hands and crying "Jessesmarren!" as it escaped her lips.

She helped him up the front door steps and fearfully shuttered the door behind them. Anna thought about the many years the children of the village had enjoyed the pond. Swimming in the summer had been their happiest recreation. She knew her husband had done nothing wrong. He had done everything to prevent such a tragedy to occur in this natural spring-fed mountain pond on his property. He had a permit from the Czech magistrate to allow children the pleasure of summer recreation, he had enclosed the property with a high fence, topped off with a string of barbwire and a padlock. Annually he had paid a hefty insurance premium. But no amount of insurance could replace the lives that had been lost. Up until this tragic event, celebrations of life and death had revolved around the churchyard in neighboring Ober-Prausnitz. All souls entered and departed from this community of saints with great celebrations within the heart of this mountain region. A hike across a mountaintop was much too far for five grieving Mamimkas who would huddle around a mass grave, mourning their children all day long and would do so for a lifetime. Merely a few yards from where they had perished the children were laid to rest on land donated by the man who had wielded the pump to become a newly consecrated mass grave. He commissioned a funeral chapel to be built to keep mourners dry on a rainy day. He commissioned a local artist who painted a picture of the Risen Christ with the inscription. "I am the resurrection and the Life." To remind the parents, that there was more glory to come in death. He made the arrangements for the funeral, paid the priests and undertakers, made unanimous donations to the families of the children as well as to hospitals and churches. But nothing was enough. He could not fill the hole in their hearts.

The enraged villagers not only viewed his generosity as appeasement, but as proof of his guilt.

The man was guilty of all that they viewed as evil…wealth. In their eyes wealth was the cause of everything beleaguering this world. They pointed to this tragedy as proof of their theory. In one breath, they raged against the man's wealth, and berated his children of privilege, as Nemci Bes (German dogs) who could wade in a cooling pond, while Ceski children were too poor to wallow in anything but their own sweat. They cursed their fair skinned, blue-eyed neighbor and the privileges his wealth could afford.

Prague ...

With no time to waste, a slender young man with a finely chiseled face, an ivory complexion aglow with the pink hue of the late afternoon sun sprinted across the cobblestones on Wenceslas Square with the agility of a young man in a hurry. His blue eyes were like mirrors of a brilliant azure sky, mesmerizing young women if his gaze happened to fall upon them. Much as they tried, none could hold his eyes, for he had eyes for only one brown haired girl with grey laughing eyes. He tossed a brown leather satchel and a woman's leather riding coat into the sidecar affixed to his new BMW motorbike. He swung his leg over the seat, fastened his leather riding cap over his wheat-blond, neatly slicked hair as a tiny tuft fell over his forehead. He tightened the goggles around his square chin, and gunned the engine several times.

With a roar, the heavy machine lurched forward and spun past the Hradschin Castle and the habitués of the square in a cloud of exhaust fumes. With youthful exuberance, he wove a path at lightening-speed past the ancient symbols of his heritage. His steady hands guided his motorbike in a north-easterly direction, toward the sweeping Sudeten Mountains, and a woman whose soulful eyes reflected his in the color of forget-me-nots. He was heading for his hometown, Mastig, taking the long way home through Klein-Borowitz, where he felt bound to the earth, and where his face and name found great recognition.

His weekly rides to and from school gave the young man time to reflect on all that he loved most, his fatherland ... his homeland. He felt indebted to his hardworking ancestors, who had labored long and hard to perpetuate this independent heritage, independent from local politics. His ancestors had brought forth good harvests in these regions, plagued most by unpredictable and severe weather, dense forests, and rocky soil.

The bike's steady roar filled the valley along the Elbe River, where it makes a knee bend just north of Prague. His eyes followed the flowing ribbon of water deep within the rolling landscape where the river has its spring. He followed the trading routes forged by his ancestors, spanning several centuries. He relished the view of such sweeping majestic landscapes that tantalized his emotions and moved him to tears.

His chest swelled with pride as he viewed the patchwork of serene hamlets of distinguished character, nestled against the hillsides with sturdy confidence. He slowed his speed and dimmed the roar of the engine as he crossed the Elbe River dam in the town of Königinhof, to engage the narrow winding roads ahead.

The forest had changed little over the centuries. The gnarled oaks and thick towering fir trees bore silent witness to the ancient tales and mythical songs of a benevolent giant, Rübezahl. By legend he was the spirit of the mountain who dwelled within the caves as king of dwarfs. His rod and staff were the roots and limbs of fallen trees. In the distance, was a view of Rübezahl's throne, the highest peak crowning the Czech-Polish border mountain range. The Snowcap summit, majestically glistened with snow above the rolling landscape far into the summer months. Here lived a mountain spirit that rose with the morning dew, and filled the pages of story books and children's songs, in which he guarded his subjects against evil, as a father does his children.

He was a young man, emboldened by a clear vision of his future, which reflected only faintly upon the ancient tales taught in his elementary school. But his heart responded to the hush the primeval setting commanded. His maiden would have to wait, for Rübezahl must have his due. The cascading crystalwaters that beckoned him, was a stronger force for the moment, as he brought his engine to a halt. A cuckoo sounded in the distance, and a nightingale by the brook sang her sorrowful songs. Alpine breezes caused the great firs to rustle together in mild but eternal conversation, harmonizing with the incessant and lovely music of the racing mountain white waters to mesmerize a young man named Josef. He knelt beside the stream, cupped his hands, sipped the fresh mountain water and cooled his face. The forest floor was neatly carpeted with needles.

The dark foliage appropriately penetrated the shadows with light and pierced them as magically as stained glass in a cathedral. Josef dropped down by the base of a tree with thick, deeply rutted bark and communed with spirits of whom he had only the slightest intuition. Yet, he felt compelled by their presence to seek their approval, their strength and perhaps their consecration. He picked a handful of blueberries growing in abundance along the fringes of the forest. He cupped his hand and with a toss of his blond head, he funneled the berries into his mouth. Feeling replenished in body and spirit, he fell back into the lush meadows and gazed the paradise that lay nestled between the shadows of Bohemian castles where kings, queens, counts, and barons had allowed this Ceski a Nemci, Czech and German heritage, to evolve over many centuries.

As neighbors, Czechs and Germans had lived in relative harmony for most of a thousand years, due to many intermarriages their cultures had become so intertwined, that it had become difficult to distinguish exactly which tradition was of German and which was of Czech origin. Most conflicts were resolved between bed sheets, until politicians became involved and the passions that were unleashed in Sarajevo and the aftermath dealt this cultural marriage a death blow.

Their story needs to be rolled back on the carpet of history, and should never be forgotten. Knowledge of history teaches us how to live in the future. Josef was a young man who was a long time rapt in the forest's lure, thinking of the maiden with the laughing blue eyes. As soon as she spotted him her eyes lit up and a sparkle danced across her face. She was as multifaceted as a diamond in the rough, mesmerizing him even from such a distance. Down in the valley, a hamlet away, he would launch his life's destiny in the shadow of the Snowcap Summit in due time, with a woman, who, when not laughing heartily, could burst forth in high spirited songs at any given moment and warm his heart, a pretty woman who shared this heritage named Emmi.

He took the long way home and passed through the tiny hamlet of Klein-Borowitz, where he had spotted the pretty brunette a while ago. From that day on he had no time to waste. At seventeen he was a young man in a hurry. Josef gunned the engine and skillfully leaned his body against the wind and the winding road along the Elbe River, until he sighted the historic Windmill of Gross-Borowitz, a stones' throw from the Lauschmann Gasthaus. He pulled up in front of the two-story stucco house, wrestled a leather jacket from his satchel, and draped it over his arm. He slipped inside, and as anticipated saw the pretty woman standing by the billiard table with the cue stick in her hand. He stepped behind her and draped the jacket over her shoulder. "Why don't we go for the eight-ball, you and me?" he whispered in her ear, as his arms fell around her waist, and he looked deep into her saucer round velvety soft eyes fringed with dark lashes.

She quickly rebuked him with a smirk. "My dear man, we have never even been properly introduced. You have not told me your name. I am not likely to go carousing around like a harlot with a man whose name I don't know." She lied with a bit of sarcasm in her voice and a twinkle in her eyes. Of course, she knew who he was. But she enjoyed playing the innocent damsel. He hesitated for a moment. He knew she knew who he was, everybody knew him in these haunts, but he let her think that he believed that she did not know him.

"My name is Josef…Josef Staffa." he responded softly as if afraid to say his last name out loud. "I am Josef junior. My mother calls me Pepiczek, my older sister Annie calls me Pepi, and Marie calls me Sef,." He added with a chuckle. "Take your pick, call me what you like, just don't call me late for dinner."

She was amused and played along looking surprised. She noticed his slight hesitation before saying his last name and looked him straight in the eyes unimpressed, and reached out for his hand. "I am Emilie but everybody calls me Emmi. People who don't like me call me Emma. You can call me what you like. I like Josef, so that's what I'll call you. Sef will have to wait until I get to know you better." She fingered the fine butter soft kid leather jacket. "And what is this? Do you buy all young ladies such fine a gift?" she quizzed with a skeptical tilt of her head.

"Only the ones I plan to marry." he said with a smirk, and then added seriously. "Someday I am going to marry the prettiest girl in Klein-Borowitz. But now I want to take you to the Spindel Mühle, have dinner there and hike up to the Krokonose."

He helped her into the jacket. "I figured you would need a leather jacket and goggles to protect you against the cold wind. I want to show you the world as viewed by eagles…and get away from your mother's eagle eyes. What do you think?"

He winked at her with tantalizing charm. His mouth curled like a rose petal into a bewitching pucker, and he blew her a kiss. He could see the excitement flicker in her eyes. The inevitable moment had arrived. A flash of a smile crossed her face and a deep furrow between her brows appeared. Josef noticed her worried look. "What do you think?" he whispered hoarsely. And she replied, "It does not befit a young woman to accept such an expensive gift from a virtual stranger. What would my neighbors say?" He unceremoniously held the jacket for her to slip into.

"I don't worry about what neighbors think I just worry about your mother. These Czech mothers can be very cantankerous. I have one myself. They like to fight like roosters in a cockfight. I try never to start an argument with my mother."

Just then her mother came out of the kitchen, wiping her hands on her apron. "Emmi! Dinner!"

Emmi replied. "I am not hungry! Give my Bratwurst to Rudi. He always looks hungry."

She quickly slipped out the door before her mother could see the leather jacket draped over her shoulder. Josef gently took her arm, led her to his bike, and gallantly helped her climb into the sidecar. Emilie was entranced by the pungent odor of the fine pig skin leather. It smelled expensive. She could not stop sniffing as she pressed her sleeve against her nose, deeply inhaling its rich odor. Her eyes widened when she saw her mother peering through the white lace curtains, knowing her mother disapproved of her accepting such a gift from a man whose family her mother despised and remembering her mother warning her on improper and unacceptable gifts. "A wealthy man spends neither a silver Thaler, nor precious time, without a purpose or an expectation for reciprocity."

But for the moment Emmi was enchanted as she gently caressed the butter soft wrinkles of the rich leather. She was overwhelmed at being the recipient of such an expensive gift. Josef fastened the goggles around her face and tightened the straps of the leather riding cap and carefully tucked her long braids beneath them. Josef loved showing off the power of his new bike. He gunned the engine to its maximum power, crossed over gurgling brooks, which spilled over rocky crevices in turbulent white-water splendor.

The wind whipped about sun-drenched faces, tugging at a few strands of Emmis' thick, autumn colored hair. Soft wisps escaped from beneath her cap as Josef spun the bike with youthful exuberance through the lovely country side, adorned with symbols of their centuries-old heritage steeped in strict Catholicism. They passed by pilgrim chapels along hiking trails, which offered a sacred sanctuary during a storm leaving behind the wooden roadside shrines and marble crucifixes adorning Alt Sankt Peter.

Josef and Emmi were awed by thunderous waterfalls bursting forth from the base of the trees Towering in awesome splendor above all human pursuits, while two young lovers strained against the mountain breezes to reach the Snowcap

Summit. Josef glanced ever so often at the young woman beside him, delighting in her high-spirited and effervescent presence. Her smile was like the sun bursting through dark clouds, holding him spellbound.

Her hair escaped from beneath the cap and whipped about her face like a halo of light. Her demureness and humility combined with a love for life was a celebration of her inner beauty. Her fiber of integrity was simply sublime and in total harmony with her physical beauty. Josef brought the vehicle to a sudden stop near the edge of a steep cliff and helped her climb out of the sidecar. Their eyes met, and he smiled adoringly, baring a beautiful set of pearly white teeth. He could not resist pulling her hand through his arm as they walked side by side. The physical nearness created a delicious sense of anticipation during their ascent to the sun gilded mountain, where the Elbe River has its spring.

Crowning the summit was an old hunting lodge where European nobility spent their vacations in a forest teeming with wildlife. Viewed from below, the lodge seemed to cling precariously close to the side of a cliff on which the two sought to find refuge from the heat.

They gazed back across the edge of paradise and to points of restful surrender of aching limbs, and simply fell in love, before they started the descend down the steep cliff.

"Emmi, I want to show you a place from where you can stand on the tri-country corner. Poland, Czechoslovakia and Germany are sewn here together along a mountain range." Josef pulled Emmi from one rocky trestle to another, alongside the razor's edge of an abyss.

Below them, civilization spread out like a patchwork quilt. Emmi stood in front of Josef and he wrapped his arms around her and pointed north. "Right on the spot on which you are standing is the border stone of three nations. Look to the north you see Poland from where my mother's family came. Then he pointed to his left side, over there is the nation of Nemcis, from where our grandfathers came."

Emmi replied somewhat amused that Josef tried to compare the commonality of their heritage. "The name, Staffa does not appear in any German name registry. I think your forefathers came from Scotland." She quipped. "Off the coast of Scotland, in the Inner Hebrides one of the islands is named Staffa.

The Romans made it all the way to Scotland, Staffa is a Latin name and means Staff of Caesar your earliest ancestor was probably a Roman soldier, Josef chuckled. "You paid a lot attention in history class." Emmi replied. "I love history. History teaches us valuable lessons for the future. Maybe a Roman soldier just wanted to go south to Rome from Scotland. He crossed the North Sea, followed the Elbe River south into Hamburg. There was no Reeperbahn then. So, he decided to follow south along the Elbe River on his way he got lost in the Sudeta Mountains." Josef chimed in with a chuckle. "Maybe along the way he met a cute Fraulein and got her pregnant. So he decided to settle down here and build his own empire, instead of going back to a decimated Roman Empire."

Their laughter was contagious as they egged each other on. Emmi mused. "I think most Germans have a Roman in their ancestry. The Romans were occupiers of Germany for many decades. They have sown a lot of wild oats here…leaving Roman nosed children behind." Emmi snickered with delight. "Some barbarian husband probably never noticed that someone had laid a cuckoo egg in his bed." Josef placed his hand over her mouth. "Be quiet, listen! Can you hear the cuckoo in the valley below on the Polish side?" Emmi listened spell-bound. "It is magical!"

Josef and Emmi were beyond the petty concerns and tumult playing out across the valley floor, as they wandered along the steep rocky path. They had to watch every step and plant their feet with care, to make sure they would not lose their footing. They reached a wooden rail which seemed to have been repaired recently. Josef stopped and pointed to a spot, just as Emmi leaned against the dry wood posts, Josef pulled her against him. "Watch out! Here on this spot on a class trip thirty children and their teacher plunged to their deaths when they leaned against a section of dry rotted wood railing and it broke away."

Emmi covered her mouth in horror and leaned in closer against Josef's broad shoulders. Here between the lofty sky and hells' abyss, Josef and Emmi had found their place of soaring love.

"I'll lend you my hand if you give me your heart." he murmured as he pulled her closer to him. Emmi's heart was racing, and it felt good and right, warm and tender to be in Josef's arms, albeit precariously close to the razor's edge of an abyss. She knew his reputation preceded him. She knew her mother felt nothing but animosity toward the man she loved and his infamous family.

They wandered back to the Flora Hunting Lodge, and chose a quiet corner on the veranda, where bright red geraniums spilled over the window sills. Josef motioned the owner to come to the table.

"Two glasses of Riesling wine, please." The owner, Gustav Kraus, placed a menu on the table. The waiter showed him a bottle and Josef nodded, while the owner's wife set a table for two, and gypsy minstrels strolled by with their string instruments. Emmi and Josef slowly sipped wine and gazed in each other's eyes above the rim of their glasses, bedazzled by the surrounding majesty of the mountains and a golden sun sinking slowly behind the most bewitching natural beauty. Two young lovers looked besotted their eyes fixated in the shadow of the highest peak.

Befitting the moment, a small band played Viennese Waltzes, Wine, Women and Song and Wiener Blut was Emmis' favorite. Vienna Blood was running through her veins. She closed her eyes to let the music wash over her like a cascading waterfall. Her head swayed dreamily back and forth, as she hummed the beloved melody. Her feet tapped lightly to the frolicking rhythm. At this moment she saw her life as an endless waltz through paradise. "Will you be faithful to me?" Josef interrupted her thoughts as he looked at the fresh-faced woman with the large laughing eyes. "Will you wait for me?" He looked beseechingly at her, held her hands tightly as he anxiously awaited her answer. "I need to know before I go back to Prague if you will wait until I am done with my engineering studies?"

Their eyes locked for a long silent moment, as Emmi solemnly pondered his request. She replied with a question of her own. "What about you? Will you be faithful to me?"

They both held their breath waiting for the other to reply first. They were each afraid to say words they might regret, words of commitment and promises made too soon, seem too eager.

Emmi felt her heart beat wildly and smiled adoringly. He was wild with anticipation as he held her close. "I want to be sure, I don't have to worry about another man in your life. Nobody will ever love you as I do."

Her reply rolled off her tongue with greatest of ease, surprising even herself. "How could I not remain faithful to you...you and those forget-me-not blue eyes?" She put her arms around his broad shoulders and planted a butterfly kiss on both cheeks. She loosened her wavy tresses and they tumbled about her gentle face, tickling his cheeks for a brief moment.

She lowered her eyelids demurely in theatric precision, but the words she gushed came straight from her heart, for those she needed no script. "Just as the mountains keep a faithful watch over this valley for all eternity, I will wait for you!"

He looked overjoyed, and playfully took the long, softly entwined tresses and piled them high on top of her head. He pulled a few strands over her eyes and formed a crown and veil. "Emmi Lauschmann, you shall be my bride! Someday I will marry the prettiest girl in Klein-Borowitz." He plucked a handful of wildflowers and with a sheepish grin tucked them behind her ear and across her forehead. Emmi laughed deliriously, tossing her head back, and letting the blossoms scatter about her in carefree abandon.

"You make me look like a Valkyrie" She reeled with laughter as he gallantly kissed her hand. "First we'll have to sweep up these flowers together. I'm not a diva like Greta Garbo. But I am not up for grabs either. You have to ask for my hand on your knees!" Josef dropped down on one knee. "What next, mein gnädiges Fräulein?" he teased in fluent German. Emmi shrieked with delight, slyly looked about the lodge at the few guests, giggling.

She looked at him with a more solemn expression. "Look, my dear man, I can't answer just now, we are just seventeen years old. I want to achieve something in my life. I don't want to wind up working in a factory."

The wine had gone to their heads, their cheeks were flushed, their sparkling eyes danced with one another to the rhythm of their heartbeats. Emmi covered her naturally rouged cheeks with her hands in mock concern over her disheveled look. "What will the neighbors think of my flushed face, my messy hair and wrinkled dress? My feet are covered with gravel. I feel slovenly dirty?"

"Put your feet on my lap." Josef ordered and Emmi complied with a sheepish grin as Josef gently brushed the fine gravel from her sandaled feet in feigned humility and servitude and replied. "My neighbors can go to hell! I don't owe them an explanation." Josef asked. "But your mother, what will she say?"

"I know what my mother will say…that man is Pepi Staffa. The Staffa men have a bad reputation as drinkers and womanizers." Emmi looked concerned. "Did you have to bring one of them home as a suitor? Do not come home with a big belly! There has been enough scandal in Mastig."

Neither of them dared talk about the soul searing drowning tragedy in the pond on his father's property. Josef mused. "I know what my Mamimka will say… She is a poor girl…must you get married?' Emmi snuggled close and chucked him under the chin coquettishly. "To which you will say, yes, of course, we must!" She clasped her chest in mock shame. Emmi wagged a finger in his face. "My dear

Mister Staffa, let me only say this…as long as you only womanize me all is well with the world."

He snatched her tantalizing finger and pulled her close. "Then all is well with the world." He cupped her face with his hands. "You shall be my bride." His arms encircled her small frame and his mouth fell over hers. She limply fell against him in total surrender for what seemed blissful eternity, she gasped for air and gaped in wonder at him at his marvelous face.

"No drama class has prepared me for this." She murmured dreamily as she smoothed out her rumpled dirndl. Josef pulled her back against him with a firm grip. "Now that we are quasi betrothed, you should know that I don't like your stage partner…what's his name?"

Emmi's eyes clouded over mysteriously, as she calmly responded. "His name is Bruno, and he is the son of the Linhart miller, from one of the finest families around. He is a friend and stage partner and nothing more…a quasi-stage prop. That's all!"

Josef's eyes darkened as he snarled. "Just so he doesn't prop up against you!"

Josef pressed his velvety smooth face against her suddenly stiff and unyielding frame. Emmi sat up straight, wet her lower lip, and replied slowly, while firmly intoning each word with a growing consternation.

"Since I was thirteen the love of my life has been singing and dancing …I am a member of a small but professional theatre ensemble, we are very good at what we do, people like us everywhere we go on tour. When I am on a stage, I feel alive with joy. Applause has been my life's elixir running through my veins. I need the theatre, and the theatre needs me to bring joy to peoples' lives in these forgotten valleys. I have played a lead role in Franz Lehar music theatre. Now you come into my life and upset everything like an applecart!"

Josef looked stern and replied. "I will not play second fiddle to your music man." Emmi's face was a cold mask as she pushed him away and snapped a smart rebuke.

"There is no ring on my finger yet. Until then, I will live my life as I see fit. I have to get back. I have a rehearsal tonight." The magic moment had fled irretrievably. Emmi was so angry she couldn't even look at him. She was so stunned at his remarks, and shrugged off his arm when he tried to help her into the sidecar and climbed in unassisted. On the ride back she could not bring herself to say another word to him.

The House My Father Built

She painstakingly had avoided mention of the theatre and her uncles' next production. Someday she would have to face the music, but not now. Emmi hated how these sour notes seem to creep into their otherwise harmonic relationship as soon as the word "theatre" came up, she fought valiantly to regain her equilibrium in happier thoughts, brushing aside her depressing disposition.

Josef pulled his motorbike up in front of the Gasthaus. He reached out to embrace Emmi, but she pushed him back. He locked her arms behind her back, and pressed her close, not giving her a chance to run off, before they had settled their differences.

He knew he had offended her, and tried to smooth things over with his charm. "I just can't stand the thought of another man kissing the woman I plan to marry." He whispered in her ear, and kissed her hand. "Because, I love you!"

Just then the stern face of an old woman peered out from behind the white lace curtains. Emmi noticed her mother's scornful eyes and pushed Josef away with a quick. "Tschüss! Drive carefully." She wrestled free of the fingers that wouldn't let her go, and blew him a kiss, just as the woman with the high-cheeked Slavic features stepped out from behind the curtain, and shouted. "Emmi! Inside!"

Emmi knew a storm was brewing and took her time to respond. Her eyes and ears followed the biker out of town. She watched him spin the bike around, cutting an escape path through the backwoods to avoid his home turf. He understood why eagle eyes were on him at every move he made. He knew his latest amorous adventures might provide fodder of unpleasantness for the girl he loved. Not only was he weary of his family's watchful eyes, he knew his well-known name provided fodder for endless village gossip.

His sister Marie had sent him a letter in Prague informing him of the drowning accident and that the village of Mastig was in an uproar. She warned him not to show his face in Mastig. His mother wanted him to stay in Prague. With a thunderous noise of his BMW he drove back to the sacred anonymity of Prague. He was enrolled in one of the few German technical schools still operating in Prague, where math and algebra was still taught in the German language, for the simple reason that the Czech school administration had failed to translate accurate teaching materials in metric engineering sciences into the Czech language.

While in Klein-Borowitz...

"**Emmi!** Get in here!" Her mother called with great agitation "Get in here now!" Her voice had become hoarse. Emmi entered hesitantly, and greeted her mother with the customary greeting of the area with deliberate nonchalance. "Grüss Gott!"

Emmis mother did not return the customary greeting instead she blocked her daughter's path. "I told you not to get involved with this guy. He will just get his way with you, then he'll marry someone with money." Franziska looked at her daughter with grave consternation as she spotted the leather coat. "Where did you get that leather coat? We don't have things like this here." Emmi replied. "It is a present from Sef. He gave it to me so I can go bike riding with him."

Suddenly, her mother's arms were flailing as she crossed herself. Ranting and lamenting about the matriarch of the Staffa clan. "With little noblesse oblige that woman has long forgotten where she came from. She was a Polska scullery maid in the only Jewish household…until she married into the wealthy Staffa family."

Fanziska sat on a chair and shook her head while Emmi listened in silence. "I am telling you the Staffa family is cursed…one scandal follows another. What does a Staffa heir want from a poor girl like you? Create another scandal? How often must I tell you, that a wealthy man does not spend time or Thaler on a casual consort, without a conniving intent? What is his purpose in consorting with a naïve girl as poor as a church mouse, he just wants to seduce you. His family won't be happy with you, especially his mother won't like you!"

Emmi put her arms around her mothers' shoulders and caressed her until the rants had ceased.

"Well, Mamimka I have a surprise! That man, Pepi Staffa, wants to marry this poor church mouse. I know my wedding will be the subject of another scandal. He said I was the prettiest girl in Klein-Borowitz he wanted for his bride someday. I will be his bride. Dobri den!"

Emmi hoisted herself on a barstool and watched Rudi fill a beer stein from the tap and placed it in front of Emmi who looked about with a puzzled face for a quiet corner where she could read her script and pretend to study in expectations of the ceaseless tirades that were sure to follow a sip at a time.

"He just wants to seduce you." Her mother intoned and followed her to the bar, still wringing her hands into her apron, berating her daughter's new love interest, and wagging a finger in her face. "I can't say it often enough. You are such a thick-skulled child. The Staffas all have a bad reputation. They are nothing but a bunch of skirt chasing drunks. They cause only mayhem. Did you hear of the murder of four children?" Emmi rolled her eyes in exasperation, and replied. "It was a terrible accident."

Her mother scoffed. "You call this an accident? Jessesmarren! If they weren't so rich they would not have a pond, if they had no pond the four children would not have drowned."

Emmi sighed. "Nobody is to blame except parents who let their children roam the streets at night when they should be in bed. The kids were trespassing." Emmi replied exhaustedly. As her mother wailed. "Who pities the broken-hearted parents? The Staffa's wealth is at fault." Emmi replied. "Mamimka these kids climbed over the fence." Emmis' face was so close to her mother's they could smell each other's breath. "Staffa Pepi will leave you broken-hearted and you'll wind up a drinkers' widow. Emmi threw up her hands in desperation. "I give up!"

She was determined to stay focused on her script. "Rudi, I need another beer…Rudi." Rudi was so much like her gentle papa, never getting excited over worldly events, often defusing ugly altercations with a kind word, or a silent wink, he knew when to keep silent. Nobody could win against his mother's tirades, lest his interference might cause her blood pressure to rise. He knew Emmi could take care of herself when he heard her say. "Mamimka, enough, already! I don't want to be distracted. I need to study my script."

Her mother clasped her hips. "So, you think life is just a romantic fairytale like the roles you play on a stage. Life is hard work!"

Emmi replied, "Subject closed!" She slid off the barstool and headed for the door with an angry. "Dobri Den!"

For indeed the subject was closed. She was in no mood to wrestle with her mother any longer about her new love or family tragedies. She had to wrestle with her own feelings, torn between her love for the theatre and her love for a man.

While she felt secure in Josef's love for her, she chose to keep his promises deep within her heart. She was distressed to see her mother wring her hands in utter dismay.

Emmi came back trying to smooth her mother's ruffled feathers. She quietly sat beside her, and said between slow sips of a cold Pilsner beer.

"Mamimka, the accident and the scandals have nothing to do with Josef. I believe him to be a good man. Josef wasn't drunk when he asked me to wait for him, and I was not besotted when I heard him say, 'Someday you'll be my bride.'"

Franziska shook her head. "His mother was a scullery maid in a Jewish household, she scrubbed floors to support her mother. Her father was a Polack from across the Polish border.

Now she acts high and mighty. Pompous as the queen of Sheba she allows herself to be chauffeured about the region by a Czech chauffeur, while her Czech fieldhands toil in fields to support her lifestyle. The Staffa family think they own this land. As if their shit doesn't stink, they have a lot of shit on their sticks." Emmi felt a rage welling up inside as she tried to remind her mother. "Your own family had its share of scandals. Wasn't Uncle Dehnert, or Dohnert, I can't remember which one it was… the talk of the town when he hung himself with his white scarf, after his shady business deals with a Jew was uncovered. When the Jew refused to pay him for his share of a deal and instead threatened to expose him for tax evasion? Remember, his wife with her chichi nimbus, had to sell her gilded rococo finery, her red velvet and gold furniture, and valuable antiques. I remember whenever I went to visit them for the summer, how uncomfortable I felt in that gilded cage. I could not sit on a sofa because every room was so pristine and elegant, gold was everywhere. Now that aunt has nothing left. She lives in abject poverty and destitute loneliness she goes begging on street corners. Was the uncle drunk when he got involved with a Jew? Every family has skeletons in a closet, some more than others."

Her mother held her head in her hands. "Just remember what I told you … and why I am totally against this relationship. And his mother won't like it either. I will not attend this wedding."

Emmi replied. "I am only seventeen. I am not thinking of a wedding. You married without Fanfare in a civil ceremony. You did not attend Poldis' wedding when he married Martha. Otto ran off to marry Hilda. They said adieu and left town. In due time comes the wisdom of sages. If I make a mistake, it will be for lack of wisdom, it won't be for lack of love. In love as in business, you have to have integrity. If you make a business deal, make sure it is an honest deal, even with a Jew. If you say 'I love you,' make sure it comes from the heart, and not just meaningless theatrics."

Exhausted from her own tirade, Emmi looked calmly at her mother, noting her worried and sorrowful look on her face. She knew life had not been easy for her poor mother after her husband's death. She always had to work hard. Maybe her mother would understand her love interests on a rational level. "Just think Mamimka, marrying Josef will have certain advantages. I'll become a household name. In every Nemci village between here and Prague, my name will find great recognition as Emilie Staffa, wife of Josef, prettiest girl in Klein-Borowitz. That's what they'll say. The way I see it, only cows in Klein-Borowitz turn their heads when they see me."

Her anger had dissipated. "After my name is changed to "Dame Staffa" I might even have a chance to perform at the National Theatre in Prague. See Mamimka, you came from riches and married into poverty, I am a poor girl marrying into riches. In the edifice of time everything is balanced out. As long as we love each other, nothing else matters. Loving Josef feels natural. Imagine, he made a veil of flowers for me, and I'll be wearing one. My wedding will be my grandest performance, yet."

Emmi proclaimed jubilantly in her final attempt to reconcile with her mother. She draped her arms around the tired looking woman and planted a kiss on her cheek. Her mother waved off her affection with a dismissive remark. "Love doesn't pay the bills." Emmi had nothing more to say. She felt drained.

The theatre was only a few sprints away next door to the Scholz Gasthaus. Emmi could lose the concerns of the day, and focus on the events that held the greatest promise for the future—-A life with Josef. Emmi prayed for compromise in which she could combine her love for a man and her love for the theater. Emmi felt befuddled. She raced to the theatre and realized that she had forgotten her script.

Startled by her own forgetfulness she ran back to the house, looked around the piano, the parlor, the billiard table, but she could not find her important script and music sheets. She remembered distinctly that she had left them on top of the piano and muttered to herself.

"My God, that man makes me forget everything." She rushed back to the theater. Slightly befuddled she managed to sing her favorite arias from memory, knowing all along that her performance would never be the same again.

Mastig...

While Annas' stepsons had grown into stately, handsome young men, she was glad their amorous pursuits were fixated upon pretty women of means. Just as his brothers were finding suitable partners, Josef, was expected to bring someone into the family fold with deep pockets, pockets full of money. His sister Annie was courted by a carpet merchant from Koniginhof, Adolf courted Minna, Karl planned to marry Ilse, whose family owned a building supply company. Emil had his eyes upon the gorgeous Hildegard next door. Hildegard was a redhead whose name was preceded by the word beautiful at every mention of the young woman. Within a few months, Emil married Hildegard in the church in Ober-Prausnitz where generations of ancestors had met, married, had children baptized, and whose maternal ancestors were laid to rest. Male ancestors had perished in foreign trenches.

During this turbulent season of first love, Emmi wanted to shout it from the rooftop that she was the chosen love interest of Josef Staffa, while villagers in the area bristled with emotion and clamored for revenge. Her cousin, the postman Bubi Scholz, delivered letters Josef sent from Prague, warning Emmi not to mention his name, and keep silent about their relationship. She pressed her lips together, wondering whether there was another nefarious reason, and handed Bubi a letter in reply. "Maybe you are embarrassed to be seen with a poor girl like me."

Josef replied swiftly. "Mastig has become a hornet nest since the accident and I am afraid you might get caught in the middle of reprisals aimed at any one associated with the Staffa name. I can feel the animosity when I drive through the areas." On nice days the people came out to assemble at every street corner, gawked at passersby outside pubs, or clustered around the village well with vitriolic accusations. Josef could feel hearts throb for revenge.

Heads turned when he passed through Mastig on his way back to Prague. In their excitement the spittle spewed from their tongues, like fiery lava, and hate filled diatribe was aimed at wide angled windows. Their fingers clamored to curl around someone's neck.

Rumors and innuendos sharpened in echoes throughout the region. Clenched fists swung into the air like arrows, as if they held daggers. Before driving to Klein-Borowitz to stop at Emmis' house Josef waited until dark or a drenching rain, when people were most likely to stay inside.

His mother had heard the rumors of his love interest and implored him in letters. "Pepi stay in Prague, until this has blown over. Concentrate on your studies. Nobody knows who you are in Prague."

Josef yearned to see Emmi, and get updates of the latest situation from his sister Marie. Emmi anxiously awaited the postman, Bubi Scholz, every day hoping for a letter from Josef. Bubi Scholz could be heard from far away as he laboriously cleared his throat as he made the rounds with his mailbag. Bubi saw the throng that was gathering every morning in front of the Narodny Vybor, Czech Nationalist headquarters, which had grown into a mob. They were out for blood and screamed relentlessly.

"Arrest the Nemci bes." As the mob grew louder and more demanding for an arrest more people gathered. One morning, Czech gendarmes surrounded the Staffa villa. Moments later, they dragged Josef Staffa from his home and charged him with the murder of four children.

The Czech villagers were jubilant and the Germans were appalled and horrified. As soon as Josef junior was informed of his father's arrest, he dropped what he was doing, jumped on his bike, gunned the engine and headed unafraid into Mastig. Josef went to see his father in his cell, who quietly sat on a strawmat with his head in his hands, but his eyes belied a calm demeanor.

He barely reflected his inner turmoil, as he pondered his fate. "It does not look good, my son." He said quietly. Josef saw, that his father had grown quiet and at peace with himself, knowing he had taken proper precautions to prevent last summer's tragedy. "I keep seeing the children as if seeing a film reel rolling through my head." He rubbed his eyes. "I have asked myself, what else I could have done, or what more I could do now, to ease the suffering of these families." He had commissioned the painting in the shelter at the gravesite to bring villagers some peace. He felt resigned to his fate, and consoled in face of his own death. He could face the firing squad with a clear conscience and at peace with his maker. He had done all that was humanly possible to prevent such a tragedy.

"They are just looking for blood." His son said and his father nodded. "Yes, they want my blood!"

"We are the scapegoat for all that has gone wrong here over the centuries, they are looking for someone on whom they can pin blame and vent their frustrations. They use a tragedy such as this to blame Germans and perpetuate hate of everything with a German association like the German Shepherd the Brits call Alsatians and kick little Dachs Hounds." His father replied. "They'll get me, one way or another."

"I don't want you to come into town anymore on your bike. They'll throw a rake or something into the spokes and cause an accident and even kill you." Josef nodded and wrapped his arms around his father's stooped shoulders. "I'll talk to mother." Josef wondered if he would ever see his father again alive or he would be shot in front of a firing squad. As soon as Josef junior walked into his mother's house, a pot crashed to the floor with a clatter. His mother screeched. "Pavel… take Pepiczek back toPrague." She shoved her son toward the door.

"You can't stay here. They'll kill you. Let Pavel Koczian drive y.ou." Pavel Koczian was her most dedicated field hand, a good looking, faithful and devoted Czech youth. Young Josef and Pavel were about the same age. Koczian showed as much respect for his young boss as he did for his employers Josef and Anna Staffa, who had always treated him like a son. He was welcome inside the villa anytime and was at all times treated like a son, it was his home

Pavel wondered about Anna Kudronovsky, the Czech matriarch who had married into the wealthiest German family, working alongside field hands as if she were one of them. Pavel escorted Josef to the Dusenberg, shielding him from prying eyes that were hanging over the fence. "What are they gawking at?" Young Josef snarled at the gawkers as he climbed into the back seat of the car. He was visibly upset over the intrusion into his private life. "Koczian, take a detour through Klein-Borowitz?" Pavel knew of the secret liaison his boss had with the young woman from the next village. He followed orders without further mention to anyone. Pavel did not mind taking orders from his young boss. He slowed the car to a crawl as they approached the Lauschmann Gasthaus.

He knew his boss needed to stop for a little rendezvous. Josef asked him politely.

"Can you pull up close to the house?" When Pavel saw Emmi pumping water from the well beside Emmi's house, he obediently stopped the engine and spread a newspaper across to shield his young boss from prying eyes. Emmi turned around as the car pulled alongside her and sat the water bucket on the front door step. She saw the familiar face peering across the front seat of the car, as he beckoned for her to come close.

She knew he did not want to be seen with her, she believed it was because of her lowly status as he tried to convince her, it might cause her grave consequences. She gingerly looked around, to see if anyone was watching, Pavel held the door open and she climbed in the front passenger seat without looking back acted as if she was talking to Koczian, as Josef crouched low in the backseat and whispered.

"Emmi, they have arrested my father on murder charges. I have to stay in Prague until all this blows over." She pressed her lips together, unable to respond in a manner she would have preferred. She would have liked to throw her arms around him, and press her lips against his. Pavel Koczian averted his eyes. He understood every German word. Emmi was not sure if this field hand could be trusted. No one trusted anyone anymore.

"We won't be seeing each other for some time. It could become dangerous for you to be seen with me. I will write to you." Pavel Koczian held the car door open for Emmi and kissed her hand, acting as if he were the one who was courting her. Emmi jumped out of the car, lifted the bucket of water and walked inside the house where she met the scornful eyes of her mother with some unease. If Josef could not show his face in her home town, people would be quick to assume with measurable 'Schadenfreude' that the son of the wealthy Staffa family had dumped her and they would be quick to say, 'I told you so.'

From behind the lace-curtained windows, Emmi watched him leave, wondering if she would ever see him again as tears flooded her eyes. She ran upstairs to pour out her heartache on a piece of stationary. The villages were abuzz as talk of the arrest of Josef Staffa senior dominated every conversation. Emmi kept her ears raised and her lips closed, knowing the rumor mills would grind fastest in her mother's pub.

She took special pains to walk past the hall of the Narodny Vybor every morning, where she could read public notices of the proceedings with great curiosity. She faithfully wrote down everything she could find out. She picked up tidbits of information, captured in casual conversations from anyone willing to share it. In each letter she meticulously chronicled every tidbit of news coming out of Mastig, and with the promise to wait for his return, she signed each letter with Eternal Love – E.

Josef responded to her in kind, addressing every letter with artful calligraphic script and telling her how much he longed to see her. With every breath she yearned to gaze again at his noble face and walk proudly beside the fine figure of the man she loved. He pleaded with her to visit him in Prague for which she needed no further prodding. He signed off with such beautiful lettering as only he could write "Josef." She ran her fingers across the letters, planted a lipstick kiss over his name, and wrote a letter to let him know, she was taking the "Bummelzug" to Prague.

She went to the post office the next morning and glimpsed a disheveled looking young man out of the corner of her eye. The man was leaning against the building, puffing a cigarette with a marked look of boredom. She walked a short distance and watched his reflection in the storefront windowpanes. She noticed how he pushed himself away from the building and followed her at a safe distance. She had seen the man lurking around a lot lately. She finally realized with a start that this man was stalking her. She decided to let him know she was not afraid of him. She spun around and walked straight toward him. "What do you want?" she snarled in fluent Czech, "I know what you are up to. Do not follow me again or I'll kick your ass," she bluffed. Taken thus by surprise, the swarthy man pulled his collar around his face to shield his identity and fled into the opposite direction.

Prague...

Rosa Jutnar, a Czech drama classmate in Prague, was delighted to put her friend up for a few days. On the first morning of Emmi's visit beneath the hundred spires of this golden gothic city, as the mist rose from the Moldau River and the lush green valley swelled with the morning dew, Emmi felt the thrill at the sight of such colossal architecture over the rivers gorge.

Emmi and Rosa linked arms and strolled down the narrow streets of the old city of a thousand spires. The two young girls in dainty pumps, gingerly stepped around the cobblestones marked with crosses, marked for those who had died as martyrs of their Christian faith.

Emmi gaped in wonder at the multitude of statues of saints, and thought that no city in the world could boast more saints, not even Rome. St. Wenceslas reigned above as Patron Saint. Emmi stopped to light a votive candle before his feet. "This one is for you, Papa." She bowed her head in silent meditation, while Rosa looked about with great ambivalence. Emmi moved on before the stone feet of St. Nepomuk, her favorite saint, and rubbed his feet as tradition commanded it. She explained her reason with her usual good cheer. "Silent Saint Nepomuk is called Silent Saint, because he kept silent even in the face of death. He refused to reveal the queens' confession to the king, so the king had him beheaded, and his body was thrown off the bridge in a sack."

Rosa responded with her own pragmatic wisdom to her wide-eyed exuberant friend."Actually he got involved in Czech politics, and that ticked the king off."

Emmi thought it best not to quibble with Rosa about faith, religion and politics.

"Say Rosa, now that we have counted all the saints in Prague, where should we go for coffee and Pflaumenkuchen?" Emmi queried. "Do you know a place where we can spend the hours, until Pepi gets out of school?" Rosa replied with a grin. "Well, that depends on what language you want to speak today…and how many coffee grounds you want to swallow in one gulp? I have had enough Hamataschen for a while.

If we speak German, we get thrown out of the Café Slavia and at the Continental Hotel we have to speak Hoch Deutsch, and pretend to have a sense of haute couture. But they do have great Viennese coffee with whip cream or cinnamon." Emmi scrambled a few Slavic words together. "Why don't we speak a bit of Ceski a Nemci?" Emmi snickered. "…and sound like bleating donkeys?" Rosa interjected. The girls linked arms and kicked up their legs, as if to do the Czardas. "Nobody will be the wiser if we kick them any higher."

The two young women decided on the comfort of the friendly Continental Hotel near Prague's National Theatre, just around the corner from the grandiose stage where Emmi and Rosa hoped to perform one of these days. For a few moments, they were satisfied to drink in the aura of the theater crowd, and marvel about the prominent celebrities as they sauntered past sidewalk cafes lining Wenceslas square.

Emmi was in love with life and relished the taste of the good life of a leisurely habitué. "I wonder if she is somebody?" Emmi whispered as she stolidly sipped coffee with pinkies extended from dainty Meissen demitasse for hours. Rosa replied somewhat annoyed and decided to leave before Emmis' paramour arrived. "Of course, she is somebody, I am somebody! I have to go home now." The girls hugged and bid each other good-bye.

Emmi continued the leisurely stroll along the banks of the Moldau River, feeling watched and sheltered by the multitude of stone saints smiling down on her. She came to know them well while waiting in their shadows before she could spend precious moments with Josef.

Emmi had enough time to daydream and count the cobbles of the square. She waited patiently for her favorite moment, savoring the seconds until the grand clock in the Mala Strana Square struck six o'clock, then the figure of Christ filed out of its lower chamber, followed by the Apostles, trailed by the figure of death turning the hour glass, at the same time the bells chimed the hour.

It was an ingenious masterpiece, known for its artistic design and precision timing. These were the landmarks in the treasured city of her heritage that would become her favorite meeting place with Josef, where they could stroll across the ancient Karls Bridge to the Orloj Clock in Old Town Square, and the Karl University tower.

But even the most illustrious, gold domed landmarks faded into a grey background as soon as Emmi beheld the sparkle in his blue eyes and the brilliant white teeth set into a big smile that spread across his face as soon as he spotted Emmi. His heavenly blue eyes would sparkle with delight from beneath a shock of wheat blond hair, whipping about his high forehead teasing the fine waxen skin that stretched tautly across finely chiseled cheekbones. Between the tolls of the hours and the lovely chimes, Emmi and Josef found time to steal away from the clamoring crowd of Prague to the banks of the river, where they swore each other eternal love while their neighbors in Mastig could only wrest eternal damnation from their breasts, upon the family named Staffa.

Josef sighed. "Time heals old wounds, but not in Czechoslovakia. My mother often said.

'Die Tschechen kennen keine Verzeihung.'

That's what my father found written in my mother's prayer book in his German language." Emmi said in German. "I know…my mother has never forgiven my father for dying…nor for getting her pregnant as his farewell gift." She clasped her mouth. "I almost forgot!

There is good news from Mastig after all this time. First, your sister Marie is getting married to Gustav Gernert." Josef looked surprised and queried. "Marie is marrying the butcher, Gernert?" "No, she is marrying his brother Gustav, the pub owner. Marie is with child, and when she told your father, he said, 'That must have happened under the Hazelnut bush'. Well, her belly looks like she ate a sack of hazelnuts." Emmi laughed. "Babies take nine months but Marie will have a seven-month preemie." Emmi chuckled. "Marie wants to make the Gernert Pub into an elegant Garden Café.

"But here is the best news of all." She read out loud from a newspaper clipping. "After careful examination of all facts, the Czech magistrate could find no fault in Josef Staffa. The justices declared him innocent of all charges and restored him to the community, as a just and honorable man, and a man of good conscience. Josef snatched the paper from Emmis' hand and shouted for joy.

"I knew it."

Mastig...

After his release from jail, Josef Staffa senior was back at work, looking weary at the end of the day. His lumber enterprise had built up a great wealth over the years of hard labor. Josef senior was glad to be home and take care of his business again. Previous generations had bought more and more land and since it took about one hundred years before a tree could be harvested for building lumber, new seedlings had to be planted to fill the increasing demand for lumber. The length of a work day depended on unpredictable and often severe weather. But the hard labor his business required also needed the labor of healthy workers.

He had to rely on them to keep his business productive. He needed them as much they needed the steady employment. He knew, the wealth of the Staffa lumber industry aroused a lot of envy among the discontented elements in their midst, who would rather sabotage his productive enterprise than work for him, therefore he had to keep a sharp eye on his workforce. He hoped to keep them satisfied with good hourly wages and a round of frothy beer from the tap at Gustav Gernerts' pub.

He reasoned that as long as a man had a sound roof over his head and bread in the oven all was well. He knew that if he didn't take care of his workers basic needs, they might look for a job in the Mandl factory who could afford to give his employees steady work. During her husbands' incarceration, Anna had done what she could to keep the saw blades humming.

When she went to the lumber yard, to discuss work orders with the men she felt the brunt of her countrymen's hatred for her, It was obvious to her that the burly men resented being ordered around by a woman. Anna complained to her husband about their attitude toward her. They sneered at her for being the boss lady, and demanded more pay all the while they spent more time lazing around the pile of wood logs as they worked in slow motion. He tried to explain to his wife the pitfalls of the business. "The lumber business is a seasonal business in these mountains I have to make the most of good weather and pay the men well. People want steady work, which I cannot give them. Adolf Mandl is my toughest competitor for low wage laborers. He can offer year-round, steady work. I can't do that."

Anna was thinking this over. "Adolf Mandl offers housing as an added incentive." Josef senior replied. "If you can call "Bretterbuden" housing, they are ramshackle huts, wooden boards hammered together with a few nails. They live in wooden shacks and have to pay rent to Adolf Mandl." Anna asked with a bit of sarcasm. "Do they have better housing in Russia?" Josef senior replied. "For a Russian worker these shacks are a Winter Palace. When the wind blows it whistles through the cracks, and when the wind blows hard enough the shacks fall apart or rot away in a few years unless they paint them every year, the Russians have no incentive and let the shacks rot. Communism has destroyed work ethics in Russia."

Anna said. "Russians are not disciplined to be punctual and shun hard work. It only takes a bottle of vodka to make them happy. They know how to live it up."

Josef senior replied. "They should learn a tool and die trade from Franz Pech, he is a tough boss and a hard worker. He owns a tool and dye factory in Ober-Prausnitz, behind the church cemetery. They should learn a trade from someone like Franz Pech. They could learn a lot from him. They need to develop discipline to make tools because it takes to lot of precision." Anna mused as she listened to her husband. "Which reminds me, Marie told me a funny story that is making the rounds at Gustav's pub causing a few chuckles. Franz Pech caught one of the Russian workers hiding in one of the tool bins. He was sleeping, snoring like a saw blade. When Franz came upon him, he gave the Ruskie a kick in the rear because the lazy guy refused to go back to work." Anna envisioned the scene and chuckled.

Josef replied reflectively. "I cannot afford any altercation with my workers. I try to be fair because it will bite me in the ass if I do otherwise. It is best to keep the peace with little men or you'll wind up giving it to money grubbing politicians."

Anna could see in her husbands' slow movements that the years of toil had bent his back. During the incarceration his spirit and high energy had died. The joy he had always found in work was gone. He could not shake the oppressive feeling that someone was out to get him. He could not trust the men at the job site that he needed. "Politicians cause all the discord between people in the first place. They start the animosity and mistrust between people then add fuel to a fire to promote their own agenda."

The House My Father Built

Anna hugged her husband "There has never been any discord between you and me, despite my cantankerous Czech nature." We work out our German and Czech problems under our featherbed." She smiled. "If only it were as easy as snuggling under a featherbed." He replied with a smile.

Anna knew her husband had tried to avoid rancor among his workers. He looked resigned at the plate Anna had placed before him.

The hatred of the lumber jacks seeped ever deeper with every peace offering he had made thus far. It seemed to affirm their belief that he sought to pay them off. The never-used Resurrection Chapel was seen by them as squander. He recently hired two strong lumber jacks, Karel and Ladislav, to meet the demands of the spring planting season. Karel Push came recommended by Rudi Shubrt, a butcher trainee in the employ of the Gernert butcher. Karel had just moved into the home of the Staffa Carpenter as a tenant, Karel and Ladislav had long sought employment and housing with a German boss to "keep a close eye on Nemci bes." The two men were members of the Narodny Vybor who sought to infiltrate the German business community.

Nine months after the drowning of the four children, on Friday, March 28, 1929, strong westerly currents were melting the icy peaks of the Krokonose Summit, causing brooks and ponds to crest with icy waters. It had been a good week for the lumber business because of the warm spring weather. Josef senior had a big backlog of orders to fill since his imprisonment. He carried a lot of money on him, especially after he had made a lot of deliveries and all transactions were made in cash. The bank was in the nearby town of Arnau. He could make a deposit on Monday morning. Every Friday he invited the mill hands to a round of beer at the Gustav Gernert Pub, after work. Slurping the frothy liquid, the mill hands stared in glum silence as their boss tried to make small talk with his new lumber jacks. The boss arched back to pull out his gold pocket watch Anna had given him on their wedding day and checked the time. He always picked up the tab

Ladislav and Karel watched every move their new boss made scarcely guessing the extent of wealth within the man's breast pocket. But they were determined to find out. The boss fanned the money from his thick wallet, and plunked down a few hundred crowns.

He counted out the wages for the men and paid Gustav for the bar tab. The two men felt the cold sweat breaking out on their forehead, and the beads clinging to their thick eyebrows. Their swarthy faces became ever more sullen, as they watched the wallet disappear again in his breast pocket, where they glimpsed the gold chain of the watch.

The men nudged each other knowing the old man would pay for their tab. He should pay. After all he was the capitalist pig who owed them. They merely saw a man with the fattest wallet, one who was responsible for their youngest brother's death. A Nemci they hated to death for his wealth. Josef ordered one more round of beer. He glanced at his watch, engraved with the initials AK. Knowing he had failed to rouse any civility, he pulled his heavy leather coat over his broad shoulders and ambled slowly home along the path he had trod all his life.

He stumbled across a wire which had been buried in the snow but stretched across the path a few feet from the swollen brook that fed into the pond. There he fell face down onto the dirt encrusted snow, and clutched a nearby tree trunk.

He felt himself being dragged down toward the icy waters of the little Elbe River by his feet. He tried to scream, but no sooner had he opened his mouth in terror, then the freezing waters swirled around him, and darkness engulfed him instantly.

The following morning, Anna noticed that her husband's bed had not been slept in. She shrugged off any concerns for her husband of twenty-six years. She saw no need for alarm, thinking that maybe he had been held up on a delivery in a distant village before nightfall. She was still in her night clothes, and her hair hung down her back to her waist in a long braid, which, during the day she usually wound into a knot in the nape of her neck. She busied herself around the stove, preparing a hearty breakfast for a few field hands who were sure to stop in for a cup of coffee, bacon, eggs and home fries.

Then she set about checking the days' pressing agenda. Since her husband's imprisonment, she had taken over a lot of his chores. She had found her own strength in her abilities to manage much of her husband's work. She had learned to take a load off his shoulders in overseeing the field hands and household help. Pavel would have to hitch up the horses soon. The ground was defrosting and several fields had to be readied for spring planting. She heard a sharp knock on the door and looked up from her musings. She bolted from the chair with a sudden jolt of panic, as an icy chill ran down her spine. Her eyes fell on the vacant chair at the head of the kitchen table, her husbands' favorite place. She looked down on her pink floral night gown. The flannel fabric shrouded her femininity in soft folds.

'It's probably Koczian,' she thought. 'He is always the first one here for a cup of coffee before anyone else at sunrise.' She chuckled to herself. 'No sooner do I turn on the kitchen light, he comes running.' Now that Pepi is safe in Prague, Anna enjoyed the young man's company over a cup of coffee. He was like a son to her. She threw on a smock over her nightgown and went to open the door at the second urgent knocking, and a voice calling in Czech, "Pani Staffawa, Pani Staffawa. Open the door quick."

Anna came face to face with a burly mill hand who with strong Slavic features and sullen, searing black eyes, covered by bushy eyebrows, stared down at her with an unabashed hatred that pierced her soul. Anna looked stunned. Paralyzing fear took hold of her when she recognized Karel Push, a member of the National Socialist Peoples Party. The swarthy young man, whose straggly, greasy hair spilled out from under a dirty cap he was twisting in his grubby hands, pointed across the lumber yard to the far end of the pond, mumbling icily without wasting time on civility. "Somebody better get your old man out of the pond, before he catches cold!"

Anna stepped outside, shielding her eyes against the glistening crystal glare of icicles that were still clinging from every bough and eave on surrounding buildings. The icicles began to melt in the early morning sun. "Jessesmarren!" She screamed and clutched her chest, gasping for air. At the far end of the garden pond she viewed the frozen statue of her husband. Still in her nightgown and smock she ran down the path, and screamed in desperation "Help! Help!" She gaped at her husband, who stood erect, propped up against the pond-side willow as if someone had stood him there for everyone to see what they had done to him. The strong current of the water pressed him up against the tree trunk, and held him there erect. Anna saw the drag marks in the snow, the gloves on the ground, and his hands that still clutched a few branches in a desperate struggle against dark forces. His eyes and mouth looked as if they were ripped wide open in a frozen scream of terror.

The terror he must have experienced the night before was clearly visible through the icicles hanging from his wide-open mouth in a silent scream. The gold chain from his pocket watch dangled from his breast pocket, but the watch was gone. His head was covered with snow that had fallen during the night. Frozen saliva clung as icicles from his mustache.

Anna's eyes were filled with naked horror at the sight of her husband. The forty-four-year old woman ran blindly, her arms flailing wildly and her breath billowing about her. She was oblivious of the freezing morning air. Anna screamed for help, running down the hill, as the flannel gown flapped around her ankles.

As she gained momentum while running blindly, she screamed her lungs raw. Her screams for help pierced the cold morning air, yet not a single face appeared in a window. The streets remained deserted. Anna staggered to the lumber yard.

She found Karel and Ladislav cajoling and playing cards in exuberant celebration of the death of the man who had employed them and their fathers. They pointedly ignored the woman's pleas for help to get her husband out of the pond. She ran up the road to Gustav Gernerts' pub, who organized a group of men to pull her husband out of the frigid water, wrapped him in a blanket and laid him on a wooden cart.

Then she ran to the police station and screamed at a bored looking Czech gendarme, who only grudgingly put down his cup of coffee with thick grounds on top, and his slab of fatty bacon rind. He slowly stood up and faced the hysterical woman, who continued to scream at him. "My husband has been murdered!" The gendarme slowly followed her to the scene of the crime, with a skeptical look. Anna pointed to the drag marks and the footprints that led to the spot where the pond overflows into the brook, which flows into the little Elbe River. The wire lay in a tangled ball stretched between the trees. She pointed out the claw marks on the tree bark, which were encrusted between the dead man's frozen fingers. She pointed to the chain dangling from his breast pocket, and the small section of the gold chain with the broken link that looked to her like evidence of foul play.

"The killers stole the watch I gave my husband on our wedding day. It was a richly filigreed gold watch, engraved with my initials *AK*. Whoever has this watch now committed the murder of my husband. My husband had a thick wallet full of money, that is gone. He had delivered a lot of wood this week, so that's why he had a lot of money on him. He had not had a chance to go to the bank in Arnau to deposit the money."

Anna looked frustrated at the bored looking gendarme with heightened agitation who seemed to do nothing more than shrug his shoulder in face of all her lamentations and protestations.

"We don't investigate crimes against Nemcis." Vainly she pointed out again the signs of a heinous crime and signs of a fierce struggle that remained etched into the icy ridges. But the bored gendarme saw no need to waste his time on paperwork. He deplored any physical exertion demanded of him by an irate Pani Anna Staffawa. Instead, he thwarted all further investigations, and put down the cause of death as a heart attack due to a drunken accident. "Case closed."

He snapped his folder shut. "Your husband has been drinking a few rounds of beer that night. He was seen by his employees in the Gernert pub buying drinks for everyone, round after round. It is common knowledge that the Staffas are all drunkards." Anna was outraged. She slammed her calloused fist on the table, and in that instant, the shy, gentle woman without guile turned into a screeching shrew, she screamed at anyone within earshot. "God is my witness. I swear that my husband was no drunkard. These men murdered my husband. Everyone knows he bought a round for workers every Friday. Even drunk as a pig on sour mash, he would never have stumbled into the pond because he knew this land like the palm of his hand."

The unchanging bored demeanor, the blank look in the gendarmes' eyes as he calmly lit a cigarette and exhaled the smoke in her face, set her teeth on edge. She screamed, cursed and cried relentlessly at the sallow face, oblivious of the crowd that had gathered around them.

"The killer has the monogrammed pocket watch. If you don't look for it, I'll search for it myself door to door, until I find my husbands' killer. I offer a reward to anyone who will help me find his killers. I may have to take this case to Prague and file a complaint against this incompetent magistrate." Her frustration built knowing she was being stonewalled by the police.

She spared no words accusing Czech authorities of gross dereliction of duty and incompetence in searing letters to officials in Prague.

Her heroic efforts seemed to fall on deaf ears, cold faces, and hearts of stone.

Anna dispatched the congenial Pavel Koczian to carry the body of her husband home and lay him in a coffin. She sat down beside it and held her head. "Think about what must I do next?" She said to herself, as she wrung her hands. "I need my Pepiczek to come home!" Anna ordered Koczian to pick up her youngest son for his father's funeral. Josef senior was laid to rest in a large family crypt.

His resting place had a large black marble headstone with large gold lettering, listing the names of the souls at rest and a black marble grave plate covered the crypt with a large embossed gold crucifix. A wrought iron fence surrounded the crypt, which had been built large enough for family members of future generations. If they were not together in life they would be together in death.

The German villagers were united in mourning the loss of a good and honorable man, and a tireless worker. After the funeral, Anna became obsessed in her efforts to find her husbands' killers. She viewed it her first duty to trek back to the police station first thing in the morning, to prod them to find the killers of her husband. She asked around if anyone was sporting an expensive gold watch and flaunting more money than before. She suspected anyone who suddenly appeared more handsomely endowed with great suspicions. Her eagle eyes scanned for signs of a gold chain protruding from someone's breast pocket, and rumors spread among the Czechs that Pani Anna Staffawa had gone crazy in her zeal to bring those responsible to justice and closure to her tormented soul.

His father's last will and testament stated that Josef junior, despite being the youngest of his eight children was worthy to become heir to the Josef Staffa lumber business. He left nothing to his brother Stefan and his oldest son Adolf, calling them drunkards and misfits who squandered what he and his forefathers had worked for all their lives. After the reading of the will, the young Josef over heard his Uncle Stefan remark with icy rancor.

"Maybe a bullet will hit him." The Last Will and Testament left the family deeply divided and perplexed why the youngest was chosen as the heir and they blamed Anna because she had named her second son Josef after her first son had died at an early age. Those who loved Josef junior knew that the will was justified. The father had seen fit to reward his youngest son because he trusted him to carry on the family name, heritage and tradition.

In becoming the heir of the Staffa lumber dynasty, young Josef recognized sorting out his family affairs was his first responsibility, paying out his brothers and sisters a fair share of the estate was a sacred trust. Josef's new responsibilities overwhelmed him, prompting him to drop out of school. He was urgently needed in Mastig to oversee the daily operations of the family business. He would have preferred reconciliation, love and family harmony above all the wealth left in bank books and property documentations of purchases and deeds and maps. He had the areas surveyed and marked the acres of land, roping off the acreage tree by tree. In the ensuing months, it became obvious that the father had been right all along. Josef acted in fairness in running the family business. Josef was meticulous in his fiduciary care and bookkeeping and his father's equal in dedication to the daily task and love of the land.

He held out olive branches to his sisters, brothers and half-brothers in equal measure. His sister Annie had married a wealthy rug merchant, and like a well-endowed princess had moved to Königinhof, where she held court like a queen. Josef gave her a monthly stipend as her share of business profits. His sister Marie was oblivious to all the family squabble. She was glad to be absolved of any responsibility attached to the name, and was simply enjoying her young family. She had married the friendly pub owner, Gustav Gernert, in the church in Ober-Prausnitz. She had her baby baptized Margit, whom Josef nicknamed "Gitchen".

Josef was determined to have order in his household. To that end he had more to wrestle with besides his family's tangled legal affairs.

But dealing in good conscience, he clung to the hope that the daggers of jealousy could remain in the scabbards. He had no desire to add oil to a smoldering fire and deeded scattered properties to his step brothers in outlying areas. They no longer viewed the choice as a father's show of favoritism, but just reward for a young man of fine character. Conversely, he reaped the jealousy of his own flesh and blood brothers, as Josef tried to appease them with good jobs and salaries. Important decision-making responsibilities as operations and finance managers in the family business. With a generous pocketbook and good intentions, he insured respectable sources of income for all.

Uncle Stefan was not married and Josef thought of his uncle as a "Nichtsnutz", a useless nobody who was often found under a tree with a bottle of beer as his constant companion and a hat he had pulled over his face to shield him from the sun. He drank himself to sleep on any meadow, where he felt safe from scolding relatives and pestering children. The children often snatched his hat while he slept. He would curse and shoo them away like pesky bugs. Josef thought it wise to keep a distance from his uncle Stefan, who was left nothing.

Josef retained customer service functions for himself, which allowed him the freedom to keep a safe distance from hometown troubles. His calm and engaging personality insured customer loyalty, and prompt delivery from the truckers. His personable demeanor earned him the respect of his laborers and field hands. Torn between family duty and countless court proceedings, Josef resolved that his family was splintered enough.

Josef missed Emmi's laughter, her high-spirited nature, without her his life in his mother's villa seemed cold and empty. Unfortunately, for that same reason, he decided that his amorous instincts would have to be put on hold. Before he could even contemplate introducing a new face to the family matriarchy, he had to have order in his house. What he faced was a tall order.

Josef immersed himself in expanding the family business to the outer limits of the German territories. Not many roads lead to Mastig, and Josef had to take long detours as he tried to avoid driving through Klein-Borowitz. He ruefully reasoned that it wasn't fair to a young girl with a heart of gold to embroil her in his many family squabbles. More than a year had passed since he last had seen her. Since then he had not been able to roll back his eyes in peaceful repose, but when he did, a beautiful face would appear before him, with a smile that spread across her face, as wide as the rays of the sun bursting through dark clouds to warm his heart. He could no longer ignore his mother's ceaseless diatribes over the poor girl, whose name she did not consider worthy to mention.

"Forget about her. You'll bring shame on the Staffa name if you bring home a penniless wench, like the village nightingale. Just make sure you don't bring her here with a big belly…you are too young."

Finally, one weekend he could not resist the temptation to sojourn through the valley with the hope of catching a glimpse of her. He drove circles around the community theater where he suspected Emmi might be performing. He avoided her mother's Gasthaus, afraid she might beat him out the door with a broom handle. To alley his fears and give him moral support, he asked his motor bike friends to ride with him through her village. The roar of several motor bikes ascended like claps of thunder in this tiny village. As they rode past the theater, Josef gunned the engine even more out of frustration when he did not spot her anywhere. His face was distorted by a nagging fear. 'What if she has forgotten me?'

There was always Bruno, who with open arms and a broad shoulder would love to make Emmi his Aida. The thought of her stage partner set his teeth on edge. He imagined them together, laughing, kissing, holding hands, and cling to each other as he and Emmi once had, whispering sweet nothings. Disheartened he drove home and stopped at the newly renovated Gernert Garden Café.

While in Klein-Borowitz...

A new theater season had begun. Emmi was preparing to go on tour with her theater ensemble soon. With a sense of relief, Emmi plunged her whole heart into her uncle's next theater production. The premiere of Franz Lehar's opera The Gypsy Baron, took her mind off her own heartache, as she poured out the heartache of a lovelorn street urchin on stage.

She could hear a familiar sound of a motor bike roaring through the valley. The steady din was emanating from outside the theater growing louder and louder as if a swarm of locusts had descended on her village. Her audience had grown used to this kind of distraction. Normally it stopped after a little while. But today the thunderous roar did not cease. Instead, it continued unabated sounding like a thousand BMW's had converged on the theater plaza, riding round and round the building without ceasing. She was waiting for lightning to strike, but then the racket outside subsided to a steady hum. Her stage partner mumbled icily. "Who could possibly be making such a racket?" Emmi muttered looking horrified. A sneaking suspicion crept into her conscious mind when a couple of goons stood in the back and booed while her audience stopped listening to her enraptured. The people looked annoyed at one another over the ceaseless and distracting din outside. Bruno paced back and forth behind the curtain looking visibly annoyed. The performance looked like a dance of the marionettes. The noise stopped suddenly and Emmi was able to capture the hearts of her adoring fans again. She could relish again the applause and smile at her audience. But, as soon as the curtain fell, she knew her heart was breaking. If that had been Josef riding around the theatre, why had he not stopped in to see her performance? Since Josef had ended their relationship a year ago, why was he tormenting her now? Had he just sought to sabotage her performance? Why was he hanging around her home turf just to torment her every time he raced through with his noisy BMW without stopping? She stashed away tender yearnings for that special someone who had set her heart on fire two years ago.

At nineteen years of age, Emmi was thinking more often about marriage. Her mother often reminded her how lucky she was to have Bruno in her life, even though he was ten years older. Bruno was a trustworthy soul who shared her love for music and the theater. He was an elegant dance partner who made heads turn when he stepped on a dance floor.

Other dancers would clear the floor so they could watch a well-matched pair doing the latest crazy dance from America. Marriage to Bruno would please her mother while just the sight of Josef made the hair on her neck stand up. Josef was so unlike Bruno, he didn't like music or dance or the theatre. He had two left feet, for which she had to prod him to get off a chair to dance. He did not know the difference between a Waltz or Tango or Foxtrot, nor the latest crazy dance, the Charleston. Josef would only get up from his chair after she threatened to dance with someone else, and his feet would move one step to the right and one to the left.

'What a poop he could be!' She snarled to herself as Bruno on the other hand, gladly provided her with a strong arm to guide her steps. How often had she left the theater arm-in-arm with Bruno Linhart, to see Josef whiz past them with a roar on his beloved BMW? One night, on their way home, she linked arms with Bruno and the entire cast to form a human chain. The comfort of Bruno's arms warmed her heart. They laughed and cajoled as the human chain stretched from one side to the other.

Emmi picked up the distinct din of a motorbike heading their way. She blushed as the din turned into a roar, reverberating from the other side of the mountain. The closer the noise drew, the more fiercely her heart pounded. As it came around a curve it caught the group in its headlights, and aimed straight for Emmi and Bruno, then swooped around the group in a zigzag formation. The group looked terrified as the biker turned wheelies and spun up gravel.

The biker came threateningly close, leaving the group to wonder if he would ever stop or run them over. Finally; he made a wide loop, gave a salute and drove across the sidewalk, then gunned the engine to its maximum, and roared away to fade into the valley beyond. Bruno cupped her face and looked into her terrified eyes, and soothingly asked. "Is your heart back where it belongs?" Emmi shrugged her shoulders and hid her face in the coat collar in embarrassment, muttering. "I don't know where it belongs." Her mother had waited and watched from the stoop. She was relieved to see her daughter arm in arm with Bruno. Now, here was a man to her liking. But, to her disappointment, her daughter politely held out a gloved hand and meekly said. "Goodnight!" Emmi saw her mother sitting on the stoop, and hated to admit that her mother's awful predictions, those ugly "I told you so's" were indeed awful reminders that her relationship with Josef was over. She pressed back the tears that seemed to burn in her eye socket a lot lately. In blind fury she sauntered up the steps to her room. She wanted to be alone, and wile away the evening hours shooting billiards to help her unwind. Her thoughts drifted back to that moment when real life with all its joys and woebegone had begun for her in the arms of the man she loved. Overcome with self-pity, she could only resort to reading his old letters over and over. The fancy calligraphic script, with which he had meticulously addressed every letter, pierced her heart. "How could such a meticulous man, behave so slovenly?" She traced every fanciful scroll he had drawn with the care of a craftsman designing official documents. His fancy lettering added to her fanciful dreams, and she dashed them all, once she faced the brutal reality of the finality of her first true love.

On stage she could play the leading role as she saw fit. She could sing and dance again to the sound of robust Hungarian folk music, which would leave her no time to ponder about what might have been. She imagined walking alongside the fine figure of the man she loved when she glanced sideways at his noble face, gazing dreamily into the most heavenly blue eyes, feeling the sensation of his presence and the touch of his waxen fine skin, and nimble fingers. The pain seared her soul like a paper cut. How could a cut so fine cause such intense pain, and tiny tears sting like fire in memory of him.

In letters to her friend Rosa, she poured out her heart over the crushing blow of her love-life gone sour. "Now our secret betrothal will have to remain a secret forever. The treasure of my love has been reduced to a subject of ridicule."

To which her mother would cut in with ceaseless lamentations droning on her ears. "I told you the Staffa men are no good. He just played you. Why would a Staffa bother with a poor girl like…just to brew up another scandal?" If only he would let her forget him. To escape the knowing looks of her mother and the awful

'I told you so!' she would have to find solace in romantic theatric fantasy, if she was not destined to lead in Josef's life. She cursed the day she had met him…the scene played in her mind over and over, how he had come up behind her and put his arms around her waist, how he had asked her to be his billiard partner but that he needed her to teach him the game, and the dubious connotation of that request. The moment when she had turned around and their eyes had locked, knowing they were in love for the first time. She knew this oh so magic moment when she knew Josef was the love of her life would haunt her for the rest of her life.

"Don't come near me again. You are a wolf in sheep's clothing." Emmi mumbled to herself.

"I won't be made a fool of a second time. It won't happen again."

While in Mastig...

Marie was a graduate of the Business Institute for Women of the year 1930 and marriage to Marie had indeed added a touch of class to Gustav Gernert's business acumen. What was once a popular pub, Marie had turned into a Rose Garden Café with a dance floor under rose trellises and in- and outdoor seating and comfortable lounging areas.

She could keep books as well as add delectable exotic spices and aromas to her new dishes. Marie was a delectable dish herself, radiating an effusive charm that she used effectively to bring in the nobles from the area.

In Marie's company, Josef felt comfortable enough to unload his agony over his lost love. "After all this time, she might tell me to kiss my ass." He sighed as Marie prodded her brother.

"Sef, just go see her. She can't do more than slam the door in your face. If she does, we are planning a masquerade ball on Rose Monday before Ash Wednesday. We'll advertise it all over the area…she'll come here. The Hample Pub is for factory workers. She won't go there." Marie winked coquettishly. "Trust me. Gourmands go where the cooking is good." Marie waved off his concern. Josef smiled. "Yours is par exemplar."

On the night of the masquerade ball, they came as Marie had promised from far and wide. It was the annual event that no one wanted to miss. The Gernert Rose Garden Café was filled to overflowing. Despite the February cold, the crowds fanned out into Marie's Rose garden where additional tables and chairs surrounded a dance platform where strings of ballroom lanterns attached. A small band played Viennese Waltzes.

Josef didn't want to be the topic of gossip, because the first anniversary of his father's death was only a month away so he sat unnoticed in a corner of the Café near the bar from where he could watch everyone as they were coming or going. He watched as the ladies dressed in satin and lace finery with flowers pinned to their bustier straps, entered the café one by one. They wore masks that hid very little of their identity.

With a little imagination, one could guess that a wall flower hid behind the mask of a ballerina. A dowdy girl dressed like a princess, and a swan was actually an ugly duckling.

Josef spotted a ballerina right out of Swan Lake. She had a good figure under her tutu and slender legs. Josef thought that this swan might be Emmi. At first thought he wanted to rush over and take her in his arms. Instead, he called on his better angels to be on his best behavior here in Marie's new domain. The look of anonymity gave the ball its allure in the final moment before the stroke of midnight, when a prince turned into a toad, and a princess into an ugly duckling.

Josef had waited for the right moment before he could ask the swan to dance with him. Josef was awash in happiness, as he led her out toward the center of the dance floor. She leaned into him provocatively. Her perfumed bare shoulders filled his head as he draped his arms around her slim body. He yearned to run his hands up her spine to the base of her neck, tilt her head back and cover her mouth with his. His lips brushed lightly against her earlobe. The mysterious woman felt good in his arms and when she did not pull away, he was sure that it was indeed Emmi, who flashed him a delightful smile. Her white teeth glistened in the rosy glow of ballroom lanterns. He felt a feverish excitement convinced that he was holding Emmi in his arms, and it felt good and right to encircle her slender frame. If only she would allow him to lead her out into the rose garden.

She barely said a word, and when she did the sound of her voice was muffled under the mask, the words were indistinguishable over the din of the music. He wanted to tear away the white feather cap and mask, and tell her how much he loved her, and to hear her say the same.

But she remained mute. At the stroke of midnight he flung off his mask and watched with great anticipation as she carefully in slow motion removed her white feather cap and face mask. What emerged was the face of an old woman, with snow white hair. Josef looked aghast, stammered an apology. "Jessesmarren! An old babitchka!"

He spun around and ran off so fast he left behind a cloud of dust, and the exhaust fumes of his motorbike. A girl dressed in the rags of a street urchin, with a sooty face and brooms for sale tied to her back—-a character out of a Franz Lehar opera—-clasped her mouth to keep from bursting out in laughter. She had watched from the sidelines as the comedy unfolded before her blue laughing eyes.

Despite the initial humor she had found in this scene, she felt betrayed and angry. Her face remained hidden behind the black mask, and a wig of straggly black hair. She was in no mood to reveal herself to anyone. Maybe she should have used this opportunity to confront him, and ask. "Remember me? What am I to make of love whispered in my ear …mashed potatoes or pig fodder?"

She knew Josef was not one to attend balls. He shunned crowds. Why had he come to this event? Was he hoping to run into her? Why didn't he show his face openly? Why had he come with a mask looking for her? Wasn't it obvious to everyone, that he had put an end to their relationship? He had ended it for all the world to see. She knew, at last, that his family had succeeded in tearing them apart, just as they were tearing up the Staffa properties. She resolutely stashed away her tender yearnings for that special someone who had set her heart on fire. She should be glad to have Bruno by her side. But, she knew her heart was the captive of another man.

In Klein-Borowitz...

Emmi was determined to forget Josef and kept busy in mindless activities. She leaned across the billiard table and expertly aimed a cue stick at a ball, as a pungent leather and spice fragrance wafted around her nostrils. A hand slipped around her waist, and a waxen-smooth face pressed against her cheek, the other hand fell on top of her slim fingers that guided the cue stick to the eight ball. Emmi succumbed to a wave of ecstasy that swept suddenly over her as a soft voice whispered in her ear. "I need a life partner. Let's go for the eight ball, you and me." Emmi dropped the cue stick and sank into Josef's arms. Holding each other tight, they gazed lovingly in each other's eyes.

Emmi whispered dreamily. "Who are you? The Angel Gabriel, bearer of good tidings?" Josef murmured. "I have come to claim my prize." She looked up at him with a puzzled look.

"Prize…what Prize?"

"I was not about to let Bruno take the lead role in your life…Let's ride up to the Switschin." Josef put his arms around her waist and leaned over to kiss her, when her mother's shrill voice resounded with displeasure, "Emmi! Dinner!" Emmi winced.

"My mother's house rule, if not home in time for dinner, you have to go hungry.

I won't get anything to eat if I am late for dinner and suddenly I am glad I'm not hungry." She wrestled free of Josef's embrace and walked toward the door with Josef in close pursuit. She poked her head in the kitchen and called out. "Give Rudi my portion. He is always hungry." Emmi and Josef ran outside before her mother could respond. Josef gunned the engine as Emmi climbed into the sidecar. They rode with glee through sun drenched fields to their favorite spot this side of heaven, up to the mountain ridge where their beloved cliff on the edge of paradise split the Czech and German communities in two separate territorial entities. Josef pointed across the lush green forests below their feet, as the sinking sun painted purplish red streaks across the horizon.

Emmi was thrilled at the sight.

"We'll have a red sunset. A deep red sunset heralds a brilliant dawn." Josef pointed across the vast forest land. "All these woods were once my father's land. Now they belong to me passed down from my forefathers who planted every tree. I followed on my father's heels from the time I was five. Here, my heart has its roots and my heart, hand and soul are anchored in this soil. This piece of heaven I want to share with you." Emmi was moved to tears by his fervor and passionate love for the land below their wondering eyes. As Josef spoke Emmi remembered how Josef had made her feel abandoned. It was time to confront him and vent her righteous indignation over his treatment of her this past year. "What took you so long to contact me?"

Josef gazed into space and glumly replied. "Family matters!" He avoided eye contact with her, afraid of that accusing look that asked for answers to questions that hung in the air, for which he had no explanation. He was hoping she could forget the past few words and look toward a future together.

But Emmi didn't budge." I'm afraid to let you out of my sight now. My heart is not tied to a yo-yo string, you can't talk about love one day and then, I don't hear another word from you for a year."

He wrapped his arms tightly around her. "I needed a clean overview of the land of which I became the owner overnight. I needed to clean house, starting with fringes of forest lands in scattered areas. I also needed to distance myself from unsavory kin like my uncle Stefan. I wanted him off my back to keep his daggers in the scabbard, that is why I gave my uncle land within Czech boundaries near Koniginhof" Josef snickered.. "Uncle Stefan can sell his lumber to his countrymen whenever he sobers up. I hope you can forgive me, but I had to put my household in order after my father's murder."

"Murder? Your father was drunk and fell into the pond in a drunken stupor." Emmi replied. Josef turned beet red, and shook his head. "No, no! That's what the Czech authorities want the public to believe. They lied. My mother saw the evidence, and she was convinced that her husband was murdered.

"He countered. "And so am I. I can't talk about this anymore."

Emmi was not easily convinced. "Will you run away again like a puppy, every time there is another hurdle in your path…or will I have to put a leash on you?"

He pulled her close. "There is only one hurdle left for us to conquer, or we shall have to plunge ourselves into this abyss." She hissed skeptically. "What hurdle?"

He chuckled, with mock concern and whispered. "My mother!"

Emmi fell silent, her heart pounded fiercely at the awesome thought of meeting his family, especially his mother. It had not escaped her notice that Josef had been avoiding his hometown in prior outings. She knew that a girl with an empty trousseau was not a welcomed guest in his mothers' house. They gazed longingly across the lush greenery, drinking in nature's bounty, high above the noise and clamor of the world, and found contentment in being in each other's arms, feeling the exaltation and reaffirmation of their love. Emmi sighed. "If only we could get old and grey right here."

Josef replied. "We might as well take the bull by the horn and face our enemies." He gunned the engine and rode without any further hesitation into Mastig. He pulled up in front of his mother's villa. "We are going to get this over with now." Josef swung the vehicle up to the front gate, and helped Emmi climb out of the sidecar.

He noticed the look of horror in her eyes, as she nervously tried to smooth her rumpled peasant dress and slick back her windblown hair. Filled with sudden trepidation, Emmi tried to resist the grip on her arm. She took a quick glance in a mirror and saw a face that was flushed from the sun, shaded by windblown hair, she cried. "I don't look proper. My hair looks like a horse's mane."

Josef reassured her with a firm grip on her elbow and pressed her close. "You're still the most beautiful girl in Klein Borowitz, even with horsehair stuffed in a potato sack."

"It's not a potato sack. I sewed it from the damask curtains that once hung in my room." Her eyes sparkled with nervous anticipation before meeting the woman who one year after her husbands' shocking demise, dressed in black and walked about town wearing the color of mourning even in the Spring. Anna could not let the world forget that they had robbed her of her life's mate.

For years Emmi had heard many stories about a painfully shy, demure Czech girl, who had married a rich German widower with four children. To make sure one of her sons would be the heir, she named a second son Josef, after the first son had died of pneumonia. Over the years Anna Kudronovsky had grown into a formidable and feisty matron, ruling over a teeming household with a velvet fist. "I never thought a child could be replaced."

Emmi was in awe, how Anna at such a tender age could take over such a lively household, and rule with a tender heart and iron fist. How she could keep the balance, between discipline and nurture. She had heard it often said that Anna K had once been the most loving mother any child could have, who had grown into her role as a tough disciplinarian out of necessity. Emmi could not understand why there was so much animosity dividing this household. How could the boys harbor so much hatred toward their stepmother and their brother that split the family into two hostile camps?

Emmi expressed her simplistic view. "Money can't be the problem, since there is enough to go around for everyone's comfort." Josef shrugged his shoulders, and waved off her consternation. "Rancor is borne out of greed and runs in proportion to wealth, the more they have the more they want. I have deeded enough land to my brothers, to keep them happy. Out of pity I gave my uncle Stefan a piece of land far away from home so I don't have to look over more shoulder any longer. We have a reputation as drunkards because of him."

Emmi shuddered in abhorrence of vulgar truth, family greed and jealousy. "Money has never done me a favor. I prefer a harmonious family life over money." Josef said with sarcasm. "So far, only one brother has done me a favor. Just think, if the first son named Pepiczeck had not died, I would not have been born. Ironic isn't it?"

Emmi responded. "God rolled the dice in your favor and I have to thank Pepiczek for your life. I might have been Bruno's wife by now."

"Until you entered my life, Marie was the only one I could trust. She's tended me more with motherly concerns than sisterly affection. Marie always looked out for me. She covers my back. She makes up for all the animosity in our midst."

Emmi loved the way he spoke of his sister in a loving manner, and looked forward to meeting her. They slowly walked arm-in arm, around the rock garden covered with creeping phlox poking through a thin layer of snow. She shuddered when she saw the drained dry ponds, which had been the focal point of family drama and children's frolic for years. Ever since the accident, frolic was banned from the premises by the woman in black.

Emmi saw his mother standing ramrod straight by the door. Her eyes were fixed with a piercing gaze on the young woman, whom Josef introduced as his future bride. The unsmiling woman promptly replied without batting an eye. "You are both too young! And your arms are too thin."

Josef didn't flinch and replied defiantly. "After my twenty-first birthday I can marry without your consent and Emmi shall be my bride!"

Anna Kudronovsky-Staffa who had married at age eighteen, now looked skeptical at the plain, homespun, and provincial Emmi. "Then you wait two more years. This place needs strong hands, not some frail and delicate whooper schnapperl like her." She pointed at Emmis thin arms. Emmis' face turned crimson as the woman with the high cheekbones and raised eyebrows looked her up and down unabashed. "Your arms are too thin. Everybody has to work here. We have no room for opera divas. How can you pitch hay with thin arms like yours?"

She looked nonplussed at Emmi, who was holding back an angry rebuke ready to spill from the tip of her tongue. She managed instead, to transport herself to an invisible stage with a disarming smile. "My arms may be thin but my muscles are made of Solingen steel. I have pitched a few bales of hay before I could sing an aria."

Anna Kudronovsky replied icily. "There is more to do here than pitch hay."

Emmi could see that the murder of her husband and the step-sons open hostilities had turned a kind woman into a bitter matriarch. The woman in black felt neither a compulsion to make incorporation into the family fold easy for Emmi, nor did she invite her to enter the house. Josef guided his reluctant bride-to-be by the arm to meet the rest of the family and teased her.

"They won't bite. Maybe I should have bought a dog collar for your neck, so I could pull you along on a leash. Instead, I bought you this." She stopped dead and marveled as he chided and slipped a gold bracelet over her arm. Emmi murmured softly as if afraid to make her presence known on hallowed ground. "You never fail to surprise me."

He opened the door for Emmi and met the expectant eyes of his sibling who sat in familiar surroundings amid lively discussions of popular themes at a round table, the men stood up to greet Josef's intended. It appeared to Emmi, that Emil and his wife Hildegard enjoyed meeting her. But his brother Karl, and his fiancée Ilse von Reichenberg turned up their noses. They hesitatingly held out cool hands, never making a step toward her. She had to walk towards them, and they were quick to notice Emmi's dowdy peasant dress, which also drew painful attention to her peasant heritage.

She was aware that the elegant glitter of the bracelet overpowered her slender wrist, and contrasted sharply with her home-spun frock.

For a moment the room was engulfed in skin prickling silence, and intolerable for a sensitive young woman who was sitting on the edge of a chair, as if on hot coals. Emmi tugged on her sleeve to keep the bracelet hidden from view of quizzical and jealous eyes. She was unable to partake in the chit-chat charade much longer, and nudged Josef to take her away to a place where she could breathe easy again. She felt uncomfortable as the others looked her up and down and pressed Josef to make an excuse to leave.

At that moment, Marie, with a blond, curly haired toddler in her arms, and her husband Gustav entered the house and transformed the stodgy aura of the room. Marie sat the two-year old down to toddle about the room. Maries' brilliant blue eyes sparkled with delight as she came toward Emmi with outstretched arms and draped them without a moments' hesitation around the thin young woman's shoulders. Cheerfully she grasped both of Emmis' hands and announced.

"Stay awhile. You can't be leaving this soon. On second thought maybe we can go to my place, the newly renovated Gernert Rose Garden Cafe." Emmi hated not being her authentic self and feeling like she had to put on airs for the rest of Josef's family, but here in Marie's company she enjoyed being who she was. Emmi understood why Sef adored his sister Marie with unabashed passion and why the feelings were mutual. Marie took her hand and led Emmi for a walk down the street to the splendid Rose Garden Café. Having heard so much about this young woman and knowing how besotted her brother was, Marie asked coquettishly. "So, when is the wedding?" Emmi felt pressured to give an answer so she whispered.

"His mother wants us to wait until Sef is twenty-one." Marie replied. "Maybe we'll have a winter wedding."

The Rose Garden Cafe had become a popular nightspot for the younger generation. Here, at last, was a cozy place where Josef and Emmi could enjoy the freedom to allow their courtship to bloom. When Emmi spotted the dance floor she said. "I agree to marry you when you can dance the SnowWaltz with me. Josef fell in step as she whispered the rhythmic long-short-short steps of a Viennese Waltz. Emmi felt free to sway in his arms to the rhythm of their generation, and giggled. "I won't ask you to dance the Charleston."

In Gustav and Marie's company the two lovers enjoyed the easy comfort of young love and family bliss. Marie exuded such warmth when her welcoming arms embraced Emmi every time she entered their home adjoining the garden cafe. Marie's acceptance freed Emmi of her misgivings about marrying into Josef's family. She felt free to show her love for life with her usual exuberance and basked in Josef's arms to show herself to the world as his chosen partner. She did not need the approval of the rest of the family. Yet, she was not oblivious to the efforts of family members to ambush the blooming courtship with rumors and innuendos about her stage life and elusive romance with her stage director, the oldest son of the equally prominent and highly respected Emil Linhart family.

Emmi repressed her fears that eventually his brothers would succeed and snuff out their romance. Josef, remained steadfastly devoted to her, and never wavered for a moment. His brother Karl cynically raised his eyebrows at the mention of her name, quick to repeat the sarcastic remarks about the poorly dressed nightingale, Josef intended to bring into the family fold. Josef was quick to respond with matching rancor. "Would a rich nightingale be more acceptable to you?" Karl continued to heckle. "Well, if your love-muffin is a nightingale, then she ought to be a rich nightingale—-rich in any case." Josef spat at the hint of nobility of Karls' wife . "Like the rich crow you intend to marry—-Ilse von Reichenberg? Von? Von What? What's with the Von? She is not someone from any royal house I know."

By the time Emmi celebrated her twenty-first birthday, the courtship with Josef had reached its climax. The more frequently the two lovers were able to sneak away to some rustic barn, or a soft patch of moss near the Fox Hollow Spring, the more urgent the desire to marry became. Every month Emmi grew more anxious to marry and Josef pressed his mother for her consent. Josef had not reached the age of maturity. His mother insisted he wait another year. Yet upon his persistence his mother felt compelled to pull the young woman aside for some frank and stern discussions on propriety. "Well, must you get married?" She queried with a suspicious glance at Emmis' belly.

Emmis' eyes widened at the veiled suggestion of pregnancy. Without a moment's hesitation Emmi whisperedwith mock urgency. "Y-e-s! Of course we MUST!" She intoned unflinchingly.

"Then you must give up the stage at once. We are a prominent family and the bride of Josef Staffa cannot be allowed to show off her legs on a theater stage for other men to ogle. After all he has a reputation to protect. Staffas' cannot allow anyone in the family to make a spectacle of their selves." Emmis' eyes widened at such hypocrisy thinking that the Staffa's were the ones always making headlines and grunted ruefully.

"Are you telling me I cannot play in a music theatre anymore?" But then she reminded herself that silence was the best defense, even though her back arched in silent protest at the intrusion into her personal affairs and this attack on her stage life. She looked beseechingly at Josef, and knew instantly that any argument would be for naught.

Josef looked solemnly at his black cloaked mother with her starchy lace collar, and nodded agreement to every word she said. Emmi knew that there was no further consideration to be obtained from him on that topic.

She remembered with disdain the night when she heard the noisy BMW ride around and around the small theater, to the annoyance of the audience and her fellow actors. Another night, young hoods from another town had booed her loudly as she was singing an aria, and drowned out the applause, as she hoped that the stage floor would swallow her up. Had these youthful pranks been engineered by the man she loved, to sabotage her bloomingcareer? She could not help but wonder now. If he had, she would have to forgive him his misdeeds, or else she would have to forget about a life with him. After all, love forgives all. The audience had loved her too, and had put up with the jealous antics of the youthful offenders, countering sick intentions with even louder applause.

Here at last was the moment of an ultimatum. His mother spelled it out plainly and Josef concurred with a final addendum. "It's either me, or the stage... and Bruno!" He said with polite iciness. Emmi had reached the fork in the road from which there was no return. She felt her heart strings being pulled in different directions.

Her legs itched to dance. Her mouth yearned to trill with operatic vibrato. But at the cost of giving up Josef, she felt the urge to burst into tears. Josef had conquered again. Life without him would remain a fantasy like the ones she had portrayed on stage. She wanted a life with a flesh-and-blood partner, not merely a romantic image. She finally realized that Josef was her life.

When she told him he was delighted by her decision to sacrifice the stage life for a life with him. He sweetened her choice by taking her to Prague on a shopping spree and a visit to a beauty shop. Gone with a snip were the long heavy braids that once wound around her head like a crown. The whimsical, if not frumpy dirndls that seemed to overpower her fair beauty were replaced by elegant garments from Europe's haute couturiers.

She emerged from fine salons with soft shoulder length waves framing her face, projecting such an elegant profile to imbue her with new confidence. As she walked arm-in-arm with Josef, visiting their favorite haunts, she relished in her own reflection as it glowed back from store windows. Heads turned and she enjoyed every minute of adulation. Emmi was able to raise her chin up high, knowing she could hold her own within the presence of Josef's family now. She had learned to elevate her nose to their level. Nobody would be able to look down their noses at her ever again.

When they passed the National Theatre, Emmi felt a tingle in her legs and an urge to rush onto the stage. Arias filled her head and she could hardly contain herself from bursting out in a joyous song. She longed to sing her heart out and play the part of Mimi the tragic heroine in LaBoheme. She felt a lump in her throat as if in mourning a lost love. They stopped by Rosa's house and as they embraced Emmi whispered. "I miss you and Aida. I thought I could have it all, a career on stage and Josef…but sadly I can't have both." She knew there would never be a compromise. Josef had become more important in her life than any career on stage.

Rosa listened with sadness to her friends' solemn musings. "I have found consolation in the inevitable. Look at the advantages I will enjoy as the wife of Josef Staffa. I will never have to grovel for a living or slave away in some awful factory, like the Mandl factory, a fate so many women suffer here."

Rosa clasped her hands in parting and whispered. "Maybe one day when Josef is out of town on a delivery we can hop on a train, and sneak away to enjoy an opera or a concert. You don't have to give up everything for a man, we can have cake and coffee."

Emmi chuckled. "Hah, for this man I'd give up my life. Maybe you can come and hear me sing in the church choir on Sunday. Besides being my best friend, you shall be my maid of honor."

Emmi never could find solace in that little compromise and whenever she and Josef had an argument her final words were always the same. "If it were not for you, I might have become famous like Greta Garbo…and married Bruno."

On January 30, 1932 four months after Josefs' twenty-first birthday, the wedding was held in the church in Ober-Prausnitz and hailed the grandest of the decade, such as none had ever experienced in this area. Josef's mother in an act of unexpected generosity lent her Dusenberg and chauffeur, and ordered six additional limousines for the bridal party and wedding guests for a comfortable ride to the church from the hotel in Arnau.

The choir from her local parish sang Emmi's own prayerful blessings for a loving family:

Bless me, Mary, bless me your child, your mother love be my guide, bless my thoughts and all my deeds,

till I make my home with thee. Bless my kin and all I love, your blessings of peace by day and night in thee.

The beautiful bride was shrouded by a tulle veil held together on the side of her face and the nape of her neck by white roses. She followed the slow procession of four pink and white gowned bridesmaids, her maid of honor, Rosa and her junior bridesmaid Anna Maria, a/k/a Anninka. Emmi and her younger sister had grown apart more than just by their age difference. Emmi was glad that the wedding brought them back together. While Emmis' time had been consumed by her love life and the theatre over the last six years, Anninka, who looked much older than thirteen years was on the threshold of womanhood, having grown into a tall and beautiful girl in the home of an isolating and stifling aunt and uncle.

Emmi noticed Anninkas' downcast eyes whenever they passed each other. She was sad to see her little sister looking shyly about herself with mistrust of everyone, shocked to see her look as if afraid of her own shadow. She was glad that she was able to bring her sister out from under the roof of an overbearing aunt and uncle who had robbed her sister of a carefree childhood and every ounce of self-esteem.

Josef was not surprised that many of his own kin did not attend his wedding. His half-brothers had made it crystal clear that they wanted no part of him and his love muffin. Therefore, he chose Emmis brothers Rudi and Otto as his groomsmen. His sister, Annie abstained for reasons known only to her and Josef, maybe because Josef had not attended his sisters' wedding. Josef's half-sister, Marie, was expecting her second child any day and was not allowed to travel on doctors' orders. Her absence was forgiven. Marie's three-year old golden-haired child, Margit made up for it as the flower girl. The sweet child quickly endeared herself to everyone with her delightful charm, especially since she was her uncle Sefs' favorite niece.

Here is "my Gitchen" he would say as soon as he saw her and giggle. Gitchen delighted in being the flower-girl at her favorite uncles wedding, strewing petals of white Chrysanthemums and Christ Roses, a white and delicate pink blossom with a fringed face which looks like a crown of thorns. It blooms in winter in deepest snow. When the snow starts to melt the face of the Christ Rose peaks out from under a blanket of snow.

Everyone with a recognizable name attended the gala affair. Josef's uncle Stefan and brothers, Emil, Karl and Alfred were in polite attendance. Emmi gritted her teeth, wondering what she had done to make them think she was beneath them. But the most painful moment Emmi experienced was the realization that her own mother refused to attend her daughter's wedding, Franziska had not seen fit to bury her hatchet of a disdain for the Staffa name.

Emmi realized that the disdain between the two matriarchs was mutual. Josef's mother refused to meet or speak to any of her many aunts and uncles. Emmi's mother refused to be in the same family photo with Josef's mother. Conversely, she wished Josef's mother had not bothered to punish everyone with her presence and stoic expression. The Staffa matriarch wore her characteristic black dress and starchy lace collar. She sat with her frozen unsmiling expression and never exchanged words with any of the other wedding guests, instead pointedly ignored the polite chit-chat of the wedding party.

Emmi whispered to Rosa with a voice filled with righteous indignation. "Why didn't that woman leave her sour-puss-face at home?" Emmi sighed. "She has no noblesse oblige. I thought she would bury her hatchet, if only for the sake of her beloved Pepiczeks' wedding…she has no cause to turn her nose up on my family." Rosa smiled benignly, and murmured. "Remember…we Czechs know not how to forgive."

As the tender lyrics and fragile chords filled the vaulted ceiling of the gothic church, Emmi could not stop the tears from rolling down her cheek, as she and Josef made their vows while they knelt on a small red velvet upholstered kneeler. She was torn between the joy she felt as Josef's wife and the betrayal of her new in-laws and that of her mother, and so were stiff-collared guests who had no clue of the animosity that lurked behind smiling faces.

The reception at the Mastig Bad Hotel, only a few hours ride from the shadows of castles of Bohemian kings, was a tastefully prepared affair, lacking nothing in comfort for the high society circles. Emmi was at last able to show off her old-world Austro-Hungarian family circle from her mother and father's side. She beamed with pride as her many aunts, uncles, cousins and spouses from Eibau, Budapest, Vienna and neighboring Nedarsch swarmed into the area.

Arriving from Austria was Uncle Johann with his wife Aunt Hermine. From across the German border came Uncle Karl Borufka with his wealthy wife, Maria of a Swiss mustard and pickle enterprise with their son Karl. Then there was the stodgy Borufka clan looking starchy with stiff white collars and heads covered in stylish fedoras, with sable-draped grand dames by their side, who nodded acknowledgment to one another with grand dignity. Emmi nudged her husband and motioned with her head. "Look around! Now you see, my dear man, I'm not a waif from the poorhouse either." Josef playfully pinched her arms. "But your arms are still too thin."

Whereas Josef's mother lacked in propriety, Emmi was utterly proud to show off her impeccably groomed husband to her Austro-Hungarian relatives. Josef's manners were impeccable and gentlemanly. Josef was a perfectionist. She pinched herself at sight of his utmost, elegant graciousness, as he mingled and chatted amicably with the wedding guests.

She glanced with utter pride at the wedding rings glistening on their right hands, matching hers, binding them forever into one unit. She waltzed with him into their new life in which she was now the wife of her own Rosenkavalier.

At last, she had found fulfillment of her dreams on the stage of life. Josef grabbed her hand and pulled her to the side. "Hold still!" He fastened a gold watch to her wrist, engraved with his initials and vows of eternal love, causing her to squeal in ecstasy.

At that moment, she caught a glimpse over his shoulder of her mother-in-law. By the downward curved mouth and pensive expression, it was obvious that Anna Kudronovsky thought her precious Pepiczek had married far beneath his position, a lowly and provincial Emmi. As her mother had often remarked, Anna Kudronovsky had long forgotten in her noblesse oblige, her own humble background as a former servant girl in Mastigs' only Jewish household.

Josef and Emmi rushed off in the Dusenberg to spend their honeymoon in Karlsbad, the luxurious Bohemian-mountain resort. They spent the days schussing down the slopes. Josef finally took heart to tell his bride that, for the time being, they would have to live under his mother's roof. Emmi looked as if struck by lightning, and waiting for the thunder roll which was sure to follow. She had never worried about where they would live upon their return from their honeymoon. Figuring that such matters were a husband's concern. With all the properties the Staffa's owned, she envisioned an empty coop somewhere. Humble as always, she would have been satisfied with Josef by her side in the pigeon coop—-under any roof—-except his mothers.

The wind defused his words and carried them away, yet she felt as if she had been hit by a sudden squall. With a quick jerk she deftly planted her skis, and braced herself on the ski poles provocatively in front of her husband. Then spread eagled, she skied backwards, formidably wagging a finger in his face. "How long is for the time being?"

She screeched hysterically against the wind. Josef shrugged his shoulder and tried to console his bride over the din. "For just a short while, maybe a year or two." Emmi's eyes widened in horror, she tore off her bindings, and stomped back up the slope with a heavy lump in her throat as tears pressed against her eyelids. "I'm packing! For a year or two, you can live with your mother and I will live with mine."

At the Grand Hotel Pupp, Josef calmly took Emmi by the arm and led her to a round trestle table. He carefully pulled out huge rolls of paper from the brown leather satchel. She had seen him carry this strange leather bag everywhere he went for years, as if it were an appendage. He pulled out stacks of blue prints and calmly spread out the thick rolls. I wanted to surprise you one day. But you might as well see it now. It will be a while before the roof is tight." He added apologetically.

Emmi leaned across the thick rolls and studied the plans Josef smoothed out before her astonished eyes and looked up at him she muttered. "What is this?" She studied the design on the paper and visualized a graceful villa with a sweeping veranda outside the master bedroom, pillars and porticos surrounded by fruit trees and flower beds. "I am speechless."

Josef pointed out specific areas. "This is a cherry tree, right in front of the kitchen alcove, so you can just reach out and pick cherries for dessert. Beside the garage is an area where you can plant vegetables. This will be our bedroom, with a view of the lumber yard and factory below, and a curved veranda outside our bedroom door. I will build my own home just as my father and grandfather had done.

My father always told me that building one's home builds character, and the discipline a man needs as a base for his life. This house will represent the strong foundation I want for my family." He totally disarmed her as he talked. She could not dispel his enthusiasm nor offend him in regard to certain family members, misfortunate as it was, that he was a part and parcel of them. In a last-ditch effort to ward off any depressing thoughts, she tried to offer mitigating suggestions.

She viewed two tortuous years in his mother's house as two years in purgatory. "Couldn't you borrow a few mill hands or lumberjacks to help you finish the house sooner?"

But Josef quickly repelled her idea with his own firm conviction. "I will build my own home. My family and my home are my life. Only I can build my life as I see fit." Emmi was deeply moved and wasted no more than a second to throw her arms around her husband as she murmured tantalizingly.

"As long as there is enough room for us under any roof or a shack, we share love." Josef grinned at her hearth and home poetry. It was her simple compass for living. "Even in my mother's shack?" He nudged her playfully. Emmi snuggled closer. "Even your mother's chicken coop …as long as there is room for one feather bed? That's all the room we need. Now that we are one heart and one soul again, we need little room for anything else."

Upon their return Emmi chose the farthest corner of the villa, down a long narrow winding hallway. Far from the noise of maddening family arguments, Josef moved Emmi's simple belongings and featherbed into a hidden corner without further ado. Emmi was determined to make the best of a bad situation, and show her friendly face in an ugly minefield as if walking on eggs.

Ignored by everyone, even by the servants, Emmi felt not only lonely when Josef was out of town making deliveries, but she felt like a trespasser as she walked past their upturned noses.

She had a hard time falling asleep in the hostile surroundings when Josef was gone overnight. She painstakingly shuttered her bedroom windows at night with uneasy trepidation, and trembled at the sound of crickets. One night she was awakened with a start. She felt the bed sag slowly beside her and realized with a start that someone was sitting on her bedside watching her. She slowly pulled the covers tighter about her shoulders and tried to scoot to the far side of the bed slowly without startling the intruder.

Just then a hand came to rest on her neck. She wanted to scream as a paralyzing fear gripped her and a hand clasped her mouth. She could barely make out a man's silhouette, and in total panic she was gasping for air. Then the man whispered. "Sh! I brought you something."

She sighed with relief when she recognized her husband's voice. "You spooked me! This place gives me the creeps. I feel nervous as a cat when you are not here." She sat up and threw her arms around his neck and smothered him with kisses. She turned on the night light and sat up straight against the headboard, and she noticed that disarming grin on Josef's face, which had never failed to unsettle her equilibrium. "Now, what are you up to?" she mumbled sleepily, as he sat the leather bag on the bed and reached inside. Emmi looked entranced. "What is in your magic bag?" She yawned, as he extracted a tiny bundle of brown fur, then her eyes opened wide as saucers when he dropped a whimpering Rottweiler puppy on her bed. Instantly, Emmi was wide awake, and screeched as Josef clasped her mouth shut. "Shush! You'll wake up the whole house." He reminded her.

Then they frolicked with the tiny tail-wagger into the early morning hours until the pup, with big black eyes fixed on them suddenly curled up between them and fell sound asleep, never to make another sound that night. Feelings of being the provincial outsider had magically evaporated with the new puppy. Emmi resolved that nothing would dismay her. Her trust in Josef was restored as he plunged head first into his daily labors in the lumber yard.

His favorite vantage point was the view of the entire lumber yard. His favorite music was the sound of board saws wheezing as blades cut logs into boards. His favorite smell was that of freshly cut lumber, which lingered on his clothes when he came home from work.

But the evening hours he spent working on the foundation of their future home. He staked out a parcel of land overlooking the quaint village that allowed a sweeping panoramic view of both his mother's and brother's estates.

It was Spring and Josef marked his itinerary on the calendar. He planned to break ground on the first of May. The perimeters of the property were bordered by three rows of white birches, which he had planted with his father many years ago and now were a glorious sight that framed the entire plot of land like a painting. Emmi worked silently alongside her mother-in-law planting potatoes and vegetables. She preferred a hard day's work in the fresh air to a day of boredom and sitting around counting raindrops until Josef came home from his labors. She never shied away from the most demeaning tasks, despite her new status, as the young wife of the new chief. Emmi knew no pride, only pride in good work, even though she knew her efforts were not appreciated.

As soon as her daily chores were completed, and when Beethoven's Ninth Symphony failed to transport her spirits magically to loftier levels, she put the puppy on a bright red leash and proudly paraded her new status down the center of Mastig. She stopped to shop at the Luschnitz General store or spent the day in the company of Marie and Gustav, where she found time to wrangle over family affairs. This was the year in which the Staffa dynastic propagation was in full bloom. His sister Annie who had married a wealthy rug merchant proudly paraded a new born son. Step-brother Adolfs' wife Minna was expecting.

Brother Karl had married Ilse von Reichenberg, who was sporting a round baby bump. Karl built his home next door to the office building of the lumber yard. Emil moved with his beautiful wife Hildegard into their new home next door to Karl's new house, and announced that they were expectant parents. His sister Marie had given birth to a blue-eyed, chunky boy with a head full of golden curly hair, and named him Kurt. Superficially, peace and plenty seemed to be the favorite motto in a fractured world. Emmi was only too happy to lend Marie a helping hand with the new baby boy, knowing she herself was carrying Josef's child. She appreciated the opportunity to practice motherly skills, while waiting for the right moment in which to announce her own happy news.

That day had come, on the day as Josef poured the foundation for their new home seemed the most appropriate to make an announcement. Josef had marked the calendar date May 1st with the notation 'pour foundation!' It was a religious holiday in honor of Mary, the mother of all mothers. Josef would not have to deliver a truck load of wood today. He could make the most of this sunny Mayday. Emmi listened to her husband explain his itinerary for the day. "I hope all the ground frost is gone. Deep ground frost would mean a delay."

Emmi poured him another cup of coffee and sat down beside him. She reached across the beautifully set breakfast table, grabbed his hand, and placed it on her belly, smiling broadly. "There will be no delay. Today you will pour the foundation of our family home—-here feel, under my heart grows the foundation of our family."

The House My Father Built

Josef's face lit up in surprise, and he rushed around the table and wrapped his arms around his wife and chided. "And I thought you were eating too many perogies. I want to hear the cooing of children, as in a pigeon coop. I want a little blond girl like Maries' little Gitchen."

Josef left for work from that day on with a spring in his step and a giant surge of energy. Emmi felt secure in her position in the Staffa household and with every centimeter in circumference of her swelling belly her confidence grew.

Much to Josef's surprise, his brother Karl unexpectedly offered a helping hand. Karl's new father-in-law owned a building supply business, and offered to procure the building materials needed for Josef's dream home at a fraction of the cost.

Her mother-in-law had suspected Emmi to be pregnant before the wedding and had cast curious glances at her tummy for months. Emmi snickered to herself when she noticed the quizzical looks. Her mother-in-law indeed felt duped, when no baby bump appeared as early as expected. But all was well with the world, animosities were buried and peace was restored after Emmi delivered a healthy baby boy, eleven months after the wedding, and four days before Christmas. He was baptized as the fifth generation of Josef Staffa.

Emmi and Josef thought of the baby boy as their grandest Christmas present and a continuation of the Josef Staffa dynasty was secured. "What else do we need, but one another and God's peace in our time? I finally feel accepted now that I gave Anna K. another Pepiczek to love."

Overnight the Staffa villa was transformed as Anna Kudronovsky gloried in being simply called "Oma Staffa." Oma could at long last cradle a beloved Pepiczek again.

Family bliss lasted until uncle Stefan was overheard grumbling to himself. "Maybe a bullet will get him." Everybody simply ignored uncle Stefan and his incessant grumblings which the family wrote off as drunken outbursts of an angry man.

Two weeks after Emmi had given birth Emil and Hildegard welcomed their son Manfred. Tragically the beautiful Hildegard died a year later of blood poisoning. She was laid to rest in the Staffa crypt beside the coffin of Josef Staffa senior. Little Fredi, as Manfred came to be known, found mothering nurture nestled against the bosom of Oma Staffa, and Anna Kudronovsky had another motherless child to raise.

So far the bells of the chapel his father had built produced only mournful chimes for funerals. The congregation planned to add a new bell tower. Josef donated the lumber for the community project in time to herald the baptism of his first-born son. "I am tired of hearing only clanking funeral sounds. Church bells should peal joyously to beckon the faithful to come into his court with singing. I want joyous music announcing my son's birth."

This fifth generation of Josef Staffa, was by the German tradition nicknamed Pepi and Pepiczek by his Czech grandmothers. The long-legged boy was endowed with blond and blue-eyed good looks, and the happy, bold, inquisitive and adventurous spirit of his mother. The birth of his first son had given Josef an adrenalin rush. With high energy and keeping only Sunday's holy, he spent every spare moment on the construction of his home. True to his father's tenets, beam by beam and cinder block by cinder block, stucco and whitewash, Josef built the house according to his own designs, with painstaking attention to details. Emmi was awed when she watched how her husbands' hands measured meticulously down to a millimeter every piece of lumber. He fit tongue and groove pieces to seamless perfection. He explained to her the need to cover the roof, eaves, soffits and drains with gleaming but expensive copper sheeting. "As the sun heats the copper the snow melts, so icicles will not form. In the end you have a safe roof that will not require expensive repairs in the future."

The marble stair wells were alit with sunshine from floor to ceiling coming through colorful stained glass window panels to save on electricity. Josef added the finishing touch and painted the exterior a pale green to blend in with the green surrounding landscape.

Josef stepped out of the master bedroom to attach a railing to the curved veranda that overlooked the entire valley. He was awed by the splendid view of the valley below, the homes of his mother and brothers'and his beloved lumber operation. He could hear the wheezing of the blades that cut timber into boards. He took a deep breath and enjoyed the scent of fresh cut lumber. He was pleased with his accomplishment and a view that was even more breathtaking than he had envisioned it.

Two years after the wedding, the Villa Staffa, as it came to be known, complete with all the modern conveniences known at the time, complete with gleaming white bathroom fixtures was ready for occupancy. The villa was surrounded by an abundance of fruit trees and the villagers proclaimed the house the grandest villa for miles around. Josef's favorite tree was the cherry tree, which he had carefully planted in front of the dining room alcove, telling Emmi with a chuckle. "I want to reach out from the window and pluck the cherries before the birds eat them."

Father Sowonsky, a young Polish priest blessed the home, sprinkling Holy Water into every room, praying as he made the sign of the cross. "Bless this home and may the family live in peace and harmony herein until they make their home with our heavenly father. Amen."

The invited guests followed reverently to watch Father Sowonsky move about the house from room to room sprinkling Holy Water. Emmi used this traditional celebration to show off her own good taste in fine décor around an elegant golden oak oval table and six upholstered chairs in the dining room.

She served plum cake with whip cream on her finest Rosenthal dessert plates. Emmi was sure to have impressed her invited guests and beamed at her accomplishments. Josef proclaimed with delight. "Now, that we have plenty of rooms to fill, we better not waste any time. A pigeon coop should be full!" To which Emmi replied. "We bought six chairs for the dining table, once they are filled I quit having children." Josef teased. "I always knew you to be a difficult woman."

They had waited two long years to live within their own four walls and fell asleep despite the fumes of fresh paint and wallpaper that lingered pervasively in every room. Emmi fell asleep immediately after the exhausting day of entertaining friends, relatives and neighbors, satisfied in the knowledge that peace would reign within their proper home, built soundly enough to establish a solid foundation for the future.

Josef awoke with a start around midnight. The pigeons in the coop were making an unusual noise. He listened intently wondering. "Maybe a weasel got into the coop." He felt groggy and hated the thought of getting out of a warm bed, but the smell wafting around his nostrils would not let him rest. He sleepily opened his eyes, and was met with the most terrifying sight of his life.

As if ignited, the entire room was bathed in flickering light. The shadows of flames danced around the room and the ceiling. Acrid smoke was pouring in from the wide terrace windows. He screamed with terror in his voice. "Fire! Emmi! Fire! Wake up! Fire!" Dazed by sleep and struggling to comprehend where the flickering light was coming from, Josef jumped out of bed, his heart raced as he yanked the down quilt off his sleeping wife to jolt her out of a deep slumber.

Then he sprinted to open the terrace windows. Instantly, thick acrid smoke slapped him back. With an aching heart, he viewed through burning eyes the billowing clouds wafting from the valley floor below. The entire lumber yard and saw mill was engulfed in flames. Emmi screamed when she opened her eyes and saw the shadow of her husband illuminated by the flickering lights darting around the room in panic. She compared it to a scene of a Wagner opera. Josef panted heavily as he pulled his pants over his pajamas and flew in a flash out of the house as if obsessed.

She could hear the wailing and screeching of fire engines, sirens and church bells ringing furiously to rouse the people of this tiny village. While horses screeched inside their stalls, pigeons cackled in the coops, her husband raced around to save what he could as the dream of a lifetime was eaten up by flames licking the raw timber with gusto. She scooped up her one-year-old son from his crib and feeling new life inside her she stood frozen on the terrace outside her bedroom to watch the terror below.

She saw Pavel Koczian dash inside the barn to release the horses in case the fire spread to other buildings. A terrified mare reared up and kicked Pavel in the groin and his thighs. The hooves dug into his flesh, tearing muscles and tendons. Pavel slumped to the ground and Emmi called the maid to care for Pepi. She ran outside in her nightgown, ripped strips from the hem and tied them above the wound on Pavel's thigh to stop the bleeding. By the time the fire trucks had hooked up the pumps, the lumber yard and surrounding buildings were nothing but a heap of charred and smoldering embers.

Josef looked defeated. too tired for his twenty-four years.

Arson was suspected because of the speed in which the whole yard was consumed. The whispered suspicions were spread around in every pub and in street corner discussions, but nothing could be proven. Josef believed also, that evil forces had been at work here. He had only one question, "who?" Who would do this to him? He had not done any harm to anyone, had tried his best to have good relationships with every kin and neighbor, he knew.

Emmi encouraged her husband not to give up and his energy rebounded especially after the insurance company paid out handsomely. Within months Josef burst with new ideas. He spread out a blueprint on the kitchen table of a larger, more efficient lumber operation, with his name Josef Staffa boldly embossed on the gable of the white washed administration building. He was filled with high hopes to optimize his operation and make up for lost time by winning new customers. He invested in the most modern machinery available from neighboring Germany. His spirits were high as he painted again a bright future for the family, of which he was easily convinced after Emmi gave birth to a second son, and named him Horsti.

Warm March winds beckoned families to spend more time outdoors. Two-year-old Pepi needed to get his immunization shots and Emmi viewed it a perfect day for an outing in a city. She thought it was a great opportunity to get together with her friend Rosa. She welcomed sister Annie's offer to care for the baby. Annie loved the cute baby boy who was three months old and full of giggly delight. She thought that the warm spring sun was a good time to dress him up, put him in the baby buggy for strolls in the garden while she curled up with a book on the sun-drenched veranda.

She became engrossed in the romantic fantasy consuming her mind. As the rays of the sun became shorter and finally disappeared behind the mountain range, a cool breeze picked up and she felt a sudden chill. With a start she remembered the infant in the garden. Her heart pounded as she raced down the stairs. She heard the hoarse wail and looked in horror at a child with a purple complexion. She wrapped the infant tightly to her bosom and raced with him across the street to the only person, she knew who had the means, to take her to the hospital in Arnau. "Pavel…Pavel!" Annie cried.

Pavel was still suffering excruciatingly with even the slightest movement, after he was kicked in the leg by a horse. Yet hearing the child suffer, he hobbled down the sloping path.

Marie was visiting with Oma Staffa when she heard Pavel's cries for help. She sprinted across the meadow, knowing Pavel could not move fast enough since the accident. One look at the tiny boy, Marie sucked in the air as she feared the worst, she knew that the baby was in grave distress. Pavel pulled the car out of the garage and drove like a maniac, taking hairpin curves through the mountain roads, as if his life depended on it. Marie clung to every shred of hope as the child lay limp in her arms, wheezing laboriously. She delivered Horsti into medical hands and prayerfully paced the floor with Pavel and Annie for hours. She looked at Pavel like a brother and leaned against his rugged frame, contemplating how she would break the news to Emmi, if her worst fears came true.

When Emmi arrived home, unsuspecting of any tragedy, the maid informed her that the baby had fallen ill. By then everybody in the village of Mastig knew that something horrible had happened. As she passed by on her way to the hospital she felt the accusing looks like needles in her back. The stares were assaulting her with blame.

"How could she gallivant around in Prague, leaving her newborn to be cared for by Annie, who had enough problems caring for herself?"

For the next three day, the whole family and village bristled with emotion. How could anyone forget an infant in the garden? Emmi kept a vigil with rosary beads slithering between her fingers and gnashing teeth as her tiny son fought for every breath. Horsti died three days later of pneumonia. The baby had not lived long enough to have a picture taken while alive. Emmi could not part from her beloved child. She needed something of him to cherish. Marie got her camera and took a last photo of a child in its slumber, dressed in his baptismal gown. The tiny white coffin surrounded with rose petals looked like a crib. Only the profusion of flowers surrounding the child in his slumber reminded Emmi that this was his final resting place.

Emmi followed the tiny white coffin of her fair-faced infant, who was laid to rest in the black marble crypt beside his grandfather and Aunt Hildegard. Emmi was devastated. She accepted blame for his death and remained sequestered for the year of mourning. The photo of her beloved Horsti was placed beside a votive candle and Emmi stared for endless hours at the picture of her child, and wrote to her friend, Rosa.

"Maybe my mother was right? Maybe the Staffa's are cursed, one blow follows another. I cannot tell my mother about this. She will say, 'I told you so.' I blame myself for everything. I should not have left the baby with one who thinks like a child. What would I do without my faith?" Rosa tried to comfort her.

"You always told me, that all of life is a matter of fate and faith, fate determines those uncontrollable events that only faith can mitigate. Fate has dealt you a cruel blow, but you are strong in your faith. You'll have more children." Emmi shook her head. "I can't replace one child with another. I can only find solace in prayer." Meanwhile, poor Anninka at sixteen-years old felt as if everyone pointed fingers at her and like the un-welcomed child she had been from birth, she was regarded as a persona non-grata everywhere.

Her mother scowled at her as an irresponsible child soon as she entered her house. Anninka responded. "Everybody thinks this tragedy was my fault, but it was her husband's sister Annie, who forgot the child in the garden." Her mother only replied without listening. "It's high time you find work and learn responsibility. Go to work instead of sneaking around with a farmhand. Aunt Maria in Eibau needs household help."

Anninka welcomed the suggestion to go away. She had never been wanted in her mothers' home. Anninka didn't want to be home with her mother who never wanted her, nor in the house of an unnerving aunt and uncle. She yearned to find an escape from her mothers' ceaseless lamentations about her 'childs' uselessness. She boarded the train to visit aunt Maria, in Eibau near Dresden, across the German border, far enough away from home to get away from gossip mongers. After her arrival in Dresden Anninka wrote excitedly to Emmi.

> My dearest sister, I have found a job as a nanny in Dresden near Rumburg . I love it here! Der Zwinger, the Semper Opera and the round Frauen Kirche. You would love the exhilarating Wagner performances. I have at last a chance to meet men in natty uniforms and shiny jack boots—-my how they strut in precision. No one ever wanted me in Klein-Borowitz, now I am wanted. I am a part of the real world. Handsome young officers are in ample supply. I am dating a young pilot of the Luftwaffe. Life is an endless gala affair, unlike anything Mastig has to offer. There is a new and exciting aura around here. Germany has risen in splendor from the ashes of the World War.
>
> German people are no longer scraping out garbage cans to survive, and I am no longer an orphan which is what I am, I have only one person who loves me, my sister Emmi " Emmi was glad thinking maybe now her sister would find a sense of belonging, and she read on. "It seems ironic that I have found work caring for children of a state security officer and his wife. I

feel safe now and no longer feel like a bird that has fallen from a nest. I am consoled at last to have found a purpose for my life. I am lucky because lately many women here in Dresden are forced into war production. That thought alone makes me quiver and cringe. I am lucky that I won't have to work in a place like the Mandl factory, as so many women in Mastig have to do. I have found my consolation, Love Anninka

Emmi found her own consolation in the birth of a third son on her own birthday, Sunday, March 13, 1938. She named him for her beloved brother Othmar, shortened to Otto and proclaimed him her best birthday present ever. She wept, for her joy was again complete. "He looks just like my fair faced Horsti." Josef sat by his wife's bedside and teased her. "Now it is about time that we have a little girl, I want one like Gitchen."

Suddenly, he could no longer listen to Emmi's exhausting chatter, with one ear he listened to the radio. Josef slowly became agitated with the crackling noise.

The clamoring sounds coming over the airwaves filled him with nervous anxiety. He fiddled with the knobs in the hopes of finding music his wife would enjoy. Emmi was the good and gentle soul in the family and the community, who enjoyed the tender sounds of love and romance. "I don't need more dramatic roles, life is dramatic enough and I have never liked brassy military music, nor the sound of marching bands. I need the music of Mozart and Beethoven to lift my spirits, not Wagner to wring my soul."

Just as she hummed a lullaby to the new baby, the music of Beethoven came to an abrupt halt. A strange voice blared over the airwaves, announcing that at this moment Adolf Hitler had crossed the border from Germany into Austria. He looked solemn as he surveyed his hometown cemetery standing at the gravesite of his parents. Glad to be home in his border town of Leonding, his Austrian childhood home and as soon as word reached him that the people of Austria had voted to make Austria a province of Germany he wept for joy.

Josef listened with grave concerns for a few moments to the insane spectacle of the screeching and cheering crowds over the radio. The ruckus got on his nerve. The name Adolf Hitler could be heard over and over. He had never given much countenance to politicians, and avoided any contacts with euphoric screeching mobs. He wanted no part in any event, that smacked of idol worship. He cringed when he heard the crowds shout. "Sieg Heil! Sieg Heil!"

For the moment, it seemed that the Austrian fox could do no wrong. It seemed Adolf Hitler was adulated like a savior by those who wanted to believe in someone to help them out of their misery. Josef reasoned Mastig was far enough removed from this clamoring world, absent of a reliable newspaper, that no one in Mastig saw the first dark thunder clouds appear on the distant horizon.

Josef cringed with foreboding and shook his head in displeasure as evil dripped like ether, so slowly, into veins no one knew what evil was to come. People just shrugged their shoulders, after all Austria was Hitler's homeland and his return was portrayed as a triumphal home coming.

Austrians had voted 99.73 percent in favor of annexation, returning Hitler to his homeland. Josef saw no logical cause to pause. He could not think of what might be in store for simple folks like his. It all just seemed like hyped up propaganda of an inevitable chain of events. Josef turned off the radio, to shut out the noise yet he could not rid himself of this sense of foreboding. "I can't listen to these idiots scream any longer! Heil! Heil!"

Josef mimicked. "As long as he doesn't come here with his brown shirts, they are likely to bring us nothing but Un-heil!" Emmi had labored long and hard to birth her third son and murmured sleepily in her earthly wisdom. "Where the wind comes from, and where it goes, nobody knows." Emmi pleaded with her husband. "Sef, can you find Beethoven or Strauss again? I don't like this screaming sound of hype and hoopla." Josef turned on the radio again, but the airwaves were filled incessantly with the same blistering noise. All other broadcasts were interrupted with crackling noises. He shrugged his shoulders in exasperation. From the moment Beethoven had been snuffed from the airwaves, news of Austrian annexation dominated. and with that news Austria had lost its independence. Emmi was annoyed by the blistering announcements only to be followed by harsh military music. Josef was so frustrated he pulled the plug on the noise.

"I have heard enough howling and bellyache noise. All that brouhaha gets on my nerves." Emmi chirped. "Wait and drink tee, as the British would say." Josef laughed cynically. "While Hitler takes over a country on a weekend, the British Chamberlain takes to the country on weekends for a spot of tea."

He snickered as he mimicked a British accent. "Events in Vienna won't affect us. Vienna has been a Mecca for dreamers, romantics and heretics. Mastig is a Mecca for no one except quiet people like you and me. Mastig is not even on a map, so it can't be found, if it can't be found, they won't come here."

Josef waved off the broadcast with a sarcastic sneer. "Listen to that howling of a mob. Jessesmarren! The Austrians have welcomed Hitler home as if he were Jesus, riding into Jerusalem on a donkey. I just hope he does not come here. Just listen…these people are insane!" Josef walked out into the backyard. Events in Vienna seemed too remote to cause any brow to furrow, and he brushed aside his gradually-increasing anxiety. Emmi never paid any attention to politics and shared with Josef only those worldly concerns that revolved around their children, born out of their love for each other. Emmi viewed the world from behind the white curtains in her living room, and shrugged her shoulders in total oblivion to the latest broadcasts. Its significance in the future was lost on her and those who had no time nor mind to listen just as Josef thought.

What have I to do with the world? A man must keep order in his own family first. If the family is not whole, the village is not whole, if the village is not whole the world is not whole. It all starts within the family." Josef concurred with Emmis' simple assessment and just like his father had an abhorrence of politics, so did he. His fathers' disdain for politicians was not lost on Josef. He had grown up avoiding political razzle-dazzle, glitz and glamour.

Since the fire of the lumber yard Josef had enough to worry about. He had to rekindle customer relations and make up for lost time on deliveries.

Despite the greater efficiency of the new equipment, he worked harder and longer hours, planting new tracts of land that would be ripe for harvest in the next generation. Two years after the suspected arson fire, he had his lumber operation in full swing. He hired a night guard, personally scrutinized every new employee, and hired an older more experienced foreman. A few young men were dismissed under suspicion. Something about their attitude disturbed Josef greatly. The question, which haunted him at night was who the saboteurs were in their midst? Who were the hotheads? Were these the men who murdered his father for retribution of the drowning of the children. Were they the same as those who set the fire in the lumber yard? Who was responsible for his father's murder? It incensed him to realize that crimes committed against Germans were never investigated and warranted nothing more than a shrug of a shoulder and dismissal as an accident due to drunkenness.

Josef surmised that it was due to the usual lack of diligence of the Czech authorities, especially when the victim was a Sudeten German. He realized that stacks of lumber of pine trees covered with thick resin would create an inferno in a flash with just a lit match. Despite leads and intense private investigations, which he and his mother had initiated after the murder of her husband, no suspects were ever brought in for questioning. After all, the Czech authorities in Prague made no bones of the fact any act of sabotage or crime committed against a German was not a crime at all, and warranted no prosecution, and no punishment even if caught in the act of murder. So, why bother investigate any misdeeds against Germans, the despised Nemcis? After all, nobody would weep if a German lost a few Czech crowns from his coffers. Josef was glad that arson could not be proven. If proven the insurance company would not have paid for his losses. But he still needed to be wary of saboteurs from within. Who were his backstabbers?

He could not trust anyone, and warily viewed everyone with ever greater suspicions. It was a question which haunted Josef in his sleep. Several times a night he had to get up slip on his pants and walk over to the lumber yard and walk around well past midnight to make sure the watchman had not fallen asleep.

Josef quickly realized that the fire had been a blessing in disguise that had eliminated a dilapidated building that all the paint in the world could no longer rescue from decay. The machinery which he had been overhauling for years, was not worth the cost of repairs. Fate had forced him to redesign the factory, purchase modern wood cutting equipment. He enhanced the building by adding more windows for longer daylight hours and better ventilation to allow for longer and healthier day and night operations.

With all the improvements he was able to give his workers longer working hours. He had a new heating system installed that burned off the sawdust and woodchips, which saved fuel and for work to continue through the winter months.

One night the new Czech foreman, Stefan Hranek, summoned Josef to the bedside of a dying mill hand. Josef had dismissed him after the fire, because he had been seen lurking around the property late at night, nights for which he had no alibi. Josef looked down on the gnome-like wretched creature, who was writhing in agony due to the cancer that was eating his guts out. Josef's anger had long dissipated as he stared into the contorted face when he saw a man whose soul had become as twisted as his body. His mouth quivered as he painfully pressed the words from his lips that tormented his soul.

"Josef, I have something to confess before I die. I am too scared to face my maker's wrath unless I make a confession." The man wet his dry lips and Josef handed him a glass of water.

The dying man strained to talk in garbled peasant Czech. He wheezed with every agonizing breath and patted the bedside, motioning for Josef to come closer. Josef gingerly sat on the edge of a lumpy mattress beside the bundle of frail humanity and with ominous foreboding, braced himself against an ugly truth.

"I did it! I set the fire! But it was your uncle Stefan who paid me to light the match." Josef closed his eyes and held his breath. "My own uncle, Jessesmarren!"

Who would have thought that he was capable of such a dastardly deed? My father and grandfather had disowned him for being a miserable drunk. Josef felt as if a knife had pierced his heart. He remembered the wicked words he had heard his uncle mumble many times when he took his small son across the lumber yard, to show him the new machines. 'Maybe a bullet will get him.' Josef had wondered at the time, who his uncle wished to get hit by a bullet. Him, Josef or his young son? Josef pulled his collar around his sunken face and silently wept. His shoulders heaved with emotion in defeat. Josef could barely hear the man's audible whisper. "I need your forgiveness!" Josef turned and left the room without uttering another word, shattered by the revelation of a relatives' treachery, he could remember his father's rage against some ill willed derelict in their midst. His father had declared some of the relatives as misfits, and unworthy of the Staffa name. He was appalled by the carousing, womanizing, and squandering lives they led and by which they burned holes in their pockets with every hard-earned Thaler.

His father had once declared that any wellspring of ill repute to the Staffa name should not reap any of its rewards. Josef instead reaped the bitter grapes of his father's wrath against a misfit brother.

Josef poured out his lamentations to Emmi between their bed sheets, for only there could he feel safe not to be betrayed. "I can't find justice in these crows-nest courts. Who do I prosecute, Brother Cain? Or his accomplice? Who deserves the punishment, the cankerworm or his accomplice. The one whom God has punished more than I ever could? Do I punish the one who lit the match for thirty pieces of silver, or the one who paid him? Uncle Stefan probably never paid the pour drunk more than the cost of a bottle of vodka."

Emmi held her husband close with the only comfort she knew to bestow with her warm body as she whispered. "You need not look for revenge any longer. God fits the burden to the back and I am glad you have a broad back. God loves righteousness and he will make everything right in due time, sooner or later, God's will prevailed."

That night the mill hand died and was buried in a paupers' grave with no one in attendance but two grave diggers. On a rainy day a few weeks after the old man's death a motorbike whipped around the sharp corner across from the lumber yard and smashed against the Luschnitz' General Store front at high speed. The bike skidded on the wet surface and slammed into the wall. Josef heard the crash and rushed to the scene. The body of the man had smashed head first against the concrete. The bike beside him was a mangled heap of metal.

Blood was gushing from beneath his leather riding cap. Josef turned the body over and recognized his uncle Stefan, killed instantly after a long night at the Hample pub.

Without eulogy Stefan's shattered body was laid to rest beside his mother Josepha, whose husband had been lost in the trenches in a war against Napoleon.

Josef reflected on past centuries in which every male in the Staffa ancestry was lost in some foreign war. None were laid to rest in the soil of their homeland as far back as the war against the Turks in Vienna in the 16th century from which only a Turkish saber was kept on the mantel in the new Staffa villa as a souvenir and a commemorative mention on a war memorial plaque. Josef hated war and reflected on the wasted lives lost in some quagmire at the behest of some monarch, while others like his uncle had squandered his life on booze.

During the funeral, Emmi glanced at her husband through a black veil, and murmured. "Everyone has his cross to bear. I think Stefan's cross was heavier than yours. God has dealt him justice." Josef replied glumly. "I feel nothing! I feel no sadness, no hate, no anger. I just feel numb in the pit of my stomach."

Josef had spent many years looking over his shoulders. He had always known he could never let his guard down, and always was on the lookout for potential war mongers and men with evil intentions. Now Josef felt a sigh of relief. He no longer felt a need to look over his shoulder at every man with a suspicious mind. Josef was relieved to see his place in the world in the quiet joy he had found by his wife's side. He saw no need to clamor for revenge. He and Emmi had plenty of nieces and nephews to charm. Josef's favorite niece was Gitchen, who often came to visit her uncle Josef and aunt Emmi, Josef recognized the adorable waif by the knock on the door. Every time he heard that tender knock, knock on their front door, Josef would say out loud so that the child could hear him through the closed door.

"I wonder who this might be? I think this can only be my Gitchen. Emmi look, Gitchen has come to visit her favorite uncle, Sef." Hearing her uncles' voice, the child could be heard giggling with delight. Her large blue eyes set deep in her angelic face twinkled with delight as she peered around the corner.

Her heart shaped cherub face was surrounded by blond ringlets in wild profusion and seeing the child, Sef would remind his wife. "It's time we have a little girl like Gitchen."

Josef's handsome five-year-old nephew Kurt, was Emmi's favorite naughty boy whom she had nicknamed Lausbub, left her shaking her head when the childish antics he cooked up seemed to drag her son into some dereliction and mischief. Josef was the favorite uncle of both Kurt and Margit and Emmi was their favorite aunt who always had something good to eat on the table. Josef was oblivious to the subtle changes in their behavior, while Emmi was busy with the new baby her keen and motherly instincts were always on high alert. She smelled trouble whenever Kurt whispered secrets into her sons' receptive ears. She looked alarmed when Pepis' eyes would light up as the two scampered out the door not to be seen again for hours. The towheads put their plans into action together, and all too often into situations that spelled trouble, much to Emmi's growing concerns. Her eyes would widen and her ears perked up in an instant full of consternation.

She was afraid that Kurt was the ringleader who would get her son in trouble. Kurt was always the brain storming leader of the pack of these little pranksters. Little Pepi tagged along too eagerly behind his bold cousin Kurt, who was endowed with worldly wisdom far beyond his years and Emmi's simplistic comprehension. What would become of a child born into their midst who was smart as a fox, and ruggedly handsome. The tall boy was endowed with a mop of blond curly hair and the largest forget me not eyes which constantly were on a look-out for mischief and adventures. While little Pepi loved tagging along with

Kurt and viewed it a moment of reprieve from the watchful eyes of his stern mother, whenever she saw that his mother was busy with a new baby.

Busy as he was, Josef enjoyed his leisure hours in a home filled with the laughter of children scampering around his ankles. As Josef plunged into his smaller but more manageable enterprise, he was delighted by the precision of the newly installed machinery, which sliced whole trees into boards in minutes. The great efficiency of the new operation made up for lost time. Filled with visions of a bright future he mapped out the landscape for truck routes and crossroads, along which he planned gas stations for his trucks, lumber distribution centers and building supply stores.

As her husband explained the building blocks of capitalism, Emmi was more concerned with the antics of Kurt and Pepi and welcomed the rainy days in blissful contentment when the boys stayed indoors and played Chess. Those were the only days when she wouldn't have to worry about Pepi. Emmi watched the boys and realized that Kurt was an expert chess player and Pepi was an eager student of more than moves and strategies on the chessboard. Kurt had taught his cousin many games and more than just chess. For obvious reasons, Kurt was the recipient of her son's hero worship. If Kurt and Pepi were too quiet for any length of time, she feared that they were planning their next coup d'etat. She could read Kurt's enormous blue eyes, which never failed to relay his intent to be the chief instigator of some mischief. She knew she had to be on guard at all times, and when she saw a need to raise her concerns, she scolded Pepi for spending too much time with Kurt.

"Kurt and I are a team, like Max and Moritz!"

"You two are worse than Max and Moritz. You two could have written the book on mischief." Emmi winced thinking that Kurt was clearly a fearless leader, whose wit baffled many an adult.

"I worry about our impressionable and easy-going son. He does not foresee the danger of a situation."

Josef waved off her concerns. "I just laugh at Kurt's daring exploits. I shudder wondering what Kurt will conjure up next." Emmi responded. "I worry what he'll involve Pepi in." Unbeknown to either of them, Kurt had found the trap doors leading to a tunnel that was connected to a castle of medieval robber barons. The two boys sought adventures where once upon a time knights in shining armor had played games of chivalry. The boys had found a place for children's playful fantasies in tunnels and caves and escape hatches that became hiding places from bullying Czech classmates who carried bullwhips and pistols.

Emmi thought she recognized a disheveled and swarthy looking young man, who every morning was leaning up against the corner pillar of their chain-link fence that surrounded the Staffa compound. A steady whistling noise followed by a ping noise, ping, ping, ping roused the boy's attention. They parted the curtains to determine the cause of the noise outside. Pepi raised his head above the windowsill and stuck his nose out of the bay window for a better view. The swarthy man spotted the boy standing by the window. He slowly swung his shoulder around and aimed the pistol at the little boy.

Pepi gasped with a quickened pulse and ducked his head out of sight. From behind the curtain, he continued to watch the swarthy man who aimed his pistol as if ready to shoot him. Instead the man slowly moved his arm and shot several times at a granite rock on the far side of their potato field. The persistent sound continued for hours as if he was target-practicing.

Pepi peeked outside, and he demonstrated for Kurt how the man had aimed the weapon at him and Kurt cautioned. "This guy is mean. We better keep away from him!" Oma Staffa prodded Marie and Emmi to look after little Fredi, the boy who had no one except a grandmother to cling to for motherly comfort.

Kurt allowed Fredi to tag along with him and Pepi because their mothers implored them to take pity on the motherless boy, but that did no spare him from being the victim of their pranks. Kurt showed Pepi how to dig trip pits along their escape routes and hidden tunnel entrances showing him how to camouflage the holes with sticks and leaves. Anyone following them to their hiding places was sure to stumble across the sticks and leaves and fall into a pit.

They hoped to trip up their molesting swarthy neighbors. But all too often, their pesky tailgating cousin Fredi fell into them instead headfirst. With wistful charm, Kurt's brilliant blue eyes would sparkle with delight at sight of Fredi crawling out of a pit, shaking the leaves from his pants. Kurt slapped the little boys back good naturedly. "Watch…where you are going little man!" Growing up in his father's tavern among grown men, swinging trays laden with frothy beer mugs, with eyes and ears that were wide open Kurt had developed faster than other boys his age. He knew how to wheel and deal in German, Czech, Russian, and Polish and all their ethnic dialects and languages of the patrons in his father's pub.

Lately he was heard practicing the English tongue because many foreigners seemed to converge on their village lately, who relished dining at the Gernerts Garden Café. British gents seemed to enjoy Marie's good cooking. Kurt was not too shy to pull up a chair, boldly asking. "What brings you to a crows' nest like Mastig?"

For lack of better housing, many of the foreign guests moved into those "Bretterbuden."

The shacks adjacent to the Mandl factory yard, for what appeared to be more than a summer vacation. Kurt was always on the lookout for little business opportunities. He spotted a novel opportunity in the chicken coop. He bartered eggs from his grandmother's chicken coop for cigarettes. He delivered not only eggs and bacon, but bread rolls and sausages, and the British gents showed their gratitude with chocolates and cigarettes. His nine-year old sister, Margit, got wind of her brothers' little racket. With a sweet smile stretching across her baby doll face from ear to ear, she managed to cut a deal with these men for plenty more than chocolates, she got oranges and marzipan pralines to boot.

Emmi knew that Marie had tried to curtail Kurt's antics to no avail. But who would have thought sweet little Margit could be a conspirator in Kurt's wheeling and dealing ventures? When Pepi got wind of the deals his cousins had cooked up, he told his mother, who let her worries be known to her husband. "Sef, I worry what Pepi is learning from this blond fox. I can' let my son out of my sight. The boys won't stay in the house unless it's raining duck weather."

Josef could not resist a gentle tease to calm his wife's concerns. "Then it's time for a little girl, like Gitchen. Girls stay home, play with their dolls or do needlepoint with their mothers."

Josef and Emmis daily lives had fallen into a comfortable routine. Weekends provided them with ample time to relax and replenish their energies for the week ahead. In the company of friendly kin and neighbors, it was easy to avoid those of a more hostile persuasion. One just had to close the door, except when Gitchen came for her daily visit. She was pushing a stroller with a toddler in it to show uncle Sef her new 'dolly.' Giggling with delight when she heard uncle Sef say as he strode to open the door to let her enter. "This can only be my Gitchen!" He said to his wife.

"I recognize her by the way she knocks on the door. I always tell her that I want a little girl like Gitchen!" Gitchen beamed with delight upon hearing that.

Emmi chuckled. "Well, I wish children were born made to order. I gave you three sons already. Once these chairs are occupied, you have lost your chance for a girl. I won't spend the rest of my life pulling up odd chairs around the dinner table!" Josef wrapped his arms around Emmi's belly.

"I always knew you to be a difficult woman. I'll have to divorce you, if you refuse to give me more children." She replied. "We're Catholics. We don't divorce. Ever! We live with what life brings us."

Gernerts Garden Café had become a regular stop after Sunday Mass for much of the congregation, including the young Polish priest. Gustav and Marie enjoyed the kind of mass appeal that kept the Garden Café hopping every Sunday. The Latin Word "Mass" means celebration, and celebrate they did with Marie's simple but hearty home-style cooking, of Wiener Schnitzel, Sauerbraten with Red Cabbage and Bohemian dumplings, and for more festive seasons, like Christmas, a goose had to sacrifice her long stretched neck.

By noon the place was shrieking with children's laughter. Festive red and white checkered tables spilled out from the Garden Cafe into Marie's Rose Garden and stoves laden with Sauerbraten and dumplings were waiting for the congregation by the time the priest announced. "The Mass has ended…go in peace to love and serve the Lord." Nine-year old Margit pushed little children around the yard in a buggy while their parents ate dinner. Cheerful families settled down at their favorite dining spots while children played hide-and-seek around Marie's abundantly blooming rose trellises.

Little Margit came around a blooming rosebush to hide and stumbled over the legs of a swarthy man. As she fell onto the lawn, she looked up and apologetically said. "Sorry! Mister."

She scrambled to pick herself up, and brushed the dirt from her white stockings, when she heard him say in accented Czech. "Someday I will bloody your white stockings." Margit ran off like a frightened little bird, shrieking in horror as the sinister looking man sauntered off down the road. Those, who had not seen how a strange man had tripped up a little girl and terrified her, believed the child's hysterical screams to be of a child at play, and no one paid any further attention to her.

The House My Father Built

Josef and Emmi were satisfied that their gravest concerns revolved around training the new nanny, Erna. What livestock could be butchered that Josef had not befriended, and what crops to plant for the next season. Fruits and vegetables not eaten in one season of its harvest were canned under the frugal motto "waste-not want-not". Potatoes were stored in cool root cellars, cabbage heads were julienne chopped, salted and cured in wooden barrels to ferment into sauerkraut.

For lack of nothing, they felt truly blessed when Emmi announced that she was pregnant again. But the world wouldn't stand for a man and woman's simple concerns and quiet contentment as evil dripped like ether into veins slowly…

Nobody noticed, with the easy annexation of neighboring Austria Hitler had been given an excuse he needed to invade Czechoslovakia, keeping in mind that many of Czechoslovakia's largest munitions factories were located in the mountains of the Sudetenland. Czechoslovakia called for mobilization and Josef was drafted into the Czech military. Reluctantly Josef donned the brown uniform of a Czech conscript and was picked up for what he thought would be military training. Instead, he was incarcerated with other Germans in a Czech concentration camp and put to work in a munitions factory, at hard labor.

At the time, Hitler's blistering broadcasts proclaimed, he could no longer tolerate the sufferings of the German minority living under Czech intimidation and terror, the German people felt vindicated and rejoiced because someone had heard their cry.

Following Hitler's diatribes, the Sudeten Germans went on strike and refused to pay taxes. Overnight, the streets in major cities of the Sudetenland were blanketed with Swastika banners, as the Masses shouted. "We want self-determination." The Czech police opened fire on the demonstrators and within twenty-four hours, bloody discord had spread throughout the mountain region. The Czechs declared martial law and more Sudeten Germans were shot.

Emmi knew nothing of her husband's where abouts. She had not seen him nor heard from him from the day he was picked up by the Czech military.

Every waking moment was spent in prayer for her husbands' welfare. She could not sleep wondering what the Czech military had done to her husband? After suffering many sleepless nights when exhaustion finally took over, she felt guilty over every catnap. She felt faint as she looked out the window, and saw a landscape of people embroiled in ethnic hatred. As a threat of an invasion by

Hitler loomed, spontaneously, in every village, citizens massed in the streets to demonstrate their determination to resist Hitlers' army.

Emmi latched the wooden shutters; taking one more glance outside and noticed again the swarthy and disheveled man leaning against their concrete garden posts. A holster dangled alongside his leg. She recognized him as the man who had been terrorizing children in the neighborhood, the man who had stalked her before her marriage to Josef at the post office in Klein-Borowitz. Did Bubi Scholz know him? She wondered how he knew where she lived now as he snarled threats of bloodying her white socks. He could see she was with child again and he was the one holding daily shooting practices alongside their house. He was the same man who was shooting at the same granite rock for hours with an evil grin on his face as he bared his rotting teeth.

It was clear to Emmi this was the man who terrorized her family as she stood and stared at him to let him know, 'I know why you are doing this. You want us to flee from our home out of fear, but I am not afraid of you!' After a while he left when he realized that he had not accomplished his goal of intimidation, at least not at this moment.

Emmi kept the terror she felt hidden from her children. She was terrified at the events she witnessed, viewed through the curtains that covered her windows. She was deeply disturbed at what was happening on both the German and the Czech sides. Threats and hate filled proclamations and propaganda leaflets were found, falling on too many receptive ears and hatred boiled over.

She saw not only the swarthy young men back in front of her house as he strutted cocksure up and down the streets with bullwhips and pistols and who became a frightful sight, but the swaying of red, black and white swastikas hanging from windows caused equal consternation.

While her husband was incarcerated by the Czech military his older brother, Emil was drafted into the German army and sent to the largest city in Greece to fight partisans there. Within a few days news reached Mastig Emil was killed in Solonika. To her absolute horror, Emmi watched from her balcony as her sister-in-law Ilse across the street, Karl's very pregnant wife provocatively hung the picture of Adolf Hitler from her balcony. Emmi was seething with rage and shaken to the core and conflicted about what to do. She hated confrontation and discord among Josef's family members. She preferred to remain quiet in their midst, always feeling like an outsider and in every argument, she knew she would be the loser. She felt as thou they thought of her as nothing more than a country bumpkin and a dimwit.

Just as she was about to follow her instincts to run across the street and scream at Ilse to tear down this poster, she heard her mother-in-law take the words out of her mouth from across the street.

"What are you doing there? Do you want to add oil to the fire? We have a political inferno here. We have no one to protect us from the carnage to come in this crows' nest." Emmi watched silently agreeing with her mother-in-law. Anna ran to Ilse's balcony, tore down the portrait of Adolf Hitler from her balcony and ripped it to shreds screaming "Because of this Schweinehund (pig) I have lost a son in the war, as she threw the shards into the wind. Emmi sighed with relief as she pulled out her prayer book and found solace in the psalm. "They have dug a deep pit before my eyes into which they have fallen themselves."

She carefully moved the curtain to the side and ordered Pepi not to venture out of the yard. "I want to make sure you are safe, when this guy is around, if you see him, you run!" She felt desperate to know if her husband was alive or dead. In the hope of a sign of life from him she had to walk to the post office pushing a six-month old in the baby buggy and telling Pepi to hold on to the side of the buggy, then she dropped him off at his Kindergarten class

The short walks with her sons past the school and post office had become a daily life-threatening venture, as she dodged from building to building for shelter, avoiding open spaces and hedges.

Instead of news from her husband there was a letter from her sister in Dresden. She was glad to know her sister was alive and well. On her way home she scanned the streets up and down to see if the swarthy man was hanging around. Emmi had not heard him walk up behind her. As she turned to go back to her house terror cursed like lightning from her head to her toes when he stood silently in front of her, his fiery coal black beady eyes stared at her in silence and blank hatred oozed out of him. She was scared to death of the dark faced man. But she dared not let her fears show. If she ran it would fill him with great satisfaction. She knew he constantly shadowed her and her children to create a constant state of unrest with intimidation. Fear and terror stalked and startled her. She was furious because children could not play outside without being frightened of this boogey man.

She was determined to put an end to his evil game. She closed the distance with a few sprints and faced her tormentor with eyes blazing. She jabbed a finger at his chest, and said in perfect Czech.

"What do you want from us? Why do you shoot at granite bolders in back of our potato field every day? Children are playing in the fields and gardens. Bullet casings are laying all over the yard, little children put them in their mouth and could choke to death."

The swarthy man snarled back at her in Czech. "That would be one less Nemci bes."

Emmi was livid and screamed at a high pitch. "Pritch! Don't call me Nemci bes. Pritch! I am not a dog, I am just one person. We are just ordinary people. Pritch! Go to the devil. Pritch! Stop scaring my children!"

Without turning around but wary of the swarthy evil-looking man who, she knew, was following behind her and Pepi, she felt his eyes on her as she tried to push the buggy faster back to her house. As soon as she saw her house, she started running to reach the front door and the security of its solid walls. She brought the children inside and ordered Pepi to barricade the doors as she shuttered the windows with shaking fingers.

Pepi was only too nosy to see what the tumult was all about outside. Emmi had to sequester an anxious little boy not to venture outside, nor to push the curtains aside so he could peer out the windows. She was determined to keep her children out of harms' way, and admonished Pepi as he tried to sneak outside pleading. "No, you stay in the house there is nothing for you to see." But the five-year old was pleading with her to be allowed outside. When she opened Anna's letter Pepi saw an opportunity to slip outside and Emmi called after him. "Jessesmarren. Come back inside."

She read Anna's letter: Dear Emmi, today is the most exciting day I ever experienced. I saw him with his outstretched arm as he drove through the streets of Dresden on his way to Prague. The people here were euphoric, and screamed "Sieg Heil! Sieg Heil!. I felt the goose bumps up and down my spine, and the chills of terror in the pit of my stomach. I felt faint as the masses swayed around me like eerie ghosts. Love, Anninka

Emmi felt faint and knew that nothing would ever be the same as a craze and euphoria spread like wildfire through the region. What all this meant to her life, she could not imagine in her wildest dreams.

At the moment she only worried about her husband, Josef. She would feel whole again if only he were here with her. She was in no mood to deal with swarthy strangers and foreigners who walked with an aura of importance around her village and leaving these people with paralyzing feelings of helplessness. When the steady pinging noise emanated from outside, Emmi knew the swarthy man was back for shooting practices as he put it. She questioned who the real target was? Her family? "Maybe one day he'll just shoot us?"

"Evil was dripping like ether into veins so slowly, no one knew what was happening until it was too late." She put the baby Otto in the buggy in hopes of walking down to Marie's house. After running across cobblestones to get back into her house she felt a searing pain and contracting cramps. She felt a trickle of blood ooze down her bare legs as she rushed into the bathroom. A thick lump passed through her loins and she knew she had miscarried. She sent her maid to get Marie, who rushed to her side immediately.

Marie helped her bathe, washed the bloody clothes and helped Emmi slip into a clean flannel gown."Lay down and stay in bed." Marie admonished. She made chamomile tea and a light snack and helped her sip the tea slowly and set the snack by Emmi's bedside. She put the baby by her side so Emmi could nurse him.

"I'll summon doctor Muecker to check you over. But I think you'll just need some bed rest." As Marie predicted, Doctor Mücker, ordered Emmi to remain in bed.

Obediently Emmi stayed in bed until she couldn't stand being shut inside. It was the first day in October 1938. She noticed a sudden stillness causing her ears to perk up like the stillness of animals before an earthquake.

The calm before a storm. The change prompted her to open her windows cautiously. All noise had ceased outside, the steady whistling of a pistol shot and the pinging of a bullet hitting the granite rock, was gone. The swarthy men were no longer in their usual positions. She peered outside through the curtains in her bedroom. The streets were eerily quiet, overnight some drastic change had occurred.

Kurt knocked on the door, calling Pepi to come outside, Pepi jubilantly scampered after his older and bigger cousin, older by only one year, but wiser by fifty. Emmi was relieved that she could let the boys go outside to play again. They no longer had to sneak around the neighborhood, or slither along walls, duck their heads at the sound of the whistling bullets and the pinging noise. They no longer feared being the target of bullets, even a stray bullet. They ran in excitement as the cloak of humiliation seemed to have been lifted. They no longer feared being beaten up by bullying Czech Kindergarten classmates, or being spit upon, or have their heels stepped on or legs tripped. No longer feared being bull-whipped off the sidewalks before being knocked into the streets with shouts of "Pritch, Nemci bes!"

The boys ran over to the granite boulder to check for bullet markings and casings at the far end of the potato field, from where the whistling noise had once roused their attention, and found a heap of bullet casings. Kurt climbed on the boulder, balanced himself atop and used his spyglass to take a closer look around. Pepi noted the changes with glee as Kurt announced. "I think all is quiet on the eastern front." Pepi replied.

"We used to turn white and ashen when we saw the goons coming toward us." Kurt chided his younger cousin. "Don't be so polite little cousin. "We used to shit our pants when we saw them coming…now they are going to shit theirs." Pepi burst out laughing at his cousin's crude antics. Pepi adored Kurt who seemed to have expert knowledge of everything going on in the world.

Whatever Kurt said or did always gave Pepi comic relief from his mother's strict and straight-laced nurture.

"We need not fear anyone, we can hide in our caves and tunnels."

Unbeknown to the people of this region on the pretext of restoring order and bringing relief from Czech terror to the Sudeten German people, Hitler had marched into the Sudetenland. Just as there was always conflict between the Czechs and Germans, the Czechs did not get along with Slovaks either and were feuding over the eastern half of Czechoslovakia. The Slovaks also wanted their autonomy. Under a pretext of restoring peace Hitler decided to take over the entire country. Hitler's convoys rolled totally unnoticed toward Hradschin Castle in Prague where he vowed to let naked terror reign against all who participated in demonstrations against him. At that moment the Czech government succumbed without a whimper in March 1939.

Hitler dismissed a moderate, appeasing Sudeten German Baron von Neurath, and appointed Reinhard Heydrich to take his place, under whose reign the Gestapo uncovered an extensive network of Czech resistance organizations, and launched executions of the Czech prime minister and the mayor of Prague. Intellectuals and army officers were rounded up and sent to concentration camps to quell further demonstrations.

The House My Father Built

But for the oppressed Sudeten Germans came welcomed reprieve from Czech terror. Hitler lifted economic sanctions, which the Czechs had placed against German industries and allowed honest business to flourish, but most important, those Germans imprisoned in Czech concentration camps, were released and freed of the brown uniforms of the Czech military.

Josef was one of them. He gladly returned home, to those things he cherished most, his wife and sons and his beloved lumber business. His business was allowed to flourish again once he was freed of Czech interference. Josef and Emmi viewed their future aglow with high expectations through the white lace curtains of their dining room alcove. The target practicing thugs were gone from the corner of their property.

Czech terror against the German minority had ceased. Josef came home again for noon meals, and afternoon coffee breaks. Emmi relished what she called their quiet time together, relieved that their daily lives had become a comfortable routine once again.

Well past midnight, Josef slipped out of bed, to take a look around. The terror of the night of the fire was still deeply etched in his psyche and he slept with great unease. Josef parted the curtains to look out over the wood logs and factory compound. His brother's house nestled close by his mother's villa, when he noticed a strange woman slipping inside his mother's house and shortly after Pavel and a women left in the quiet of the night. In the morning he noticed that the Dusenberg was still not in its usual place. He wondered if Pavel Koczian might have driven his mother somewhere.

"Maybe my mother went to visit my sister in Königinhof. Maybe my sister is having another baby?" The next morning the car was back in front of the house, and he thought no more of it.

No one had a clue of the horror to come on a balmy morning, April 20, 1939, when a noise and clamor roused a Pepi and a toddling Otto into action they raced out of the house just as a flock of white pigeons were spooked from their roost. They lifted off and headed for the forested mountains. The boys stopped to watch the panicked birds. Little Otto screeched in baby talk,' Lele Pepa la Taua to which Pepi replied in understanding of his baby brothers babble. "Jaah! See? Lauter Weisse!"

Josef was reading the Catholic Newspaper, when he heard the noise outside. He parted the curtains and gasped in horror when he saw the street blanketed with red, black and white banners and his nephew Kurt running ahead of the band swinging a baton.

Josef looked ashen. "Jessesmarren!" He jumped off his chair and ran to the door.

"I don't want my children to be poisoned by Nazi propaganda and all their razzle dazzle."

Pepi ran to the garden gate and Otto scampered after him. Pepi climbed on top of the concrete pillars that anchored the corners of the white garden gate. From his vantage point he had a great view over the major intersection of Mastig. He lifted Otto on his lap. There the two boys clung like innocent sparrows and caught sight of the streets below that were blanketed with swaying swastika banners and marching bands.

To Pepis' surprise, his eight-year old cousin Kurt was racing ahead of the parade, marching to the clanking noise of harsh military music. Kurt exuded such excitement and pride, acting like the grand marshal of the parade. Pepi wished he could join Kurt and march alongside him. He loved a parade and looked envious at his cousin. Josef ran out of the house and against his sons' childish protests lifted them off their pedestal, chiding them. "Come, come, this is nothing for you!"

Pepi knew he would not be allowed to participate in the excitement of a parade. One he was not even allowed to watch from afar. Josef glanced toward the marching band and saw among the marchers his brothers Karl and Alfred, carrying Nazi banners and Josef scowled at them as they passed his house. "Big shots!" Josef looked across the street and saw Karl's wife, Ilse von Reichenberg, quickly hang pictures of Adolf Hitler on her balcony in "honor" of Hitler's birthday. Seeing Kurt swing the baton as if he were the leader of the band greatly alarmed Josef, and he called out to his favorite nephew. "Come inside. You don't belong with these people. You can teach Pepi the Chess game. You are not one of these people."

Kurt replied with a big smile. "Uncle Sef, I just love a parade!" Hitler's troops left deep footprints across this dewy, spring fresh peasant landscape, and Emmi and Josef became increasingly filled with an ominous foreboding.

As swiftly as German troops marched through the quaint village, the Czech gendarmes were relieved of their uniforms and sent home forthwith and replaced by German sentries. The Czech mayor was dismissed and the former German mayor, a benign seventy-year-old gentleman, was reinstated. His pious, white-haired wife beside him glowed with pride during the brief ceremony on the steps of the new community hall.

All radical measures were believed to be for the protection of the German population against Czech retaliation. The train station in Mastig was placed under constant guard, and occupied by a newly installed "Gauleiter," named Ernst Lochmann. As Gauleiter it was his job, to secure the patriotic loyalty from the citizenry to the Nazi party and ordered to vow a pledge of allegiance to Adolf Hitler.

Propaganda posters and placards of Hitler and his proclamations appeared suddenly on buildings, lamp posts, and the cylindrical Litfass Obelisk daily. Josef winced at the slogans and propaganda and he knew that nothing good could come of this and nothing would ever be the same again. He had no time to ponder the changes around him. He was too busy with his own business affairs. He had just bought a new fleet of trucks with which he hoped to deliver his lumber more efficiently.

One morning there was a sharp pounding on the front door. A stranger, dressed in a trench coat who nobody had ever seen before, introduced himself as Ernst Lochmann. He informed Josef quickly that it was his duty to make sure that people towed the party line. He had taken up his residence in the upstairs loft over the Mastig train station. The whistle stop was the perfect place from where he could monitor the comings and goings of the befuddled flock. Josef knew in fact the man was the newly installed Gauleiter, the Nazi henchman and Hitlers appointed enforcer.

Josef understood the man's mission in this town and what this demonstration was really all about. Here, as in the smallest Sudeten German community these Gauleiters were men whose job it was to control every person's life and march in goose steps to the party line with arms raised high in a Hitler salute. It was this man's job to enforce loyalty to Adolf Hitler and membership in the Nazi Party, the NSDAP, with its full name and weight of National Socialist Workers Party of Germany.

First on Lochmanns agenda was a visit to the homes of prominent families with a recognizable name, to garner support for the cause. As soon as he had arrived in Mastig, which Ernst Lochmann labeled a crow's nest he learned that the Staffa name ranked high in prominence in this region. That put the Staffa family name on top of his list. He had already enlisted the loyalty of Josef's older brothers, Karl and Alfred. They were in his party's pocket as loyalists.

Now he had to enlist the one hold out, Josef Staffa. Much to his annoyance Josef Staffa was not an easy prey. Every time he paid a visit to the Staffa villa the maid answered with a curt. "Sorry, Herr Staffa is not home." Ernst Lochmann tried again on Sunday. To his annoyance nobody answered his knock on the door. He walked around the village, his keen blue eyes looked skeptical as he toured the hamlet. It was obvious that the youngest of the Staffa clan was avoiding him. He walked up the road toward Mastig Bad with its spas and recreational facilities.

On a hunch he entered the Gernert Garden Café. There he spotted the families, who had gathered around festive Sunday dinner tables, for a friendly neighborhood get together with good food and light laughter and conversations. Ernst Lochmann stepped up to the table nearest the entrance. He showed his badge as his credential as the party functionary of Mastig.

He touted his well-rehearsed propaganda line to the patrons. He had the feeling his words were falling on deaf ears as Josef paid scant attention and kept on eating. Josef could not be swooned into socialistic fervor and made no motion to show anything but polite indifference as he dug into his sauerbraten and dumplings with a hearty appetite.

Emmi was annoyed at the persistent intrusion into their family time. She could feel a paralyzing trepidation that pierced her soul. She could feel the constant encroachment of goose-stepping strangers into their little world, and felt as if her breath was being squeezed out of her chest. Emmi shuddered with dread as she read new decrees that were posted on every pole and pillar filled with threats of doom and gloom and warnings of war.

Whenever someone rang the doorbell persistently followed by loud pounding on the door, the maid was not allowed to let them in and only say. "Nobody is home." Emmi resented that Josef had to slip out the back door, run into the woods in the back of the property, to avoid the man with the trench coat and badge and she had to keep the children quiet about their fathers' whereabouts.

Many days Josef was afraid to come home all day, afraid of running into one of the goons. and now the man with the badge had followed them here to their favorite dining place only to disturb their Sunday dinnertime. Ernst Lochmann knew that Josef Staffa was avoiding him.

Now in front of all the assembled patrons of the restaurant, he dressed him down with a stern voice, reminding him of his patriotic duty to his fatherland. Emmi cringed at the man's words but was even more afraid of her husbands' reply. "What is my patriotic duty, to love my homeland, that I do. I love my fathers' land and its history." Lochmann stepped closer to the table. "I must remind you! You must stop at party headquarters without further delay." Josef waved Lochmann off and chewed unimpeded, unwilling to let this man ruin his life and time with the family.

"I have no time for your nonsense. I am having dinner with my family first, and during the week I have to make a delivery to customers." Lochmann replied. "I am reminding you for the last time, you must first thing tomorrow become a member of the NSDAP." Josef shook his head and waved off the steely harassment and intimidation as blackmail, threats, and encroachment on his precious time with his family and snarled. "To the devil with you and your ilk!" Lochmann's steely eyes bore into Josef's. "I am warning you! If you love your family and fatherland, it is your duty to be obedient to Adolf Hitler's authority and mine. I am his representative here, and I order you to join the Socialist Workers Party of Germany. Lochman klicked his heels together, raised his outstretched arm and snapped. Heil Hitler!" Josef swallowed hard and hissed. "I have no time for your pig shit."

Lochmann shouted. "That will cost you a fine of a thousand Reich Marks." With a click of a heel and an outstretched arm Lochmann turned his attention on Father Sowonsky without the usual reverence for a priest, he slapped down a piece of paper. "These are the new instructions for prayers and sermons you are allowed to use." The young polish priest read the instructions softly to himself. His eyes widened and his fair face turned red with disgust, he read out loud for all to hear the pledge of Allegiance to Hitler

"Adolf Hitler, you are our great leader, Thy name makes the enemy tremble, Thy third Reich has come, Thy will is law upon the land, Let us hear daily thy voice and lead us. We will obey you to the end and with our lives. We praise thee! Hail Hitler!

The young priest looked down on the paper in stunned silence, then he looked up at Lochmann, handed him back the paper and said in his soft voice. "This is not the Lords' prayer. It is a hideous piece of Socialist brainwash. I will not have my parishioners say these words because it is not a prayer, it is a blasphemy." He folded his hands in prayer and softly and reverently recited the Lord's Prayer in defiance. Our Father who art in heaven, hallowed be thy name.

The families who had looked forward to dinner looked down in silence on their dinner plates until the priest ended with 'Amen.' Ernst Lochmann slapped the paper back on the table, he stood up, flipped his arm high and with a heel click shouted. "I will be in your church next Sunday, to make sure, you read it as you are told. Heil Hitler!" He turned around abruptly to make his exit, and the priest called after him. "Grüss Gott!"

The old familiar salutation used in Catholic regions had just recently been outlawed.

A small child stepped up to the priest with a snappy salute and shouted, "Heil Hitler." The priest looked surprised and replied softly and unafraid. "But in this land when we greet each other we say, Grüss Gott!" A painful silence followed, all knowing that a new stranglehold law had been decreed, and children were the first to be brainwashed and indoctrinated into an ideology they did not understand and one which a simple priest had dared to challenge in open defiance.

Josef gathered his family to go home and said under his breath to Emmi. "I am afraid these filthy dogs have invaded our fatherland. I am sick of their hooting and howling along with a bastard like Lochmann. This is all Socialist propaganda. People have sold their soul to the devil. I will not sell my soul to the devil."

The next morning Josef rushed from one customer to another, spending no time on friendly chit-chat. It galled him that he was expected to flip his arm and shout hail Hitler to everyone he met. He refused to do as he was expected to do. So he said nothing. He no longer tipped his hat in civility and ducked his head at every passerby. He noticed that others did the same and nodded wordlessly. He felt trapped in the whirlwind of changes sweeping across the region.

Catholic schools were closed, roadside crosses and shrines were removed and replaced by the hooked cross of the Socialist regime. The Ctholic newspaper, "Volksbote" was outlawed; and replaced by political posters filled with slogans, and propaganda. Reading the Bible and the Lord's Prayer, and the music of Beethoven were outlawed and so was listening to foreign broadcasts.

These were on the list of forbidden subversive materials, under threat of the death penalty by firing squad. Josef knew at last his ominous foreboding had become reality and that one evil had replaced another.

The following Sunday, those parishioners who dared attend Mass shifted nervously in their wooden pews for a long while, waiting for Mass to begin. They looked at each other with faces etched with fear. To their surprise a Czech priest, Anton Rohaczek, stepped up to the pulpit and celebrated the Latin Mass followed by a homily in the Czech language.

A hush fell over the German congregation as they filed out in fearful silence, solemn reflection and awesome foreboding. Father Sowonsky had vanished. No one dared ask what had happened to the young Polish priest or his whereabouts. Beset by a quiet understanding that it would be a futile attempt with serious consequences to ask questions. Rumors spread that Father Sowonsky had been dragged from the church rectory in the middle of the night and arrested. The best a person could do was to remand his memory to a higher authority. Naked fear was etched on sunken and sullen faces.

Josef felt chilled to the bones as the words droned on his inner ear like a jackhammer. The keen sense of danger his father had honed in him for dirty party politics allowed him to quickly recognize the changes in people. Josef was quick to suspect any one of being a party goon, and trusted no one. A bitter gall filled his mouth from the pit of his stomach. With stoic paralysis he refused to flip his arm and shout hail Hitler. The law demanding this greeting sickened him to the core. He kept his head low and his mouth shut

Emmi no longer rushed to the door in joyous anticipation of a welcomed visitor. Instead, she cautiously parted the curtains from behind bolted doors, and cautioned Pepi not to blab to anyone, especially not to cousin Kurt. The boys were inseparable in their constant quest for mischief, and Emmi was afraid that Pepi was too impressionable. "You and Kurt may be one heart and one soul, but keep your thoughts to yourself, and keep quiet about anything you hear your father or I say to each other. What Kurt doesn't know may save our lives."

Emmi tried to maintain her sense of good cheer and family harmony as meticulously as her wrinkle free Battenburg tablecloth. She had been so proud to show off her finest Rosenthal serving plates as she served coffee and Pflaumen Kuchen to friendly kin and neighbors or anyone who might stop by on any given afternoon. One sunny afternoon, Ilse von Reichenberg, came for an unexpected visit. So unexpected was the visit, it knocked the cake right off her plate. Having never considered Karl and Ilse as anything other than highbrowed snobs, Emmi tried to smile knowing her face might look like a frozen grimace. She knew this was not a social call and she did her best to hide her disdain for this woman. Looking mildly pleased to see Emmi standing in front of her, Ilse wasted no time and said. "I just want to introduce my new twin baby girls. Meet Heidi and Ingrid." Emmi smiled at the darling tow heads glad she could avoid the eyes of the woman who had taken every opportunity to make her feel inferior. Emmi crouched down to take a closer look inside the carriage, and said to the little girls. "Grüss Gott!" But Ilse sternly responded to this Christian greeting, with a snappy Heil Hitler salute. Emmi was caught off guard. She looked startled, and snickered to herself at this unaccustomed greeting in her home with nervous trepidation, and tried to compose herself.

Yet in her naiveté, Emmi innocently replied. "And what should we do about the Good God? Just forget him?" Seeing the stern expression on Ilse's face, Emmi knew instantly that she had made a mistake. Her eyes became round as saucers. Her heart throbbed like the foot of a rabbit, caught hypnotically by the eyes of a snake. Ilse began questioned her with a sharp tongue. "How come Pepi is not in the Hitler Youth?"

Emmi was ill prepared for this inquisition, shrugged her shoulders and mumbled a vague excuse. "I'm too busy with my household, my children, and I have to take care of my husband. The church choir is my only recreation." Ilses' steely blue eyes bore into Emmi's. "Even with twins, I have enough time to serve my fatherland." She replied with a stoic expression. "I serve as Hitler's Youth Group leader. Pepi is now old enough to join the Hitler youth. Pepi belongs in the Hitler Youth. We have enrolled Kurt, and it is your responsibility to enroll your son also. You should also convince your husband to become a member of the NSDAP. It will make your life easier as soon as you are one of them." With trembling fingers Emmi poured another cup of coffee, and cloaked her fear in silence. She pressed her lips together to prevent any slip of the tongue, as Ilse repeated the words that would strike terror in Emmi's heart and give her sleepless nights. "You still have not told me, why Pepi is not in the Hitler Youth?"

Emmi looked down on the floor, her eyes filled with tears, as sudden terror pierced her soul. Since the disappearance of the young parish priest, rumors mounted that people were being dragged out of their homes at night, loaded onto army trucks at gunpoint, branded and shamed as traitors. Emmi feared looking at Ilse, afraid of revealing her naked soul, and helplessly shrugged her shoulders again. She weighed her words cautiously knowing at last that every word would be placed on a scale, and her life was in its balance. Meekly she replied.

"Sef and I don't understand the world of politics. We have never paid any attention to it. Our world revolves around each other and our children." She looked beseechingly at her sister-in-law, pleading with her eyes hoping that Ilse would not turn her in to the Gestapo.

Ilse stood up flung her fox cape, with dangly fox feet, over her broad Hun shoulders and left in a huff. Emmi was greatly relieved, albeit for no more than the moment. Her stomach roiled in revulsion as shivers ran down her spine at the prospect of future visits. Shaken to the core, Emmi called for the nanny. Erna, a beautiful dark-haired young woman stood before her with dignity and solemn poise. She kept her hands calmly folded over her white crisply starched apron as Emmi spoke. "Erna, in the future if that tall blond with the fox cape comes knocking on our door you have to tell her 'Missus Staffa' is not home.' I don't want this Peitschen Weib in my home again."

Josef and Emmi were making many changes to their lives to safeguard their family. Josef walked home after dark and quietly slipped inside the house which was kept in pitch darkness, where Emmi sat in the dark, afraid to turn on the light. She flung herself into her husbands' arms, as soon as he entered. It seemed to him, that she had been waiting in the dark for his home-coming all afternoon. He noticed that her face was tear-streaked and her eyes looked tormented.

"Sef, I have the feeling, that the Gestapo sent Ilse here to spy on us. She knew for instance that you have notjoined the Socialist Workers party, and she wants me to prod you to join the NSDAP. She also ordered me to enroll Pepi in the Hitler Youth. What is happening here?" She whispered helplessly.

Josef replied. "These filthy dogs have a stranglehold on our people. I will not succumb to these terror tactics. I will not join these bandits, and our son will not become one of their pawns."

He shook his head resolutely looking on the floor. "I am afraid we have become political pawns in this chess game, Emmi. "Sef, be careful what you say. Don't voice your opinion boldly. I am so scared that someday they'll come and drag you out of the house. I have heard of summary arrests and executions." Just then Josef saw the maid enter the house and he murmured. "Don't get too gabby with the maid either. We don't know if we can trust her. You have to curtail Pepi. I love Kurt like my own sons. But I worry about the influence Kurt has on Pepi."

"Did you know Kurt is in the Hitler Youth? Maybe Gustav was pressured as you are being pressured now." At that moment the maid walked into the room after a quick knock on the glass door and a little curtsy. Josef folded his arms around Emmi and whispered in her ear. "Let's make another baby, a girl this time." Erna blushed at sight of Josef nuzzling Emmi's neck and left with a deep blush across her innocent virgin face.

As soon as Erna was out of earshot, he cautioned. "From now on, we have to be careful of what we say to each other."

Emmi replied as she snuggled close to her husband. "We will have to whisper in bed." Josef took her by the arm and led her up the stairs to their bedroom. "You are right. We cannot trust anyone, not relatives, friends or our nanny. To avoid Ilse, you have to make a big loop around her. That woman is not a Girl Scout leader. She is a Nazi enforcer with a whip." Emmi looked perplexed and grimaced.

"What is a Nazi Whip?" Josef whispered. "She indoctrinates children into Socialist ideology and enforces loyalty to Adolf Hitler even to the level to make them snitch on their parents."

After this day Emmi dismissed the maid before darkness set in. She did not want the maid to know that lights were not to be turned on after dark. Emmi used flashlights and candles to get around the house after dark. The house felt spooky and eerily quiet. Emmi felt relief as long as Josef was around. With his ethereal calm demeanor, he exuded a balm for her frazzled nerves. In the past, Josef's staunch resistance against the changes to their culture and traditional values, had restored Emmi's confidence that all would be well in the end. As long as Josef lay beside her in bed and they could whisper in the dark, she felt safe in his arms. Yet, even as he held her, she could feel his fears and tremors, as he talked, she heard the quiver in his voice, and realized that Josef was just as scared as she was knowing something ominous had happened in this little village and nobody knew why or how it all changed so suddenly.

Emmi felt an increasing anxiety over the changes that seemed to happen at rapid fire speed. Josef was leaving in the wee hours of the morning before breakfast and returned home after dark. When he had to ride out of town, he took the back trails he knew so well since childhood on his motorbike to dodge the devil he did not know, but knew that he was out to get him. The people of this village had run up against an insurmountable evil that dripped like ether into the veins of simple folks. Josef whispered reassuringly as best he could, knowing his wife was scared to death. "We just have to keep our eyes and ears open. I never thought, Mastig would be of any ones' interest. For some reason we have lost our anonymity. I think that Mastig was put on the map when my father sold the property to Adolf Mandl." Josef said and Emmi questioned. "Why did the Mandl factory put Mastig on the map?" Josef whispered. "Because it is huge, and Mandl put a rail line in that put Mastig on the official industrial map.

I have seen a strange woman going into my mother's house. My mother does not welcome strangers. I wonder what this mystery is all about?" Emmi looked puzzled as Josef shook his head.

"Maybe it's best if we do not know everything." Josef had seen a strange woman go inside the house one night and then he saw Koczian leave with her in his mothers' Dusenberg. He never told Emmi of the incident because he did not want to give Emmi more cause for concern. The less she knows the better. "How do we know whom we can trust?" Emmi muttered suddenly and Josef snapped angrily without a moment's hesitation. "No body!" Emmi looked aghast as treachery seemed to find its way to their door with every knock. Ever since the altercation and subsequent disappearance of the parish priest, a sick pallor hung over Gernerts' Garden Café, where only a few weeks ago families gathered in joyful abandon of daily concerns. The Café had lost its charm since that dreadful day, when the entire village had fallen under a cloak of dread. It swirled unseen like a dark cloud, from the day Josef was accosted amidst a bunch of strangers, who were wearing jackboots and armbands with swastikas.

Josef's sister Marie could identify the strange loners in civilian clothes, who wordlessly sat in the corners of her cozy cafe with a single glass of beer for hours. She knew they were not local people. She guessed that they might be Gestapo. She surmised that they frequented her cozy inn not only because she served the best dumplings and sauerbraten in the area. They were here to keep a watchful eye on the locals, which they referred to as riff-raff. She saw the men jotting something down on a notepad as they kept a sharp eye out on every man, woman and child.

Then there were the other strangers who looked a lot like Sherlock Holmes in their wrinkled trench coats, floppy hats, and pipes dangling out of the corner of their mouths, looking bored, or pretending to read a newspaper or looking around at the beautiful landscape and being amused by jolly good folksiness.

Kurt was a broadly smiling, blond, curly-haired youngster, who towered above the rest of his peers with such confidence, as he helped Marie serve bowls of steaming soups, platters piled high with sausages and sauerkraut and mugs of beer to hungry patrons. The young lad caught every one's immediate attention. His bold curiosity and daring exploits had not gone unnoticed by these silent men. He was the kind of lad who would give parents sleepless nights and his mother prematurely grey hair.

Marie had warned Kurt not to ask too many questions, and not to talk to these men like a child that knows-it-all around these strangers, some of whom spoke languages nobody could understand. But that only added to their mystique. Marie could hear that they did not speak any Slavic languages, which would have been recognized by the locals for their familiar sound. But for some reason Kurt understood what they were saying. Endowed with worldly wisdom, he eagerly shared his knowledge and pointed out the silent observers to an open mouthed Pepi. "Those are Brits."

The local Czechs did not come to this pub. Kurt was proud that he could converse with these Gentlemen. He also understood an order for a round of beer in various Slavic languages. He could clearly identify the Poles, the Russians and Hungarians.

He nudged Pepi and whispered. "See, these guys, they never say much, but when they do, they speak schoolbook-German. They pay good tips, though. I know they are British."

He squinted with one eye. "I bet they are spies. But why are they here?"

Pepi looked quizzical at his cousin. "What are spies looking for in this crows' nest?"

"Look at these men! It looks like they are keeping an eye on each other, but they never talk to each other. I know one thing, they did not come here for pilsner beer," Kurt quipped, looking puzzled.

"I'll find out! I wonder what both groups find so interesting in our crows' nest about each other?" By the time they knew the truth, it was too late. On September 1, 1939 a German cruiser on a "courtesy" visit to a Polish peninsula began shelling a military depot. Simultaneously, artillery fire crashed along the German Polish border, followed by a massive surge of the German Army. Agents had been swarming like thick and black locusts, moving north from Austria like thunder clouds from the distant horizon right above unsuspecting heads into the Sudetenland.

Hitler's easy conquests of Austria and Czechoslovakia, was seen by him as nothing more than a weekend excursion, executed by him with precision, which had emboldened him to trust his self-reliant intuition. He predicted that the British and the French would leave the Poles in a lurch as they had Austria and Czechoslovakia. He wasted no time to broadcast his case against Poland. In the streets of Germany hung a deathly pallor, people had not forgotten the horror of the last war, which had solved no nationalistic problems for them. They expected another war to make life worse just as Britain and France handed in their ultimatum to the German government, which called for war unless German troops were withdrawn from Poland by noon.

Fifteen minutes later, Britain declared war on Germany and France followed. That first September morning, trucks pulled up in front of the Staffa villa. Uniformed men of the SS jumped out, and ordered Josef to hand over the keys to his handsome new fleet of trucks to other uniformed drivers. Josef learned later that the confiscated trucks were used in the invasion of France. For his refusal to join the Nazi Party, Gauleiter Ernst Lochmann handed Josef a notice of a fine for 1000 Reich Marks.

A caravan of trucks moved in front of his mother's house ordering the Staffa matriarch, who long ago had worked as a maid for the Mandl family to produce her Czech citizenship papers. She gesticulated wildly and kept shaking her head as pictures were held under her nose. From his office window, next door to his mother's house, Josef could see the duress his mother was suffering and rushed over to see what the commotion was all about. Pictures of the Mandl family were passed around. Josef noticed that his mother's face had become ashen. It was the picture of the woman he had seen slipping in and out of his mother's house a few times.

Anna clasped her mouth in horror. She quickly composed herself and gave the picture back with a shrug. "I don't know these people." She insisted muttering as she turned her back on the men. She tried to go back inside her house to busy herself around the stove. In relentless pursuit the Gestapo followed her into the house.

"We think you do!" The man insisted. "You worked for them over thirty years ago. We don't believe you. You must tell us where they are."

Anna shook her head. "They were fine Jewish people, who did not associate with peasants like us." Josef knew his mother was in trouble and he took the pictures to draw attention away from her to scan them one by one. "I think this is the Mandl family." Josef shrugged his shoulders. "You won't find them here. They have left long ago for America." The man spun around and ogled Josef curiously. "Who gave you this information?"

Josef shrugged his shoulders. "Rumors…all we know about these people are rumors. The Mandl family never associated with us. They did not bother us and we never bothered them. They were an enigma in this community."

The soldiers appeared to prepare for departure, and Josef looked relieved. He hoped the ceaseless searches for "Enemies of the state," as Hitler called them would end and not put anyone in needless jeopardy. Josef watched the trucks leave knowing he would have to find a way to reenforce a rumor. He walked down to Gernerts' Garden Café and sat down underneath the rose trellis in the lush green garden. He plopped down in a lawn chair and let the sun bathe his face. Kurt came running when he saw his uncle Pepi and brought him a beer. Josef pulled out photos from his breast pocket and showed them to Kurt, who was always eager to know everything. Josef showed him a picture of Oma when she was known as Anna Kudronovsky, a young Czech or Polish girl who worked as a scullery maid for the Mandl family in the only Jewish household.

"This was Oma Staffa as a young girl. She is actually your step-grandmother. But she treats all children like a good grandma." Kurt nodded and replied. "Oma is the Best. She sprinkles sugar or shaved chocolate on a piece of buttered bread and a piece of bread tastes just like a slice of cake."

"A long time ago, Oma as a young girl worked for these people." He showed Kurt a picture of an attractive dark skinned and raven-haired couple, and a young boy.

"They went to America." Josef said it with a low voice and so nonchalant the 8-year olds' curiosity was peaked even more. To hear he had to lean in and asked impressive questions.

"Ah, jah. America, I want to go there someday."

A few days later a caravan of army vehicles stopped in front of the Gernert Garden Café, the officer flipped his arm up and shouted to passersby. "Heil Hitler!" He sauntered up the steps and slipped inside. Soldiers with their weapons drawn were conducting a door-to door search, starting inside the Garden Café.

They flashed pictures of a family, but at every table the people shook their heads.

The House My Father Built

Gustav Gernert was in the kitchen with flour up to his elbow, he looked astonished and annoyed at the man in a midnight blue uniform, who was waving a picture in his face. "Have you seen these people?" Gustav shook his head, and pushed his belly past the uniformed man. "By the order of the Reich, you may not provide refuge to these people nor feed them. You are hereby commissioned to cook for the engineers of the former Mandl factory. You can thank the Führer that you'll be spending the war time in service of your country and fry Bratwurst and Wiener Schnitzel. Heil Hitler!"

Gustav waved off the greeting like a pesky gnat, as he lifted a pot of boiling water from the stove and grunted to himself. "Get out of here before I spill noodle water all over you. I cook, that's all I do. I don't care who eats my food." Kurt walked up to the soldier and looked at the pictures and blurted out his latest find. "These people have gone to America."

Later that night, Kurt watched the frenzied activity in the Mandl compound where bright flood lights lit up the entire compound, as if it were daylight. During the midnight hours German soldiers dropped a 10-foot high fence around the Mandl villa, the factory and the "Bretterbuden" that had housed the Russian and Polish factory workers.

The next morning, much to their surprise, the men in trench coats and floppy hats, found themselves imprisoned like fish in a net. Uniforms were handed over the fence—prisoner of war uniforms. Gustav Gernert was ordered to cook simple meals for the foreign prisoners. No doubt his soups were the best prepared by his expert hand. Gustav would only serve the best, without regard to status, rich or poor, villager or prisoner of war, it made no difference to him. Gustav was a busy chef, because Marie had just announced that she was pregnant with their third child and Gustav would have to delegate more chores to little Margit and Kurt.

He assigned them the duty to deliver canisters of oatmeal, chicken, split pea or lentil soups for lunch and dinner every day to feed the forty-seven gents imprisoned behind the fence of the Mandl factory yard.

While Ernst Lochmann ordered Gustav and Marie to prepare meals for the engineers of the Mandl factory such delectable meals as Schnitzel and Sauerbraten with dumplings and red cabbage. From his bedroom window Kurt had noticed that the Mandl villa and factory was under heavy guard day and night. The compound was well lit by day and by night, and swarming with German Reich Army vehicles.

Curiosity always got the better of Kurt. He had to know what was going on and discovered a great business opportunity for himself. Every morning he counted out additional items for the forty-seven imprisoned gents before he delivered the canisters of oatmeal or soups. In between these tin canisters he stashed eggs, bacon, sausage, cheese and butters. He knew how to work up a barter deal for cigarettes. These men appreciated the smuggled goods and knew what rewards the boy was looking for.

Undaunted by the grey uniformed soldiers surrounding the compound, Kurt chatted amicably with the men and quickly endeared himself to those behind the fence. Margit's friendly innocence played into Kurt's hands. Her lively chatter distracted the guards' attention, while Kurt doled out the extra goodies he had stashed between the canisters. Then he sauntered over to the guards at the gate of the Mandl villa. The guard looked bored as Kurt came up behind him and inquired unabashed.

"So what brings you here? Why do you have to guard this place, the people who lived here, went to America long ago." The guard looked up. "Who?" He queried.

"You know the people, who lived here!" Kurt smiled broadly. "How do you know that?" The guard asked just as Margit approached the fence. I'm Kurt, I know everything and everybody here. This is my sister, she knows nothing." The guard looked the lad up and down, and became visibly annoyed as he felt compelled to listen to the constant chatter of this brazen know-it-all. He had to concentrate on his duties and these kids distracted him from doing his job.

"You brazen brat, get out of here, before I fill your belly with shrapnel, and take your sister with you. Now scedaddle."

The guard pushed the obnoxious children back from the fence at rifle point. Margit fled like a frightened little bird, her long braids flapped behind her, but Kurt did not flinch. He only chuckled when he saw Margit run. Kurt walked off slowly unafraid, whistling through his teeth some unknown tune. "By the light of the silvery moon…I'll see you soon." He ran his sleeve up against the fence to allow it to snag a few threads, then he sauntered nonchalantly out of view.

Every night and every day trains rolled into the tiny train station in Mastig at a steady stream and under heavy guard. After sundown Kurt crept along the fence to his designated post along the Mandl factory yard. He noticed the frenzied, ceaseless activities and it made him quake with excitement. 'I'll have to get Pepi and show him what I have discovered."

He crept back to the Villa Staffa, and whistled the familiar signal for Pepi to come out. Pepi was quick to respond and slipped unnoticed out the door. The two boys crept along the fence to the Mandl factory yard, were enormous cylinder-shaped equipment was being transported, covered by huge tarpaulins, surrounded by heavily armed soldiers who were standing guard all around.

Pepi shuddered for fright at the sight and asked. "What are these huge cylinders for?"

Kurt whispered. "V-2 rockets!" He was filled with a great pride in his feeling of superiority, knowing he was the smarter of the two. "I'm going to try and get a closer look. You stay here. Don't let anyone see you." He admonished his timid cousin and crept along the fence to the same spot, where he had left a swatch of cloth.

Nestled between thick tufts of tall grass, Kurt found chocolates and cigarettes, and crept back to where Pepi was waiting. He broke off a piece of chocolate. He was about to extract a cigarette from inside the cigarette pack, when he found a note tucked inside the small carton. He held the piece of paper toward the flood lights of the factory yard until he could faintly make out the scratched message. "One of our gentlemen has died." Kurt felt sad and held his head in deep thought. "Now what should we do?"

"I know that if the burial is left to these guards, they will bury him like a dog in the factory yard. We cannot let that happen." Kurt needed to think this over. In this tiny hamlet where everybody is laid to rest with great fanfare, he needed to do something.

Everyday Pepi tagged along with Kurt to find new adventure. But this conundrum was too much for him. He decided to heed his mothers' stern warnings not to get involved with Kurt's daring mischiefs. Pepi had no clue what to do about a dead Brit and thought it best to hightail it home. He was plagued with curiosity and a guilty conscience for disobeying his mother in the first place, knowing that in her eyes Kurt was simply too bold to understand the gravitas of their new life under the vice of swastika dominance and oppression but also for leaving Kurt to deal with a problem alone.

New laws and ordinances seemed to change constantly, and extreme caution was advised as a necessity for survival. The bold and daring adventure-spirit of his cousin created such excitement to make it impossible for Pepi to stay home and not tag along with him. For an impressionable seven-year-old his cousin Kurt was the most exciting person in contrast to his strictly regulated life in his stoic mother's house.

As patrons enjoyed their morning brew and breakfast Kurt jumped on a chair in his parents' restaurant. "Attention, every one! Listen, I have an announcement to make!" The villagers stopped sipping their beer, turned around with bemusement, wondering what Kurt had up his sleeve now. "One of our gentlemen guests has died. I think it will be up to the people of Mastig to give this man a proper Christian burial, one befitting every human being even if he is a British gent."

The bar patrons wiped the beer froth from their faces and clapped as they followed Kurt to the Mandl compound to claim the body of an unknown patron whose name was not known. He was just a British gent number 47. Kurt marched ahead of the villagers straight up to confront a befuddled guard. "We are here to claim the body of one of the men who has died behind these fences so he can be buried at St. Anna's cemetery." The silent villagers nodded agreement. The sentry went inside the fenced compound and checked the man's pulse to ascertain, he was actually dead. The guard was relieved that he did not have to dig his grave, and loaded the dead man on a cart and covered him with a blanket.

Kurt with the help of villagers pulled the cart with the corpse to the Staffa lumber yard. "Uncle Sef, I need a wooden coffin for a man so we can give him a proper burial in Saint Anna's cemetery." The next day nobody was surprised to see Ernst Lochmann strutting boldly into Gernerts' Restaurant. He slapped a glove into his palm as he confronted Kurt's father.

"You better reign in your son. Your boy has to stop talking to foreigners. Let this be a warning to you and your wife. You better put your son on a short leash!"

Gustav retorted angrily. "My son is not a dog. I won't put my son on a leash."

Wagging a finger in Gustav's face, Lochmann replied. "I can shut down your kitchen." As soon as Lochmann slammed the door shut behind him Gustav pulled his son to the side and wagged a finger in his face. "Kurt, you are getting yourself in trouble as well as our entire family. Stay away from these foreigners, I told you not to say a word to them."

Gustav knew all too well that threats never intimidated Kurt, but merely aroused more curiosity and resistance to authority. Now Kurt had to deliver soups and goodies for only forty-six gents. But first he had to bury number 47. Kurt went from door to door and rustled the villagers together to pray for his soul and pay their last respect to one of the silent visitors from his fathers' pub.

Kurt called out six strong farmhands to carry the simple wooden box, which his uncle had hammered together in the night from the chapel to his final resting place. He instructed a brass band from his father's pub, to lead the funeral march to the gravesite. The black cloaked villagers followed a brass band playing songs befitting a fallen comrade, as the coffin of an unknown gent only known as number 47 was carried to his final resting place in Saint Annas' cemetery. Kurt led the procession swinging a baton and as he passed the Villa Staffa he saw Pepi sitting on a pedestal and called out to his cousin. "I just love a parade."

The mourners prayed in the solemn procession until the gent was buried near the tomb of Kurt's grandfather with full honor and dignity accorded every human being.

A few days after the funeral, the twenty-nine-year-old Josef received the order to report for military duty while his brothers Karl and Alfred were rewarded for their loyalty to the Socialist party.

Josef's brothers were allowed to stay home to take care of the local Socialist Workers Party and administrators of the Josef Staffa enterprises. Josef read the notice and moaned.

"I was born between two chairs and now I have to exchange the brown Czech military uniform for the grey rag of a German conscript." His refusal to join the Nazi Party earned him the draft into Hitlers Army. He was the first man in the village to be picked up for military service.

"No matter which way I want to move, I am doomed by accident of my birth between my German and my Czech heritage. Now I feel like an invader within my own home."

Thrust from one political camp to another, Josef felt no allegiance toward any nationalistic interests, only anger for the disruption in his daily life. His allegiance belonged to his wife and children, his home and the land he loved. He whispered to his wife. "A soldier is trained to kill. How can I be a soldier? I can't even shoot a rabbit. I can't stand the sight of a deer head hanging on the walls in Gustavs' Gasthaus. I look into their vacant eyes, and think of how the animal must have enjoyed running through the forest, enjoying his freedom. How can I shoot a man, who like me, just wants to be home with his wife and children?"

Josef was sure of only one fact, that one evil had replaced another." His older brothers Emil and Franz, had lost their lives fighting partisans in Greece. Josef was driven north into Poland, as the turbulence of the region spiked ever higher.

Emmi was surprised to see her mother Franziska at her doorstep seeking the comfort and safety within her family harmony. She spent time helping with the children and the harvest. Emmi was glad to have her mother around while Josef was away for military duty. She was relieved to know that the mother had agreed to help the nanny care for little Otti.

Pepi was capable of caring for himself. Marie reassured Emmi that in case of an emergency she was available to take charge. Emmi surmised, that the reason for her mother's generous offer to care for the children was because Josef would not be around for some time to come. Emmi missed her husband and felt free to board the train and follow Josef's deployment to Poland where she planned to spend precious moments with Josef for a few weeks.

Josef was overjoyed to have Emmi stay near his army barrack and thought himself lucky when a Polish woman offered him a room to rent for his wife's visit. Emmi had planned to stay for a two-week visit, as long as there was a clean sheet on a bed and a tub to bathe in.

Josef paid the rent in advance with Zlotys and gave the woman extra bread and butter, sausage, milk and eggs for breakfast. Emmi arrived in the evening and deposited her suitcase in the assigned bedroom. She freshened up and met Josef in front of the house for an evening stroll. They dined, and danced until midnight, then Josef brought her back to her room before his curfew.

Emmi reached up to plant a good night kiss as she slowly opened the door and said lightheartedly. "All good things must come to an end…but you don't have to be back at the barrack until 1 a.m. Why don't you linger a little longer?" With a sensuous smirk she opened the door wider until the light from the hallway fell into the bedroom, she stepped inside and screamed.

"Ah what is that? No! There is a man in my bed!" Emmi screamed hysterically, and gesticulated at sight of the greasy tousled head tossing between the blanket and the sheets.

"There is a man in my bed. Who is that? Get him out of here." Josef ran to the bedroom of the landlady, and pounded on her door. The woman was clad in a tattered robe, shuffled wearily from her bedroom to see what the commotion was all about. Emmi pointed into the room.

"There is a man in my bed? Who is that?"

The old woman waved off Emmis' frantic lamentations. "Oh, that! He is my son. You can lie down beside him. He won't bother you." Emmi shrieked in horror and backed out of the room. "That, I can't do! I can't sleep with a strange man in my bed!" Well after midnight Emmi and Josef walked the streets of Krakow in search of another room. They knocked on every house with a sign "Rooms to Rent." There were no vacancies. They walked over to the army barrack to see if fellow soldiers had any suggestions. They did. Josef's buddies hoisted Emmi to the second-floor window with ropes, where they draped blankets around Josef's bunk to give the young couple a little privacy.

To her surprise, her husband's buddies stashed food and a bottle of champagne into the cubicle. Emmi was feverishly excited but also afraid of being discovered by the night watchman or the commandant. Despite her jittering fears nothing would deter her from enjoying the time she had in the arms of her beloved husband.

The night watchman was making the rounds, as she lay there with baited breath. She saw him peer through a slit in the blanket. Their eyes met as Emmi felt the goose bumps rise on her arms and chills run down her spine, wondering what might happen to her. The watchmen never said a word, just turned on his heels and left.

In the morning Josef's buddies lowered Emmi back down to street level. She spent the days exploring the dark streets of Krakow while Josef was assigned to guard a bridge. When his duty ended in the evening Emmi returned, to be hoisted up into the barrack and waited for Josef. She realized that her husbands' buddies would not rat her out. She didn't have to hide nor be scuttled down with ropes every day. On rainy days, she waited in the barrack until Josef was done with sentry duty at a bridge. She never got tired of this game of duck and cover, as long as she could spend the evenings in Josef's arms.

Emmi trekked from one barrack to another within earshot of screeching Stuka bombers and terrifying masses of tanks and Polish cavalry with lances, wreaking havoc across the Polish landscape, who were no match for German military might. Daytime hours she spent watching the events in the streets below, and listened in horror to screeching Stuka bombers overhead. From a distance she saw a caravan of black open limousines.

Emmi recognized the man standing up in one of the cars from the propaganda posters hanging on every lamp post and house facade. Now she saw him with his tautly outstretched arm and a chill ran down her spine when she saw Adolf Hitler riding by to the front lines with bombastic pronouncements. Emmi shuddered when she heard him proclaim. "A leader must share his people's deprivations, rank and file officers must share the simple diets with a conscript and not allow themselves special privileges."

Not even Hitler's family members were allowed special privileges. In a show of benevolence toward his chosen people, Hitler's adjutants tossed out cigarettes to the front-line soldiers cheerfully as Hitler chatted amicably with them. But when the first trainload of wounded soldiers arrived, Hitler refused to speak to them. Hitler explained his action in a broadcast that the sight of suffering was intolerable for him to bear. Emmi looked astonished. "He can't bear the sight of suffering of which he is the chief architect."

Josef shrugged his shoulders. "A wounded soldier is of no use to Hitler any longer. To Hitler we are all just cannon fodder." He explained. "We are the countless pawns in this scheme. Nobody pities pawns."

The turbulent days Emmi had spent with her husband in and around Krakow gave her a long-legged souvenir with which she could remember the two weeks frolicking around Krakow, in the birth of a fourth son, the following May. Josef was allowed to come home on furlough to welcome his new son, Rudi. Josef sighed in wonder, as he beheld the peculiar looking, long- legged boy who with long spiked black hair filled Josef with serious misgivings.

"Couldn't you have arranged for a little girl with little blond curls, just once, as a little homecoming present?" Emmi threw her arms around his neck and chuckled. "Well, those arrangements are made in heaven!" While Pepi and Otto glowed with good health endowed with blond, blue-eyed good looks, the boy Emmi named Rudi in honor of her favorite brother, was a frail child with spindly arms and legs, whose head was covered with a shock of black hair that stood straight up like quills. Josef laughed when he saw the baby.

"He looks like a hedgehog". Thus, the brothers saw it befitting to nickname the baby "Hedgehog." Emmi moaned at sight of her baby boy. "No wonder he looks as he does. The screeching Stuka bombers made his hair stand up on end in my womb. It made my hair stand up from morning to night. What should I do with that hair? I tried slicking it down with a greasy pomade, but the hair just springs up like quills. He can't wear a hairnet." Josef chuckled. "What can I say? I think you have a real problem there! If I were you I'd shave that stuff off. This is not hair. These are bristles for a brush or a broom. That's it, a brush!"

Emmi and Josef laughed out loud at sight of their peculiar looking son, whose eyes became round as saucers, and his lips formed a constant pout. Emmi trimmed the broom into a brush, to spare her child the threat of constant teasing. She proudly strolled her new baby boy through the center of the village for all to see the baby peering out over the rim of his baby buggy, neighbors sucked in the air and smiled politely.

Thus Rudi became the first child in Mastig to make a fashion statement with a stylish brush cut. Josef remained unconvinced that such an awkward child would ever amount to much, and chuckled with good humor when his son wobbled as he tried to stand and his long fingers could not hold his toys. "How will he ever be able to stand on these thin legs, they are too thin and too long.

Look at his fingers, they are too long. How can he ever hold tools when everything he touches falls to the floor. How can such a clumsy child ever learn a trade? He will never be able to hold a hammer? I think he will break the hammer."

He laughed and Emmi chimed in the silliness of the moment. However, generous her sense of humor Emmi would not tolerate any criticism of little Rudi, even if voiced in jest. "You can't expect all your sons to take after you and become engineers. Only Pepi has your talent for precision craftsmanship. Just like you he is precise in everything he does. Otti is a sweet sensitive child, he likes music and delicate creatures, like birds and bunnies and pigeons. He is sensitive and takes after me."

A year after the sweeping annihilation of Poland Josef and Emmi listened to radio broadcasts in which Adolf Hitler proclaimed that he was prepared to rid the world of the breeding ground of Bolshevism, the Jewish people, who posed a constant threat to their lives and to the German empire in the East. He announced that the Operation Barbarossa would deliver a grateful world from the greatest of all evils, Communism. The world held its breath at Hitlers' proclamations as the lives of simple people and peaceful days of family bliss were short-lived in exchange for jaunty diatribes blared over the airwaves. "People of Germany the hour has come. I have laid the fate of the German Reich into the hands of our soldiers." Hitler boastfully predicted a Russian collapse within three months, the likes the world had never seen before."

Josef came home for one more short furlough. It was to be a last Christmas measured in austerity and overshadowed by fear. The first family casualties had brought home the terror of war in simple announcements as when the family learned Josef's older brothers Emil and Franz had been killed in Solonika during a sweeping incursion that was to assist the Italians in their conquests of Greece and Albania. As the human losses and suffering struck blow after blow at German invincibility into the heart of families, as they listened to pompous broadcasts at Hitler rages of diatribes against the enemies of the German people; who, if not brave enough to fight for their own existence to the finish, should cease to exist themselves.

Such banter deeply alarmed Emmi and she cried. "Who is my enemy? I don't quarrel with anyone except Ilse, I avoid her like the black plague. I don't want to be any braver than that." She lamented to Josef.

"If you fall at the Russian front, I don't want to live any longer, either." She hastily sewed a medallion of Saint Anthony of Padua into the lining of his heavy field coat. She clung to him and the memory of his last smile and didn't want to let go. An army truck stopped in front of their house. Her heart was pounding heavily while she held on to his arm until Josef was forced to leave her embrace. He was again the first man of the village who was picked up and sent to the embattled Russian front, along with three million of his German comrades. Emmi joined a prayer group organized by Franziska Linhart who invited women of the village to pray the rosary with her for the welfare of their husbands, sons and neighbors. Emmi poured out her worries in letters sent daily, venting her hope to keep Josef's spirits alive.

She wrote stories of the home front and her elusive dreams of family harmony. She tried to maintain a decorum of normalcy for her boys, and garnered new energies whenever she spied a letter from Josef in the mailman's pouch. Only then could she sigh with relief but only for a moment. The next day, she spent again every waking moment anxiously waiting for a sign of life. Days of waiting became longer and days turned into weeks and weeks turned into months. She waited for precious letters addressed to her in his beautiful calligraphic script.

Emmi wrung her hands in despair, before she wrote him. He had left behind a souvenir again, and urgently begged him to come home safe and sound.

"Dearest Josef, I'll never forgive you if you don't come back to me. I am pregnant again. There is no place to go, no place to hide. I feel like a steamroller is heading our way, and I can't escape our fate. The Vice of evil is closing in on us all around. Mastig has become a beleaguered camp and so threatening with army vehicles rumbling through day and night. I dare not venture out any more without trembling in fear. I don't feel even faintly secure within our four walls. Walls seem to have ears. One terrifying story follows another. To whom do I whisper my sorrowful stories in bed? For even the slightest infractions, people are being rounded up and without a court hearing, are summarily executed. One man was caught stealing a loaf of bread from a Jewish baker. Then the thief was executed for stealing a loaf of bread from a Jew. I am just as afraid of the stranger in the streets as I am of our relatives in my home. I don't know whom I can trust. Karl and Alfred came in and out of our house as if it is their own. From our bedroom window I can see Ilse hanging the picture of Adolf Hitler outside her window and balcony. Your mother became so incensed. She ran into Karl's house, ripped the picture off the balcony, tore it into a million pieces and screamed 'Because of this filthy dog, I have already lost two sons in this war, and maybe I will lose Pepi too." She flung the pieces into the air and they were carried away by the wind. There is no need to turn on the radio, since the music of Beethoven has been declared subversive and I can't stand the blaring propaganda. It frays my tender nerves. Life has become unbearable, just come home so life can be worth living again. Love eternal-E"

Emmi had made it a habit to keep curtains drawn tight, louvers closed, and windows shuttered, following the terror that did not seem to end. Emmi was panic stricken upon hearing of the assassination of the Reich protector, Reinhard Heydrich, whose assassins and five accomplices were trapped in a church in Prague, and executed along with thirteen hundred Czech male inhabitants of the village of Lidice, and Lidice was razed from the face of the earth.

To Emmi's surprise one thing had changed for the better, her relationship with her mother and Josef's mother, which had always been a tense relationship for her.

Emmi was astonished when Anna K came to the house almost every day for a friendly visit. Oma Staffa simply stated that she enjoyed watching the children at play. Emmi knew better, she knew her mother-in-law was just as anxious for signs of life from her beloved Pepiczek as she was. The first question her mother-in-law asked upon entering the house. "Have you received word from Pepi?"

Oma Staffa as everyone called the old matriarch was a big puzzle. Her demeanor had changed from a once shy, demure and pious Czech girl to that of a feisty old lady, whom Emmi had once feared and avoided at all costs. In her deepest fears Oma Staffa kept busy and found relief in the company of her grandchildren.

Since her husbands' murder, the stoic old woman dressed in the same black outfit every day even in the summer. The only changes to her dress were the removable stiffly starched white lace collars. Every day she plopped herself on a kitchen chair and made herself at home, canning fruits and vegetables which were her sons favorite like cherries and plums in season. She snipped beans, peeled potatoes, or julienned cabbage heads to fill wooden vats for sauerkraut. She chatted amicably as if she and Emmi had always been the best confidantes. Each sought comfort in the others' company.

From the day the Mandl factory had been taken-over by the Reichs Army, the compound had changed into a war production facility. A steady feverish activity day and night surrounded the factory and in the adjacent Mandl villa, smartly dressed SS officers marched in and out daily, cloaked in darkest secrecy. Public warning signs appeared in rapid succession on fenceposts, gates and obelisk pillars to keep people informed. Posters warned of deadly punishment to disobedience of the new rules. UNBEFUGTER ZUTRITT STRENGSTENS VERBOTEN UNTER TODESSTRAFE. Such threatening words alone jarred the people into blind obedience. Nobody dared question these warning notices against trespassing, nor did anyone ask what was going on inside these factory buildings who only a few years ago had manufactured colorful textiles. It was best not to ask, better yet, not to want to know anything.

In her naivete' Emmi often spoke her mind without thinking of consequences, her mother-in-law had once worked as a maid in the old Mandl villa, she was not afraid to ask her. "Do you know what happened to the Mandl family who used to live in the Mandl Villa?" Anna whispered in her raspy Czech dialect filled with a mixture of local dialects and rolled consonants and very few vowels so that the words sounded like gibberish. Nobody but Emmi could understand her. "I heard that the old Mandl family has fled to Vienna, from where the son went to live in America." Emmi felt the heat in the kitchen and it was not coming out of the oven. "The Mandl brothers smelled trouble after Hitlers' annexation of Austria, and sent their son to live in America. I was told that the old couple died in Vienna."

For an unknown reason Emmi asked. "Did they die a natural death?" Anna K. shrugged her shoulder and shook her head ambivalently. After a long pause, she added. "I hope so." Emmi murmured. "I think of them although I have never met them, I wonder what happened to them, because of their stately villa I can't believe that anybody would voluntarily leave an estate and opulent wealth behind."

Nine-year-old Pepi was always glad when Oma came for a visit, because it gave him a chance to slip away from under his mother's watchful eyes. He listened to the women's hushed voices for a while, the lower they whispered the more his ears perked up. He could barely understand the Czech language and got bored trying to figure out what was being said.

He waited until he was sure the women would be absorbed in lamentations on the ways of the world for a long while. Then he took the chance to slip silently out the door. Emmis' rounded belly interfered with the tight grip Pepi needed.

The boy was too eager to roam through the area, to explore it footloose and fancy free from any motherly constraints. He met up with cousin Kurt down the road, around the bend and out of view whenever an opportunity arose after school. The two boys crouched low against garden hedges and watched everyday with eyes wide open as huge cylinder-shaped tubes were being transported from the former Mandl factory to a cavern in the mountains.

For an instant, the heavy tarp slid off the huge objects that looked like hollow tubes, and allowed the awed boys a glimpse of a V-2 rocket in transport to a testing site in these mountain caverns. The boys pressed their lean bodies into the shadows of rocky crevices and watched the explosive force of Germany's newest wonder weapon. Kurt explained to an excited 9-year old about the intriguing ways of the world they lived in.

"I didn't think so many of our British guests were tourists, when they swarmed into our crows' nest for Pilsner brew on tap. I bet Hitler wanted the tea sippers to find these contraptions. He probably wanted them to quake in their boots?" Pepi looked wide-eyed and replied. "I am shaking in mine."

Emmi was blissfully unaware of the boy's follies and foibles. Had she known that these daring lads were sneaking around the neighborhood, exploring caves and tunnels, and had discovered the munitions depots built into the mountains and the V2 rocket sites, she would have died of a heart attack. She looked out the dining room window, noticing with a start once again the same disheveled young man leaning against the corner trestle of their fence. He ducked his head back behind the pillar, when he saw that she had spotted him. She had the distinct impression that he carried a pistol in his pocket by his side, and shuttered the windows quickly from the inside.

She was heavy with child and the daily trek to the post office was becoming a chore.

But in the hope of receiving word from Josef, she painfully pushed her bulging belly ahead. Oma Staffa invited Emmi and Marie to ride along with her to Arnau. Pavel Koczian drove them to the shopping district where Oma had to take care of some business. Pavel dropped the women off at the corner near the village square right by the monument of the two Giants. Buckets were hanging at the famous fountain beneath four water spouts for every one's convenient use.

The women spotted a caravan of army trucks and gasped at the sight of trucks covered with heavy tarps. Skeletal men peered out from under the tarp covers. The women stopped dead in their tracks and looked quizzically at each other. The truck was surrounded by soldiers with drawn weapons to bar onlookers from approaching. The truck had stopped for refueling. The women looked horror struck as they focused on the gaunt looking men with ashen grey complexions. They had never seen such misery shrouded in skin and bones.

Emmi threw her hands over her mouth in disbelief, her jaw dropped in horror as she gasped. "Jessesmarren! My God this cannot end well. Jessesmarren." Emmi mumbled barely audible the religious exclamation which had recently been outlawed. Emmi could not calm herself and whispered it over and over. She was shaken to the core. Her face masked her inner terror revulsion and fear of what horror was yet to come. Tears pressed in her eye sockets and blurred her vision. She pressed a handkerchief over her mouth to keep from crying. Her chest felt heavy with pity as she saw the outstretched arms and heard cries for water.

Not thinking of consequences, Emmi mustered all her strength her bulging belly allowed, hoisted a bucket into the village well, and pumped the lever until the bucket was full of fresh mountain water.

The other women followed suit and dragged the heavy buckets a few steps at a time toward the truck, across the cobblestoned square. Within a few feet of the truck a guard blocker their path with rifle butts pressed against the women's bellies and pushed them back. Emmi looked beseechingly into steely eyes. "It's just water. Nothing but water." Emmi pleaded as the other women milled around to see what was happening. Emmi felt the rifle butt press ever harder against her and the tears welled up in her eyes. She sat the bucket down with a heavy sigh and looked around at the other women. She felt a courage building in her when she saw more and more women doing the same. Emmi turned to the women. "Maybe together we can give them water. They can't chase us all away."

The women pumped water, one after another, and like a bucket brigade, approached the trucks. Suddenly they were surrounded by several guards and Emmi whispered. "Lord, have mercy." Shots rang out and the women screamed hysterically. More salvos were fired into the pavement before their feet, propelling the women to drop their buckets. They all ran in different directions and without looking back, Emmi scrambled a safe distance to a grassy knoll behind a wood pile, and peered back.

She felt her belly roiling, its load weighing her down to the ground. She felt a sharp pain in her back and wiped her face, staring into the blue yonder. "This can't be happening. It is too soon." Her trembling fingers fumbled inside her deep pocket for her rosary, a heavy sigh escaped her lips, as her belly heaved nonstop. She lay prostrate on the prickly grass as it dug painfully into her flesh. Emmi felt a sudden urge to relieve herself and a grapefruit size lump passed between her loins, a warm, oozing stickiness between her legs. She clamped her skirt between them tightly. She cried out for help and waved her white handkerchief above the wood pile and scooted her body to lean against it.

Pavel Koczian had been looking for the women and when he saw the white kerchief fluttering frantically over the grassy knoll. Emmi saw Pavel and screamed for help. Koczian thought she had fallen. "Koczian! Koczian! You have to take me to the hospital."

Pavel recognized Emmi and hobbled as fast as his lame leg would allow. He reached down to help Emmi stand up. As her skirt slid to the side, he saw her bloody calves.

"Stay here. I'll get Marie and Anna." Emmi slumped back unto the grass and passed out. She woke up in the hospital in Arnau.

"Well, Frau Staffa, you should know better than to lift sacks of potatoes in your condition." The doctor admonished. "I wish it had been potatoes." She mumbled. "Well, you are healthy and at 31- years young you will have more children." Emmi reached for his hospital smock. "Doctor, can you tell me, what it was?" The doctor replied. "It was a girl." Emmi cried softly. "I carried a girl and lost it. From the day we were married all Sef talked about . He wanted a girl just like his niece Gitchen. A cute little girl with blond curls. I wanted to do my husband this last favor."

The pristine white tiled hospital walls were like a blank movie screen. The pictures of the suffering people, and the images of their torment was etched in her memory, and flashed before her eyes and haunted her by day and by night. She stared at the walls ashen faced, and those who came to visit thought she was grief stricken over the loss of another child. The other miscarriage was in the first month before she knew she was pregnant. This was different; she knew she had carried a girl.

Sobbing, she finally told Marie, knowing her words were safe with her. "With what is going on around here, I don't think I want to bring another child into this world. Everything has become so deadly frightful. We are being squashed between two steamrollers. From one side we are pushed by the steamroller of the NSDAP and on the other are the Czech National Socialists in Prague and their Bolshevik cousins in Moscow. "What chance of survival do we have?" Marie shook her head. "I don't understand what is going on here either. I've had my own nightmares lately. Bright flood lights from the Mandl yard shine right into my bedroom all night. Huge cylinders are moved about constantly at deafening noise. I would like to know what colossal horror is hidden within these monstrous tubes. I have already instructed my children, that if they come for us, to flee across the rooftop and hide between the gables." She stared transfixed at the floor, and clasped her mouth to silence herself.

Emmi murmured. "What is to become of us with all this evil. Someday evil will demand its retribution. Like my husband said, we are pawns in an evil scheme. We are being bartered into oblivion."

After her release from the hospital, Emmi erected a small altar in her bedroom and gazed at the beatific face of a smiling Madonna in prayerful pose with an infant Jesus in her arms, Emmi prayed ceaselessly I need a sign from you before I lose my faith. The one to whom she had prayed so many Hail Marys for years, was silent.

She prayed for peace and understanding within the family, even her sister-in-law, Ilse, for better neighborly relations, good health for her children, and most fervently the life of her beloved husband. But there were no signs from heaven or the post office. She wondered if prayers were of any use any longer since the evil powers were the more dominant force at the time.

Emmi dared not give up her prayerful vigils. She dared not go outside, and smell the flowers and fresh air, or the richness of the earth. Her miscarriage rendered her imprisoned in her peaceful home, the only place, where she felt safe, in which her body had become worn and weak and her soul weary. She had enough to keep busy with her three boys. Caring for Rudi and Otti was easy work for her. Otti was a pensive child who was scared of his teddy bea who was sitting in his crib with a pipe hanging from his mouth. The child preferred to play in solitude and limited his friendship to pigeons. He gleefully chased after chickens and geese in the yard. Such an easy-going child was sweet solace. Emmi could do needlepoint all day.

Pepi was another matter, Emmi had to keep a watchful eye on him every minute. He was increasingly impossible to control and needed a father's firm hand more than ever to keep him on the straight and narrow. "Damn this war! I need my husband here at home with me!" She mumbled to no one but herself as the Russian Winter of Barbarossa—-came across the mountain early with the first gust of cold Siberian air, that drove October rains, which changed into snowy blizzards.

With the first snowflakes the boys couldn't wait to rush outside in the morning. The slushy muck turned into frozen ruts and gullies. Emmi was keeping warm and busy knitting hats, scarves and mittens that would wind up under the Christmas Tree in two months. The old ones would have to endure the boys rough and tumble sledding at least another season. Pepi was almost ten years old. He loved spending every winter day schussing with Kurt on the Switschin mountain ridge or any hill worthy of a good climb.

Pepi was in his element feeling the peace and serenity of the mountains and was unperturbed by the happenings in the valley below. Early in the morning as soon as the sun came up over the mountains, Pepi hoisted his skis across his shoulders, grabbed a piece of buttered bread, sprinkled sugar on top and clamped it between his teeth before the long trek up the hilltop from where he had a panoramic view over Mastig.

Even from such a great distance, his father's house was prominently visible among the other homesteads because of the red glistening copper roof. He could see the factory smokestack where white billowing tufts of smoke curled into the crisp mountain air as piles of logs were being cut into boards. Much more imposing and dominant over Mastig was the Mandl factory and Villa. He could see the clear outlines of property from a mountain ridge where the three rows of white birches his father had planted marked the property line between the Mandl Administrative building, in clearly defined parameters.

Every morning as long as there was even a thin layer of snow, Pepi went skiing on the Switchin Ridge while the nanny, Erna dressed Rudi and Otti to play in the yard, they were happy to go sledding across the gentle slope alongside the house.

Emmi was glad she could watch her boys from her kitchen window while she was recovering from the miscarriage. The boys were her joy and her world. She was satisfied to see the boys frolic in the snow through the wafting steam of a cup of coffee. She sighed as her eyes drifted like a helium filled balloon that followed the crest of the Carpathian Mountains, beyond the Caucasus into the desolate plain of the Ukraine.

She imagined Josef fighting for his life in the barren tundra. She could not imagine anyone risking life and limb to conquer this land.

The months since Josef had kissed her good-bye seemed like an eternity. For irksome reasons nobody could understand, Josef, like millions of other young men had been drafted into a war, code named by Hitler Barbarossa for a 12th century red bearded emperor who had gained a mythos for his heroic conquests. The winter of Barbarossa was anything but a heroic conquest. It was a death trap for German Soldiers.

Emmi listened to Hitler's blistering broadcasts. Her spirits were lifted in moments when she heard that the Russian troops were surrendering in masse. The steady flood of Nazi propaganda, filled with proclamations of initial conquests in the trenches, and that entire units of Russian officers and enlisted men were reported to be deserting, as German Stuka fighter planes mined the Volga River, pounded Stalingrad, seized its railroad station, and that the German battalions had driven as far as the Volga waterfront.

Such blaring propaganda across the airwaves were posted on public buildings, and justified the peoples' high hopes of the war coming to an end. Emmi hoped against all odds that Josef would be coming home soon. The last sentence rang in every one's ears, as refugees from the Ukraine were cluttering the roads with livestock, and farm equipment signaling that a Russian collapse was imminent. All Emmi could think of, was that her husband would be home soon and the horrors of the war would be relegated to the history books again as they were in 1918.

What the propaganda did not tell was that the pelting October rains had turned the Russian tundra into a thick muck. It did not report that the rains had turned into freezing rains, nor that the heavy rain had turned into thick blinding-snow, or that the blinding snow had turned the desolate landscape of the Ukraine into a deadly quagmire as the muck froze, and defeat of the German Army was not at the hands of the Russian soldiers, but the Russian winter.

Winter conditions for German troops had become just as unbearable and deadly as they had been for Napoleon's troops. The heavy German equipment got stuck in the frozen ruts. The German advance was halted by father frost and the German soldiers froze to death in the muck in which they were left to die.

As the war raged on at the Russian Front, sinister faces loitered again around the neighborhood as thick as flies on a compost heap. Emmi paced the carpeted floors with great impatience, as the waiting for news lengthened and the worry worsened to heart wrenching numbness over her husband's life and limb. In sleepless nights, she touched the cold and empty pillow beside her face, and felt the bitter loneliness.

She had little to smile about, with the exception of the occasional antics of the children, which at times brought a weary smile across her tired face. She could only wring her hands in prayer and dismay, pleading that the nightmare would end. It all would have to come to an end sooner or later, she told herself, as she watched her little boys as if in a trance. The boys were her sole reason for holding on to every shred of hope for a new morning.

She opened the window a crack and called out to the nanny. "Erma, keep the boys away from the trees." The nanny waved back and continued to play with the children in the snow, pulling them around the yard on the sled. The boys had found an ideal little slope along the property line, a narrow winding gully that diverted the mountain waters to run off into the brook. The gully was covered with ice and snow, and formed an ideal little bobsled run.

Suddenly Emmi heard a scream and looked out the window. Rudi lay sprawled between the trees, and Otti was lying alongside the narrow slope. She rushed outside, screaming, when she saw the blood oozing from beneath the boys knitted hats.

The snow slowly turned into bloody slush. Luckily Otti had rolled off the sled and was able to scramble to his feet unharmed. Rudi lay motionless beside the base of a birch. Koczian heard the boys' cries and Emmis' screams and hobbled across the powdery snowdrifts. Emmi crouched beside the profusely bleeding child, and together with Koczian picked up his limp body. They carried him to the car.

Emmi climbed in and Koczian laid the child across her lap. She bandaged his head and applied handkerchief compresses to stop the bleeding as they rushed to the hospital in Arnau where she watched in horror as his swollen face turned black and blue. Emmi felt Rudi's fingers curling around hers. Between her muffled sobs she heard his tiny voice. "Mommy, I can't see you anymore! It's dark here. Turn the light on. I can't see you anymore."

Emmi wept even harder, glad he was alive, but knowing her darling son was blind. Every morning, Koczian drove Emmi to the hospital, and kept a faithful vigil by his bedside. She prayed for a miracle, while rosary beads slithered through her fingers without ceasing. "Blessed Mother of God, restore my child's sight, spare him a life of darkness."

The morning of the sixth days after the accident, at the sound of her approaching footsteps, Emmi heard her son jump up and down in his crib. She heard him shriek with delight all the way down the hall, and as soon as she entered the room, he screeched.

"I can see you, Mommy, I can see you!" Emmi was filled with joy and her faith in the power of prayer was restored. Emmi wrote Josef. "So you see, our Blessed Mother has interceded on behalf of our son, thus, with that same faith. I plead for the miracle of your return into my arms, when your faith is tested, hold fast to mine in prayer. Eternal Love—E

As the list of fallen soldiers was becoming longer every day, resulting in a deepening despondency among neighbors and friends, who were anxiously awaiting word from their loved ones, Emmi prayed that her strength of faith would endure now.

Christmas was nearing and she felt it her duty for the sake of her boys to make it a joyous celebration of Christs' birthday, despite the deep despondency she felt the brunt of despair, she did not want to rob the boys of their unbridled joy and unburdened laughter. How could she feel any jubilation when an intense agony over her husband's welfare weighed her spirits down so low, she couldn't get off her knees. Her faith and her spirits had hit rock bottom. The light of the Advent candles reflected in her children's trusting eyes, simply disarmed her and she told herself, "Emma, pull yourself together." Despite her depressing moods she knew what her responsibilities to her children were. How could she deny them that wondrous dulci-jubilo moment once a year?

It was bad enough wondering what Josef was enduring in the fight of his life in a frozen hellhole somewhere in the tundra of the Ukraine or Russia, where she imagined his struggles for every breath in blinding snowstorms and blistering cold, where he needed every ounce of strength as he dodged mines and bullets, while she huddled in numbing fear around a makeshift altar, mumbling prayers of a lifetime.

If she stopped praying guilt would consume her, fearing she might be slacking in her faith, believing that only prayers would bring her husband home from the vast Russian war frontline along the tundra that had become an icy snow swept graveyard for her husband's fallen comrades.

While Josef was frozen in a quagmire from which there was no escape, knowing that thousands of his comrades had not been struck down by bullets, but had suffered freezing deaths in this frozen hell. The only thought that kept him going was the memory of Emmi. He was obsessed with only one thought of her.

He clung to every thread of life, and celebrated every day as a miracle. Emmi's thoughts and prayers were with Josef every waking moment, while Josef became increasingly despondent. He was not fighting Hitler's war, he only fought to survive the Russian winter, to live another day and go home to his beloved mountains and Emmi.

As he listened to a thousand mournful sounds in a starless-night he knew he was only dreaming when he thought he saw his wife waving to him, when he heard a balalaika's mournful sound along the Western shore of the Volga River, as soldiers huddled in the piercing cold around a warming horse manure fire built inside a lone barrel drum.

The starving soldiers extracted undigested kernels from animal droppings off the frozen tundra. With frozen fingers, Josef scrawled his last reply from

Stalingrad, not knowing if his wife would ever receive his message. My beloved Emmi, I stand alone on distant shores, keep watch in endless nights. Lonely I have been ever since my youth, my heart is filled with grief as a heavy burden dims my mind. The mist of lonely tears, shroud the icy hell around. In darkest night too far from human sounds, I am alone and cry. No moon, no stars shine her for me. Has he above forgotten me? Does He not have enough angels up there? He could send one angel here for me, just one Angel for me? Love Sef.

It was the last soul piercing letter Emmi received. The balalaika faded to dead silence.

Moments later, in a barrage of artillery fire Josef was brought down. He could feel the shrapnel pierce his thigh; a moment later darkness engulfed him. His soul hovered over an insurmountable abyss filled with deepest despair.

He regained consciousness as comrades loaded him on a truck. He knew not where they were taking him but was glad to be transported away from this frozen hell. He touched the spot beneath the coat lining and felt the cool medallion of St. Anthony, which Emmi had sewn into the inner lining. It was a symbol and reminder of her faith and that obscure assurance of sweetness awaiting him in the arms of a beautiful woman. He could have wished for angels to transport him from this icy hell and endless bleakness into the heavenly world beyond. Instead, he was delivered to a field hospital near the Slovak border so he could fight another day.

The hospital was overcrowded with wounded soldiers, and being so close to home, the doctors sent him home to recover. Josef would have crawled home on his belly. His heart raced across the Slovak plain to a quaint village in his beloved mountains, ahead of the westward rumbling Soviet trucks, for a two-week short furlough—-on Christmas Eve 1942.

The streets were blanketed with snow, not a soul appeared in a window and lights were out. Nobody took notice of an army truck from where Josef jumped down and wished the driver a blessed Christmas. He hobbled up the short walk and softly opened the frost covered door. Emmi screamed for fright as the door opened softly. But as soon as she recognized her husband she screamed in jubilation and called the children, who scampered around him while Emmi sank to her knees, and wept uncontrollably.

Christmas—the most splendid feast for families around the world was a day that pressed so much emotional yearning upon souls with heart-throbbing high hopes and family togetherness.

Despite the joy of his home coming, the air was filled with a dull ache knowing that this Christmas had to be measured in austerity, and a numbing foreboding hung in the air, knowing this might be their last family celebration. All around the region suffering faces emerged, of those whose lives had been torn apart by this horrid war, for a cause that surpassed their own understanding.

Emmi and Josef knew their days of family bliss were numbered. The Russian front was an ever-present memory, a memory straight from hell. Josef knew the truth, knew how the German people had been lied to. He knew they were doomed. He knew the Russian front had moved close. He dismissed the preposterous lies of Hitlers' propaganda machine that predicted a Soviet collapse for the purpose of deceiving the German people. Hitler needed the soldiers to keep fighting, as long as they believed they were winning the war they would do as ordered. They did not know Hitler was leading them into the abyss with false hopes.

To spare his wife more heartache he kept his fears to himself, cloaking it in silence. Emmi and the children did not need to be burdened with disheartening truth. He cherished the brief muted family celebration, cherished every tick-tock and ding-gong of the grandfather clock, and nights spent in Emmis' arms. He was sitting on a simple kitchen chair, watching Emmi pull out trays from the oven filled with warm cookies that filled the air with such a delicious aromas of cinnamon, hazelnuts, cardamom, vanilla and butter wafting throughout the house, which brought the children running into the kitchen.

Home was his idea of heaven. "This is where I belong and I long for no other place on earth. I want to barricade myself here from all intrusions of the outside world."

He stretched out on the plush maroon velvet sofa, and Emmi snuggled up against his emaciated frame. She gently caressed his finely chiseled face, and traced the contours of his lips and kissed him gently.

"Josef, I have to tell you something. I was pregnant but I miscarried. The doctor said it was a girl. I am so sorry. I would have loved to place a baby girl into your arms as a homecoming present. I know a girl like Margit would have been the grandest Christmas present I could have given you."

Emmi saw the tears in his eyes and brushed her own tears as they rolled down her cheeks."We have cried enough tears already. I cried for both of us." She was too glad to have him home. She was not willing to spend these precious moments consumed with worries and grief.

"I know I should be satisfied to have three healthy sons." Josef responded. "Emmi, you and the children are my anchor. I clung to thoughts of you every day. You were my lifeline."

Christmas Eve dinner lacked nothing in aroma and festiveness. Emmi spared nothing her magic hands and skillful hands could serve up, starting with the traditional beer soup, followed by a Christmas goose with red cabbage and Bohemian dumplings. For dessert she had prepared for each child a colorful goodie plate with oranges and butter almond Kipferl. For good luck and peace and plenty she had placed shiny gold and silver coins under every dinner plate to be discovered after the dinner plate was clean. The shiny gold coins were a valued traditional addition to children's piggy banks. After dinner Josef put on a coat to follow the boys out into his beloved woods.

Later they came back with cheeks aglow from the freezing cold, dragging a nicely shaped pine tree into the living room.

Emmi mysteriously disappeared for a few minutes and locked the door to the living room. Josef set up the tree, while the children freed themselves of the bulky winter clothes, boots and sleds in the garage. Emmi used some of the pine branches to decorate the living room, hung ornaments and tinsel, then she fastened candle holders to the tips of the branches.

Before the children were allowed to enter the living room, she lit the wax candles on the tree. Gaily wrapped presents lay beneath the tree. Swiss chocolates covered in gold leaves dangled from the branches. The rustling noise behind closed doors aroused the boys with excitement.

Josef held the boys at bay until the magic moment had arrived when the double doors slowly opened. The living room was bathed in candlelight, as the door opened Emmi started singing. Oh, come all ye faithful… it was the signal to the children to come and embrace the magic of Christmas. In moments the presents were unwrapped. The boys tried on the new sweaters, scarves and mittens and thanked their mother for the new winter wear, knowing she had spent hours knitting all year. Otti and Rudi exuberantly climbed on their new sleds and Pepi examined his new skis with expert eyes. He knew these skis were the best money could buy.

Emmi bundled the boys up in new knit wear and Josef wrapped them with blankets to the sleds, so the boys would not fall off. Church bells still beckoned the faithful to come and worship, as the war raged on the other side of the mountain and the war front was coming closer to their home front. Streetlights, churches and schools were not allowed to turn on lights for fear of bomb attacks. They lit torches to guide their path on the long walk across fields and forests on their way to church. Other neighbors joined them, and soon they formed a glowing trail across the frozen landscape to the beautiful gothic church in Ober-Prausnitz.

A few old men and widowed women sat quietly prayerfully in wooden pews.

It seemed Midnight Mass would be celebrated in total darkness until the nave gradually filled with flickering candlelight, adding warmth for a worshipful celebration. As the family walked down the aisle to their favorite pew Emmi noticed the vacant seats beside quietly weeping women. White handkerchiefs wiped the tears that rolled unabashed down a few sunken cheeks all knowing, the war had torn another gaping hole into the heart of a family. They were a simple, pious flock, who grasped naught what the world had in store for them. They could not know that their young men had been seduced and led to slaughter and were left to die at the Russian front, listed as missing or frozen to death in the quiet of the loathsome Russian tundra. Such were the wounds German families suffered, souls who found respite before the feet of saints, here in a sanctuary where the main altar was dedicated to the Holy Family.

Around the altar of Saint Josef flickering votive candles lit the nave in commemoration of a beloved husband and father. Despite the beautiful choir anthem In Dulci Jubilo, and the lovely baritone solo of Transeamus, the faces of the listening parishioners bore only burnt-out reflections of resignation to a fate over which they had no control.

The boys had fallen asleep during the somber and dignified Mass before the candles were extinguished. Emmi and Josef bundled their boys on the sleds and pulled them home in the dark. They clasped their frozen fingers together, sharing one big mitten between them, clinging to the frazzled ends of the rope, while Pepi raced ahead on his new skies.

The tall firs cast black shadows against the crunchy snow, looking peaceful beneath the endless firmament of stars, giving no clue to the raging war beyond the mountain peaks. Emmi murmured. "I wish this night could last forever. I want to remember what peace there is in silence, all I want is peace in our time again, like the peace we have right here. I can live without the clamor of the world."

She smiled meekly and looked with sad eyes at Josef. She could no longer hold back the flood of her own tears when she saw tears rolling down his cheeks as he wiped them with his handkerchief. Emmi and Josef spent a fortnight in each other's arms, not daring to think about tomorrow and beyond an inevitable moment of a sad good-bye. For two weeks neither had talked about that dreaded moment of farewell. Josef couldn't stand the tears. He quietly slid out of the warm featherbed before being sent back to the Russian front, which in two-weeks-time had pushed back the German onslaught.

Before Emmi could wake, he quietly slipped out the door. Outside an army truck was waiting and he slipped inside the back of the truck and it sped off into the night as the angel of doom loomed ever larger for German soldiers. Hitler's generals suggested a retreat. But their suggestions were quickly dashed by the man who vowed never to give an inch.

As the Russians gained in confidence, the German soldiers lost their will to fight to the finish of a mad scheme which had been foisted on the German people for what many had come to belief was nothing but Hitler's insanity, with a dread of the horror that was to come. Hitler's rejection of his General's suggestions to retreat degenerated into panic flight. Emmi dreaded the long days and nights of waiting for news from Josef. Day by agonizing day turned into weeks, then months without a letter from Josef.

Walks to the post office for news from the front became a daily pilgrimage for Emmi. She had given up listening to the radio broadcasts long ago, knowing they were being fed nothing but lies by a well-oiled propaganda machine. The fever pitch voice of Hermann Goebbels with his front-line news rattled her nerves.

The sweet romantic music she had always loved to sing on a stage was in her memory of a long gone era. The only music she enjoyed was the music she could still sing herself, the music that filled her inner ear gave her the only peace her soul was yearning. Every morning she walked to the new town hall to read through a veil of tears the list of fallen soldiers, many of whom were friends, classmates and neighbors, she shuddered as she recognized familiar names, as one shock followed another. One of the names among the fallen was her first boyfriend and theater director, Bruno Linhart, who had been killed in an air raid. She fondly reminisced on his marriage proposal when she was only seventeen.

He had been her dance partner on stage, with Bruno she had shared many good times in her youth, until she married Josef and Bruno married Hilda Haase. "My God, had I married Bruno I would be a widow now. I am too young to be a widow, I'm only thirty-three." Thinking of her time with Bruno she wept bitterly.

She would never become accustomed to sweating blood and trepidation, as her fingers slid over the 'S's of the list of fallen soldiers. She was relieved when she could not find the "Staffa" name among those listed as missing or dead. As the list of fallen soldiers grew longer and longer, day by day, Emmi looked crestfallen, she felt a seething rage at the injustice perpetrated against young people who had sacrificed their lives for the power-hungry madness of others.

How could the architects of the world inflict such suffering while they lived in comfort, and those who had put up the slightest resistance or criticism of murderous socialist regimes, were shot before firing squads or sent to the Russian front in expectations of becoming one more nameless cannon fodder.

Emmi decided to visit her childhood village, Klein-Borowitz, to express her condolences to Franziska and Emil Linhart for the loss of their oldest son Bruno.

Emmi spotted Franziska at a roadside alter, which she had decorated with red Geraniums in honor of her son Bruno. She prayed the rosary fervently and Emmy sat beside the crestfallen woman and prayed silently with her.

While the godless scoundrels, who embraced socialism as their "patriotic duty" were allowed to walk in and out of her home as if it were their own house. She felt like a stranger in her own home as if it were no longer hers. These men had made themselves at home in her living room. She dreaded going home because of the constant intruders violating the sanctity of her home. They knew her comings and goings.

On the pretense of working on Josef's journals and bookkeeping, his brother's treated her home as if it were their property. Ilse could be counted on to follow on their heels, not to chit chat with Emmi, but to spy on her and prod her to enlist Pepi into the Hitler Youth. Emmi waited for the snake to rear her Teutonic head, steering clear of her brazen intrusions.

It was not enough to have the maid inform Ilse and Karl, that the "lady of the house was not home." Most days she sequestered herself in her own bedroom to avoid her husbands' intrusive clan. Emmi slowly walked home but as soon as she opened the door she saw Josef's brother, Karl, sitting on her living room sofa uninvited. He looked so relaxed and comfortable as if he had been waiting for her return home. She knew something was wrong as soon as she stepped inside without the customary "Gruess Gott."

Karl patted the seat beside him "Come, sit here." He invited Emmi to sit down on her own sofa. With an ominous foreboding she lowered herself on the sofa with great unease. Karl shoved a wad of documents under her nose. "You must sign these papers. Here!" She picked up the papers with trembling fingers as she scanned the pages.

As Emmi read each page and paragraph with great care, she realized in horror that Josef's brother had connived to disown her and rob her children of their rightful inheritance. The documents he shoved under her nose would have deeded the lumber business, forest land and the house Josef had built, to his brother Karl in the event Josef was killed in the war.

Emmi felt a rage boiling over at the audacity and ultimate betrayal. Emmi stood up, tore the documents into pieces then hissed. "What do you take me for, a stupid little country bumpkin? Get out of my house. Don't set foot in my house again! Keep your wife out of my sight." She held the door open and screamed. "Out!" Karl stood up and walked toward her. "Emma, everything is lost here. I want to secure our future on the other side of the border in Germany." Emmi screamed again. "Out!" and slammed the door shut behind him.

She slumped against the sofa cushion, covered her face with her hands and wept. "What treachery and deceit are these people capable of? Do they really think I am that stupid?" She had always known that Josefs' brothers and their wives thought of her as inferior. But she was even more incensed over the injustice seeing how Karl had been rewarded for his party loyalty. He had been allowed to "serve the fatherland" as "party file clerks" right here in the safety and comfort of his home, while her husband was sent away to fight for his life along the Russian front.

While she feared for her husbands' life and prayed for Josef's safe return, she realized she and her children had to fear for their own lives as well. She feared the sinister motivations of those hanging around her home, how slyly they had maneuvered to disown her and rob her children of everything her husband had worked for.

She rendered herself unable to function unless the rosary beads slithered through her fingers because she was pregnant again.

She feared the rest of nine months she would have to spend in solitude, and the hours kneeling by her bedside altar while praying for a healthy baby girl, before she could slip into her cold bed, waiting for the down comforter to warm up and keep her teeth from chattering. She reminisced on the days when she and Josef had met and she had hummed an aria from a Franz Lehar opera. 'Dein ist mein ganzes Herz, wo du nicht bist, kann ich nicht sein. So wie die Blume welkt wenn sie nicht kuesst der Sonnenschein.'

Yours is all of me, my whole heart, where'er you're not, I cannot be. Just as flowers wilt, when not kissed by sunshine.

She could not be where Josef was not. How the words of that aria had once moved her to tears on their strolls along Wenceslas Square. She remembered the old wrought-iron lamps that cast their glow upon saints she once had admired. But now they were steeped in silence, only earworms of favorite melodies reminded her as to why we pray. No place on earth had more saints than Prague which reminded her of Josef. But those declared holy as they graced the bridge tower across the Charles Bridge, gazed out on a brutal world in stone cold silence. In those lonely hours she beseeched all saints to pray for her husbands' safe return so she could feel his loving arms once again around her bulging belly. She sighed and whispered woefully. "We have the misfortune of living in Hitler's time."

Another wet October had arrived with driving rains where Josef fought, not to conquer but to stay alive, mostly shooting in the air at invisible enemies. He had no desire to kill anyone. Instead, when he was wounded a second time, he hailed it a miracle. He had no desire to return to lice, mud, and disease-infested trenches, instead this time he was not sent home, instead he was driven with other wounded soldiers to a field hospital near Munich. He was in no hurry to recover, thinking of his injuries as another miracle.

He was merely wounded and lucky to be away from the vastness of windswept tundras. "Yes, there is a God in heaven. If only he could fix the calamity the world is in." He laughed cynically just as a telegram was dropped on his chest. Despite the horror all around him he was buoyed by a sign of life from home, he read the news from home out loud to his smiling comrades. "Yes, there is a God after all! Today, he blessed me and. I'm happier in this hell hole than I have ever been in mother Russia and Ukraine.

Today is my thirty-third birthday and yesterday my wife gave birth to my daughter. The best gift a man can get. God blessed me with a daughter!" His wounded comrades cheered and celebrated with whatever meager field rations were left. His joy was short lived.

The wound in his leg had barely healed, when Josef was sent back for active duty. By now, the front line had moved close to home. He did not have far to go. He was assigned sentry duty of a bridge crossing over the Tisza River, in Hungary near the Ukraine-Slovak-Hungary border. Along this eastern front he saw timid signs of Spring. The harsh winter was breaking, the ice was melting, and white birch trees began to show pale green buds.

While in Mastig, signs of spring popped up in meadows where crocus and snowdrops peeked through the snow. Emmi was determined to maintain a semblance of normalcy for the sake of her children, and kept the horrendous sounds of war that screeched over the airwaves from penetrating with frightening clamor. Most of the men of the villages were away fighting a war or had fallen victims of it already. She had stopped turning on the radio long ago ever since the music of Beethoven had been outlawed and snuffed from the airwaves. Singing her favorite hymns and operatic arias, between cooking and baking the children's favorite foods, provided an aura that all was well with the world, Emmi planned to celebrate the baptism of her daughter as norm of her faith.

She spent an entire week baking an apple cake, a juicy plum cake, a cheese cake and a butter cream torte for this family celebration. Her daughter's baptism would bring relatives together around a festive coffee table. She had invited them all but since Oma Staffa was the only person in Mastig who owned a car, Emmi wondered who would walk a long way to the church in Ober-Prausnitz and back to her house. She could count on Josef's sisters Marie and since his sister Annie was the baby's god-mother she was sure to come. She was not sure of her mother Franziska because she would dread the long walk ahead.

A soft knock on the door brought her out of her thoughtful preparation of this great family celebration. To her ultimate surprise her sister, Anninka stood in front of her with a suitcase by her side and a fox fur slung across her shoulders. Anninka had nowhere else to go after the bombing raids over Dresden and Berlin. She came to the only place where she would feel welcoming arms around her. She was sure she would find refuge under her sister's roof.

Emmi burst into tears for joy as she wrapped her arms around her sister. The sisters hugged each other for a long time until Emmi said. "Let me take a good look at you!" Emmi screeched excitedly, seeing that her "little" sister had grown into a tall slender and utterly beautiful woman who knew how to turn heads. Seeing her sister look worldly elegant, poised and self-assured renewed her faith in miracles. She remembered how she had worried about the once shy little sister, who as a child was afraid of her own shadow.

Emmi now took a good look at a sophisticated beauty endowed with a nicely rounded baby bump. "Well, I see life in Dresden has been very active and interesting for you!" Emmi noticed the buggy sitting behind Anninka alongside the front porch. A baby girl was peering out from under the hooded pram. "What have we here?" Emmi looked surprised and overjoyed as she lifted the toddler from the pram. "This is Eva." Anninka dropped a few bundles inside the foyer.

Emmi realized that her sister had not just come for a visit, but had come to stay. All the hugs and kisses were now for little Eva. Emmi was delighted to see that her sister's baby was only two months older than her own baby. She put little Eva down in the playpen beside her baby she had named Jenna, who was quietly playing with a rag doll Emmi had sown and that now would have to be shared by two.

Emmi innocently asked "Where is your husband?" Anninka sighed and murmured. "He is dead. He was a pilot and was killed in an air raid over Berlin. His name was Peter Schmeck." Anninka pulled out a photo of a gorgeous Luftwaffe pilot and settled down on the sofa, and talked about her life and dread of fire bomb raids over Dresden. Emmi asked about the father of the child she was carrying in her womb.

Anninka told her it was the child of another man. Emmi was getting confused and couldn't keep the names straight of the men in her sister's life. "Now, who is this baby's father?" Emmi looked totally confused, trying to learn the paternity of her sisters' children. She reiterated bits and pieces of what Anninka had told her.

"So, you were in love with a gorgeous fighter pilot? You became pregnant before you got married?"

"Yes, we planned to get married, but he was called into active duty, we were married by proxy. He was a very handsome man, I loved him, I was pregnant when he was shot down over Berlin during an air raid." Anninka looked sad as she went on. The war ruined everything. When I got the news of his death, a friend took me out to dinner in a dance café, to keep me company and comfort me. Instead, while there, I met a young soldier and I found comfort in his arms. I was five months pregnant with Eva at that time, so he knew about the pregnancy as soon as we began to dance. I told him everything, and he promptly accepted responsibility for my unborn child." Emmi's curiosity was aroused and she inquired. "Then what happened?"

Anninka waited. "He was sent back to the front shortly after the baby's birth. He came home one more time, we spent a few months together and I became pregnant again with this child." She rubbed her softly rounded belly. "I am now waiting for an annulment from my first proxy marriage, so I can marry again by proxy, before the father of this baby gets killed. But with the war raging in Berlin, paperwork takes forever." Emmi could see her sister's distress. She looked aghast as she questioned her sisters lack of prudent judgment. "Why did you get involved with someone right after the pilot was killed? I could never sleep with any man but Josef."

Anninka scoffed. "It's easy for you to criticize me. Since you were seventeen you had one man in your life. I used to watch you and Pepi make out on the leather sofa late into the night. You always had someone, I had no one. I needed someone to help me in these times. This is war, I clutched at every opportunity to protect my child and survive. The war has ruined many lives in Berlin and Dresden where war is an everyday reality. In these mountains I see no sign of war, I hear no air raid sirens. You never had to fear British bombs dropping on your head like I did in Dresden and Berlin." Emmi shook her head and cautioned her sister.

"Jenna will be baptized on Sunday. I don't know if our mother will come for the baptism. It is a long walk from Klein-Borowiz to Mastig. If our mother does come, just don't talk about all these men, different fathers of your children, say nothing about a proxy marriage and proxy annulment. She'll never understand such family discord."

She intoned and winced as Anninka shook her head. "I know she will call me a slut, an easy girl." Emmi tried to understand the confusing family arrangement and said in bewilderment.

"Oh, God! Proxy marriage? Proxy annulment? Proxy fatherhood? What is this world coming to? I know who fathered my children. If our mother does come, just don't try explaining anything to her. Tell her you are married. He was a pilot who got killed, period." She shook her head in disbelief as Anninka looked around the room and whispered.

"Well, Emma, everything was well planned in your life. My life has been chaotic from my birth. I have always pulled the short straw." Emmi could hear a touch of envy in her sister's voice and tried to smooth things over. "Has Eva been baptized?" Anninka shook her head. "Maybe we can have both babies baptized on Sunday." Despite all this confusion about fatherhood, and proxy marriages, Emmi eagerly prepared a joyous family celebration with a double baptism of her daughter, Jenna together with her niece, Eva.

Emmi was glad and sad at the same time. She was overjoyed that their babies could be baptized together in the church in Ober-Prausnitz. She felt sad because her mother did not bother to attend the children's baptism. Her disappointment waned over cake and coffee and ceaseless lamentations in family togetherness for a moment of reprieve from their daily worries over the war.

Once the cakes were eaten the boys, Kurt, Pepi and Fredi got bored listening to the women's chatter and went outside looking for trouble, and they found it.

Anninka knew she would never have to plead with Emmi for a roof over her head in these difficult times. She and Eva were welcomed in her home as long as Anninka wanted to stay and allowed her sister to move all her belongings into a large comfortable apartment in the mansion that used to be the maids quarters. Anninka and Eva would have a comfortable place to live and conversely Anninkas' presence gave Emmi great comfort.

She no longer felt alone in her misery, now that she had a kindred spirit to commiserate with. She could have adult conversations and no longer felt restricted to baby talk. She felt needed and busier than ever, especially when her sister's due date was close. Emmi ran to get the midwife and doctor Muecker helped Anninka deliver a healthy baby boy, she named Peter. Anninka, Eva and baby Peter needed a safe place to live. Emmi was only too glad, she could help. Just like

Eva's father, Peter's father was also lost in the tragedy of war in one of the many air raids over Berlin. One night Emmi was awakened from a fitful sleep by frantic knocking on her front door.

Emmi heard a steady tapping on the glass paned door, but was afraid to leave her bed to open the door, but the ceaseless tapping gave her no choice to ignore the intrusion. She did not want the noise to wake Anninka and the babies, who were sound asleep. Reluctantly Emmi scrambled out of bed, wondering who might the intruder be so late at night. She quietly descended the stairs and parted the curtains. She saw a stooped shadow and slowly opened the door.

There stood her mother carrying a small suitcase and her only valued possession, a crystal rosary. With her usual stern demeanor, Franziska explained with a tremor in her voice. "I am scared to stay in my house alone." Emmi embraced her mother, realizing that her mother was trembling with fear, looking just as frightened as Emmi felt herself. "I couldn't come earlier in the day. I waited until dark. I walked the lonely wooded path between Klein-Borowitz and Mastig. I had no other means to get here. Whom can I turn to, where should I go?" She mumbled over and over and Emmi answered. "You did the right thing in coming here. You stay at least until this nightmare ends."

Emmi realized that both women had come to her house for comfort and security. For every bodies sake Emmi realized she could not allow her own fears to show. She calmly asked Pepi to move his bedding and bunk with Otti. "Oma Borufka can sleep in your room and make herself at home."

During the day, the women huddled under a comforter seeking warmth and security in shared fear and anxiety. Emmi was glad to keep her mother safe here. Her sister Anninka, was non-plussed about her mother's presence and an unwelcomed surprise. Going to church on Sunday was no longer a refuge for the soul, but a life-threatening venture. Even a short walk to a store had become a treacherous excursion for the women.

Emmi built a little altar in her bedroom with a velvet kneeler before a rose trellis adorning the picture of the Madonna with the Christ child who was feeding white doves. She gathered the children around it and led them in their daily prayers around the make shit altar. It was the serenity this painting conveyed which had given Emmi great comfort in this turbulent time, a serenity she wished for her own life. Because of the turbulence outside Pepi and little Otti were relegated to stay inside the house.

They played Chess every night. But Pepi found it difficult to concentrate and listened with one ear to the women who sat around doing a lot of needlework. To keep their mind from worrying about worldly events, the women spent many hours sewing clothes for the children, knitting socks, scarves and mittens, Emmi crochet doilies and table clothes amid a steady murmur that aroused even more curiosity.

"I came here to let you know I overheard rumors, that the Russians are coming here."

Anninka cried hysterically. "What? I'm terrified! I barely escaped the bomb attacks of the Brits on Dresden. I came home relieved that the war was finally over. Now the Russians are coming? They like to rape German women as revenge!"

Emmi murmured prophetically, "I'm afraid, for us the war has just begun. All we can do is pray." Anninka scoffed. "Praying doesn't help us anymore. Berlin is finished. Dresden is finished, even its famous church Frauen Kirche is a heap of rubble, the Zwinger, and the Semper Opera. Nothing is left, but heaps of charred piles of stone and twisted steel girders." Emmi couldn't even imagine how such beautiful buildings could be targets of an air raid.

She shook her head in disbelief. Anninka dropped her head on her chest. "Those Brits didn't just want to destroy Hitler, they wanted to destroy the German people and culture. Only the Brits would sink this low as one who sits on a gold toilet made for a pompous ass with a cigar in his mouth. I worry about what else the world has in store for us? Our children can't go outside. What should we do now?"

Emmi shook her head, murmuring sadly. "Where should we go? We have nowhere to go except to the Lord in prayer."

Anninka cried in exasperation. "Nobody will hear us! I ask you, who is going to hear us? God?" Emmi knew her sister had lost her faith during her tortured youth and life in Dresden while working as a nanny in the employ of an SS officer's family.

Emmi stoically defended her own faith with a confident voice. "Who else but God? We have no one else to lean on. To whom should we turn to, where should we go?"

Anninka hissed sarcastically. "Mark my words, no one will care, not even God.

The world will not say a word not even the Pope, about the atrocities we have to suffer because we are German by accident of birth. We had the misfortune of living in Hitler's time."

Emmi had nothing more to say. Her eyes took on a haunted look as she thought of Josef, and smiled at an invisible image somewhere across the mountains on the Eastern horizon. There Josef was assigned to guard a bridge, which delivered him from the most heinous acts of war—-killing another human being.

There was nothing to guard against any longer. Josef saw no sense in standing guard at a bridge. He saw nothing but charred earth and shattered lives. Josef had known all along, no war made any sense to him. He was wasting his life in a war that should have never started and was lost long ago at the cost of many million lives. The steady flood of caravans of covered wagons rolling across the barren Ukraine fields heading west, were jam packed with refugees. A downtrodden humanity was fleeing from the Russian onslaught that could no longer be stopped.

Josef followed the Ukrainian caravans at a safe distance, carefully avoiding being seen by men or beast. He felt almost peaceful and serene in his solitude as they neared the Slovak border. The treks of refugees got longer as they moved in solemn processions across the barren terrain and leaving a trail of scraps and garbage imbedded in the frozen tundra. Josef was feeding off their refuse, scratching the frozen ground for a turnip, a potato peel, a carrot, or a half-eaten beet. A miserable humanity was fleeing westward afraid of partisans, militias and the Red Army.

Germany had run out of food and Hitler had given his Generals the order to shoot enemy combatants rather than take them alive as prisoners of war. Any German war-weary defector or disobedience to Hitler's orders or sparing the life of a prisoner would cost the soldier his own life. To be shot by a firing squad.

Germany no longer could feed its own people, its own soldiers, let alone a prisoner of war. Straggly remnants of war-weary soldiers in tattered uniforms followed the caravans at a distance. A lone soldier looked around in his emaciated state, as he spotted another man looking as war weary and spent as he felt. The color of his uniform was barely recognizable.

The soldier wearing a grey uniform collided with one wearing a brown uniform, who had just settled into dry rushes along the Tisza River. One soldier had the jump on the other as he aimed a rifle at the chest of a young soldier wearing tattered rags that were barely recognizable as an army uniform. As the soldiers looked at each other they recognized each other as enemy combatant by the color of their uniform.

Each looked as spent as the other felt. They stared into each other's eyes and saw their own reflections in the face of a frail humanity. They both bore the haunted look of men who had been pushed to the edge. Neither man had the strength to cringe in the face of death in total acceptance of an inevitable fate. The soldier in the grey uniform dared not look in the eyes of the soldier in a brown uniform as a cloud of doom hung in the air. One question mark bound them to each other.

"Who will it be? You or me?" Knowing that he risked his own life if he spared the life of a Russian soldier, the German soldier raised his weapon with a do or die determination.

As the Russians' face and chest came into focus, a picture of a young woman surrounded by small children flashed before his eyes. The woman carried an infant in her arms and walked toward him, waving a white kerchief with her free arm, calling out to him "Josef…Josef."

He felt a paralysis in his arms as little boys scrambled to greet him. He could not shoot and carefully scanned the immediate area and then, convinced that nobody was within earshot he called out in Russian.

"Drop your weapon and run. If I don't shoot, the SS will shoot me. Run." Josef called out. "Drop the gun and run!" The Russian soldier looked surprised, and replied barely audible. "Da…da." The Russian soldier tossed his weapon, and ran blindly into the scrubby brush, as gun pellets exploded around him, aimed at nothing but the air above his head. Josef nestled back into the underbrush thicket and scanned the horizon with his field glasses. He was relieved that all the noise and clamor of war seemed to have ceased.

A woman waved to him in his dreams and the memory of her kept him moving westward. He slumped down wearily into the underbrush thickets, crawling and creeping along the edge of the shrubbery. His eyes were fixed on a small village, nestled deep in a valley within the Slovak territory. He ran a gauntlet between white birch trees, and crouched in the bushes. He cut a few strands of barbed wire leading to a nearby barn and slipped unnoticed inside. Panting heavily, he rolled up a Russian field coat he had taken off a dead Russian soldier to keep as a bedroll and tore off the tell-tale epaulets. He cut off the silver buttons emblazoned with a swastika from his German uniform, grabbed a shovel and buried every tell-tale-signs of his nationality in the pigsty, as the disturbed sows squealed and grunted. He smeared their dung on his uniform, tore the lining and fastened his field glasses, army knife and wire cutters inside the coat, and wiped his stubbly bearded face. He felt old and emaciated as he dragged himself toward the railroad track among smelly, grimy humanity and moved wearily along with the down trodden masses to the train station. He boarded a cargo train, filled with refugees, and nestled in among the westward fleeing Ukrainians, Rumanians, Hungarians, Russians and Volga Germans. Volga Germans are an ethnic German minority group who had been brought to Russia for their skills and craftsmanship by Empress Catherine the Great upon her marriage to Czar Peter III.

Catherine the Great was a German Princess before she married the Russian Czar Peter III. She became the revered Mother of Russia. She ruled Russia from 1762 to 1796 after she had her husband killed, because he was insane and the edicts he decreed were a subjugation of the Russian people. Nobody on this train cared about nationalities. Everyone just wanted to get away from the war and the mayhem to come under Soviet subjugation.

Josef mingled silently among old babitchkas of varying nationalities, who with colorful kerchiefs tied around their full faces, sat on their bundled belongings, to guard against thieves who were eagerly looking for anything of the slightest value. They had no shame as they victimized others with their sticky fingers. Josef was unrecognizable as a German soldier and snuggled deep within the wave of corpulent comfort, where he was hardly noticed among their hefty frames.

As soon as the train strained with its first chug, he sighed with relief and fell asleep. Suddenly the train jerked to a halt. The doors rolled back and several black-uniformed men of the SS jumped aboard, pulled along by ferocious barking German Shepherds called Kettenhunde. Tethered to long chains the dogs ran ahead of their handlers to ferret out war-weary German soldiers, all knowing, if caught the soldier would be dragged off the train and shot on the spot.

Soldiers nervously pulled up collars and clutched blankets around their weary faces. A Ukrainian babitchka noticed one who was sitting close beside her wearing a Russian coat and smelling like pig manure and stinky cheese. The emaciated wreck looked as war weary as she felt. His eyes looked wearily up at her through his thick collar pulled over his ears. She was filled with pity for him, when she saw his forget me not blue eyes and without a moments' hesitation she threw a blanket over his head and piled her bags and baggage around him.

She knew that soldiers like the one beside her was the reason the train had been stopped and he was doomed if discovered.

The SS officers scrutinized the faces of these miserable people huddling close together. He lifted blankets and peered beneath them to find any who might be hiding their faces. The closer the dog came the more the people winced in fear. As the officer neared the babitchka she cackled good-naturedly, her broad Slavic face smiling toothlessly, trying to beguile him as she gummed. "He's an old man, don't bother him, he is sleeping. He is just an old man, let him sleep! Leave him alone." She waved off the uniformed man, away from the soldier, who huddled motionless next to her in the darkest corner beneath her bundled belongings. The heat and stench must have gotten to the SS guard. With the click of his heal he made a quick exit.

Soldiers huddling on the train had imagined their luck running out and being dragged off the train and shot any moment, knowing this would not be the last inspection stop, knowing there was no mercy for the likes of those found hiding from the carnage. Not until the train moved forward with a jerk, did soldiers sigh with relief. Josef peered out from under the blanket and whispered a mild thank you. The old woman winked at him, smiling broadly with that knowing look. "You are tired too, like me. I know, we are all tired of war."

She gummed a toothless smile. Josef nodded, blinked back tears and sighed. At every stop he trembled with fear of another SS sting operation and his luck running out. As they neared Ölmütz, a German enclave within Slovakia, Josef jumped off the train. He anticipated another search by the SS. He feared his luck running out. "I spared the life of a Russian soldier, and an old babitchka saved mine."

With his head cloaked by the blanket, he sauntered out of view, with cautious sideway glances and deliberate nonchalance, as if he were a homeless nomad. He cautiously slipped inside a nearby barn, stripped off the stinking coat and jacket, retrieved his field glasses, his army knife, and wire cutters from their hidden compartments. Then he buried the German uniform inside a haystack. The shadow of a man with a pitchfork fell over him. The prongs pointed straight at his chest. The soldier quickly turned and grabbed the handle and pressed the prongs away from him.

As the two wrestled for control of the deadly weapon, the soldier with a quick jerk was able to turn the pitchfork around and pressed the prongs threateningly against the farmer's throat. Josef whispered in fluent Czech. "I don't want to harm you. I just want to go home, where I belong." The soldier gave the farmer a little smile, as if to convince him of his good intentions.

The farmer looked at him with great suspicions, and strained agonizingly against the jabbing pitchfork, as Josef tried to explain his intentions.

The farmer queried. "Where did you say you are from?" Josef replied. "I'm from Mastig nearHohenelbe. I own a lumber business. My wife and children are waiting for me at home. My wife just had a baby girl. I just want to go home to my wife and daughter." What is your name?" The farmer queried unconvinced. "I'm Josef Staffa. The Staffa lumber business is mine."

The farmer's eyes lit up in surprise as he pointed up at the steep hip roof of the barn and exclaimed with relief. "I know who you are. I know all about the Staffa lumbermen." He pointed to the roof, chuckling with great relief. Josef moved the pitchfork away from his face. "See that roof. I built my house with your lumber! Every shingle on the roof was delivered by your uncle Stefan.

He paused a moment. "I have also met your brother, Adolf, from Königinhof?" Josef grasped the famers hand. "I am Josef the youngest of the Staffa brothers, Stefan was my uncle." The farmer clasped Josef's hand. "I have known your father and his brother Stefan for years. They delivered all roof shingles and barn wood years ago." Josef couldn't believe his luck as the farmer guided him to the house.

"Well, what do you know? Josef Staffa, I am pleased to meet you!"

The two men shook hands once more. Josef shook his head in disbelief about the coincidence that had just saved his life, the fact that an uncle who had once wished him dead, now unwittingly had saved his life.

"To get home now you will need a shirt and pants, so you can make it. You won't get far with these rags." The farmer thrust the pitchfork into the hay, and dragged the uniform out to the field and put a match to the tattered rags. "Partisans come through here regularly. If they find this uniform in my hay, they'll think I am a German collaborator, and pritch. They'll put a bullet between my eyes, just like this." He snapped his fingers. "Wait here!" The old farmer headed back to his house and returned moments later with a bundle of clean clothes.

"Here, take these, they were left behind by partisans. This is a Russian field coat and fur cap. You'll have to be doubly careful because you are sitting between two chairs. If you are caught by the SS they'll shoot you on the spot for having aligned yourself with Czech partisans. If partisans find out that you are a German soldier, they will hang you on the nearest lamp post. Partisans are radicals, revolutionaries without an ideology, misfits, discontented bad boys. They are all a bunch of communists out for blood. They don't care whose blood they shed."

Josef chuckled with relief and nodded with understanding of the double jeopardy he was in. "I know my lot in life, I was born between two chairs. In either case I am a cooked goose. I will take my chances with the partisans. I have no chance with the SS. They don't ask questions, they just put a bullet in my head."

He pointed two fingers at his forehead, mocking his own execution. Josef winced as a rickety old wagon pulled up in front of the barn. The men were singing in a drunken and euphoric stupor. The farmer whispered. "Partisans! They come through the area in search of remaining German soldiers hiding out in the area. They are stealth hunters who rustle soldiers like quail out of hiding, then shoot them on the spot. It no longer is a question of winning a war. It is all motivated by revenge and a thirst for blood. Let me do the talking." The farmer was well-known to the partisans. He enjoyed their confidence and no iota of doubt crept into their conscious mind, as he introduced Josef as one of their comrades. Josef pumped their hands and jovially spoke a folksy Czech. "Pozdrav pan buh!"

"Dejz pan buh! Dobr den…potch key…prosim…yakuyu." The farmer winked coquettishly and chuckled as the partisans proclaimed a hearty welcome to their new compatriot. "Dobri den! Comrade Jusep is on his way home to visit a wife and new baby. He deserves our sympathy…eh? Potch key…Potch key. Here take this cat as a gift for the children." The farmer leaned forward to bid Josef farewell, clasped his shoulder, and as he kissed Josef on both cheeks he murmured softly in his ear in German. "Gott beschütz Dich." Josef tucked the black and white cat under his coat and then said out loud. "Nas Sledano." Josef whispered.

"Yakuyu." The partisans cheered their new comrade to join them, cajoling with him lustily and helped themselves heartily to the German field rations Josef divvied up with aplomb and gave a few morsels to the little cat. He explained that he had looted the remains of dead German soldiers along the Russian front.

Josef instantly had endeared himself to these roughnecks. He shared his rations with his new buddies, slice for slice, and tit for tat, with an intermittent swallow and a hearty. "Nas dravidzgo."

They laughed deliriously when Josef said. "Well, man cannot live by bread alone. A sausage goes well with it and a bottle of Pivo…Nas dravidzgo! I give you a slice of what I have and you give me a slice of what you have." The partisans slapped Josef on the back and responded. "You are right, comrade, man cannot live by bread alone but, in the most-dire need, a sausage tastes good enough to eat." Josef felt comfortable among the partisans. When he had nothing to say he played with the cat and put on a good show of camaraderie. If he hadn't, he might have suffered their swift and merciless, "Yate dum par futzig."

While In Mastig...

Far removed from the noise and clamor of a war that was nearing its' end, Josef's picturesque hamlet appeared serene and unscarred by the ravages of war. The Czech broadcasts ordered that the German population was to turn in all weapons or face the firing squad. Emmi was not concerned about the order to turn in weapons. She knew of no weapons in her home. A Turkish saber hung over the fireplace as a souvenir from a war fought a few hundred years ago in Vienna by an ancestor.

She was more concerned for the children, Kurt, Pepi and Fredi when they went trout fishing along a gurgling brook, a tributary to the Elbe River. Suddenly Kurt saw something metallic glistening in the water, and he called out to Pepi and Fredi. The boys jumped into the water and carefully fished the object out of the water. Kurt examined the object carefully. Their curiosity was peaked and their hearts pounded wildly. Fredi gasped. "What is it?" Kurt replied respectfully. "Jessesmarren! It's part of a German Mauser. Where did you find it?" Pepi asked as Kurt pointed into the water. Immediately the boys waded back into the brook in search for the parts, clips and ammunition. They quickly put together a German Machine pistol. As soon as the last piece clicked into place, the boys looked wistfully at each other.

"Now, what?" Fredi whispered. "I can't bring this thing home. Oma will pull my ears" Pepi replied. "My mother will beat my ass with a cooking spoon. She does not want to see guns."

Kurt nodded. "We must think of a hiding place. We'll have to find a dry place, there are piles of wood chips and sawdust in the factory. Pepi throw the thing into the pile of saw dust."

The boys chortled with excitement and mischief. Kurt handed the loaded weapon to Pepi and the boys raced each other down the hill. Pepi suddenly stumbled and the gun went off, as he fell the gun went off with a loud bang and missed Fredi by a hair. Panicked even more, the boys ran inside the factory building to where the bark of trees was shaved off and trees cut into boards. The boys took a quick look around and seeing nobody and hearing no sound, they searched for a dry place where they could stash the gun in a dry place.

Suddenly they heard feet shuffling. Kurt quickly grabbed the gun from his timid cousin's hands, and dropped the weapon into a pile of sawdust and wood shavings, and kicked a pile of wood shavings over the mysterious find.

The boys ran outside as a craggy old man pressed his wiry body into the shadows of the building. The boys ran up the hill and disappeared inside the Staffa Villa to join again the women in joyous celebrations over cake and coffee.

The face of a crotchety old man appeared as he stepped out of the shadows. His eyes followed the boys with a puzzled look until they disappeared inside the majestic building on top of the hill.

In the Spring of upheaval...

A rickety truck, carrying Josef and the cajoling partisans rumbled along until it reached the outskirts of Mastig. From a distance Josef could see the Mandl smokestack, and opposite that compound was his lumber business. Josef begged to be dropped off in front of wooden shacks along the Mandl factory yard and several yards from Marie's home, he waved a final 'Yakukyu,' hunkered down and waited, waving good bye to make sure the robust rabble rousers were leaving.

He did not want these guys to see in which direction he was going. He crouched in the underbrush thicket and waited until the din of the truck had dissipated. He expected the announcement that the cursed war was over any day. He was one of the few men who had survived the carnage of the Russian frozen and hot inferno. He would be home in minutes and the arms of a loving wife would fall around his neck, he would swaddle his baby girl, and his boys would clamber across his knees. He would surprise Emmi and the children when he let the cat out of his coat pocket. His children would screech for joy over a new playful kitty. He had so much to do, so many wasted years to catch up on. He had his life to rebuild. He had years of accumulated memories he spent in agony and suffering at the Russian front to overcome.

He would continue were he left off. He had his business to run, trucks to roll to haul the timber, cut from his fathers' land into boards and delivered to customers.

Trucks need fuel. He would dot the landscape with gas stations to fuel the trucks that hauled the timber. He saw his lumber business as the springboard of dynamic enterprises he had envisioned since his youth. He would build on his inheritance, like his father and grandfather had. He was lucky indeed, lucky to be alive, with all his limbs and mind intact, having survived the most treacherous war of the century.

Now he was free to pursue his own dreams again, albeit seven years later than he had planned. So far, the best of engineering education his father had afforded him had been for naught. At every moment in his young life, he had found himself at loggerheads with a world run amok, with historical diversions that did not fit into the orderly plans for his life. Hell had sought him out, found and followed him where ere he went. His eyes swayed across the beautiful landscape he felt emboldened with determination to put the past behind him. Adrenalin of pure joy took hold of him and he sprinted like a deer with giant leaps across the dewy meadow toward Marie's house and her beloved garden café.

He saw a young girl contentedly pushing a little girl in a buggy around the yard. He recognized his favorite niece Margit by her sweet smile, stretching from ear to ear as she looked up momentarily. He called out to the girl. "Boidsem! Come here." At sight of the ragged, bearded man, wearing a long tattered Russian coat, the girl ran like a frightened little bird, frantically pushing the buggy ahead into the ice cellar, screaming hysterically. "A Ruskie is here. He is coming to our house! Mama! A Ruskieee!"

As soon as Marie heard her daughters' hysteric screams, she rushed outside, shielded her face against the glare of the sun and stared aghast at a strange, straggly, bedraggled looking man sprinting across the field, waving his arms, flashing a jubilant smile and calling. "Marie! Marie! I'm home."

Then Marie recognized her beloved brother by the quick flash of his smile and his pearly white teeth. She shrieked at the top of her lungs. "Gustl, Jessesmarren! Come quick. It's Sef! Sef is home! Jesusmaranjos!!" (Jesus Mary and Josef) She opened her arms wide, raced toward her beloved brother and jubilantly screamed.

"Children come here. Uncle Sef is home." She met his embrace and he twirled her around. Josef saw three blond curly haired youngsters peering out from the cellar door. Josef could not stop laughing as he watched from a distance the children slowly crawl out of the cellar. He took the kitten from his coat pocket to beckon the children to come closer. He hardly recognized his favorite nephew, the thirteen-year old tall, muscular Kurt with a shock of blond curls falling over his large witty blue eyes, standing next to him was the pretty sixteen-year-old Margit. He had recognized her by her sweet, gentle, heart-shaped face, surrounded by a halo of blond ringlets and long braids as she peered out from the cellar door. Marie pointed to a small child in a stroller. "This is Christa. She is almost five years old now, children come here! This man is not a Ruskie!" She chuckled. "This is our Sef, your uncle Sef is home."

The House My Father Built

As soon as the children heard their mother say that the man was their uncle, they ran screeching with outstretched arms, each trying to be the first to leap into their uncles' arms. Josef's homecoming called for a family celebration and Marie ordered her son. "Kurt! Run and get Aunt Emmi. I want her to come quickly. But don't tell her, Uncle Sef is home and don't say anything about the cat."

Josef stopped the lad in his tracks momentarily and put the kitten back in his coat pocket. "Kurt, potch key, potch key for a few minutes! I want to clean up a little bit first. I stopped here before going home. I want to use the bathroom. I don't want my wife to see me like this." Marie walked ahead to show her brother where he could clean up. Kurt waited patiently until Uncle Sef reappeared looking cleaner and refreshed. He still had a full beard and was hardly recognizable as the uncle he had last seen years ago.

As Josef was leaning on a cane he looked like an old man. He waved to Kurt to go-ahead with a swift command. "Pritch ! pritch!" Kurt sped off on his long legs, and Josef followed slowly, stopping often to look around as he supported himself on the cane. He felt rejuvenated as he slowly wound his way along the tree lined road along the little Elbe brook and the spot where his father had been dragged into the icy waters and where a memorial plaque had been mounted. He gazed at his house in the distance with the gleaming copper roof that was lighting up the hillside and savored the view with acknowledgment and a satisfied smile "Yes, this is the most beautiful house on earth." He slowly walked past his office building, the lumber yard and factory, where timber waited to be sawed into boards and building supplies.

The Nazis had confiscated his trucks but not his life. He could rebuild on what was left behind. He walked across Mastigs' largest intersection past the Luschnitz General Store and the Mandl Administration building. He walked slowly up the grassy knoll toward the house he had built. His eyes absorbed the clean lines of his beautiful villa with the wide angled veranda, surrounded by lush gardens in which he had planted an abundance of fruit trees that appeared to be budding into bloom. The cherry tree with its delicate pink blossoms was his favorite. It was the one he had planted in front of the dining room alcove.

He looked forward to the day when he could pluck the first fruit with a wildly pounding heart. He smiled to himself as the peace of his homeland filled his soul. He sighed deeply. "Oh, what peace there is in silence, the peace of God that passes all understanding."

No bombs or hand grenades had fallen on this landscape. No shots had been fired in this region. The people of this area had gotten away unscathed. He was relieved at sight of his lumber piled high that soon he would cut into boards and he would hear again the buzzing and wheezing of saw blades. The buildings stood like fortresses that had given his life a firm foundation, on which he could rebuild. He breathed deeply and exhaled slowly.

"This is the most beautiful sight on the face of the earth, my house, my home, my wife and life." Josef had crossed the fork in the road just below his estate and saw a young woman, whose brown hair softly framed her beautiful face. She walked hesitatingly toward him. He could see the fright in her eyes. She did not recognize him and that she was frightened the closer he came. He stopped advancing toward her, leaned his chin on his cane to let the beauty of the moment soak into his eyes as the wind gently caressed her face and blew her hair into wispy strands. He whispered to himself.

"There is nothing more beautiful than the beautiful sight I have seen now." It was the moment he had dreamed of and was determined to live for. Seeing his beloved wife gazing at him with a dazed look, harkened his sense of humor. He had to smile when he realized that she could not distinguish a dream from a nightmare.

Emmi saw an emaciated beggar with a full beard like those she had seen on the truck at the village well. The beggar looked emaciated as he dragged himself slowly up the hill toward her house.

Emmi stopped dead in her tracks as the man looked at her like he didn't have an ounce of strength left in his weary bones, his tired eyes looked old. Paralyzed with fright at the strange man's pathetic condition, she clutched the fencepost, ready to run back to the safety of her house. For a moment they just stared at each other. He was stunned to see Emmi tremble in fear. She wondered if she could run fast enough before the man could grab her. She hoped to run back to the house and bolt the door. Yet, the pity she felt for this wretched creature made her wonder. "Maybe I can give the beggar some soup."

Seeing her frozen in terror, he spread out his arms, smiled saying. "Don't you recognize me? It's me!" At that moment, the puzzled look fled from her face, her eyes opened wide in sheer joy, as she recognized his smile by his pearly white teeth.

She dropped to her knees and burst into tears. She gathered her strength to get up and with arms raised high, her hands clasped together in prayer, tears streamed down her face in torrents.

"Josef, my Josef, somehow, I knew God would spare my beloved husband. My prayers have been answered." Blinded by tears, with arms outstretched, she ran toward him, her torment had found relief. She stumbled and fell to the ground. Josef rushed to help her get up on her feet. Josef caught Emmi in his arms, and the sudden impact caused them both to fall onto the grassy knoll.

Crouching on the embankment, they embraced, oblivious to the curious onlookers of the world. She helped Josef get up on his feet, reached for his arm and draped it over her shoulder, as if she planned to carry him home the rest of the way. She realized how thin he was and knew she would have to be his rod and strength for some time to come. Josef reached inside his coat.

"Here, I brought you a souvenir as a homecoming present." He pulled out the small black and white cat and put in Emmis lap.

Josef breathed in the fresh spring mountain air. "Home! Sweet, Home. Here is where my heart is anchored. This is my home where I belong, where my children cluster around me, where we will celebrate new life and joyous family events. It's all I could think of on the cursed Russian Front. You and me in the house I built." As soon as he entered the house Josef realized how much his sons had grown and how much the family had expanded, when he entered the house. He saw that Emmis mother and her sister Anninka, with her two children Eva and Peter had moved into his house. He tousled his boy's heads, bounced his baby daughter on one knee and baby Eva on the other knee. He let the small cat out of his coat pocket to the delightful screeching of the children.

For a few days Josef could relax amid family harmony and around the dinner table he told endless stories of babitchkas, a Russian soldier whose life he had spared and chained dogs called Kettenhunde, while the children played with the cat. Family bliss was his idea of heaven, but he realized that his business affairs could not wait any longer, unaware they would give him new nightmares.

He went to his office to check out the cash receipts journal, but no sooner had he turned the first pages he discovered that certain pages were missing. "Emmi, did you tear out any pages from this journal." Emmi looked puzzled and shook her head as Josef quizzed her. "Look, this is the last entry, I made five years ago. Nothing was logged after that date." Josef looked dumbfounded and fingered the frayed edges where once other pages had been. "Here, see this! From here several pages have been torn out." Emmi clutched her chest. "Your brother Karl came here almost every day. One day he shoved documents under my nose and asked me to sign them.

"Josef looked alarmed. "Did you sign anything?" Emmi exclaimed. "No! I asked him why he wanted me to sign documents, he acted strangely evasive. So I read the paperwork. He talked about purchasing property near the border to the Netherlands. He wanted me to sign something in case you were killed in the war.

Because of the problems with the Czechs, he wanted to relocate the lumber business near the Netherland border after the war. To secure loans he needed our house as collateral, he told me that I should sign the house over to him, so he could use it to buy for us a house in Germany." Josef looked aghast. "Are you sure you never signed anything?" Emmi shook her head again.

"Absolutely not! Karl tried to convince me that he needed to be named as administrator so he could act in the best interest for our family. I did not trust him. I told him I would not do anything without your approval."

Josef grabbed the business receipts journal and raced to his office across the street. The doors were locked, so he pried them open. To his horror, he discovered that the safe was open and cleaned out, the desk was empty. He found a letter addressed to his brothers' new place of business, Karl Staffa Lumber, Lengerich, Deutschland.

He walked to the office of the land registry, and discovered that his brother had sold off valuable pieces of woodlands. The clerk told him that his brother used his power of attorney for the transactions and even tried to transfer the deed to Josef's house, into his own name. It all became crystal clear to Josef what had happened.

"Because your wife's name is on the deed, your brother needed her signature, which Emmi would not give, so he sold other properties, over which he legally could exercise his authority to sell.

It became clear to Josef that his brother, Karl thought his wife was too dumb to notice that he was conniving her into signing the house over to him. His brother, Karl had not expected Josef to survive the Russian Front and was ready to sell his house out from under him, and leave his wife and children homeless. His plans were thwarted when he couldn't get Emmi to sign the papers.

Josef went to the bank next, and was shocked to find that the account was nearly depleted. The business proceeds for the last three years were gone. Fuming inside, Josef went to Karl's house ready to confront the whole family clan. He was not surprised to find that Karl was not home.

Ilse was home alone with four children, looking nonplussed to see him alive and well. It appeared to Josef that Ilse looked sorry to see that he had survived the war at all, and barred him from entering the house with her full corpulent frame. The children ogled him and queried about the strange man who confronted their mother with an angry voice. While Ilse appeared to compose herself and proudly introduced her four blond and blue-eyed children, her only son Karli, twin girls Heidi and Inge, and a baby Judita.

Josef was beyond pleasantries and admiring Ilse's offspring. He was livid and snarled.

"Where is Karl? Where is Alfred?" Ilse shrugged her shoulders. "I don't know?"

Josef flung a piece of paper under her nose. "Let me refresh your memory. He is somewhere near the Netherland border?" He read to her the address and shouted. "Karl and Alfred fled the country because of their Nazi affiliation. Now that the tide has turned fearing retribution of the Czech militias who will string them up on lampposts!"

Ilse's fair skin glowed beet red. "If you know where Karl is, why ask me? All is lost here. There is nothing left for us here. When Karl realized that the war was lost, so he rescued what he could." Josef was fuming while he waited for her to finish. "Karl and Alfred conspired against me to build up a new lumber business in the west. They sold all they could and took with them the family fortune, leaving me and my family with merely an allowance in my bank account." Ilse shrugged her shoulder. as Josef blasted her nonchalant attitude.

"While I wasted my productive years in muddy trenches in the battle of Stalingrad, for a cause that was not mine, I paid the price for your idiocy and barely survived a hellish existence, while my brother and you, who were the arch believers in Socialism lived in relative comfort through this bloody war. As my brothers on the pretense of minding the store, plundered it instead. To hell with all of you!" He slammed the door in her face and opened it once more. "Don't ever set foot in my house again. In my eyes my brothers and you are dead."

Heartsick over his brothers' treacherous deceit, he poured all his energies into repairing the damage. However, there was little he could do. Josef never got the chance to wrangle with his brothers over the missing money and the sale of properties. With a world in disarray and Berlin in ruins, there was no court in which he could seek redress.

Josef enjoyed the leisure of his home for no more than two weeks, when hell sought him out and found him again. Josef and Gustav along with former German soldiers were arrested by the Czech military and partisans herded them along, with whips cracking against their naked backs. Rubber mallets and truncheons crashed about their heads. Josef was assigned to a group of prisoners of war near the Switschin Ridge, were the German captives had to clear the region of all tank barriers and all other remnants of war. Josef along with thousands of his countrymen were herded along on a foot march toward Prague.

The men were prodded along with bullwhips and rifle butts, many were shot along the way. Finally, those who endured the march were incarcerated and interrogated in countless Czech concentration camps, where the Sudeten Germans were treated just as brutally by the Czechs as Jews had been under Hitlers' reign of terror.

Germans were chained to one another, forced to wear armbands with Nemec (German) smeared on them, hair was shaved and their foreheads smeared with black swastikas, vengence was the trigger mechanism of ancient hatred that went all the way back to the 10th century King Wenceslas and his brother Boleslav, or Hus doctrines, or Cains' jealousy of Able. Canons were silent and the war was declared over. For the Sudeten German people, the war had just begun. The Czechs made no distinction between Nazi guilt or the innocence of being born German by accident of birth, or of one born between two chairs. Those who survived the carnage of war were assigned to work as slaves for Czech farmers in beet fields. Josef angrily plowed the hoe across the new seedlings, defiantly telling the horrified farmer in the Czech language. "I know nothing about beet farming. I only know the lumber business!"

The farmer wrote an assessment of Josef, as one unsuitable for farming.

Smert Nemcum ...

Death to Germans on the morning of May 5, 1945, overnight "Death to Germans" was the cry that blared and echoed over bullhorns of the Czech militias throughout the Sudeten German villages, which had become a witches' cauldron that instant. In the smallest Czech villages mobs angrily ransacked and looted the cavernous rooms of the old Nazi party buildings covered with old Swastikas and Nazi propaganda posters.

Josef was sent with the next caravan of prisoners of war to a concentration camp near Prague. There in the Prague spring of 1945, Josef witnessed the gruesome destruction of his culture and the tragedy of his people while he prayed. "Lord, whom can I turn to where can I go?"

The mob pried open file cabinets, tore pictures, posters, flags, emblems and all Nazi propaganda to shreds. No sooner was the face of Hitler consumed by flames behind a red draped podium, new pictures were hung up surrounded by golden hammers and sickle banners of the old Communist guard, Stalin, Lenin, Karl Marx, and the new Czech Premier Eduard Benes.

Eduard Benes had successfully seduced the British under Churchill's influence to accept the forceful deportation of Germans from the Sudetenland in a "Humane and Orderly Manner." Knowing all along there was nothing humane and orderly to witness, as the red-faced mob shouted relentlessly for revenge. Revenge for what? What had the ordinary person done?

The old foreman from the Staffa lumber yard, Hranek was caught in the midst of the mob. He listened quietly to the instructions ordered by the National Czech militia. The Narodny Vybor distributed lists of names. "Arrest all Germans. We have to rid ourselves of German sub-humans. We have to kill them all if they don't leave voluntarily. Every single man, woman and child will be lined up. Make them dig their own graves. Pritch, pritch!"

Hranek tried to intervene with a moderating voice. "We should find those guilty of crimes and put them on trial. German villages have nothing left but women and children and a few old men. They won't harm us." Despite his moderating and reasoning appeals he could not keep the venom from flowing as Hranek pleaded mournfully. "This will not bring us any blessings."

A roar filled the old party house, and his pleas for moderation were dismissed as the whining of an old babitchka. "You whine like an old babitchka. We have the party's blessing. Benes swore revenge for Lidice, and to use every opportunity to kill Germans." He screamed. "There is no such thing as a good German. If you kill a German, nobody will be prosecuted. The Benes Decree allow us to rid ourselves of the German colonists.

The old foreman, Hranek waited until the streets were steeped in midnight silence. Panting heavily, he ran up the hill toward the Staffa villa of his German employer. He knocked softly but persistently until a light shone on him from inside. Through the glass paneled doors he could see the maid rushing down the stairs. As she opened the door a crack, he stepped inside the door so the light would not shine on him. He grabbed the arm of the maid and covered her mouth with his rough hands to keep her from shrieking in terror.

"Shhh! Don't make a sound." He whispered with a barely audible raspy voice, as she struggled against his grip and felt his arm tightening as he held her against his chest. "Don't make a sound or I have to kill you. Go get Pani Staffawa, quick. Get the misses, hurry!"

He pushed her away from him. Erma rushed up the stairs and called softly with a fearful tremor in her voice. Emmi had heard the commotion downstairs. She appeared on the top of the stairs in her nightgown, visibly shaken upon hearing her name pronounced in the Czech language. She sleepily looked over the banister, and recognized her husband's trusted Czech foreman.

Frightened to the core, she whispered. "Hranek! What are you doing here at this hour?" He placed a finger across his mouth and whispered. "Pani Staffawa, we have to bury the machine gun, everyone in this house will be shot if that gun is found by the militias."

Emmi looked stunned and ever more frightened. "What gun? We don't have guns. We have a few hunting rifles that have never been used, because my husband can't even shoot a rabbit. We have a family heirloom it's a Turkish saber, a souvenir from the war against the Turks hundreds of years ago." She hastily replied in panic. Hranek hurriedly replied unflinching,

"I saw the boys a couple days ago, Pepiczek with that blond tall Kurt and little Fredi. I saw them with a German pistol. I implore you to find it tonight, we have to get rid of it, or you will all be shot tomorrow morning."

At that moment, Pepi ran past his startled mother and Hranek gave chase through the back door, yelling over his shoulder at the maid. "Have Koczian bring shovels and a pick axe. Gather all rifles, guns, and that Turkish saber over the fireplace, everything that can be seen as a weapon." Pepi and the old man ran toward the factory building across the road.

The maid ran across the street to wake Koczian, who had a permanent apartment upstairs in the old Staffa mansion with Oma Staffa. Emmi still in her night clothes scrambled to fetch shovels from the cellar and gathered the never-used rifles and the antique saber which had been found after the battle of Vienna against the Turks.

Koczian hobbled up the road, pulling his suspenders over his shoulders. Hranek briefly explained what he had overheard. Koczian cried out. "Jessesmarren!" He understood immediately the gravitas of the situation. He crouched down grimacing in pain, and wrapped the entire assortment of weapons into oil cloths. Hranek and Pepi hastily cut away a square piece of sod and dug a hole under the threshold of the garden gate, throwing anything that could be seen as a weapon into the hole. They carefully placed the old sod back in its place and tamped it flat.

The only sounds heard that night were frantic heartbeats and labored breathing. Emmi turned to Hranek to thank him with a squeeze of her hand. But the old man waved off her gratitude and quickly disappeared into the pitch-black darkness. Emmi whispered to Koczian. "Thank you! You good and faithful servant." He nodded and quickly disappeared. Emmi followed him with soulful eyes and wondered. "Lord, whom shall I turn to? Where should I go? What evil is heading toward us now?" But there was no time to ponder of what was to come. She darted back into the house and called her son. "Pepi, you have to help me crate some stuff." They hollowed out the cinder block walls in the attic. Emmi stashed her jewelry, wrapped silver, crystal and valuables into the hollowed walls along the attic rafters. Pepi sealed the walls up with mortar. Emmi could not part with the watch and bracelet Josef had given her on their wedding day, she sewed them into her undergarments.

The basement was divided into a cool storage cellar for apples, cabbage and potatoes, a coal bin, storage racks for canned goods, a smoking chamber for meats and sausages, and curing barrels for sauerkraut. Pepi helped Emmi dig holes in the basement's coal cellar, wrapped Josef's pride and joy, his BMW motorbike into heavy oilcloth, then shoveled layers of sand and coals on top to cover up the pit. Emmi went to bed late that night and slept fitfully until the rooster crowed the dawn of a day of horror.

Karel Pusch was leading the mob. The man stood tall and intimidating with thick, black oily hair, slicked straight back before the trembling women and children. Wearing the symbols of their membership in the Communist militia, the Czech Socialists and Narodny Vybor, wore red bands around their arms and legs as they marched six abreast into the streets. Their small sinister eyes squinted in the morning sun, as their bushy mustache bobbed up and down while the names were read out loud of those they were specifically looking for.

Karel Pusch and conspirator Stanislaus Shubrt reached the old Nazi party building. The building was teeming with frenzied activity. The jostling goon squads distributed lists of addresses of former Nazi party members. Armed with whips, rubber mallets, and shotguns and fists flying in the air, the mob went from door to door, searching throughout every neighborhood to raid and plunder for valuables, and a bloody carnage ensued.

Loudspeakers blared new orders. Every male over the age of fourteen had to step outside. Then they stormed the homes of unsuspecting people in search of weapons, watches and jewelry, dragging women and children out of their beds into the streets in their nightclothes.

The mob confiscated even food supplies, and clothes hanging on laundry lines. When Emmi was asked to identify everyone, Emmis' mother Franziska shouted "I am a Borufka!"

Oma Staffa likewise used her maiden name. "I am Anna Kudronovsky." Both grandmothers produced their Czech citizen papers and both women were allowed to go back in the house.

Emmi and Anninka clung to each other as they watched a scuffle ensue over a box of baby food between Ilse and the disheveled militant goon squads. Emmi felt sorry for her sister-in-law's babies, as Ilse struggled to hang onto a box of baby formula. It was the only food she had left for her baby, and screamed. "I have nothing left to feed my children."

Emmi saw the scuffle over a box of baby cereal. She ran across the street, stepped in between the men who were harassing Ilse and in fluent Czech implored the men. "My God let babies have their food!" Emmi tried running back to her house as the men turned their attention on her and tried to frisk her and Annika for valuables, they scattered their belongings including the underwear on the clothes lines. Emmi had prepared herself for the loss of material possessions, but nothing had prepared her for the cruelty of the ensuing terror and massacres.

The mobsters painstakingly studied the list for the names of former Nazi party members. They read the names out loud among them was "Karl Staffa a member, Alfred Staffa a member. And asked where are they? We watched them as they carried flags in parades."

Emmi dared not blink or show emotions when she noticed that the man's feet stood exactly where the gun lay buried beneath the sod. She felt considerable unease as beads of sweat formed on her brow and running down her face. Only one thought occupied her mind. 'I hope he won't notice that the sod is softer on that spot on which he is standing.' Emmi harnessed the attention of Karel Pusch.

She knew her life and the lives of her children was at stake. She was pleading for the lives of children, her sister Annika's and her own. "Leave the kids alone. They have done nothing."

The man snarled belligerently. "Kids grow up and then we have to deal with them later." She implored the men with the talents of an actress, and in fluent Czech she steadfastly maintained their staunch defense in a feverish frenzy. She beseeched him with her wide grey eyes and fervor in her voice, while he smacked the handle of the whip against his boot in nervous agitation. Emmi shook her head. "I have not seen them, the last notice we had from my brother-in-law was from a place in the Netherlands. They will not come back here."

Karel showed no sign of anything amiss, as he scanned the S's with his fingers, meticulously. Emmi knew who the men were looking for. "If you are looking for my husband's name, you won't find his name on any membership list. My husbands' name is Josef Staffa. He never joined any party. My husband hated party politics and all its hateful diatribe, hype and hoopla so much he wouldn't even let my boys watch military parades. He had to pay fines every year in the thousands because he refused to join the Nazi party. He never listened to political broadcasts because he had an abhorrence of their propaganda. Karl and Alfred are his brothers and they have already fled to the Netherlands.

His brothers carried flags in parades because they wanted to look like big shots. That was all they did. They joined the party because they did not want to get sent to the Russian Front."

Emmi astonished herself, when, despite the tremor in her voice she was able to convince these men, that she was telling the truth. The men looked relaxed and placated with her explanations.

Anninka listlessly clung to little Eva's hand and soothed baby Peter with a rocking motion of the baby buggy. Emmi stood by her sister's side with her own baby girl in her arms. She swayed back and forth to calm her child, just as gunshots and screams could be heard from around the neighborhood.

The next morning the swarthy and disheveled young men were back. They had stalked and haunted their German neighbors for years, keeping them all within the visor of their binoculars and shooting across their wheat fields at one big granite rock in the distance just to make a lot of frightening noise in the hope of scaring these people into panic flights. They boasted in pubs how they had successfully terrorized their Nemci neighbors at every opportunity.

It had been their aim to intimidate these simple folks in the hope they would leave voluntarily. These folks had become very nervous at their sight, but stubbornly refused to leave. Over the years, they realized that it would require a political solution to rid the country of all Germans. These terrorists had always known that their day of glory would come.

Emmi recognized three of the men among the mob. One of them was the employee from the butcher shop. Others whose faces and names she knew from her husband's lumber business Stanislav Shubert, Rudi Kostial and Karel Push. Czechs who now drove the cries to a fever pitch, relentlessly chanting the newest slogans coming out of Prague "Smert Nemcum!"

Karel had moved into the home of a distant Staffa clan member. He was known as the Staffa carpenter, who had used his skills to fit cabinets, doors and windows of many of his neighbors' homes. Karel paid his rent knowing he was just biding his time until the moment was right in which he planned to become the rightful owner of the house. Karel used the latest Eduard Benes decrees that stated that anyone caught with a weapon would be shot. Karel had concocted a sinister plan to confiscate the property under the new decree. He stashed a weapon among the belongings of his German landlord, knowing when the weapon was found, his landlord would be shot and he would be able to spread out his belongings over the entire house and call it his own. Today was his day!

He would cleanse the nation of Czechs of all Nemci colonists. His brother had died in their pond. This was the day when he would avenge his brothers' death. He would bloody their white stockings, and free the land of these capitalist pigs. In Czech schools the children had been taught that the Germans had colonized this area for a thousand years. The trauma of the Hussite defeat after a thirty-year war had never left the psyche of the Czech people.

In the eyes of the Czech people, the Germans had never been sufficiently punished for the lost Thirty-year war. They were determined to turn the moment of retribution into a slaughter and blood bath. As they chanted along with the cries. "Smert Nemcum, Death to Germans!" We cannot let these pigs sniff around our Socialist Garden of Eden." Their swarthy faces were covered in sweat and grime.

Dark curly hair fell in thick coils across their deeply etched faces. Bushy eyebrows formed one straight line across their downward slanting eyes and broad noses, which they frequently wiped against the back of their dirty shirt sleeves.

Gustav Gernert had been released from the Switschin prison. The Czech war crimes tribunal and interrogators could not find any party connections of Gustav, hard as they searched the party files. Gustav had merely cooked meals under the orders of Ernst Lochmann, the local Gauleiter and commandant. Gustav's atrocities amounted to no more than arms covered with flour up to his elbows, and spilling boiling noodle water. But the local members of the Narodny Vybor, Karel and Stanislaus were nonplussed by Gustav's quick release from prison.

Emmi worried about Josef's sister, Annie, who lived in Koniginhof where the slaughter had begun, Germans were beaten about the head, neck and torso and marched to their ultimate destiny. If they survived the beatings, they were tossed over the Elbe dam while children clung to their mothers. The baby buggies were tossed after them.

Those lucky enough to survive the fall over the dam were shot as they struggled to swim away. Many lamp posts had become gallows from which even old men, even those who were known as staunch resisters to Socialist regimes, were not spared. Others, rather than give the tormentors a chance to kill them, jumped on a stool beside the lamppost, placed the noose around their own necks and kicked the stool out from under themselves. Throughout the Sudetenland a blood bath had ensued that cost the lives of more than 240,000 people, about 10% of the Sudeten German population.

Emmi shuddered in horror when the men pressed a rifle at her belly, ordered her and Anninka to come along with them. The two women clutched their children close to their breasts, wondering if they were going to be shot next. As they were herded along, they saw their German neighbors as they were driven at gunpoint from every house. The children attending Mastig's only Elementary school, among them five-year-old Reiner and Christa in Kindergarten, and seven-year-old Otto were marched in a two-by-two formation, into the clearing of a wooded hillside.

Sirens blared from the Mandl factory for a long while, as the workers were ordered to march out of the gate. A bus pulled up in front of the factory gates, and the workers were ordered to put white armbands on. The armbands had been smeared with the name Nemec (German). The workers were driven to a clearing between Mastig and Klein-Borowitz, there they were pushed with rifle butts off the rickety bus. There they had to wait wondering if they would be summarily shot, or what was about to happen to them. Moments later, Emmi froze in terror when she saw a truck pull up.

A white-haired woman emerged from the truck and Emmi recognized Franziska Linhart, mother of Bruno Linhart, the friend of her youthful years.

The old woman and her husband, Emil were pushed from the truck with rifle butt. The old couple had been the first to be arrested and dragged from their home in full view of the villagers. One of the militias had once been a millhand in the employ of Emil Linhart.

He had set his eyes on the Linharts' three-hundred-year-old estate. Their ancestry was emblazoned in church and cemetery archives. Their rich properties, gracious home, trout pond and flour mill were the envy of the neighborhood. The mill hand often bragged to his comrades that the villa with a trout pond, a flour mill belonged to him. After the war ended, he stashed a pistol under the couple's belongings, knowing this would secure the couples death sentence. Emil Linhart and his wife Franziska paid the price for the crime committed by another evil doer.

The House My Father Built

When the weapon was indeed discovered by the militia, they were sentenced to death by firing squad, despite the couple's protestations and their insistence of innocence and swearing under oath repeatedly. "The gun does not belong to us. We have never owned any weapons." Their protestations of innocence were of no avail. It was a forgone conclusion, that the court would find the couple guilty and sentence them to death. Emmi tearfully remembered the goodness of Franziska Linhart, whose five sons had been drafted into the German Army and had lost already Bruno in the war. How Franziska decorated German war memorials on sunny days before the German Army marched into the area, how she decorated her window sills with fresh Geraniums and sung Viennese favorites "Vienna Blood", and "Wine Women and Song."

From spring through summer months Franziska Linhart planted flowers around public roadside altars and crucifixes. Her disdain for the Nazi war mongering and military complex and men in uniform was obvious when she stopped planting flowers where soldiers of the Reich had covered the crucifixes with Swastikas. She was known as a godly pious mother of five sons, one of whom, Emmi's friend and music theatre director, who had been killed at the Russian front. She was known as a hard worker who never had an unkind word for anyone. During the war, this shy and endearing woman often invited other women in the area to come and pray the Rosary with her.

They prayed for hours for the safe return of their husbands and sons to no avail. Nobody could imagine that this woman had done anything to deserve what these men of the militia were doing to her now. This little woman and her husband were dragged from the truck like criminals. Franziska's eyes looked at the weeping women and children lining the narrow path. She recognized her neighbors and kinsmen. She saw the sadness and pity and horror in their teary eyes, knowing that these old neighbors were forced to witness the massacre of an innocent woman and her husband. Franziska whispered to her husband. "I think they are going to shoot us here in front of all these poor people." At gunpoint the white-haired couple was ordered to dig a deep hole, what would become their own grave at the edge of the forest clearing. At one point Franziska could be heard sighing and heaving with exhaustion. "I can't go on anymore." She sat down exhausted on the dark earth behind her. The guard paced behind her with great impatience and ordered the woman to keep shoveling. As she tried to stand up again, her knees buckled and a neighbor named Walsch jumped into the shallow hole and took the shovel from the doomed woman's hand. Franziska turned to the assembled villagers and said for all to hear. "Tell my sons…we died innocently. We have never owned a gun."

As they shoveled the husband and wife could be heard praying together over and over "Hail Mary…full of grace, blessed art though among women…pray for us sinners now and at the hour of our death." In the last seconds of their lives, the ccouple reached out for their hands and held them until...

One highly decorated Red Armist, a Narodny Vybor with the red armbands and one who stood beside the Czech militia commander as the death sentence was read in an unrecognizable language.

Franziska and Emil Linhart were still praying as the executioner stepped back and signaled the Czech commander, who raised his arm, and when he let his arm drop, shots rang out that echoed through the valley. Emil and Franziska Linhart slumped together into their shallow grave instantly, still holding hands.

The next victims of the Narodny Vybor rampage were the old German mayor of Mastig who with his white-haired wife, had been the mayor of this German village before 1918. They had been replaced on the day of the birth of the new Czech Republic by a Czech Administrator. When the German troops marched into the Sudetenland the former German mayor got his old job back, but at a cost. He was forced to join the Nazi party, just as many government employees including teachers, were forced to do. Emmi thought about the many times her husband had been accosted and pressured to join the Nazi Party. Hitler's stranglehold over the Sudeten German people had pressured those in the lowest government positions to join the party or lose their jobs and pensions.

Emmi thanked God now for her husbands' fortitude in that her husband staunchly resisted joining the Socialist party, even at risk to his own life. He referred to these Socialist party henchmen as Schweinehunde. He had made no bones of his disdain and refused to flip his arm and shout 'Heil Hitler.' It had galled Josef to be pressured to pander for economic advantages, if it meant he would have to adhere to Socialist party doctrines, that had galled him most. He displayed an open disdain for what he labeled the hooked cross enslavement, with his own brand of abhorrence for any stinking political ideology.

At the time, the constant demand for unswerving loyalty to Hitler, the never-ending threats and intimidations had seemed such a noose around her husbands' neck, not to mention the hefty fines he had to pay every year.

Emmi had pleaded with her husband to acquiesce for the sake of keeping the peace with the local leadership, and appease people like her sister-in-law, to join the party, just so they would no longer live in fear of imprisonment or the firing squad. Now she thanked God, that her husband had smelled the rats and had resisted becoming one of them.

Her husbands' keen instincts and clear vision of what he had perceived as pure evil might just have saved their lives now. Emmi realized that Josef had resisted Socialist pressures to join the party and had rejected the clamor of idolatry that attributed to Adolf Hitler the status as Savior of the German people. She pitied those who had no choice but to join the party if their lives depended on a government salary or a well-earned pension in old age, and those who feared imprisonment and the firing squad and who now had to pay an even more bitter price.

Gustav Gernert was home for merely two days, when he was dragged out of his house by the Czech militia led by Rudi Kostial, the 24-year-old Mandl factory worker. Kurt was watching in horror as his father was shoved aboard a rickety Soviet truck. Rudi sneered at 13-year-old Kurt when the truck drove off. "Now, you will never see your father again."

While women like Emmi and Anninka and their children were forced to line the streets to watch the spectacles of executions, Pepi crawled behind Kurt along the wooden underbrush dodging the militias who were looking out for anyone in hiding. From their hiding place they had a vantage point. They could watch the gruesome massacres in the villages below without being seen. Kurt couldn't get his father's image out of his mind with plaguing questions, what had these Czech militias and goon squads done to his father? Kurt scanned the faces of people who were being lined up for executions to see if his father was among them, wondering what these people had done to be massacred like this. He watched people slump against bullet riddled walls behind the Elementary Schools.

Margit was pushing a six-old around in a stroller in their Rose Garden Café, playing on the sidewalk drawing in the sand hop-scotch squares with a stick. Designs and crosses, symbols and pictures of anything her young eyes had seen.

When the mob saw the child drawing what looked like a swastika a bullet in her head ended her life. The tool and die machine shop owner Franz Pech, from Ober–Prausnitz, just down the street from Holy Family Church, whose wife and son had fled to Germany before the end of the war, was chased out of his house. Russian laborers in the employ of Franz Pech had never forgotten the kick in the pants he had given one of their Russian comrades for sleeping on the job. The mob exercised such brutal revenge on Franz Pech, calling him a capitalist pig while they beat him up, spat on him, they dragged him to the edge of the forest, tied him to a tree, cut out his tongue, then they beat him to death.

The women shuddered when they heard the crackling of machine guns amid the terrified screams of elementary age school children. At gunpoint, the German Kindergarten children were marched outside, among them Otto, Margit, Fredi, Rudi and Christa. They had to form a single line along the parameters of the sports field behind the school building to watch the gruesome spectacles of executions taking place where they once had played soccer.

In the final years of Hitler's insane war, boys as young as fourteen years had been drafted into the German army. One of these children was Franz Mintner, who was no more than fifteen years when he was drafted and sent to the Russian front. He was glad to have returned to his parents unscathed. He was only seventeen-years old, still wearing the grey uniform of a conscript as he lay on his mother's sofa and thought how lucky he was to have survived the Russian front. He was glad to be in his mother's cozy home.

The shaggy facial growth hid his baby face and belying his age of a boy as he was dragged from his parents' house. He was kicked to the ground, pulled up again by his blond hair and beaten about the head and torso. Anninka recognized the boy as one of her classmates before he was drafted into the army. Franz Mintner, was the son of the German school chancellor. The boy screamed and struggled as they tied his hands behind his back, and nailed him by his tongue to the barn door, there they beat him to a pulp.

At last, they dragged the boy out to the sports field behind the German Elementary School before a nine-man firing squad. They put a blindfold on his face and waited until all the children had surrounded the sports field. Franz Mintner, in the last seconds of his life, ripped the blindfold from his eyes, tore open his uniform jacket to expose his bare chest. Instantly, a hail of bullets from nine machine guns sawed his body to bits and pieces. The children shrieked in naked horror, as blood spurted at them from all directions.

When Anninka saw what they had done to this boy, she burst into tears. "I remember the day when Franz Mintner started kindergarten." His parents the German school chancellor and his wife were executed next.

Emmi and Anninka watched helplessly as they heard other women screaming, only to be caught, dragged into some barn, where they were raped. Husbands' who tried to help their wives fight off an attacker were shot in the head. As soon as the militia had finished their blood bath in Mastig, they moved on to neighboring communities and left villages in chaos as people rushed to reach their own homes and then an eerie stillness returned.

Emmi looked around for her oldest son. She screamed the name of her son to no avail. Pepi had become ever more difficult to curtail and she thought it best to take the younger children to the safety of her home. Emmi and Anninka hightailed it back with their young, traumatized children, and barricaded the doors. There would be no school any time soon.

Kurt and Pepi stayed hidden in their secret caves and tunnels from where they could watch the terror spreading throughout the small communities of the Sudetenland to a fever pitch. No one knew why the baker and his daughter were shot among the assembled villagers. The villagers were forced to watch as the baker and his daughter were killed. They were standing beside his wife who was clutching the youngest son. After witnessing the brutalities against her husband and daughter, the mother and son committed suicide together, fearing they would be next. Another daughter fled for her life and lived to write about the tragedy of her people.

Other families were found slain in their beds, in one room they found the parents. In another room they found the children with a bullet hole in their heads. One could only hope that they never saw it coming. Finance executive Erich Seidel, was chased and beaten then shot and buried where he died. His wife, Maria Bönsch, owner of a mountain inn, and her daughter were bludgeoned to death. Wenzel Lauer, owner of a hotel was beaten bloody before being shot. Gustav Kraus was beaten to a pulp, until he couldn't stand up any more so the militias tied him up with ropes to a tree before they could shoot him. The forest ranger, Engelbert Lorenz, carried a rifle as all forest rangers do, he was brutally beaten and shot. The Schubert family had just come to terms with the tragedy of the loss of their oldest son, who had fallen on the Russian front. Now the father was shot by the Czech militia.

Karel Pusch stashed a weapon beneath the confiscated belongings of his landlord, the Staffa carpenter, when the gun was found and despite the man's assertions that the gun did not belong to him, he was shot by the Czech militia. His tenant, Karel Pusch proudly declared himself the leader of the local militia, and promptly claimed the house as his own.

His lust for blood was satisfied that day, as he leisurely made himself at home. One of the last victims, which Pepi recognized was Hranek the Czech foreman in his father's employ. The old man paid the price of good conscience with his own life. The moment Pepi saw the old man slump to the ground he could not contain his emotions.

He burst into tears, knowing a good man had saved his family's life the night when he came to warn them of what was about to happen to any who owned weapons. Pepi was shaking as he slinked quietly through the back door into his house. His chest was heaving uncontrollably as he was throwing up vomit. His hands trembled so violently he could not press the door handle down. His mother heard him and rushed to helped him, glad to see that he was alive. Pepi slumped against his mothers' chest and whispered between sobs.

"Mamma, they grabbed Hranek and shot him. He saved our lives and couldn't save his own." Mother and son held on to each other silently and cried on each other's shoulders over the lives that had been lost and the life of the man who had selflessly sacrificed his own to save their lives. The world they had known was out of control. Emmi could only find release of her inner turmoil within a flood of tears. She prayed so long her knees hurt as the rosary beads slid methodically through her entwined fingers.

Emmi was unable to find solace in her grief over the evils of this world that had foisted so much sorrow and pain on ordinary lives, a world that had taken her beloved husband a countless time from her side, a world she feared had gone berserk. Emmi could not move, lest a moment without prayer might be a surrender to a fate she dared not ponder.

Pepi could not sleep and sat down beside his mother and said to her. "Nobody will ever know what we have suffered and nobody will care to know."

Emmi held her rosary between her fingers. "Nobody will talk about our suffering. We are a forgotten people on the frontline of chess boards like pawns in the scheme of world events. We are being moved about by forces we cannot control. That is why I can't stop praying to the highest authority. Because, I am afraid to stop! God brought my husband back to me from Russia twice, and as long as I don't know what they have done to him, I have to pray for his safety. No bombs have dropped on us, but the arrows of hatred are aimed straight at our hearts."

Anninka heard the whispered exchange and protested mockingly. "Praying won't help us any more now! God turned a deaf ear on us long ago. If he even exists? If he does exist, why does he allow so much suffering and injustice? The many hours you have spent praying hundreds of rosaries have all been for naught."

Emmi shook her head at her sister's lack of faith. "There is a lot of injustice in this world. I remember that the murder of Josef's father was never investigated. They didn't bother because he was a German. His murders are still walking the streets and are probably the same who are doing all the killings now." She paused a moment and then said, "Since I have known my husbands' mother, she made no bones of the fact, she believed these thugs also murdered her husband. She, a Czech herself accused the Czech magistrate of shirking his responsibilities in the investigation of his death, because he was a German. I am sure she was right in her assessment. He was murdered not for any wrong he had done, but for his wealth, the watch and the money in his pocket. I don't believe there will ever be justice for Josef's father. But I still believe in God!" At that moment Pepi tipped the chess board upside down, sending all the chess pieces flying through the air as he yelled, "Check Mate."

Otto looked startled and protested. "Hey, you always tip the board over, when you are losing." Ever the inquisitive boy, Pepi had to find out what had happened to his grand-father. He pulled up a chair beside his mother who was in conversation with the other women, to interrupt their diatribes. "What proof do you have that these thugs murdered my grandfather?"

"Well, if your grandfather had suffered a heart-attack he would have fallen into the brook face down. The murders stood him up erect and propped him up against a tree. These evil men wanted everyone to see what they had done to their boss. He was a gruesome sight with icicles hanging from his body. Afterward they celebrated his death, cajoling around the logs inside the factory as if they were proud of what they had done." Anninka smirked. "I told you, there will be no justice for us in Czechoslovakia."

Emmi dipped her fingers into a vessel of Holy Water and crossed herself. "I cannot listen to this banter anymore. No earthly being will come to save us. We need divine intervention. We have to pray for help to the Almighty God."

Anninka waved her off, and turned her attention to a book. " No, not even the Pius Pope will say a word about the genocide here." Her mother was incensed and raged at her daughter. "You godless waif!"

Anninka snickered with a taunt. "Tse, tse. Mamimka! Why are you angry with me?" Her mother snapped.

"Anninka you talk like a slave of the devil about a man of God." Anninka snickered. "My sister was right! We are pawns in a political chess game. Even the Pope is a politician and he won't say one word about our suffering."

Franziska turned away, crimson with fury, and knelt beside the makeshift altar. With a childish pout, Anninka curled up in a ball on the plush divan and nervously pulled the fringed tassels. "Nobody and nothing will save us."

Emmi desperately sought to maintain a peaceful repose within her bedroom. She calmly replied "Hopefully, this nightmare will pass like a storm in the night, and tomorrow will be a sunny day again. Just as all good times must come to an end, so do the bad times."

Anninka could not forget what she had seen. "I am sad over the injustice when I have to watch a child soldier getting shot by a firing squad. He was a child, when he was drafted and once the war was over, he was shot upon his return for wearing his grey uniform. Franz was younger than I am when they shot him. I remember the day he started kindergarten. Was he any guiltier than I am for being born German? Was it my fault, that I was a burden to my mother from the moment of my birth?" Painful silence followed.

An accusing finger seemed to point at her mother. Franziska sighed deeply, she had been filled with guilt and now the enormity of the accusation sank in. All Franziska could remember from the time of Anninka's birth was the tiredness she felt every day and all day and her inability to love her child and give her the nurture she deserved.

Emmi put her arms around her sullen sister and looked into her forlorn eyes. "We have to stick together whatever befalls one befalls all of us. I have my faith to cling to. What about you? I believe that all will be well in God's time."

Anninka scoffed. "What am I to have faith in? What has the world taught me thus far that I should have faith in anybody? I have been rejected from the moment of my birth by my own mother." Emmi shook her head resignedly. "I don't have any answers, but may the world never bring you to your knees. You have no refuge."

The Ruskies are coming!

They were on the war path heading straight toward their village. Emmi awoke with a start to a sudden stillness. Even the birds were hushed. She was laying in her bed when she heard a faint creeping noise. She looked at her mother who was sleeping on the far side of the double wide bed, snoring. That was not the sound she had heard. She saw the sun rise like a red fireball, heralding a stormy day and threw back her comforter and put on a robe.

From his room on the opposite side of the villa, Pepi could hear the unfamiliar sound of wheezing and creeping of vehicles coming closer and closer. Overcome by his endless curiosity, the young boy quickly threw caution to the wind and slipped into his pants and ran out the backdoor. He crawled on his belly in the drainage ditch along the garden fence all the way to the fork in the road, and listened toward the noise as it got ever louder. He cautiously raised his head above the grassy knoll and came face to face with the turret of a Russian tank aimed at him.

Soldiers riding on tanks, trucks and wagons drawn by horses rumbled up from the nearby village of Arnau into the sleepy hollow of Mastig. The women and children were still sleeping. They were awakened by the sound of robust Russian music.

Pepi felt a sudden paralysis taking over his body and an uncontrollable urge to defecate into his pants, right where he was crouching down in the overgrown grassy ditch. For seconds that seemed like an eternity he could not move a muscle. He could only feel the uncontrollable shaking of his knees and his heart fiercely pounding in his chest. Panic-stricken, his mind racing as he pressed his belly flat to the ground. He fought for self-control, as he cautiously crawled back to the house. He slipped inside through the backdoor and yelled. "The Ruskies are here. They're headed straight toward our house."

The women quickly abandoned their morning chores, gathered the children around them in the bedroom, and barricaded the doors with heavy furniture. They shuttered windows, pulled down the shades and huddled together trembling around a makeshift altar. Oma Borufka and Emmi frantically snatched their rosary beads off the hook on the wall and prayed silently before a portrait of the Madonna and Child serenely feeding doves.

Anninka muttered under her breath. "That's not going to save us. I'm telling you. This is all for naught. The Russians will just shoot us." Emmi could hear boisterous raspy voices of soldiers.

She could hear the front-door glass crashing against tiled floors, and knew that they had broken through the door. Then she heard their footsteps coming upstairs. Emmi grabbed the children around her, and clutched her baby girl in one arm and with the free hand clamped her mouth shut, just as the Russian troops burst through the barricaded door, yelling, as they pushed the furniture aside. "Uri! Uri! Dawai! Dawai! Hand over your watches quick." The soldiers trampled across the thick Persian carpets with muddy boots, sliced open mattresses, clawed and ripped the wallpaper from walls, in search and seizure of valuables in the wall safe and ripped the watches from the arms of the women.

A large imposing man wearing a general's uniform stepped into the bedroom. The women and children's eyes were filled with terror. He bellowed out a command for the peasant soldiers to leave the house. The peasant soldiers scattered and scurried, like chickens aflutter in the hen house as a fox raids their coop. The Russian general decked out in his richly decorated uniform made an impression of power and ultimate authority. He unceremoniously made himself at home in the luxurious surroundings before the women and children could exhale, who huddled startled and frozen in panic and fear.

He stretched out on the plush velvet divan, lit a cigar and allowing the smoke rings to drift around the room. He motioned for his adjutant to pull off his boots as he leaned back leisurely. His eyes scanned the room and as they fell upon a portrait hanging above Emmi's head, his eyes shifted back and forth between the portrait on the wall and the young woman clutching her baby girl to her bosom.

With an unexpected motion of his head to the picture on the wall, he asked in Russian. "You?"

Emmi could not help but smile to herself. It was clear to her that the Russian general had mistaken her for Mary and baby Jesus. Because as she herself posed a similar image and like Mary was holding a baby in her arms. A blush covered her face as Emmi shook her head in slight bemusement at the mistaken identity, and murmured softly with the few Russian words she knew. "Nyet!"

"This is Maria, mother of Jesus. Our Blessed Mother with the Christ Child." Knowing the General had been raised as an atheist under the Soviet communist regime, she tried to explain, thinking he would not know anything about the icons of her faith. But the general surprised her with an acknowledgement of her explanation with a slap on his knee. "Da! Da! I know da! Yes, the picture looks familiar. I remember my old babitchka had a picture just like this."

The general, with a show of magnanimity smiled broadly, clenched the cigar between his teeth, and trying to hold the eye contact with Emmi, who kept her eyes averted as she could feel his scrutinizing eyes on more than her face. He scrutinized everyone in front of him. Then he calmly reassured the visibly terrified women and children in the Czech language.

"Ne boidjes! Fear not." He produced a small Matrushka doll from his coat, unstacked the dolls, and playfully pointed to the smaller dolls as he sat them around a small table. "Babitchka, mamimka…matrushka. He intoned in German the genealogy of grandmother, mother, I have wife and children!"

He pointed to himself and Emmi understood with relief to know that he was a family man. Then he explained that he had no intention to harm the women, nor let anyone else lay a hand on them. Knowing the reputation of Russian soldiers raping women, preceded them. He stepped out on the balcony, inhaled the cool morning air, stretched himself up and spreading his hands he pointed over the landscape, explaining that he had chosen this particular house, to serve as his Russian Headquarters, for its strategic location and high elevation from which he had an optimal panoramic view of the terrain.

He interrogated the women briefly. Then he concluded with reassuring words that they were safe and no one would be allowed to harm any of the women and children in this house, as long as he was here. He winked at the children who buried their faces behind the skirts of the two young mothers and the corpulent frame of the grandmother. He formed a cradle with his arms, and asked if he could hold the baby, but Anninka clutched her baby to her bosom only tighter and refused to hand her baby over to the general.

Without further ado the Russian general informed the women what he planned for them. He liked the spaciousness of the bedroom and without further ado ordered the women to pack their personal belongings. "You women and children will have to sleep in the cellar at night, but you are free to move about the kitchen and the bathroom during the day. Take what you need for personal comfort, blankets, etc.etc."

Emmi took one last mournful look from her bedroom window. She stepped out on the balcony, and saw the Russian peasant reservists with horses and wagons, scrambling for space until the entire area was covered around her house, front and backyard, driveways and surrounding potato fields and forest area. The factory yard and Oma Staffa's house and gardens, Gustav and Marie Gernert's Garden and Café were covered with military equipment. Grounds were trampled by horses and wagons. She watched in amazement, as Marie's children climbed out of their bedroom windows, climbed over the rafters and crouched behind the roof gables, to hide from the Russian soldiers. Suffocating stink of horse manure and swarming flies forced her to step back inside her bedroom with tears in her eyes.

The Russian general chuckled with a wink. "Don't forget your chamber pot!"

He and his officers made themselves at home within the first hour, they had installed radio and telephone communications equipment. The peasant soldiers with their horse and buggies and pitched tents that covered the entire property, potato and wheat fields, vegetable and flower gardens, lumber yards and forests and all roadways to overflowing, spilling out into the side roads, but not before they had raided every smokehouse, butchered all the livestock, foraged the storage cellars, scattered undergarments from clothes lines and confiscated all items of even the minutest value.

One of the soldiers found the bracelet and the gold watch Josef had given Emmi on their wedding day. Emmi screamed when a soldier snatched it from a hidden pocket Emmi had sewn into her undergarments. A scuffle ensued when another sought to grab it. Pepi seized the moment and grabbed the watch and bracelet. Instantly, two soldiers pointed bayonets at the lad, and Pepi reluctantly let go of his mother's prized possessions.

The officers slapped eggs they had found in the henhouse into a huge frying pan. The pan covered the entire stove top. When the eggs were cooked, the pan was placed in the middle of the table. The soldiers pushed and shoved each other to get a bite of the delicious curds before the general stepped into the kitchen. The general had brought his own cook and never took a bite of anything unless it had been prepared exclusively for him. Even as the cook had prepared the food in front of the general, he had to take the first bite to ensure that the food was not poisoned. He waited a few moments to make sure the cook did not keel over, only then did the general leisurely sat down and delved lustily into the heavily fried foods. Even when other foods were prepared, the cook had to take the first bite of everything.

Every morning such lusty feasting occurred around the kitchen table, to make the children's mouths water. The women and children were not allowed to participate in the feeding frenzy. They were given dry bread and water. The frightened women and children ogled the feeding frenzy with utter dismay as hunger pangs churned their bellies. Pepi bravely stepped amid the chess playing soldiers, clamoring around the kitchen table laden with fried eggs, bacon and sausages. The tall lad brazenly challenged the soldiers with a jocular tone in his voice.

"Chess anyone? I challenge anyone to a game of chess. If I win you give me some of what you have. I will give you a slice of what I have. Drushba, nas dorowie! Here is to friendship and good health!" He chuckled good-naturedly, and raised a glass in a mock salute.

The soldiers laughed uproariously, tousled the boy's blond hair, and pulled up another chair to the table for him. They passed a bottle of home-brewed vodka around the room and motioned for Pepi to take a big gulp. As the bitter brew ran down the boys' throat, he shook with disgust and grimaced, and the soldiers laughed even more and slapped him on the back good naturedly. But with every checkmate the soldiers amid raucous laughter, shared with the lad sausages and bread slice for slice. Pepi eagerly stashed away the sausages into his bulging pockets. The soldiers delighted in the clever boy and good naturedly gave him far more than what he had bargained for, while down in the cellar, which was always locked behind the family at night, Pepi divvied up the booty with the family.

Every morning, the soldiers forced the twelve-year-old boy to drink home-brewed vodka to their knee-slapping bemusement. Before the soldiers would give him the food for the family hovering in the basement, he had to barter for every crumb with another swig from a bottle. Little boys Otto and Rudi milled around, as the soldiers pulled up chairs for them and they too were prodded to take sips from the bottle of Soviet camaraderie.

The higher-ranking officers delighted not only in the clever lad, but in his fancy bikes decked out with all the latest high-tech German gadgets. Ultimately, they confiscated his most prized possession, and gleefully rode around the village, marveling at German engineering.

Adjacent to the kitchen was a bathroom. One morning Pepi and his younger brothers watched the peasant soldiers wash potatoes in the toilet bowl. One of them fondled a ceramic pull that was attached to a chain that hung from a water tank near the ceiling. With great curiosity, the soldier asked Pepi. "What is this for?" Pepi shrugged his shoulders with deliberate nonchalance. "I, donno, pull it!" Pepi made a jerking motion with his arm. The soldier did likewise. With a great whoosh and whirl, the potatoes disappeared in the gurgling flush of water. The soldiers looked dumbfounded at each other. Pepi hid his snickers behind a face masked in feigned surprise and with icy sarcasm, mumbled. "It must be a capitalist conspiracy? Checkmate."

The Soviet Army had succeeded in stopping the vigilante killings and chaos. Order was restored in this region by Soviet design. The board cutting machinery and sawblades was stripped from their foundation and all mechanical accessories was shipped off to Russia. The raised lettering, Josef Staffa, was chiseled off leaving only the shading of scrape marks where once the letters were clearly visible from a great distance. The vacant hull of the factory was filled with hay. Hammers, sickles, rakes, shovels and scythes were removed and the potato field and farmland were turned into a collective farm.

Fancy ornamentations of the villa, porticos, terraces, pillars, rose trellises, trout ponds and symbols of wealth were torn down, destroyed, discarded or left in a heap of rubble. From the windows facing the main road huge posters of Josef Stalin, Ilyich Lenin, Karl Marx and Eduard Benes were prominently unfurled from windows and balconies.

When a tall willowy Anninka emerged from the house to push her children in a baby buggy around the court yard, the hungry soldiers' eyes followed her everywhere. The soldiers nudged each other, whistled through their teeth, made crude remarks, ogling spellbound this beautiful woman as she walked about with deliberate nonchalance.

Although, Anninka was used to men's admiring glances, she slapped their fingers as they reached out to touch her. She couldn't do much about their crude remarks, but the stench swelling from their mouths, sickened her and she reeled back when they came close enough, and their breaths slapped her back in the face.

The fear of being raped kept Emmi sequestered in the safety of her house. She kept watch by the window. Emmi could speak a little Russian. She had understood the general's authoritative command to his soldiers. "The women in this house are off limits. Find amusement somewhere else." And they did to abandon. On the order of the general the women in this house were free to move about unhindered and dignified, but other women in the village were not so lucky. From a safe distance of their own yard, they could hear the screams of other women who were being raped by an overbearing Russian soldier.

Emmi and Anninka considered themselves lucky in comparison to other women. They could hear how women had to fight for their dignity, as they tried to fight off a Russian soldier or a man of the Czech militia. The women gave each other knowing looks and shook their heads in helplessness. The women squirmed and shuddered with an uneasy feeling, comprehending the atrocities of what was happening to these women in some barn. As husbands who tried to come to the aid of a wife's attacker were shot dead. No one dared say another word about a rape of an unfortunate victim.

Anninka loved to hang out the laundry without fear instead she felt protected and free to play with her babies in the yard. She could take them out for some fresh air, ride them in the stroller up and down the long driveway to the garage and back to the house. It was about as far as she dared to go.

Emmi dared not go before looking up and down the deserted streets and across her shoulders. One morning in early July, the women sighed with an uneasy relief, when the Russian Army broke camp and moved on toward Prague, leaving mountains of their debris behind.

Emmi watched them leave with a sigh of relief with the hope that life would return back to normal and she could tend to her normal household routine and chores uninterrupted. Her heart skipped a beat for joy as she watched from behind her white lace curtains hanging in the dining room alcove that the cherries on her husbands' favorite tree were ripe.

It promised to be a smoldering hot day, and Pepi would be only too happy to pick cherries before the birds got to them. Her itinerary for tomorrow was well planned. She would make the children's favorite dish, cherry filled perogies with browned butter and cinnamon. She would make cherry jam and fill canning jars with the luscious fruit. The children would eat cherries until they complained of belly aches. The rest she would bring to Marie. It was a day to look forward to after her sequestration in her cellar during the Russian army's encampment.

She looked across the valley floor and witnessed as Marie and her children, Kurt, Margit and Christa, were herded unto a truck as a rifle point pressed against their ribs.

Emmi was shocked to see in this July heat, the children were all wearing thick layers of winter clothing and insulating felt boots, as one would have to wear in Siberia.

"Oh, my God! Now what is going on here? Is the Gernert family being sent to Siberia?" Emmi whispered and clutched at her chest. She pondered their fate with tear filled eyes. A shiver ran down her spine as she watched the flap of the truck closing behind them. Then the truck sped off in the direction of a concentration camp.

At seven o'clock the following morning Emmi tore the calendar date and greeted the new day, July 11, 1945 with an ominous foreboding, just as loudspeakers blared throughout the village. Messengers pounded on every door, handing out sheets of paper with the order that all Sudeten Germans, must assemble at the train station at eight o`clock this morning, with no more than 50 pounds of personal belongings—-no more than what could fit into a small handcart. No more food rations than what was necessary for survival for one week. All valuables had to be left behind. The Czech militia gave the German population merely one hour to gather their belongings and leave their home. Nobody voiced an objection to this ethnic cleansing in process as unreasonable and impossible on such short notice. Emmi shook her head in disbelief.

"They are inflicting revenge on us for Hitlers' atrocities." The Czech Prime Minister Eduard Benes, had labeled the Sudeten Germans colonists, never acknowledging that their ancestry dated back a thousand years. Now, within an hour they were to leave everything behind, all they had loved and worked for all their lives and passed on from generation to generation. Unable to think rationally Emmi felt totally at a loss, wondering what to take. The cherry tree glistening with red ripe fruit, would have to be left for the birds to eat. Emmi would have loved to bake a few cherry perogies. She rushed around the house like a headless chicken, wondering what of her prized possessions was most important to secure.

She packed family photos and her prayer book. On second thought she packed a few pots and pans and the featherbed, while Anninka and the maid dressed the children in layers of warm winter clothes. Now she knew why Marie Gernert had dressed her children, Kurt, Margit and Christa in layers upon layers of warm winter clothing. Even felt boots for winter covered her children's feet the day on what promised to be a sweltering hot July day. Marie must have known that they would never come back here to get their winter clothes, and winter was sure to come.

Any items weighing over fifty kilos the children simply had to wear on their backs. They would need the layers of warm sweaters, hats, mittens and insulating felt boots, in less than six months to survive a harsh winter, which was unthinkable at the moment.

The militias started at the house of the matriarch. Oma Staffa showed them her Czech citizen papers and she was allowed to stay in her house. Oma Borufka showed her Czech citizen papers and she was allowed to stay in the country, but she was not allowed to live alone in her big house alone. She was told that the house was too spacious for one old woman. A gypsy family was allowed be move into her house instead.

Oma Staffa whispered to her. "You can stay with me." The mob moved on the short walk past Oma Staffa's house to the old Mastig Cemetery. Emmi saw a group of Czechs tearing up the family graves of prominent Germans. They were convinced that the Germans had hidden treasures in these graves. A black marble crypt covered with a giant gold crucifix was lifted off the Staffa family tomb, wherein all the Staffas' had gone to Rest in Peace. But now they were not allowed any peaceful repose. A little white casket was lifted out of the tomb and ripped open. All that was found therein were the tiny bones of a tiny baby.

With a tearful farewell embrace, Emmi clung to her trembling mother. "Why don't you come with us!" Her mother shook her head. "I will die soon. And I want to be buried beside my husband, Wenzel." Franziska clutched a rosary to her chest, and mumbled resignedly. "Go with God!"

Emmi nodded sadly. "I have no one else to go to."

With heart wrenching sobs Franziska turned to her grandchildren, hugging, and kissing their little faces as they tried to understand the incomprehensible. For a woman, who had never shown much affection, she uncorked her bottled-up love for them, which was finally spilling out over her grandchildren, knowing she would never see them. Her last words to those whose births she had attended, and had loved. She passed loving words of wisdom as her face looked contorted with grief.

She whispered. "Be good to your mother and never forget Czechoslovakia is your home."

Franziska stroked Anninka's face, as she clutched her tightly. "I am sorry I was never here for you, I was too old and too tired and now we will never see each other again. Farewell my child, God be with you." Anninka burst into tears, and clutched at her mother. "What is going to become of me? Where should I go? Why do I have to leave, I am your flesh and blood."

Franziska replied. "I cannot help you anymore. I am too tired and just want to die." She turned abruptly and clutched the fence post with both hands and dragged herself away to a garden bench.

Anninka looked forlorn at her mother, picked up her few belongings, heaved them onto the baby buggy and followed Emmi and her children who joined the thousands who were trekking the long and winding road out of town. Millie the children's black and white cat, followed them at a distance, meowing mournfully. She sat down to look back at the house every now and then while the children beckoned her to follow them with bacon morsels, luring her all the way to the edge of town.

Then the cat sat still, meowing ever louder, as the trek of humanity kept moving forward. She pitifully looked back and forth between the house and the children, torn between loyalty to domain and love for the children. Millie finally headed back to her domain and the children cried. "What about Millie? Who is going to feed our cat?" Emmi replied. "Cats take care of themselves."

As the family was swept away by wave after wave of a faceless humanity, they passed the torn up graves in their cemetery, Emmi stopped for a moment, looked with sadness at the huge family crypt whose marble grave plate was emblazoned in gold lettering with the names of the deceased family members who had been laid to rest in her beloved soil, including her little son Horsti. Emmi bowed her head and crossed herself, placed a sprig of forget-me-nots on top of the torn grave and bade her final farewell.

Pavel Koczian watched the family from the window of the Staffa matriarch's mansion. The Staffa family had employed him since his youth and had treated him like a son. He looked on with deep sorrow as the family walked by under the guard of a rifled Czech militia. Emmi pulled a white handkerchief from her pocket and waved Pavel Koczian good bye. His eyes filled with tears at sight of their plight, as the women pushed the baby buggies across the rough dirt road with a few bundled belongings tied on top, as the children dragged their tired feet under the weight of winter clothes toward the train station in Arnau.

Pepi pulled the handcart, and Otto pushed from behind. Emmi and Rudi pushed the baby buggy with bundled belongings, a featherbed and pots and pans and the eighteen-month-old toddler was sitting on top of it all.

Koczian knew that those Czech countrymen, who had given any aid to the German people like Hranek, had paid a bitter price for their good conscience. He knew the Czech militia had shot Hranek the foreman from the lumber yard because he had been loyal to his German employer.

Koczian said to his Slovak wife. "I want to help but I risk getting shot myself." His wife tried to stop him, but as he watched the wretched carnage, he brushed her aside and threw caution to the wind. "I'll drive them to the train station." Koczian hitched up his horse and buggy and rode up beside the family. Wordlessly, he took the family's bundled belongings, hoisted them on top of the handcart and the baby buggy. Sat the children on top and, like the obedient servant he had always been to the family, Pavel Koczian gave the family their final thirty-mile ride to the train station in Arnau, the town where years ago two giants had been brought down by a swarm of little people.

The Sudeten Germans assembled along the railroad tracks. Again, the militias searched their belongings for valuables. Struggles ensued again and again, over anything from baby cereal to wedding bands. A gun found under any bundled belonging of any family meant a death sentence for the entire family. People cringed as cries and pleas rang out constantly. "No, this is not mine. I don't know where the gun came from." But there was no salvation and no mercy. Nobody could help. Shots rang out against a nameless faceless humanity, trembling women and children and a few old men were herded into open livestock cars, the floors of which were covered with lice and feces infested straw. Yet, as the train began to roll to an unknown destiny, they sighed with relief, glad to have gotten away with their lives, squashed inside a wagon reeking of sweat, feces and urine.

While in Mastig, Franziska Borufka remained seated on the bench in the garden which her daughter Emmi had lovingly tended for years. She was oblivious to the beauty of the colorful abundance of silver and purple bearded irises, magenta peonies and bright-blue delphiniums that surrounded her. Their intoxicating scents gave her no solace. She wondered where she had to go as she listlessly stared into nothingness. Suddenly she felt the presence of another person and looked to the side. Anna Kudronovsky sat beside her on the bench and reached for Franziskas' hand.

The two old women sobbed on one another's shoulder, then they sat silently and stared into space motionless, grieving their loss of home and family. Crystal rosary beads slithered slowly through entwined fingers, catching the rays of the morning sun. The tears had long dried, crusting down their deeply lined faces, cutting even deeper furrows into their parched skin. From far away Arnau, they heard a train whistle blow. Anna felt as though a dagger pierced her heart at that moment and she whispered. "Now I have nothing left." She clutched her chest, writhing in agony. Anna penned her pain into her little book of psalms and prayers she had carried on her wedding day forty-three years ago. The same book into which she logged the most commemorative dates of the greatest loves of her life, the deaths of her mother Maria Kudronovsky nee Reidel. First-born son Pepiczech and her husband Josef Staffa. Sighing deeply, she murmured barely audible in German.

"Ach das Gottlose Czechische Volk!" Oh, those godless Czechs

On August 2, 1945, at the palace of Cecilienhof, in the Berlin suburb of Potsdam, within a few miles of the ruins left by the war was the shattered seat of Nazi power. Agreements regarding the realignment of the borders of Eastern Europe were hammered out between tea and crumpets and billowing cigar smoke. A line was drawn from the Baltic Sea to the Balkan Mountains.

Winston Churchill bemoaned the fate of "these unfortunate people and of a great tragedy happening behind an Iron Curtain," which was splitting Europe into two hostile camps.

Victorious Allied personnel had been ordered to permit the brutalities perpetrated against the German people without interference. The fate of three-and-a-half million Sudeten Germans was sealed with the agreement obtained by Czech premier Edvard Benes at a roundtable conference, with Winston Churchill, Josef Stalin and Harry Truman. Benes sole intent was to obtain legitimacy for the annihilation of the Sudeten Germans in the eyes of the world-for a fait accompli planned by the Czech government since 1918 and perpetrated with its execution in 1945.

For these unfortunate people, a fait-accompli had been perpetrated three months earlier, even before the agreement to expel all Germans from Czechoslovakia was reached.

The agreement called for the expulsion in an "orderly and humane manner." It was anything but humane. Three million people were expelled in a brutal manner, driven by unrelenting hatred, ancient jealousies and greed. Beastiality had been unleashed to descend upon the German people with uncontrolled fury, resulting in the gruesome murders of over 240,000, about 10% of the German population.

Sweaty flesh of a crushed humanity was squeezed into every corner of the stench-filled pigsty on wheels. Open cargo trains that once were used to transport pigs, now lurched forward to deliver the Sudeten Germans to their ultimate fate. Packed with wretched and writhing women and children, the train headed northwest toward the German border with accelerating speed.

Only small children seemed to be able to separate themselves from a cruel reality. Otto elicited from his harmonica the soulful ancient songs of blue mountains and green valleys and of the mythical giant Rübezahl and his dwarfs, the tales of the Sudeten Germans favorite heroes of folklore.

The children, who were not tall enough to reach the air vents held their noses. Emmi wiped the tears that slowly rolled noiselessly down her cheeks. Tall lads like Pepi gaped through the air vents at the disappearing mountain range, gasping for breaths for fresh air.

After a four-hour ride, the train came to a screeching halt. The human cargo had arrived on Soviet occupied East-German soil. The doors were unlatched and rolled back. Militiamen with rifle butts shoved the frightened women and children from the train down a steep embankment into a ravine. Their belongings were tossed helter-skelter after them. After picking themselves off the ground, the dispossessed searched in the scorching heat for their meager scattered belongings.

The mass of expelled Germans aimlessly followed caravans of families heading west along torturous railroad tracks. Peasant carts jammed the gutters and gullies. Baby buggies and bicycles caused intermittent traffic jams. The refugees pulled their wagons through muck and sand, only to get stuck again and again in the pea-sized gravel.

Exhausted and numb with fear, Emmi and Anninka dragged themselves with the children into an empty railroad depot. Through the broken windowpane they searched for any familiar face among the hordes of people. They all looked alike in their naked horror. Forlorn and dejected, the women had no idea in which direction they were to go.

Emmi knew only that she did not want to venture too far from the border. She maintained the hope for the political winds to change direction, and looked vainly for signs from heaven in ceaseless prayers for a return to her beloved home. But mostly she prayed for a reunion with her beloved Josef. Emmi fastened blankets to a tree, stretched one tattered grey army blanket across her children, tucked the ends under them, to keep them warm. But before she could let them fall asleep, she prayed for a miracle, the miracle of a return home.

Anninka, ever the doubter balked sullenly. "With all the time you have wasted in praying…the many hours you spent praying the rosary, your faith has done us no good. I've been telling you, praying won't help us anymore."

Emmi shrugged off her sister's comments. "That's all I have left. My faith!"

Anninka pooh-poohed impatiently. "I'm a realist. That's good for nothing."

If refugees wanted to survive, they had to avoid capture by the brutal Russians and head West. Word spread quickly among the huddling masses that Russian tanks were closing in and riding around encircling the westward fleeing masses, rounding them up to stop them from fleeing. The captured refugees were put into concentration camps, were Russians ransacked what little possessions the refugees had left. As the vehicles crept near, the refugees dodged the onslaught to avoid being mowed down by Russian tanks. The refugees fled into ditches, only to be rolled over by tanks, who moved back and forth until the hapless victim was buried alive.

Emmi shook her head resolutely. "I can't go far from here. How will my husband ever find us?" But Anninka heeded the suggestions of other refugees. "The parents of little Peter's father live in Cologne, that's where I should go. I'll hitch up with the next group going West." Emmi replied dejectedly. "You do what you think is best for you. But I can't go far from this border. I have to stay and wait for my husband right here. How in the world will he ever find us in this chaos?"

The next morning the women and their children parted, crying and wishing each other Godspeed. "God be with you." They wiped their eyes with white handkerchiefs, not knowing if they would ever see each other again. White handkerchiefs fluttered farewell in the wind for a while until Emmi felt abandoned in her misery.

She remembered the childhood summers she had spent in Eibau and Rumburg, a little village across the Czech border, when she visited a Swiss aunt, Maria Pfenninger, uncle Karl Borufka and their son, Karli. Uncle Karl was her mother's brother. They owned a mustard and pickle factory a mere foot march from the border. Emmi remembered that the mustard factory was near a railroad depot. She slumped on her few bundles and wracked her brains, trying to remember the way to the home of these relatives. She had to rely on her keen instincts, as she bundled the few belongings unto the baby buggy and followed the railroad tracks, not knowing which was east or west. She tried to find orientation in the landmarks and was overjoyed whenever she recognized certain familiar characteristics of the terrain.

Drudging along with the masses, her heart skipped a beat, when she spotted a huge Swiss flag fluttering invitingly atop a roof as if it were the residence of an ambassador. It seemed to beckon from a great distance those refugees seeking shelter from the hordes of ransacking Russian troops. Emmis' eyes fixed on the white cross on a red background and she hastened her pace.

By the time Emmi arrived with the children in front of the villa, the stately mansion was already overflowing with refugees.

Maria Pfenninger spotted her niece among the homeless trekkers and ran to greet her with open arms, and Emmi yielded her tired body to her warm embrace. "Emmi, come in, as you can see, I have only one room left in the basement. But you can stay as long as you need a roof over your head. How is your good Mama?" Emmi sighed deeply and wiped the tears from her eyes.

"Terrible! She suffers from high blood pressure. I couldn't bear to leave her behind, but she insisted she wanted to die in her own home, and be buried next to my father.

My sister and I thought it best to let her stay. We were afraid she would not survive this ordeal." Maria Pfenninger whispered. "I know she had heart problems. High blood pressure. We had our own ordeals here. When the Russians came through this area, they mowed everything down. They mowed people down with their tanks as they were fleeing the onslaught before them. Even as we thought,

Berlin was finished and bombing raids would stop, the Allies decided to give us a coup' de grace, which Germany no longer needed. The war had been lost long before. The bombing raids over Dresden were just another nightmare we had to endure, borne of Churchills revenge for the Blitzkrieg.

The British let loose fire storms and incinerated people in the air raids and burned everything to the ground, even churches. We could see the fires lighting the sky from here. Luckily no bomb was dropped on our house, because I flew the Swiss flag on top of our roof, we were spared that nightmare. This flag saved our lives. But now, refugees from all around come here for shelter during air raids. Which still are blaring even though the war is over. I have opened my doors to all who need our help."

The kindly aunt never turned anyone away. She gave generously of whatever she had in food and shelter, a hot chamomile tea, a blanket and a pillow, and tried the best she could to provide some means of comfort to the steady flood of a miserable humanity the war had pushed to the brink. Emmi squeezed her aunts' hand in thankfulness for the food and shelter she had given them. But every day, more and more refugees squeezed into every nook in the basement until the arrangement became unbearable.

After two weeks in the overcrowded basement, Emmi decided to head west at last, as hopes for a return to their beloved Sudetenland dimmed with every new wave of uprooted humanity which moved into the crowded basement. Emmi carried the bundles on her back, packed the featherbeds into the buggy and put her toddler on top of the soft downs.

Pepi and Otto pulled and pushed the handcart. Rudi was ordered to push the toddler in the baby buggy. The family trudged along the railroad tracks as long as the sun was in their eyes. Then drifted aimlessly along with other caravans, hitching up with this group then deciding on another group. They went from one refugee camp to another not knowing where to go next. During the night they scavenged for food in the fields farmers had left behind to find an old carrot or turnip, a beet or potato, any leftovers from a prior season. The boys snuck into barns hoping to find a goat or cow that could be milked. They searched in fields for green nettles, berries, anything that could be chewed, or juices that could be sucked from whatever could be plucked from any bush along their path was a valued find.

Emmi sank down on her knees overcome with exhaustion, plagued with hunger and tiredness, berries filling her growling stomach and fearing the diarrhea to follow. Seeing nothing but bombed out bridges across the Elbe River and Russian troops following behind them, Emmi had reached the point of utter despair and total hopelessness, the point of no return.

They were doomed, unable to go backward nor forward. They were stuck at the banks of the swollen Elbe River. Emmi lost her will to go on. She cried out, her face twisted in a bottled-up rage, as she burst into tears, screaming and pounding the ground with her fists, as tears streamed down her face.

"I can't go on anymore. My legs have given out. I cannot move my legs anymore!" She cursed the architects of global engineering, foisting such horror and misery on the world to the lives of innocent people along with nothing but shame, degradation and humiliation…we are paying the price for the crimes of these criminals." She scanned the silvery ribbon of the Elbe River, wondering where they might be able to cross, she caught sight of a mass bobbing up and down in the water, floating north toward them.

She stared transfixed, into the swirling waters of the once beloved mother of rivers, the Elbe River. Then she recognized what she was seeing. She could not believe her eyes. Corpses thousands of them were floating in their watery grave. It was a sickening sight as countless faceless bodies floated north surrounded by their meager bundles and children's buggies. Horrified she stared at a nameless humanity with white faces cloaked in death. The mother of rivers, their mother lode of life, had become the angel of doom.

Traumatized into a trance Emmi saw the hopelessness of their place in a world, that no longer had a place for them. The fleeing masses along the banks of the Elbe River, had seen no way out but a slow march into swirling waters. They simply had allowed the swirling waters to carry them away to a more peaceful place, where the strong currents had swept them under the waves and spit them out as corpses. With a feverish yearning in her eyes, Emmi became transfixed and even enchanted by what she saw. "See here, boys look how peaceful they appear! They just float away. See that? All their pain is gone." She mumbled hypnotically transfixed. "Maybe, that's what we should do too? Everything will be over in moments. Maybe it's the only answer to our misery? Maybe it's better where they are going?" Rudi clutched her hand tightly, looking at her with large and trusting eyes. His mouth formed a droll pout as he replied with childish faith, knowing she would make everything whole again. "Yes, Mommy, maybe it is better where they are going."

Pepi jumped up with agitated impatience and shouted at his mother. "No, we will not wade into the river! We are not going to die like this. I will not give up as long as we have an ounce of breath left, we keep going!" Emmi stared in wonder and awe at her twelve-year old son, whose tall handsomeness and stoic determination to bring any problem to a successful conclusion had always given her a great sense of pride.

He was a perfectionist in whatever task he had undertaken. She smiled meekly and replied.

"You remind me of your father who always took charge of difficult situations, and never gave up. You are such a handsome young man you will accomplish great things. I don't want you to lose your life because of my weakness, if you have a chance to survive this ordeal. Go."

Pepi stalked off defiantly. Emmi called after him. "Pepi, you go on without us. You have a chance to save yourself without us dragging you down. My beautiful boy, I just can't go on any more. Go on, and let us stay here. I am finished. The little ones are too weak, they won't survive."

Pepi replied over his shoulder looking around for edible weeds from which they could suck nutrient rich juices. "Either we all survive or we perish together. I am determined to survive. We have so far." Emmi gaped at her son in wonder as Pepi shook his head with stoic resoluteness. "I will not go anywhere alone, if we go, we go together. If we die, we die together. I will see if there is a bridge up head. Rest your legs here for a while. Let the children sleep a while.

I have been thinking, somewhere there has to be a railroad trestle that is still intact. I can hear the sound of heavy train activity in the distance, heading north toward Berlin. The Ruskies wasted no time in taking over the entire Eastern part of the country. The trains are running constantly and somewhere they are crossing the Elbe River. We have to find that spot, which means we cannot avoid the Ruskies any longer. We have to get close to them and wait for an opportune moment when a train crosses the bridge. The trains run very slow over a bridge, and make clattering noises over the trestles. That is the moment when they can't see us or hear us walk alongside the train." He paused a moment and looked around. Pepi was ready to leave impatiently.

"I will come back to get you after I have found the crossing and clocked the train schedules."

Emmi smiled at her son resignedly. "You are a mother's pride and joy. I am very proud of you! How can I falter as you fight for our survival?' Pepi slinked through the reeds along the banks of the river impatiently, hunkering down in the reeds at any rustling sound. A day later he returned to find his mother looking anxiously for his return, relieved at his sight. With renewed hope Emmi gathered her last ounce of strength, pulled herself up and pushed the wagon from behind, while the boys pulled in front.

Rudi pushed the buggy along the banks of the river, until they finally saw bridge girders that were still intact. They crouched low in the overgrown reeds and crawled to the top of the embankment.

Pepi raised his head to look around. "We have to wait here under the bridge girders until dark. We can observe the intervals of trains. How often the trains are running. In the meantime, I'll see if I can find some berries or mushrooms." Moments later he came back shaking his head. "There is nothing to be found." When night closed in Pepi hoisted bundled belongings on the hand cart and waited in readiness for the first train.

"Mother we cannot go together, we make too much noise, we might attract unwanted attention. As soon as the first train approaches, I'll take the wagon, and drive with it alongside the train track. As soon as I am across the river, I'll drop a pebble into the water, to let you know I have made it. Next the boys have to cross in single file as long as the train is rolling. You and the baby wait until the boys have made it across." Emmi feared for her sons' life and interjected. "Let me go first with the baby, if the Russians lay in wait to shot refugees as they cross the bridge, I'd rather they shoot me." Pepi waved her off but Rudi wailed. "I want to stay with Mama."

Pepi took Rudi by the shoulder. "You do as I say. You walk fast without making a sound, you got it?"

Rudi nodded with a pout. "All right!" Pepi ran alongside the first train across the bridge without a problem, and quickly dropped a stone into the water, the boys followed one at a time in the shadow of the train cars. At last Emmi followed with the baby buggy. They spent the night sleeping under the bridge on the west bank of the river.

The next morning, they trekked westward following again along the railroad tracks through sand and gravel, clattering across railroad ties and granite rocks. Emmi pushed and pulled the hand cart and Rudi pushed his little sister in the baby buggy. After a while, his frail and tired arms let go. He numbly trudged behind his mother and older brothers, leaving the buggy sitting on the railroad tracks. Pepi turned around and screamed. "Where's the baby buggy?"

Rudi looked forlorn at the ground, kicking the sand from his worn shoes. Emmi threw her arms over her head, as the light of a train appeared on the distant horizon and a train whistle could be heard as she screamed. "Jesus, Mary and Josef, my baby?" Pepi raced back on the track and snatched the buggy off the tracks, a minute later, a freight train loaded with tanks and trucks roared past them. As the click-clack of the train faded away, Pepi hoisted the baby on his shoulder and with a furious kick hurtled the buggy down a steep ravine.

The nights were spent looking for food, and the days were spent looking to stay alive, hiding in bushes along the edge of a forest, a shed or a barn, but always in sight of a train track, so they wouldn't lose their sense of direction, in the hope of getting to the West somehow. Someday!

Always on the lookout for Russian troops who were looking for scattered remnant refugees, to round them up and transport them to a labor camp to pick potatoes. During the day, Pepi went to farmers, asking them if he could help with chores. He worked tirelessly cleaning out pig-sties, he offered to help with the farm work, tilling hay, in exchange for some milk for the baby, or just to be allowed to sleep in their barn when it rained only to be chased off the property like pesky gypsies. A few times they got lucky and were allowed to stay overnight in a barn. Pepi worked during the day in a farmers' barn, pleading for some eggs from the hen house.

Sometimes the farmer allowed the children to drink milk from a few goats. He loved squirting the milk directly from the udder into every one's mouth. The warm milk gave them new strength and even caused some chuckles as the spray covered their faces.

Pepi was relentless in his pursuit to provide for his mother and siblings some means of survival. Every morning he was the first to hunt down an opportunity to find something to eat. The moment he was out of sight Emmi could feel her deep despair as she worried that her beloved son might not come back. The moment his tall dark blond hair came into view, a beam of light crossed her face.

Just the sight of him raised her hope, that someday this nightmare would come to an end for her, and her children would have a chance at a life without fear. Her son's restless zest for life, all his hopes and dreams, all those qualities that once had been her own, she now saw inherent in her sons drive to succeed. He was determined to save their lives at the very moment she was ready to give up the fight. Her son's boundless energy was their salvation the moment she had lost all hope. If only her legs would not ache and her stomach not feel so empty, which had stopped growling long ago.

In September the family's luck ran out. Russian troops swept up scattered refugees, rounded them up and herded them into wire fenced enclosures. Emmi and the children were driven along with a multitude of women and children into a labor camp in Belgern. First, they were given a douche of white powder, to kill the head lice. The straw covered bunks were infested with fleas. Flies swarmed around the children's faces and bit into their bodies, until the bite marks had become infected. Their tender skin soon was covered with boils. Emmi tried to keep her children clean, but there was no facility for bathing.

She swatted the flies and fleas off her children, knowing that diseases are spread through insects. The fleas caused the deadly typhus spreading throughout the camp.

A Russian doctor in the Gulag had no medicines to dispense to the sick instead he could only sign death certificates. The shovels that were used to dig up potatoes during the day were used to dig graves by night. The rest of the night was spent scratching flea bites until the boils festered.

Blistering fall winds heralded that a severe winter was on the march and fast approaching from the East. The wool blankets were not sufficient to survive the blistering cold oozing through the wooden slats. The winds started to howl threateningly through the creaky sheds made of linear boards.

Pepi remembered with longing the warm down covers they had left behind at the villa of Maria Pfenninger in Eibau. At the time it seemed more convenient to leave the bulky comforters behind, thinking they could get them later. Knowing they would not survive a severe winter, Pepi decided that he would back trek to Eibau. One night he whispered to his exhausted mother who looked at him with feverish eyes. "I'll be back in a few days! I am getting our feather bedding. We'll either freeze to death or die of Typhus."

Emmi dreaded to see him leave, fearing what might happen to him. "Promise me that you will be careful." She whispered knowing that without sufficient covers they were all doomed.

"I'll be back…with our down comforters."

Pepi clasped his mother's hand and gave her a reassuring wink. If she could count on nothing anymore, her son could be counted on to deliver what he promised. He had become her rod and staff. All she could muster on her own was a prayer for his safe return, knowing, without Pepi she would have given up her will to live long ago, and the younger children would be doomed as well. She reached up to bless him. "God be with you. May the mother of God protect you on your journey". She kissed him on the cheek and made the sign of the cross over his forehead, folded her hands in prayer and watched him leave.

Pepi left, dragging the empty handcart as the winds howled from the East. At the train station, he mingled easily with other refugees assembling on railroad tracks heading west. Peasant carts mingled with mud and rust encrusted army vehicles. He was the lonely camper heading east and they were quick to point out his mistake. "Boy, you are going in the wrong direction, boy where are going, boy? You are headed east straight into the arms of Russians."

The weary refugees shook their heads as they watched in amazement the determined lad single handedly struggle to hoist the empty handcart onto railcars to hitch a ride to Eibau. Many offered to give the lad a helping hand, but he winked them off fearing that somebody might rip the cart from his hand. Even when he was too tired and needed sleep, he sat inside the cart while he was waiting for a train. He slept sitting up inside the cart, he dared not leave it unattended for a second. He slept in it to make sure, nobody would steal it because he trusted no one and kept his distance from everyone.

Once he had secured the down covers, it was an easier ride back to the camp. He could wait for trains curled up in the warm down blankets. A week later Pepi walked into the gulag's barrack. At sight of him, Emmi dropped to her knees and murmured.

"Holy Mother of God, you restored my faith and my hope." A few days later Emmi was overcome with a scorching fever and placed in the building marked "Quarantine." She was separated from her children and isolated from many who were already on their deathbed. One by one, the children joined her in the 'Quarantine' barrack, because all had become infected with typhus, except the youngest child. The child was handed over to a Polish woman to be cared for. Emmi could hear the child's screams coming from the adjacent building. "Mommi! Mommi!" The screams and sobs tugged at her heartstrings.

She found the strength to sew a rag doll from the tattered edges of a field blanket, and asked the Russian doctor to give the doll to her child, Emmi heard her baby cry and as soon as the doctor handed her the doll the child stopped screaming and curled up with the doll tucked in her arms and fell sound asleep. The Russian camp commander increased the milk rations for the Polish woman, so she could feed it the baby left in her care. Instead, the woman fed the extra milk supplement to her eight-year-old son, and fed stale bread crumbs soaked in black coffee to the child.

Every night, Emmi could hear the thud of body bags being tossed into holes outside the wooden shacks, followed by more shoveling and yet another thump, as another body was dropped into a hole. Emmi could hear the moaning of the sick and the shoveling interrupted by sobs and wails in the night, as another lifeless body was carried out for burial. She murmured to herself. "We are tossed away, like bags of garbage, as if we had never existed." She was sure she would suffer this fate. She knelt beside her cot and prayed. "Hail Mary, full of grace. Blessed art thou among women, save my husband and my children and pray for me in the hour of my death."

A gaunt looking man with crystal blue eyes strode into the gulag one evening. His eyes flickered anxiously as he scanned the emaciated humanity. He had searched every refugee camp along his route. He had run the gauntlet from barrack to barrack, searching the faces of those huddling on cots. He shoved outstretched arms out of his way with irritated impatience. Suddenly, his tormented expression softened as a look of recognition crossed his face.

He saw a strange woman with a Slavic face wearing a bright floral printed kerchief, holding a baby with tiny blond curls ringing her face. The woman was prodding the baby in a strange language full of shushing and rolled R's to eat bread that had been soaked in black coffee.

The baby pushed her hand away, and cradled a rag doll instead. The man sprinted over cots and snatched the child from the startled woman's lap, knocking down the coffee cup. "How dare you give my child black coffee? You were given extra milk rations so you could feed her the milk. Where is my wife?"

The startled woman pointed to a building marked Quarantine. "They won't let you in there…they are all sick. They have typhus fever." The woman cackled as the man's eyebrows furrowed when he saw the warning. He darted across to the building with the child in his arms to the barrack marked in bold red letters

"QUARANTAINE. ZUTRITT STRENGSTENS VERBOTEN."

A Russian doctor blocked him from entering the barrack. "Nyet! Nyet! You are not allowed to go in there. They are all sick and highly contagious." The man pushed the doctor aside. "Don't tell me what I am allowed to do." The man shouted and a kerfuffle ensued. "They all have typhus in there! You can't go inside!" The man pushed the doctor back against the wall. "I'll shove your ass into this hole, if you don't let me go inside. You horse doctor!"

He shouted and with his last ounce of strength felt a great adrenaline rush and pushed the doctor aside, who stumbled back and nearly fell into a pit which was readied for yet another victim of the deadly disease. The man pulled the door open, and ran from one cot to another, until he spotted Emmi and his three sons huddling together on one cot. As soon as Emmi saw her husband, she whispered barely audible. "Josef, my dear Josef."

He scooped up his wife in his arms as the three boys scrambled to sit beside their father. He reached out to hold them in his arms and sobbed. "I have searched everywhere for you between hell and back. I have searched every labor camp listed by the Red Cross. I never gave up trying to find you even to the ends of the earth." Emmi's feverish eyes still could not comprehend that a miracle had occurred, as she beheld her husbands' face with wonder, and murmured. "Who are you? Are you the Angel Gabriel? Have I died and you are taking me to heaven?" Josef held Emmi close and whispered in her ear, as tears rolled down his cheeks unabashed.

"I feel more like Saint Nicholas. I brought a cake which your mother packed for you and the children. Here is the Bundt cake she had baked with lots of eggs." Emmi choked up with tears, she swallowed hard, before she could respond. "How is my mother?" Josef didn't answer right away.

The boys clambered around him, looking starved and waiting with hungry eyes as he tore off the wax paper from a golden yellow cake. Josef cut off slice for slice with his Swiss knife. While the children were busy devouring every morsel, Josef looked in his wife's eyes, and whispered in her ear. "I have sad news! Your mother baked this cake and died in my arms shortly after. Her poor heart just gave out. I buried her beside your father in the cemetery of Klein-Borowitz that was her dying wish. The Communist administrator would not allow your mother to stay in her house, because, he claimed, the house was too big for one person. Your brothers had fled to Germany before wars end. Instead, they moved four gypsy families into your old home. When your mother had no place to go, my mother took your mother in until my mother was ordered by these criminals to move out. She could no longer stay in her house either.

When Koczian drove my mother to live with my sister Annie, your mother had no place to go. She went back to her own house to live among the gypsies who bullied and shoved the poor woman around. Then my sister and her children were deported and my mother went with my sister to live near Marburg. After I was released from the Czech concentration camp, I went back to Mastig and found out that the Czech policeman who had terrorized our family, had moved his family into our house.

Our house has been turned into a police station. I found your mother living in her house with four gypsy families, where she was allowed to stay in one room. The shock of losing her entire family, having no place to go then being chased from one place to another, shuttled homelessly from one place to another caused your mother's heart to fail. She died in my arms and it was her dying wish to be buried next to your father." Emmi cried softly.

"At first, I had to bury her in her own backyard. Because these criminal elements had removed the marble grave plates from the graves of Germans as if we had never existed, so I had a hard time finding out where your father is buried. Some old guy told me and I reburied your mother next to your father".

He handed Emmi a small white Bible, no larger than the palm of her hand, adorned with small flowers and a mother of pearl cross, a small clasp at the side held the silky fine, gold rimmed pages together. Emmi opened the tiny clasp and fanned the pages. She looked astonished as dried forget-me-nots fell out onto her lap. It was her mother's final farewell. Emmi cried softly as she told the children of their grandmother's death.

As the rosary slithered through her fingers, Emmi rested her head against her husband's broad shoulders, and whispered solemnly. "Holy Mary, Mother of God, save my children and my husband. Pray for me in the hour of my death." She repeated the last words over and over until Josef retorted impatiently. "You're not going to die." Emmi looked up at him with sad, tear-filled eyes. "Josef…I will not live much longer. Look at me. How much longer do you think I have?" She threw off the covers, baring the sight of her grisly swollen, once beautiful legs of a woman who in her youth had been a singer and dancer. Josef grimaced and looked away at the sight of the purplish, puss filled boils and thickly swollen varicose veins. "I can't walk anymore!" Emmi cried.

Josef replied defiantly in the face of death. "I better get you out of here and fast." He heard the shovels outside, preparing again another grave. "If I don't, I will lose you." Emmi covered her face and shook her head as he continued saying. "We have to make it to the West and get away from these Bolsheviks." He knew this was a Soviet labor camp and those imprisoned here were worked to death, those who fell ill simply were left to starve to death.

Josef knew once his family had fallen ill, they were no longer given food. They were given thin watery flour soups and black artificial coffee made from roasted wheat. Since the sick could no longer work in the potato fields they would not be entitled to eat either. Food was only given to those who were productive. In time the disease would weed out those too weak for hard field labor, and allowed to starve. Josef waited until everyone had fallen asleep. He could not allow himself such luxury, as a multitude of images and queries continued to plague him.

Foremost on his mind was how he could save his family from the fate so many of the refugees suffered as the disease was raging through this fenced in compound. He had resolved that he would first have to recover his family's health and strength, before he could even attempt an escape from this hell hole, nor could he tell Emmi or the children of his plans.

The following morning, he turned himself in to the commandant of the labor camp to work for food. His picture was taken and his name was logged into the camp records. He joined the others working in the fields, but at night he slipped out to forage for food. He stashed his field glasses into his coat lining. Whenever he was sure nobody was looking, he slipped the field glasses out, scanned the terrain, looking for farms where he could work for a few morsels of food, clean out a barn for some bread for his family and a little milk for the baby. During the day, he crawled on his knees along the fence, weeding and hoeing the furrowed fields, and as he did, he snipped through the wires anchored deep in the ground. He worked close to the wire fence and out of view of the armed guards who walked the parameters of the camp.

The House My Father Built

One day he cut off two low hanging tree branches and stashed them under his cot. At night he whittled off the bark until they were smooth poles. He tied field blankets at the ends of the poles to form a makeshift stretcher. Late one night, as the camp was steeped in silence, Josef crept close to Emmi's cot and roused her to sit up. He placed a finger across her mouth and whispered "Sh!"

He carefully helped her slide to the floor and lay down on the stretcher and whispered to his son. "Pepi take the baby." Pepi heaved the baby on his shoulders and silently followed his father outside. The boys had learned to move about in silence over the last year. Quiet as mice they followed their father's lead. Josef dragged his wife out of the labor camp, pulling the barbed wires he had cut before over their heads, to let the children slip through the fence. Pepi carried the baby on his shoulders, and crawled silently behind them.

They fled across fields and forests, carefully avoiding major roads, inching across the girders of bombed out bridges, and across logs that had been laid across gurgling brooks, taking particular care to avoid Russian troops, but always heading west toward the setting sun. During the day Emmi and the children foraged for food in the woods, picking berries, and leftovers in the fields. Josef ventured out alone to scout out the terrain, leaving Emmi and the children hidden in the dense forest. He ventured toward villages, farms and houses, knocking on doors, begging for a day's work, only to find the doors slamming shut in his face. On rainy days, he begged farmers for shelter in a barn or a night's sleep in a shed, milk for a baby, only to be chased off as "Gesindel." (bums)

Months had gone by, another winter was approaching and Josef knew they could not go on this way they had to find permanent shelter. They reached the outskirts of a small village surrounded by thick forests, where a line had been drawn between East and West.

"Over there are the Americans. That's where we have to go, and get away from the damn Ruskies." He took out the field glasses, studied the terrain and noticed guards patrolling the area with German shepherds. He sighed deeply and shook his head. "We are not going to make it, they'll shoot us all. We can't go any further. We are stuck here, and have to make the best of it. I don't see any chance of getting across unnoticed. We'll have to make this our home for now. I have spotted a lumber yard, maybe I can find work there. Emmi said with a voice filled with high hopes and expectations. "Maybe we can even make a new life here."

Josef replied. "I'll go into town and see what is cooking there." He again left the family in the shelter of the thick forest and calmly strode into town to inquire at the mayors' office about housing and a job.

Josef approached a desk, and was informed that the man seated there was a Socialist party functionary who interrupted Josef's inquiry about work and a place to live, abruptly. "Are you a member of the Communist Party?" Josef looked startled, calmly shook his head, glanced at the name plate and politely replied. "I have never belonged to any party, Mr. Gerber."

The functionary looked the emaciated man up and down and gruffly responded. "What can you do?" Josef replied unruffled. "I owned a lumber operation, I have studied engineering in Prague. My expertise is in the production of building lumber."

The functionary cut him off gruffly, "We need no engineers and wood workers. We need workers and farmers. You can show your gratitude to the Communist party as a logger at the railroad station and shave off the bark with a planer."

The functionary put his official stamp on the assignment, and continued undeterred. Josef inquired.

"I need a home. Where can my family stay? "

"There is an unoccupied kindergarten building on New Street, Number 2. Our Communist Party has confiscated the Evangelical Church. You can move into one of the rooms there." Josef winced at the functionary's harsh words. "Mister Gerber, I need housing for my wife and four children, three sons and a baby girl, how are we to fit into one room? We need…"

The functionary cut him off, stared coldly at the man through his thick rimmed glasses.

"That is your problem. It is none of our business. You are lucky to have a roof over your head." He handed Josef food ration cards for one week and keys to the house. Josef went back to the woods to fetch his family. Emmi was exited to hear the good news and overjoyed thinking that their odyssey was finally over. At last, they had a roof over their heads. Hopefully this was a signal of better things to come.

The family gingerly entered the building. The entrance was covered with black and white tiles. The "school room" had once been used as the schools' administration office. In one corner was a small pot belly stove, and a glass sliding door to the assembly hall, but this door was locked and the glass was covered with thick paper. Around the corner of the room was a tiled wash-up area with several small sinks, that hung very low above the ground. The toilets were perfect for small children, but awkward, to say the least for grown-ups.

As soon as word spread around the neighborhood that a family had moved into the old 'Kindergarten' building, the neighbors brought old furniture, a crib, a table and chairs, field cots to sleep on and old clothes, and best of all a wash tub. Emmi hung a thick blanket in front of the windows to keep private matters private. Josef took a look around the small town, past an Evangelical Church, the school, the lumber yard, a grocery store where he bought bread and margarine with the meager ration cards. The margarine was rancid and the bread stale.

Then he went to the dump where he searched for discarded or damaged household items. An old man joined him there and pointed proudly at a yellow building set into the woods, and told the newcomer about the community. "That house once belonged to one of Hitler's closest friends, Hitler had visited this village for the baptism of a child who had a birth defect." Now the house is an orphanage. Josef winced and spat on the ground. He was in no mood to listen to stories to remind him of the Schweinehund.

He told Emmi what he had learned on his walk about town. "I don't want to remember anything about this Schweinehund, who has caused us enough trouble. I wish they had caught him alive so they could hang him like Mussolini on the highest tree. He knew what would happen to him and that's why he committed suicide. He escaped the justice he deserved, and we are paying the price for his crimes."

Josef went to work the next morning at the railroad yard, where he was assigned to shave the bark off felled trees with a planer. Gone was the machinery he had used at his own workplace. Before coming home after a twelve-hour workday, he walked to the scrap yard, where he found discarded items that were fixable. In the shed behind the school building, he turned everything into functional items for living.

He found pots and pans worn thin with holes into which he pounded metal plugs to seal the holes, and Emmi had a cooking pot. He found rusted springs of a mattress which he tied together. A farmer gave him bags of horsehair which he stuffed into the springs. He inserted a metal tube into the small potbelly stove, so that the flames would curl around the tube and distribute the heat evenly across the entire cooking surface.

Emmi marveled at her husbands' ingenious ways, with which he brought order into their lives. His engineering know-how was put to good use and every item brought a certain comfort to their lives.

One day he found a rusty Singer sewing machine. Josef cleaned and oiled it until it was free of rust. Emmi was in her glory sewing clothes from old hand-me-downs her neighbors had discarded. She took old duds apart at the seams, cut off the frayed and worn sections. In a few hours one of her children had a new garment and nobody knew the difference between old and new, rich and poor.

The meager food rations allocated for a family of six were a source for much discontent. There was never enough to eat with which to fill the bellies of hungry children, and the children were always hungry. Emmi knew if she wanted to find something in the store to buy, she had to get to the store early. She got up at four o'clock, bundled her little girl up, knowing the boys, especially Rudi would harass her if she were left at home alone. She clasped a folding chair under one arm and held on to her child with the other. She hurried to the tiny grocery store in the bitter morning cold.

A few people were already standing in line at this early hour. She knew from experience that in the next four hours long lines would form, always with the hope that there was something eatable to buy. But all that was ever left to buy was slimy green fish from the Black Sea. She unfolded her chair, sat down and with her sleeping child on her lap waited for four hours. After the store opened, customers pushed and shoved each other for every crumb and morsel, snatching up everything from rancid margarine to the slimy fish her children hated and within an hour the shelves were empty.

With the ration cards Josef's family was allotted, Emmi bought flour and margarine. Empty noodle boxes remained on the shelves and they were for show only to give the appearance of plenty. Yet, despite the empty shelves inside the store, the lines in front grew longer and longer, as bellies growled louder and louder, month after agonizing month.

To fill their bellies the boys went out at night to forage for food. They had developed an eye for eatable weeds which added valuable nutrients to daily soups. Mushrooms and nettle could be found in the forests, which Emmi cooked into "creamed spinach". The boys had become very apt at finding potatoes, sugar beets, and carrots left by farmers in the fields.

The House My Father Built

Farmers no longer cared about bringing in a harvest before a storm, or what was left to rot in the fields at the end of their required work hours, because farmers no longer owned the land. They merely worked on state owned collective farms. They could care less after their workday ended, the farmworkers left the rest for hungry scavengers and wildlife to devour. The neighbors were beginning to wonder why this new family of refugees had more to eat than they did.

One factor could be attributed to Emmis magic skills in the kitchen. Josef teased his wife. "Nobody has your magic touch. I know you can make soup from stones." Emmi's rustic simplicity had taught her early the art of survival. There was a wonderful fruit orchard next door. The boys had watched the apples ripen over the summer. They could not resist the temptation of the red ripening apples.

The apples beckoned to be eaten. One night the boys waited until the lights were out in every house in the neighborhood, then the boys crept out of the house, crawled through one loose board of the picket fence, climbed the trees like monkeys and started shaking the trees.

Even the youngest child had learned of her brother's nightly scavenger hunts and scampered after them to watch from behind the wooden fence as her brothers' shook down the fruits of the trees of the collective farms. The noise of the falling apples caused the farmer to turn on floodlights and suddenly the orchard was bathed in a silvery glow. The boys clung to the branches in dead silence as a man stepped out of a building. He walked among the trees, shining a light up into the thick branches, yelling, "Is anyone out there?" The boys held their breath in fear of rustling leaves. Even the youngest knew she had to hide behind the wooden fence and knew not to make a peep. But as soon as the lights were turned off, the apples pounded the ground like hail again. The children filled sacks with apples and pears to the brim, even the youngest filled up her apron in a hurry.

The boys dragged the booty home and Emmi looked stunned and gushed. "Where did you find these apples?" The boys shrugged their shoulders and Pepi replied with a chuckle. "They are just laying around on the ground. I figured, since the state won't give us anything to eat, except moldy bread, rancid margarine, and empty noodle boxes. Since everything is owned by the state and the state belongs to the people, we, the people have to help ourselves." Emmi laughed heartily. "What would I do without my ingenious boys?" Pepi was indeed the most inventive genius. Not only did he know, what weeds were eatable, but knew the difference from eatable mushrooms and those poisonous enough to kill."

Emmi quickly exhausted her recipes of every apple dessert imaginable until the house smelled of apple dumplings, apple strudels, apple cakes, apple fritters, pies, breads and apple sauce. The next day, Pepi surprised his mother as she prepared the daily flour soup. "Look what the farmer gave me for cleaning out the stables." He held a huge egg under her nose. Emmi looked surprised.

"A large egg like this must be a goose egg," Pepi mimicked a waiter reading from a menu with stilted sarcasm. "On today's menu, we have our usual flour soup with one egg. Tomorrow, after I clean another pig stye, we can vary the menu, and serve one egg and flour soup."

Emmi ruffled her sons' hair good-naturedly and, with a lilting voice said. "With one egg I can make egg drop soup?" The next day Pepi brought home a burlap sack. "Look mamimka, nettles grow all over in the field, and here is another egg the farmer gave me today."

She looked surprised. ""I am beginning to feel rich. I can make creamed spinach today and top it off with a fried egg. God gives every bird its' food, but he does not throw it in the nest."

"Pepi replied, 'That's right Mamimka. Even birds have to find their food and so do we."

The family sat down feeling blessed and thanked God for the food they had found, as they simply stared at the friendly looking sunny-side-up egg, looking like a crowning glory atop a bowl of nettle soufflé. The wondrous egg looked so beautiful, nobody dared eat it. They had not seen a fried egg in years, and didn't dare eat it. Pepi finally broke the impasse. "OK, everybody can savor the egg for another second. Say Ah." They all echoed, "Ah!" And laughter filled the room. Emmi divided the large egg into six bite size portions. "Everyone can have just one big bite." The laughter was uplifting as the six pieces disappeared amid gleeful smiles in seconds. Josef pushed his egg portion toward his little daughter.

"Here, little one, you can have my portion." The little girl clapped her hands and eagerly leaned over to open her mouth for the extra portion. Rudi's droll mouth turned down at the corners in disappointment and said ruefully. "She always gets everything!"

Josef turned his back and looked out the single window. He smiled contentedly at the merriment one egg had created.

As anticipated, the functionary stopped by the "school house" without waiting for an invitation to enter. With cold eyes he surveyed the lively scene before him and boldly strode around the sparsely furnished, yet cramped room. He took note of the field cots leaning against the wall, with bedding neatly stacked on top. The crib by the front window, the goldfish bowl on top of a cabinet, the stove with an enlarged cooking surface, and a pot of sugar beets bubbling over until it turned into an amber syrup. The aroma coming from the cellar, gave the room a pungent smell of abundance.

The children sat around a kitchen table, which Josef had just painted white, waiting with hungry eyes for Emmi to ladle the soup into the bowls before them. The youngsters lustily gulped down the mushroom soup. They still looked hungry after the pot was emptied.

The functionary had a few carrots dangling in front of their noses. "Well, I see your family is doing well in this Socialist Workers Paradise. We can make life even better for you." Emmi politely offered the man a seat at the sparsely decked table. All the while, Josef kept his back turned and pointedly ignored him, as he stood by the window gazing out at a bleak landscape.

It was as if the functionary only talked to Emmi. He implored her to think of her children's future.

"We could give your husband an administrative job, in an office with a nice desk. We can see he is an intellect. His capabilities are in his head, not his arms. He is not fit for logging." He paused a moment and then said." But he would have to join the communist party. International Socialism is the future."

Of course, your sons have to join the Communist Youth Group called Young Pioneers and your oldest son must become a member of the FDJ—-Free German Youth."

Emmi listened intently. She knew in her simplistic view of the world, there was nothing free in political allegiance, everything had its price, but she had no clue what that price was. Dead silence followed as Emmi watched Josef with grave concern. He turned around to stare silently at the thick, horn-rimmed glasses of the functionary, who, in Josef's view was a local communist enforcer, just like Ernst Lochmann had been the enforcer for the National Socialists. Nothing had changed. One evil had replaced another.

Emmi could feel her husbands' bristling animosity toward this man building in his eyes. The crystal-clear-blue eyes, the windows to his soul, revealed nothing but pure revulsion. His jaw muscles twitched with restraint, and his fists slowly opened and closed. The functionary continued undaunted, unaware of the storm about to unfurl. "I could do a lot for your family. We just ask for a little cooperation. We can send your son to Moscow to study nuclear physics." We know he is a brilliant student with a very high IQ. Unfortunately, during the war schools were closed, so he was only able get a sixth-grade education. He is not going very far with such minimal scholastic achievements. He will have to work as a glassblower all his life. Maybe we can send him to Moscow where he can study, whatever he missed during the war. But first, you have to join the Communist Party and your son must join the FDJ, the Free German Youth."

At this moment Josef lurched forward and shouted. "Out!" He took two steps across the room and with one kick knocked the chair out from under the startled man. Josef grabbed him by the collar and dragged him to the door and said with loathing. "I will not live like a radish, white on the inside, red on the outside, only to dance to your tune. I will not hoot and howl with the masses in order to perpetuate your deceit. You are no better than the National Socialists were. You have one thing in common you are all criminals." The froglike eyes of the functionary bulged out of his head in fury, but his voice was that of a squeaky mouse.

"You'll regret this! You have no choice you will have to join the Communist party. We can make life very unpleasant for you if you don't. You have no options. The future of your children belong to the Socialist workers paradise. Their loyalty belongs to the Communist Party."

Josef shoved the man out the door and down the concrete steps. The man screamed when he hit the pavement. "God damn it! You will pay for this. You don't know who you are dealing with?" Josef ran down the steps and replied with an eerie calm. "I know who I am dealing with—-a blood red swine." Josef gave him one last shove against the black wrought iron garden gate.

The functionary picked himself up and ran off waving a fist in the air. "You'll pay for this!"

Josef calmly closed the door and Emmi looked mortified. Clutching her chest in horror, she shrieked. "My God, Josef will this ever have an end? Must you be so antagonistic toward every man? Can't you make peace with this man, and go along with their ideology, if not for you but for the sake of a better future for our children. I don't like this constant discord and hatred."

Josef waved her off and scoffed. "You can never make peace with a communist. These people are the same criminals who have robbed me of my home and my livelihood. Now I have to work as their slave, but they will not enslave my soul or my children's."

Emmi shuddered as her husband's voice became more passionate. "He said he could make life easier for us." Josef shook his head and replied adamantly. "Lies, lies, nothing but lies. They lure people with utopian propaganda. Don't you see, people are like lemming and mindlessly follow a messenger who dangles a carrot before their eyes with phony promises into their abyss. I will not sell my soul to the devil and follow these evil prophets."

His voice softened a bit as Emmi continued to sniffle. "People fall for their bullshit, before they realize what it's really all about, it is too late!"

Emmi whispered. "I am just so afraid for you… someday they will pick you up and haul you off to a gulag in Siberia. I will never see you again. I don't want to lose you again. All you have to do is put on a pleasant face, a facade in an evil scheme."

"I can't do that…you're the actress! Put on a facade for these gangsters." Josef had more important things to do. He had children's shoes to repair and drive a few nails into the soles of their shoes. He left the house slamming the door behind him and went into his shed. Emmi lowered her eyes and bit her lips knowing the subject of appeasement was closed. She was afraid of saying words she might regret later. She watched how Pepi scraped out the last bits of caked-on soup from the pot.

She had grown used to the rumbling in her stomach and the numbing fears for the future of her children. But the children had not grown used to the hunger pangs. Pepi with his flair for dramatics and humor sniffed the air hanging over the empty soup pot.

"Mmmm! there is nothing like the smell of flour soup!" The other children giggled in anticipation of hearing Pepi say. "And one egg!" Pepi frowned mournfully. "Sorry! No egg today!"

The tension was broken and Emmi smiled to herself, thankful to have a son with a sense of humor and a cool head, who in dreadful moments of hunger provided them with rare moments of laughter. Pepi never failed to make everyone laugh, although his humor had become very cynical. Failing one day to surprise everyone with a new food source, the next day he doubled up when he brought home a young gosling tucked under his coat.

"Look at this bird! I cleaned out the pigsty for a farmer and he gave me this little gosling because the other geese were picking and harassing the poor thing. He thought, the goose could not survive the meanness within the pecking order. He said it was a Christmas present. Behold our Christmas goose!"

Rudi murmured softly as he petted the tiny bird. "I could never eat the goose."

Otto listened, quietly whittling for hours on a piece of willow branch he wanted to turn into a flute. Now he looked up and calmly said. "You will eat the goose when your stomach growls long enough. "

He picked up a small harmonica and played the mournful song of 'Blue Mountains and Green Valleys' the anthem of the lost Czechoslovak homeland. Emmi was thankful for the roof over their heads, yet the memory of the home from which they had been driven so brutally wrenched her soul.

They had made a start with which she hoped to make life better every day. But her homeland and the four walls, she had called home for all of her thirty-five years was always on her mind and in her prayers.

Emmi questioned the wisdom of keeping a goose, knowing that a permit was required for everything short of taking a breath of fresh air. "Where can we keep a goose? We don't have a cage. We won't be able to hide her. She'll make too much noise as she grows up." Pepi thought for a moment and firmly said. "I'll have to figure something out."

He loosely put a rubber band around the gooses' beak. "She can't go around advertising her existence, we'll have to make a cage in the back of the yard, and take her out at night so she can eat grass to fatten her up." Emmi wrinkled her forehead. "Gerber will come around to check on us and if he finds out that we have a goose. He will confiscate the goose. He will never permit us to keep her." Pepi waved off her concern. "I will not let this weasel take one measly goose from us."

Emmi marveled at her oldest son for his bold and cool calculating odds in difficult situations. Pepi went outside with the other children in tow. He took the yellow-downed chick into the back corner of the yard, dug a deep pit, lined it with straw and covered the whole contraption with chicken wires, twigs and loose leaves.

"At night we can let her out, we'll take the rubber band off, so she can drink water, and eat grass." The boys looked dubious. "What if Gerber finds this pit?" The children waited and watched Pepi think things over. Pepi scratched his head thinking. He started digging a second pit in the middle of the school yard. "We'll have to dig another pit as a diversion in the front yard. Go fetch more twigs and leaves." Emmi looked dubious as Pepi explained his ideas and asked. "Who taught you all these tricks. How do you always come up with such clever solutions." Pepi replied. "Kurt taught me everything."

Emmi nodded and it became crystal-clear, despite having only six-years of elementary education Pepi had learned more from Kurt than from any teacher. He had learned survival skills in the school of hardships. Emmi went back in the house as a multitude of neighborhood children gathered and Pepi instructed them to pick up sticks and leaves. The children gleefully complied and tossed everything into the pit. They were excited to be allowed participation in a conspiracy.

After the pit was filled, Pepi covered everything with chicken wire, then covered the chicken wire with additional thick twigs and leaves. "I think even Kurt would be proud of me. I can imagine Mister Gerber strolling around the yard. It is his job to check on his radishes and keep them towing the communist line in compliance with his communist authority. He'll wonder what a pile of leaves is doing in the middle of the schoolyard, and he will fall into it." The children roared with laughter at the hint of sabotage.

"Mister Gerber will be so embarrassed he won't bother checking out the pile of leaves in the back corner where we hid the gosling." The children cheered ever louder in wild anticipation of what was bound to transpire.

Thankfully their father was unaware of what the boys were up to. He had spent every spare moment in the work shed to avoid any confrontation with Mister Gerber. The shed had become his refuge. It was his place of solace, where he could dedicate himself to work in peace and quiet contemplation about ways to make life better. Just as he had expected, the Socialist Democrat party functionary paid regular visits to enlist Josef's loyalty. This time he sought to confront Josef in his shed alone. As the functionary was about to walk into the back of the school yard. Josef slammed the wrought iron gate shut in front of Gerber's face, and walked toward his shed in the back. But the man sauntered after him in relentless pursuit.

The children of the neighborhood started to gather, clinging to the spiked iron fence like sparrows in anticipation of a show-down. Their eyes filled with anticipation of gleeful mischief as the functionary tried to catch up with Josef with bold strides, and heckled. "It's about time your sons join the Young Communist Pioneers, comrade Staffa!" Josef lowered his head as he turned around and snarled. "I'm not your comrade!" Josef kept his back straight, his head high, and walked even more briskly toward his shed. He passed the pile of leaves, picked up a hammer and pounded a metal plug into a hole in the bottom of a cooking pan. The functionary hurriedly sought to catch up with this stubborn man.

"You foolish man, you are depriving your son the chance to go to Moscow and become an academic. He could study atomic science. The Socialist state needs clever young pioneers like your son. He could become a party official in the Communist Party!" Josef spat on the ground and shouted.

"You mean a goon like you? Get away from me! I did not bring children into this world, so you could turn them into radishes, I rather my son becomes an idiot, than a radish!"

Just then the functionary let out a scream as he stumbled and fell face down into the pit filled with leaves and sticks. His feet got tangled between the wire mesh and the twigs. The children of the neighborhood shrieked with laughter, and the parents came running to see the cause of this commotion.

Josef just grinned at the man's pathetic misfortune and turned back to mind his own business. He was busy mending pots and pans so Emmi could cook another flour soup.

Gerber struggled to climb out of the pit, shook the leaves off his pants and jacket, stalked off red faced, leaving the snickering neighbors behind. Emmi had watched the event from her window, deeply dismayed. While Josef smiled contentedly as he entered the house, Emmi wrung her hands in his face. "My God! Sef, we'll all wind up in Siberia. Can't you make peace with this man, so that he will leave us alone!" Josef retorted with a wave of both hands. "I have told you already, you can never make peace with a communist." He brushed off her pleas, and changed the subject which seemed to be on everybody's mind. "What's to eat?"

The children had just entered and shouted in one accord. "Flour soup and no egg!" Emmi looked stung and embarrassed for she was sure her children blamed her for their meager, uninspiring meals. "I can' help it. We are not getting any ration cards because we don't belong to the Communist Party. But even if we did get ration cards for flour, sugar and margarine, the store shelves are still empty. How does the elite get everything for their creature comfort? When there is nothing to buy."

Josef wrapped his arms around Emmi's waist and purred contentedly. "I can't expect you to bake a Bund cake from rocks, but I can expect a loving arm around my neck."

Emmi turned around, somewhat appeased and with a broad smile on her lips, she murmured tantalizingly. "…and this, I guarantee you! There are no ration cards of my love." She wrapped her arms around his neck and kissed him passionately, then draped the blanket once again before the window.

May Day!

The functionary returned to the neighborhood on a regular visit, as on this sunny day. He knocked on doors, and prodded children to climb aboard the hay wagons which were lining up in the streets. The wagons were colorfully decorated with rainbow colored crepe streamers. The children jammed unto the wagons, singing the praises to the Socialist Workers and Farmers State. The wagons rolled through the streets, swaying red banners with the golden hammer and sickle encircled by a wheat stalk, were blazing in the sun. The banners proclaimed the accomplishments of the Socialist Workers and Farmers with laud and jubilation, and the boastful proclamations.

"Without God and without sunshine, the harvest we will reap in time!" Emmi bristled at the bombastic claims aimed to cut God out of people's lives. She wagged a paring knife in the air.

"Without God and without sunshine? They won't do anything. God will let it rain to wash out the harvest. He did. It rained throughout the summer and washed out the harvest." Josef snarled. "Make sure our children do not participate in these activities Keep them at home. I don't want them poisoned by this spectacle of communist propaganda." Josef responded absentmindedly, as he listened to the loudspeakers' announcements extolling the virtues of the Socialist Democratic State.

"Calm down. The boys are playing soccer in the yard." Emmi reassured her husband. "I wish it would rain on their parade. Oh, boy, here comes the weasel. I am so sick of that frog faced radish." Josef sneered as the functionary came up the steps and barked his order.

"These young pioneers should join their young comrades in celebration of the Socialist Workers Paradise." Josef spat on the ground. "Paradise? You call this paradise?" Josef was filled with utter contempt. "This place is a dung heap? My children are not allowed to frolic around on your manure pile. I will not let them cajole with your radishes. I don't want my children contaminated by your hype and hoopla indoctrination."

The functionary was not intimidated. He reminded Josef of his obligation to the state to bring up children in communist doctrines and that his resistance would cost him dearly. Josef snarled as his blood vessels bulged and his face turned into a frustrated grimace. "I did not allow my children to be poisoned by Hitler's propaganda machine. They were not allowed to join the Hitler Youth and they are not allowed to join your Radish Brigade, so that the likes of you can poison their minds the way Hitler did."

Josef chuckled cynically; his eyes sparkled passionately during this tirade, as the youngest child used the opportunity to sneak out the back door. Around the bend and out of view the little girl climbed quickly aboard a hay wagon before her Papa would notice her disappearance and command her to come back.

She nestled in quickly among the other children, some of whom were her little friends from her street. She wanted to share in the fun with the songs of the cajoling children during the ride to the fairground. She was thrilled to sit beside her unsmiling friend, Karen Bergmann from across the street. Karen Bergmann had a somber face with a bright red kerchief tied around her head, which was in sharp contrast to her pale face and her blond braids. Unruly locks spilled out from under the red scarf above the saddest puppy dog, water-green eyes. The little girl smiled at her friend and said, "Smile, Karen! Why don't you ever smile? " But Karin shrugged her shoulder and looked even sadder. "I have nothing to smile about."

It puzzled the little girl how Karin could look so sad on a day like this. This was no ordinary day. It was a thrilling day. A day when all the girls wore red dresses, red kerchiefs or neckties, and the boys wore red neckties over white shirts, surrounded by red flags and red banners.

The girl looked around and saw red everywhere, even Karin's dress and kerchief were the proper color of a Communist patriot.

She was oblivious to the fact that she was the only child not dressed like a Young Pioneer. Papa had never allowed her to wear red. She was always dressed in pink. Today she was dressed in her favorite frilly pink butterfly dress, her mother had embroidered around the ruffled collar and skirt. A large white bow adorned her blond braids which made her stand out even more in a crowd dressed in red. The little girl looked down on her pink butterfly dress. Because she wore a pink dress, the other children called her Christliche Gesindel, Christian Bums. She had always known she was different in her pink dresses. But she was oblivious to the stares and taunts. She liked her pink dresses, because her mother had sewn them for her. Besides, she knew she looked pretty in pink, especially when her long blond hair was banana curled. She was too excited and delighted to care. She wanted to take part in all the excitement. She laughed and clapped her hands to her heart's content and listened intently to the strange songs her little comrades were singing. She enjoyed being able to partake in what Papa had labeled the Radish Brigade, in the company of her kindergarten classmates.

She was too happy to be seated beside Karin, because Karin had never been allowed to play with a Christian riff-raff, like her. Conversely, her Papa never allowed her to set foot in Karin's house either, because, he said, that they are painted Red across the street. The little girl hated coming face to face with the stern woman from across the street, whom she knew to be Karin's mother and who like Karin, never smiled either. Instead, her stern face put the fear of the devil in her. She knew that Karin's father beat her black and blue if she ever set foot in the house of the Christliche Gesindel.

Whenever she wanted to play with Karin, she threw small pebbles against her bedroom window pane. Then she ran quickly around the corner of the house in the hope Karin would come out to play out of view of color-conscious grownups, and, my, oh my, if Karin's mother found out that they had played hopscotch or played hide and seek, Karin was in red hot trouble. Karin's parents were nothing like her own. Her mama was forever singing, while Papa fumed only about the red poison. The little girl thought she saw an association with the color red, it was the color of blood. She hated the sight of blood.

But now the red bows, red scarves and red dresses worn by her friends were greeted with excitement by her feeble spirit. For the moment, she enjoyed being among children who were entertained with games and contests, playing for prizes of candy, fruits, cookies and sausages dangling from a colorful May wreath. The likes of which were never in stores available for anyone to buy.

First, the children had their hands tied behind their backs. Then the May wreath was lowered over the children's heads by a man with a pulley. The children were instructed to jump in an effort to snatch a bite of the tempting morsels. The man with the pulley yanked the wreath back up quickly as the children had to jump, higher and higher. The little girl realized only the tallest boys were lucky enough to snatch a bite from delectable sausages. She stood by the side to watch the game. At that moment a stone was hurled at her and hit her in the forehead, and she heard a boy shout. "Piss off, you Christliches Gesindel!"

She fingered her forehead and felt the stickiness of blood trickling down the side of her face and a large boil swelling up. Some unknown assailant had attacked her, because she was different from the rest,—-she was dressed in pink.

Exhausted from jumping and disappointed for not winning a treat, she trudged along the road holding her head. She was unable to contain her sniffles, and ran blindly along an unknown path. She had no idea which way she was to go now.

The banter with Gerber had so antagonized Josef; he could feel his blood boil and his mind replaying the ugly scenes over and over, now his anger had fizzled and he turned to Emmi with a start. "Where is the little one?" He paced back and forth in heightened agitation. Emmi replied with a veiled accusation.

"I haven't seen her since your discourse with Mister Gerber." Her words seemed to imply that Josef should have paid attention to their little girl instead of fighting with that man.

Josef anxiously looked up and down the narrow street. Emmi made a suggestion. "The boys are playing soccer, maybe they saw which way she went." Josef walked into the "school yard" where his sons were playing with other neighborhood boys. "Has anyone seen the little one?" He got angrier by the minute as no one could give him more than a shrug of the shoulders.

He fumed and started running in the direction of the village center. Down the narrow winding streets and past the old farmhouses with their characteristic stucco and cross beam facades. He walked along the banks of a swirling brook, past the church and the grocery store, and toward the school building and soccer fields.

He swore to himself, "I'll beat her little fanny, if she went to that parade of comrades." He was filled with fury for having been disobeyed. His fury was replaced by fear, thinking of what might have happened to her.

On the outskirts of the village, near the People's Festival Grounds he saw her sitting by the side of the road, holding her head with a blood-soaked handkerchief. When she saw her father coming toward her she burst into tears.

Josef's anger had dissipated at the sight of the watershed. He picked her up and looked at her tear-streaked face, as she sniffled painfully. "Papi, I didn't win anything. They made me jump and jump with hands tied behind my back, but I couldn't jump high enough or run fast enough in the sack races. The others were taller and faster at everything, and then someone threw a stone at me and called me a Christian riff-raff. I think it was Karen's brother."

She wiped her nose on her sleeve. Josef handed her his handkerchief. "Here blow! Or your mother will pull your ears." He wiped her face dry with the clean ends of his handkerchief. "Hold it to your forehead until it stops bleeding. Today you learned the lesson of a lifetime. Now you know that everything worth having has to be earned. Contests are concocted by charlatans for simple fools like you, who put their trust in lies and deception instead of hard work." Josef lifted his daughter on his shoulder for a piggy back ride home.

Now we have to go home and face your mother together. But at least I have my Gitchen back. Let all the other fools jump with hands tied behind their backs. You will not have to spend your life jumping around like a monkey. I promise you that." He took the child in the back of the school yard, where he built her a sand box, near where a goose was kept in a hidden pit.

Emmi watched from the front stoop. "Now, that's a good idea. It will keep her from wandering off. She needed a place to play in, a place that is all her own. The boys have each other. They are busy playing soccer or chess; they pay no attention to her."

The little girl was in her glory. Playing contentedly in a place where she baked sand cakes and built sand castles. In the early morning hours, she couldn't wait to run outside to let her fantasies flow free. The sandbox was just within a few feet and within view of the shed, where Josef was repairing the children's shoes, just the way his grandfather once had. The child felt safe within view of her Papas' shed. Sometimes she skipped across the yard to watch him work with a myriad of tools, as he hammered and chiseled at an object to turn it into something useful. A week went by in blissful peace, but the peace was illusive, and too short lived.

The man with the stern face and thick horn-rimmed glasses stopped by the yard one day. He never missed his weekly rounds to keep his lemmings in line. He looked over the fence and watched for a moment. He saw a little girl at play in a sandbox in total oblivion to her surroundings. He walked briskly across the yard, took a shovel and knocked the boards of the sandbox down and raked the sand into the dirt. The startled child let out a piercing scream, and howled as she saw her castle smashed and leveled with one fell blow.

Josef heard the scream and crossed the yard still holding a sledgehammer with his arm raised high over his head. Enraged at seeing his daughter's distress and seeing what had caused such an ugly scene, Josef sprinted across with the hammer swinging wildly as he ran with his arm in a striking pose. Emmi had watched from the window and screamed in horror when she saw what was happening. "No! Josef, don't!" That instant and not a moment too soon, Josef dropped the hammer. He stared at Gerber for a second numb with rage, holding unto every ounce of sanity by a thread, when he heard the man's cynical taunt. "Little comrades don't play in sandboxes." That instant Josef was beyond control. He grabbed the functionary by the collar, lifted him off the ground, and hooked him by his collar to the wrought iron fencepost.

The functionary screamed as he dangled as if he had been fastened to a meat hook. Josef walked away and left the man dangling and screaming. "Help!" Upon hearing the commotion, the neighbors came running from every direction and laughed uproariously at the spectacle before their disbelieving eyes. Emmi came running out of the house, wringing her hands, and imploring her husband. "Josef please, put him down! You'll be hauled off to Siberia for sure this time."

Josef ignored his wife's pleas. He was beyond reasoning and so enraged he shouted loud for all the neighbors to hear his rants and raves. "I've had enough of communist diatribes and this man's incessant harassment. I never flipped my arm in a Hitler salute. Never shouted Heil Hitler, nor did I march in goosesteps to the tune of Socialism. I will not cow tow to the red vermin in Moscow!" Josef entered the house.

Emmi was embarrassed to have to ask neighbors to help her lift the struggling man off the fence hook. Gerber shook off the helping hands as they sat him down and took off running as fast as he could. Emmi went inside to confront Josef. She shook her head and sadly whispered in dismay. "Josef…" She sat down by the window in silence, and wept. Josef kissed his wife on the cheek and whispered, "Goodbye!" He stepped toward the front door.

"I am leaving. I know they will be coming for me, so I might as well spare you and the children the drama and embarrassment of my arrest. I will go to the police station, and turn myself in." He did just that. He remained incarcerated until the trial. In the interim, food ration cards were suspended pending the outcome of the trial.

It was October, the birthday month for both Josef and his little Gittchen, as he lovingly called her. Every year they both celebrated their birthdays together. But this time, there was nobody to celebrate with. Josef was in jail. Before his incarceration Josef he made her a birthday present cut from an old pair of shoes. Her feet had grown and shoes were too small. Much to the child's delight he had fashioned a pair of sandals for her. He had simply cut out the front and the heels so her toes could peek out. Emmi bought a small bowl of grapes at a high price from a farmer. The child was delighted when told, she would not have to share the delicious grapes with her brothers.

Judgement day was upon them and the mood was subdued as Siberia loomed large on Emmi's mind as the most dreadful place on earth, to which they might all be sent. The trial started the next day and Emmi was present during every proceeding. But all she knew how to do, is pray. The prosecutor called five key witnesses who were neighbors who had presumably seen everything as it happened. The first witness was the highly respected Doctor Rudolph Messerschmidt who took the stand and told the court. "I saw nothing." The next witness was the doctor's wife, Hedwig who was a nurse, and she responded also with. "I saw nothing." Neighbor after neighbor repeated the same words and the court saw no option but to set Josef free. Emmi beamed in amazement at Josef, as they walked out of the court house into a beautiful sunny fall day. "At every moment of tumult and strife, I've met an angel, today I met five."

Mister Gerber's zeal for retribution did not wait long. Without wasting a moment, the functionary stepped up to Josef and handed him an order to report for work at a uranium mine in a distant town. It was a place far out of commuting range, even on a weekend. Josef looked puzzled at the address he was given and queried. "What provisions have you made for my wife and children, where will they live?" The man said coldly. "No provisions were made for the family."

Later that night, after Emmi had covered the windows with blankets and the children had fallen asleep, Josef wrapped his arms tightly around his wife, and whispered in her ear. "I have been expecting a knock on the door any day, I didn't think it would be this soon." Emmi replied softly. "Well, I am thankful they are not shipping you off to Siberia. During Hitler's time you would have been hauled out of bed and lined up against a wall without a trial. I was afraid every day of that dreaded knock on the door. I thought any day would be the last day for us."

Josef cut in calmly. "You don't understand! I am not short sighted like you. You like to appease people so you can have peace for the moment. I know what these bastards are up to and what the end result will be. This is the end for me. Mining radioactive material is a death sentence, and that is what Gerber handed me today, my death sentence. They will never let me out of these mines alive. You see, once again one evil has replaced another." These were the last words Emmi heard Josef say before he disappeared into the night without another sound. Without him, the house was eerily quiet. Emmi stopped singing, and a little girl kept vigil by a window, wailing. "Where is my Papi?"

An Iron Curtain Christmas...

was just around the corner when a little girl sat by the window, staring out at the wintry scene. Through windowpanes thick with frost and icicles hanging low from every eave, the five-year-old kept watch by the window on her world for the beloved face of her father to appear. She stared glumly at a caravan of slow, creeping vehicles winding their way through the lifeless streets. A thick blanket of snow muffled the rumble of tanks and trucks creeping in slow motion through the otherwise deserted streets of the tiny village nestled deep within the heart of the Thüringian Forest. The softly falling flakes veiled the creeping caravan, veiled the show of intimidation to the people of East Germany, who watched in solemn resignation, remaining hidden behind crystallized window panes.

A beleaguered people, imprisoned by a strangling coil like that of a giant python, which stretched from the Baltic Sea to the Balkan Mountains, lived in paralyzing fear as in a giant mausoleum. Pressing her nose against the icy panes in childish curiosity, the girl stared in awe at the eerie procession. The snow clinging to the soldier's furry caps and the red star fastened to them gave them an almost comical look. To her they looked like droll bears in a circus parade.

There was not a single face in the streets, not a flutter of a kerchief, to cheer or greet the soldiers. She scratched the frosty crystals for a better view. Just then her mother blocked her view by covering the window with a thick dark green blanket. The child looked disappointed and sighed deeply. "I am looking for my Papi. I am waiting for him to come home. Why doesn't he come home?" Emmi tucked and fastened the blanket tightly around the window frame and whispered. "Hush! Don't ask any questions. I don't have any answers. You know walls have ears." But the child remained disconsolate. "I don't see any ears on walls." The corners of her mouth curved down more, as she vainly fought back the tears. "I just want Papi to come home. I miss him. Why doesn't he come home?" Emmi could only answer with a sharp hiss. "Hush, don't blab! If you blab, we will all wind up in Siberia." The child whimpered, "I can never ask anything! Never! It's always hush…just hush!"

She mimicked her mother's voice and asked. "What's Siberia?"

"It's a terrible place where Stalin sends the people, who don't obey his orders. People have to toe the line. People disappear now and nobody ever hears from them again. Stalin makes people work to death or they freeze to death in gulags. We always have to be careful what we say to anyone, so we don't get hauled off to Siberia."

"Who is Stalin?" The child persisted. "Stalin is an evil man like Hitler was. A Russian dictator. Now hush. The walls have ears. I should not tell you anything. You might blab to your little friends. Gerber will come knocking on our door and some day we all get sent to Siberia like Papa." Emmi admonished her sulking child. "In any case, cheer up, it will be Christmas soon!" But the child mumbled glumly. "Not without my Papa!" Pepi impatiently cut in. "Not without food. I can't find anything in frozen fields. Do I dare ask, what's left to eat, considering it will be Christmas soon? Even our Christmas dinner will be nothing better than our usual flour soup…and you know what!"

Emmi slumped exhausted on a chair and shook her head in utter dismay, while the children mocked with one voice. "Flour soup and no egg?"

Pepi grumbled. "It's better to make a joke of ones' misery, than to bemoan it. Christmas Eve used to be a time of feasting not fasting. I can't imagine feasting on flour soup. I am filled with a most unsavory foreboding that this Christmas Eve we'll have to sit around with a growling belly."

Emmi looked beaten down. She knew her children were hungry, while she felt exasperated in the daily struggle for anything to eat. Two months ago, she paid a farmer a fortune for a small bowl of grapes as a birthday present for her little girl. Now she put her head on her arms and wept, wishing she still had that money.

"What do you expect from me? Miracles? I have no money left. Even if I had money, there is nothing in the stores to buy, the shelves are empty. Empty noodle boxes are on display, and there is plenty of flour, rancid margarine, and green slimy fish from the Black Sea nobody wants. Nothing else! I can't perform miracles. Maybe you should pray for a miracle?"

Pepi retorted, as his stomach concurred. "I'm hungry and I know praying won't fill my belly. You always made us pray for a return to our home someday. It has been almost four years, and there has not been a single miracle. All the praying you have done has brought us nothing. I pray for Stalin to die! That's the miracle I pray for." Pepi had always evoked a certain hero worship in the younger children. In their eyes Pepi could do no wrong. He was always right about everything and his prophesies always came true. The little girl sat by the window and prayed for Stalin to die, and for Papa to come home.

Pepi continued to vent his anger over his never-ending hunger. "If this criminal were dead, maybe we could get something to eat. Forget about praying for a return to Czechoslovakia. The Czechs won't let us move back home, I heard they have moved gypsies into home vacated by Germans. We have been played like pawns in a chess game. And we lost Check Mate for communism! We have always been the pawns for politicians to kick around like a football."

Hunger pangs became more acute as snowflakes piled up on window sills. The thick snow-cover and frozen ground gave up nothing for the children to scavenge anymore. There was nothing left anywhere. They grumbled more and more, but, at last they had stopped complaining about the daily flour soup, for even flour soup was better than nothing.

Emmi knew how to make the simplest meals delectable, if only she had the ingredients. In the summer she could add tasty mushrooms or greens and herb cuttings from the fields, or onions and potatoes. She was desperate to get some food in the house and bundled up her little girl for the long trek to the store to sit again for four hours before the store opened in the hope of buying something to eat as allocated to her and the children on the ration cards, even if only flour and rancid margarine.

On the morning of Christmas Eve, the little girl sat on her usual perch watching Soviet tanks roll through the bleak, snow-covered streets. She observed the mailman struggling through the knee-deep snow covering the sidewalk. He had to dig a passage from door to door, until he reached the top steps of the school house. With a jubilant cry, the child slid off the chair.

"Yippee! It's for us! The mailman has a package for us!" She clapped her hands for joy and raced to the door, but Emmi cut in front of her with quick strides. The boys were quick to follow and ogled the disheveled looking package. The children's eyes lit up like sparklers at the familiar sight of beautiful calligraphic script, naming the family as recipients.

"It's from Papa, isn't it?" The little girl jumped up and down in one place with cries of jubilation. Emmi hissed sternly. "Hush…" The child clambered on top of the table, stubbornly ignoring the elbow shoves from her brothers. She sat like a statue as Emmi frantically tore at the rope and wrap, till both flew about her in shreds. Moments later, treasures lay before their hungry eyes; the youngest had never seen anything like this before.

The boys could remember a time of plenty, a time when oranges, chocolates, candy, butter, sugar and spices were always in a kitchen cupboard in ample supply. But after four years even for them a time of plenty was becoming a cherished memory. The children shrieked in wonder and quickly sized up the huge navel oranges and chocolate bars, which Pepi divided among them to insure fair and even distribution.

The children were as euphoric as if they had received an early Christmas present in an atheist land which had not celebrated Christmas and Saint Nicholas had been exchanged for little Father Frost.

They did not notice what transformation had taken place as Emmi frantically dug with a wooden spoon inside the butter tub. With a great sigh of relief, she extracted what looked like a wad of rumpled paper, which she held to her bosom for a second. She closed her eyes in a silent prayer of thanks, slipped the paper wad quickly into her apron pocket, and assembled the baking ingredients, humming to herself.

Every now and then she snapped instructions at the children. "It's time you swing into high gear and create some Christmas cheer." She turned to her oldest son. "Pepi take the goose to the butcher for slaughter." The children including Pepi had grown fond of the goose and protested wildly. "I can't kill the poor thing." Emmi insisted nonplussed. "Take her to the butcher, have him cut the head off and pluck the feathers. I need a new pillow." Pepi grudgingly complied, tucked the wing-flapping bird inside his coat. An hour later he was back with a blood dripping carcass and a look of disgust on his face. The other children burst into tears at sight of the bloody carcass of the dead bird, which had chased them across the yard to nip at their thighs.

Soon delicious aromas filled the dinky room as soon as the poor gooses skin sizzled and Emmi's spirits soared. "Sing! It's almost Christmas! It's time to make music." She started humming her favorite Christmas carols to lift her children's spirits, seemingly to no avail.

The House My Father Built

The memory of the goose haunted them into sullenness and tearful outbursts. Pepi finally broke the silence, grumbling. "It's still a miserable Christmas! We have nothing to eat, except a goose nobody wants to eat." Rudi shook his head with gruesome disgust and wiped his eyes dry.

"I can't eat her." Emmi cut in cheerily. "Just wait until she is browned on all sides." Otto murmured solemnly as he looked up from tuning his hand-carved flute.

"Maybe you'll eat the goose when your stomach growls loud enough!" He chuckled.

Pepi ranted as he turned to a more pressing problem, the pressing of his pants. He laid the pants straight across the kitchen table, placed a board across them, and then sat on the board, in the hope of creasing the pant legs. "I don't want to look like Gesindel." He sneered, looking under his behind now and then to see if a crease was forming.

Emmi wanted to set the table, while Pepi behaved like a hen on her nest. She looked on impatiently, getting visibly annoyed over such a tedious process. She wanted to prepare a festive Christmas table, the likes she had not been able to in years. "Pepi, how much longer will it take before you lay an egg?" The children started to snicker, as Emmi teased. "I am waiting to see you lay an egg. You are looking constantly under your seat to see if you laid an egg."

The children shrieked uproariously, and Emmi joined their laughter. But Pepi only looked frustrated. "It's the shabby fabric; it's good for nothing but a scrub rag."

"Pepi, I would rather you get a tree now. Your pants look good enough to impress the Fräulein from the glass factory. What was her name? I need to set the table now." Pepi bristled with sarcasm. "You don't need to set a table. Whatever there is to eat, we can eat right from the frying pan."

Emmi smiled mysteriously. "Take the little one with you on the sled, the fresh air will do her good." The children bundled up and left for the nearby forest, Emmi started decorating the room. She hummed to herself, as she graced the table with a frayed but clean white tablecloth. The room slowly filled with the aromas of freshly baked cookies. Magic filled every corner, as she lit a few candles and again covered the windows with a thick blanket.

The children were awed by the magic of the snow-laden trees and scampered through the deep snow, looking at pine trees from every angle, to find the perfect tree for Christmas. Rabbits scurried about, and the wind whipped the snow playfully into diamond sparkles, as the sinking sun shone with slanted rays through the trees.

It was a magical day for a little girl when the boys built a snowman and showed her how to make snow angels, and she twisted and twirled as if she were one.

Suddenly, a sharp object seemed to pierce her eye. A searing pain caused her to slump into the deep snow. She curled up into a ball, writhing in agony and screamed until she finally lay motionless. The boys, who had just cut the perfect tree scrambled to where their sister lay unconscious. They carefully lifted her onto the sled, tying her down with ropes. Then they hurriedly headed home, across a narrow gurgling brook. The boys eased the sled across a rough tree trunk that lay across the frozen water.

When Emmi saw the boys coming back without a tree, and seeing her child lay motionless on the sled she screamed. "My God, what happened?" The boys shuffled awkwardly about. "Something always happens to her." Rudi replied.

Emmi turned to Pepi. "You have the longest legs, run and get Doctor Messerschmidt. Otto and Rudi help me carry your sister inside." Emmi laid the unconscious child on top of the kitchen table. Moments later the doctor entered the room with his black bag. He adjusted the kitchen lamp and shone a bright light over the child's face. The area around the eyes looked inflamed and swollen. He took out a pair of tweezers, carefully lifted the eyelid, and extracted a large pine needle. He reassured the handwringing mother. "She'll be fine, I see no damage to the iris." He covered the eye with gauze and a black patch. "Just leave the patch over the eye to rest the eye and avoid any irritation." He turned to Rudi. "And don't make your sister cry." He winked at the mischievous boy, took his black bag and left.

When the child regained consciousness, she looked about the room and instantly queried. Where is the tree?" Pepi gave her the earth-shattering reply. "It is in the woods where we found it. We are unlucky at everything. Something always goes wrong. No tree… no Christmas." Rudi added glumly. "Yep, no tree, no Christmas!"

The girl screeched. "No! We have to get the tree." Pepi shook his head resolutely. "No, it is too late. It's already dark out. We can't get across the brook in the dark." The child began to cry. "We are not going to have a Christmas?" Emmi cradled her daughter in her lap, "Hush, don't cry! Even without a tree it's Christmas. The doctor said you should not irritate your eyes." She rocked her child gently, soothing the sniffling child with a lullaby. "Still, still, still a little child wants to sleep as angels sing a lullaby, while Mary nurses a sleepy baby." The fragile melody visibly calmed the child.

One lonely tear stubbornly clung to the side of her cheek, as she sniffled. "Mommy I just want my Papi to come home. My eye hurts." Emmi brushed the child's tousled curls from her face, braided her long blond hair. Took off the eye patch, and slipped her favorite pink dress over the child's head. "The doctor said you should not cry. So don't!" Emmi admonished her.

"Don't rub your eyes. You are lucky you did not damage your eye. In the meantime, you can pray and hope, someday we will all be together with our Papi. Singing will help you forget all pain."

Emmi busied herself around the stove, carved up the goose, smothered the meat with gravy, scooped out potato dumplings from boiling water, and plated up the evening meal. The children just stared down at their plates, and poked at the goose meat. Pepi sprang to his feet and slapped his forehead and said. "This is crazy! Even I have lost my appetite! We are practically starving to death, but we can't eat the goose because we have grown fond of the bird. Emmi gave up trying to prod her children to eat the luscious meat and frowned as gobbled down the cookies instead. Otto busied himself with his flute and managed at last to extract a few recognizable melodies from his carved contraption. Emmi sang louder and louder, and the child listened while choking back the tears, meekly trying to chime in, reading her mother's lips to help her follow the verses. Emmi prodded the boys to sing along. "Sing boys, it's Christmas, time to be merry and joyful!"

Pepi looked nonplussed. "We have nothing to be merry about. We left the essence of Christmas in Czechoslovakia in a house on a hill."

Emmi retorted sternly. "I beg to disagree. We have our life and each other. In every difficult moment of our life Gods' mercy has revealed himself with grace. Our souls rejoice in Gods beauty made visible on Christmas Eve! Where is your essence of Christmas? It is in hope that we find the spirit of life!"

After Emmi's stern reprimand, in an attempt to appease their mother, they sang half-heartedly, with croaking voices. As a crescendo rose slowly to harmonious singing, the child noticed the door opening slowly. She slid off her mother's lap and scooted under the table. Rudi scooted smack behind her and pulled down the table cloth to hide behind it. Through the holes in the table cloth, they peered at a bearded old man, dragging a sack behind him. A tiny Christmas tree with a multitude of flickering wax candles fastened to a sled, instantly filled the room with magic. The child whispered to her brother. "It's Saint Nicholas!"

Saint Nick said, with a mysteriously deep voice. "Come out from under the table, children. I can see you hiding!"

The child grabbed Rudi's suspenders and clung to them for dear life. Both children slowly crawled out from under the table. They cautiously ogled the old man from a distance. Saint Nicholas asked sternly. "Have you all been good to your mother?" The child stared into those clear, forget-me-not-blue eyes that looked all too familiar and nodded dutifully, as Saint Nicholas prodded her to sit on his knees.

"Let me hear what you have learned in kindergarten. Can you sing a song for me?" The child smiled, "I sang this one for my kindergarten class. Mamma taught me one. I am a little Saint Nicholas, here to bring great joys. In my coat are two big pockets, filled with horse, rider and a wagon, soldiers march with drum and fife. I forgot the rest." She mumbled shyly and Emmi applauded.

Saint Nicholas lifted the sack by the ends. The most beautiful toys tumbled to the floor, the likes the child had never seen before. Two dolls, one blond with blue eyes, the other a brunette with green eyes that opened and closed like magic. When she tilted the dolls head the doll cried Mama.

A red hand-painted doll stroller, a dollhouse filled with tiny wooden furniture. The child shrieked with delight, clapped her hands and jumped up and down in one spot. She had prayed to see her beloved Papa but instead Saint Nicholas had made her forget Papa and the world around her.

She was lost in a world of her own. She took no notice as Saint Nicholas stepped into the shadows of the room, where he gently put his arms around her mother and the two stood silently side by side and watched the children's merriment.

The children paid no attention to the tete-a-tete, least of all the little girl, who was content to play out her fantasies, as Saint Nicholas slipped out the door and Emmi followed him. He whispered to her. "I couldn't let Christmas go by without seeing her eyes sparkle with delight. She never had a Christmas celebration. I hope this is one she will never forget." Emmi gently stroked his face. "She'll remember this one for the rest of her life!"

At this moment Rudi smashed the face of the child's favorite doll and screamed as she struggled to yank the doll back from her tormenting brother. He let go of the doll as soon as Emmi entered the room. The girl cradled the doll with the scared face, which now looked cross-eyed at everyone with a stupid grin. The child tried to repair the scare that ran down her forehead and along her nose to no avail.

She felt sorry for the doll with the battered face, and refused to let her out of her tight grip, even when Emmi tried to pry it from her hands. "We have to get ready for church." Emmi dressed her little girl with greatest of care, gussied up and banana curled the child's blond hair and slipped the pink dress over her head. Bundled in warm winter clothes she skipped alongside her mother, while her brothers drudged along with less enthusiasm, because the pews had been removed by the communist government and the electricity was shut off to churches to discourage church attendance. The boys grumbled all the way to church for "Midnight Mass."

They entered the church in pitch black darkness as the priest handed lit candles to the worshippers. Rudi sneered. "Why is it called Midnight mass, it's not midnight."

"Why do we have to stand all night?" Rudi hated standing for an hour, in this packed crowd of worshipers in the pitch-black darkness. Otto responded pragmatically. "The mass is held earlier because the communists cut off the electricity to churches, and removed all the benches, so little wimps like you get discouraged to go to church." As worshipers entered, a warm glow filled the nave, which mingled with an intoxicating scent of incense wafting around their nostrils.

The boys snickered and jabbed each other, shifting their weight in agitation back and forth, until Emmi admonished them when the Mass began with a frown and a "hush," until the music ended with a multitude of glorious alleluias. The little girl stood near the front, clutching her doll and looking down on the porcelain figure of the baby Jesus, lying on crude straw, with his arms out stretched and a benevolent smile on his lips. She bent down low and whispered in his ear.

"Thank you, baby Jesus."

After mass had ended, Emmi and the children continued singing all the way home. Their hearts were filled with an ode to joy swelling their breasts. Songs of faith, and glory alleluias of the heart rang out and echoed through the night, hymns, which the government of East Germany under Soviet influence, had banned long ago, followed them home, and remained in their hearts all their lives as the very essence of Christmas.

They sang jubilantly, without fear through the sparkling Christmas night. As they turned the corner to their street, Emmi gasped and held her breath, and stood ramrod still. The children's laughter turned into pin drop silence. There, in front of her building were armored vehicles, and floodlights were aimed at them.

"God! Oh God! It's the Stasi!" Emmi whispered. She looked frantic, wrung her hands and clasped her child's hand tighter. Grappling for calm, she looked toward heaven. Her heart sank to her knees, as she saw the functionary amid the armed men.

She prayed for composure, and gingerly took a few steps forward. She saw uniformed men were inside the brightly lit house. They were not only searching their one room, they searched the three-story building from basement to the attic. "What is going on here?"

She asked boldly as if she had nothing to be afraid of. Nosy neighbors had stepped outside their front door or watched from behind the safety of their curtained windows, watching Emmi's dilemma, as she was suddenly surrounded by policemen. The functionary stepped forward and replied sternly.

"We are looking for your husband. We have had your house under surveillance ever since your husband did not report for work as ordered."

Emmi shrugged her shoulders with deliberate nonchalance. "I haven't seen my husband in more than two months. Now if you excuse me, I have to put my children to bed." As she turned, she blotted the sweat from her forehead. "You stay right here." The functionary said as he held her arm in a tight grip. While inside the house the Stasi tore floorboards apart, pulled cabinets from the walls, looking for any possible hide away. The functionary looked sternly at the little girl beside Emmi, who was hiding behind her mother's coat. "Tell me! Little comrade, didn't little Father Frost visit you tonight?"

The child voiced her confusion at the unfamiliar communist invention intended to replace her beloved Saint Nicholas. "No!" The child protested. "That was Saint Nicholas." The party functionary yelled at the officers. "Keep looking, he has to be here. The building has two attics and a cellar."

The State Security Police also known as Stasi, obeyed the order with unrelenting zeal, tearing the building apart. Emmi sat stiff-lipped and sore-footed on the door step. She was so tired of running, and hiding, and never feeling the freedom from fear. An old man stepped forward and approached the functionary.

"I am Doctor Rudolph Messerschmidt. My wife is a nurse. We live next door and with this commotion my wife and I cannot sleep. We are old and need our sleep. My wife is seventy-five years old. We can't sleep with all the lights shining in our bedroom and the noise you are making. What is going on here?"

"We are looking for Josef Staffa. We have ample reason to believe that he came here last night, disguised as Little Father Frost."

At that moment, Doctor Messerschmidt slapped his forehead chuckling with great animation. "You people have nothing better to do than to cause such hoopla. I am an old pediatrician and I played Saint Nicholas for the children. I look so much like good old St. Nick with my white beard, don't you think? I like to play pranks on little children to make them laugh." He was revered by children not only because he cured their belly aches and fevers. The children in the neighborhood liked to think of Doctor Messerschmidt as their good uncle Rudi.

The child stared at 'Uncle Rudi' for a moment and then looked at her mother. Her mother held her lips pressed together in a silent message not to say another word. She had learned long ago never to contradict or interrupt an adult while they were speaking, so she remained quiet. Doctor Messerschmidt's eyes held the child's curiosity as he talked, because she remembered Saint Nicholas, who had forget-me-not-blue eyes.

Uncle Rudi winked at her with his brown eyes. With his white beard he looked like Saint Nicholas, but she thought of the good doctor only as 'Uncle Rudi' because he often played magic tricks to make her laugh, plus he always gave her something to eat, an apple or a piece of candy. She heard him talk to her mother with unusual formality.

"Frau Staffa, forgive me. I did not mean to cause you all this trouble. You see, I wanted to make sure your little girl had a joyous Christmas, she still believes in miracles, the miracle of Christmas."

The policemen turned to the functionary to discuss this unexpected turn of events. Emmi breathed deeply and suppressed her own relief as moments later, the police left. As soon as they were gone, she expressed her gratitude with her eyes to 'uncle Rudi.' She clasped both his hands, and pressed back the tears that threatened to burst forth. She was too choked up to speak. She could barely whisper. "Merry Christmas, Rudi!

You were more than a Saint Nick tonight! You have been our guardian angel countless times in the last five years since we came to live here." In those years Doctor Rudolf Messerschmidt, had indeed become more than a good neighbor. He had become a good and trusted friend to the family who never tired of helping out in times of need. The children enjoyed the wisdom of this sage, who had become a great substitute for the uncles they had lost.

"I don't know how we would have survived without you. Thank you again Rudi. You are an angel!" The good doctor squeezed her hand and chuckled. "You could never convince my wife of that. I am no angel." He kissed Emmi on both cheeks, and bid the family. "Good night!"

Later that night, after the children had fallen asleep, Emmi scooped up the toys into her apron. The one with the battered face and blinking eyes, which her daughter had clutched all night and refused to put down, she stashed into a small knapsack. She ran across the street with the other toys wrapped into the apron frantically ringing a neighbor's doorbell. When the woman opened the door, Emmi thrust the armload of toys at the startled, sleepy woman. "Here, these are for your little girl, Ella."

The neighbor came out of her stupor in an instant. "I don't know what to say. We don't have such wonderful things here. Where did you get them? Where?" Emmi couldn't explain why she was giving her daughters' toys away in such ample show of generosity.

"My husband made them in his workshop in the backyard." She felt uncomfortable about the lies, yet felt compelled to do just that. "What about your little girl?" The neighbor persisted, and Emmi replied. "She won't need them, where she is going." The woman looked ever more perplexed. "But where is she going?"

Emmi dared not give any more answers for fear of saying too much and quickly replied. "It is late. I have to go." She ran back across the street without another word, and disappeared into the night, leaving the neighbor shaking her head in disbelief. In total darkness, Emmi stashed their few belongings, including the dismantled sewing machine, into several knapsacks, together with the remaining pieces of bread and covered them with the last bit of rancid margarine.

At three in the morning, she roused the boys and ordered them to dress. She packed knapsacks with parts of the sewing machine and stashed the last slices of bread with rancid margarine in each bag. Then she woke a sleeping child and pulled several layers of clothes over her head and a coat over the layers of dresses. She strapped the smallest knapsack to her child's back. Emmi strapped the heaviest knapsack with the sewing machine head over her own back. Then she fastened knapsacks to the boy's backs. In the still of the night, they silently filed out of the house and left behind a sleepy village on cat feet and angel wings.

Emmi pulled out a crumpled wad of paper, and followed the directions scrawled on it to an old barn along the Iron Curtain border. She and the children slipped inside the barn wordlessly. After a long foot-march they fell exhausted into the hay and instantly fell sound asleep. The barn door creaked open and a sharp hissing sound "Psst!" rustled the family up. The silhouette of a man dressed in black appeared in the doorframe and motioned with a wave of his arm to follow him, whispering hoarsely. "Don't make a sound and follow in my footsteps as fast as you can."

The man's dark face remained unrecognizable, hidden behind the turned-up collar of his jacket and the visor of his cap pulled low over his forehead. The boys were wide awake, and on their feet instantly. Emmi struggled to pull a soundly sleeping child out of the hay. She had to drag the child along, whispering. "Go, go, go…move your feet already!"

In total silence, they trekked in single file after the mysteriously dark man, whose steady hissing sound commanded them to, "Hurry up!" He spurned the group to move faster and faster. In the pale sliver of moon light, they saw the shadow of the man scurrying between bushes and tree trunks. In the dense forest the snow was not deep, but tree stumps and exposed tree roots were very slippery. "Step into my footsteps, so we don't leave too many footprints." He warned.

The group followed the ominous stranger obediently. The boys' long legs were able to keep pace with the man's footsteps with ease, but the child stumbled and fell over tree trunks and slid on snow covered leaves with every step. Emmi and her little girl struggled to keep up and trembled for fright at every sound the breaking of twigs under their feet was making. To everyone's horror whenever the child fell, the doll in her knapsack wailed mournfully. "Mama! Mama!"

Emmi felt the eerie wail cut through her bones. She realized she had made a terrible mistake in trying to save at least one toy for her child. Suddenly they all heard the distinct sound of a large animal running through the thicket.

They all stood frozen on the spot in bone chilling fright. Trembling like leaves the boys whispered. "What was that?" They could only guess what it might have been, a deer or a boar? The worst fear was, what if the animal was a German Shepherd of the border patrol?

The man motioned for them to stop and wait and motioned for them to crouch down behind bushes. They waited with baited breath until all was quiet again. Emmi was sure, that the cry of the doll had rustled the animal out of the thicket into flight. Emmi in anger with herself tried to remove the doll and toss her away. But the man stopped her with a scornful hiss. "Leave it alone…we have no time for this…you can't discard it here? We leave a trail. We are leaving too many foot prints, as it is."

The unrecognizable stranger spurned the group to keep going fast. "Hurry! Before border guards find our foot prints in the snow!" They were not given any time to think. The man got up again and Emmi and the children had to run to catch up to him. They scurried from one tree to another, always in the man's footsteps so as not to leave more tracks.

The layered clothes held the body heat and sweat and made running difficult. Despite the cold of a winter night, the sweat was running down the middle of their backs in rivulets. The little girl whimpered. "I cannot run any faster and I am hungry! " Emmi pulled her wordlessly along, until she had reached the limits of endurance herself. She sank to the ground, exhausted. Wrestling with herself for strength, it almost did not matter to her anymore, whether or not they were caught or not. At this time, she would welcome a quick death, perhaps a shot in the head. She was ready to surrender to her fate, whatever that might be. She waved the children on. "Go on without me! I cannot move my legs anymore. I have reached the limits of what I can endure. But I cannot let my children die like this. Take them as far as you can go. I will stay here! They will probably find us all and shoot us anyway. But the children deserve a chance to survive. "

She crawled beside a thick tree trunk, and leaned her back against it. "They'll just shoot us! The children clustered around their mother, not willing to leave her to die. She was prepared to wait until she could hear the sounds of machine pistols. The child whimpered. "Will they shoot us?" The dark cloaked stranger grabbed Emmi by the arm and forced her back on her feet. "Come on! Get up we are almost there, only a few meters across the little mound up there, then you are close to the west-border. " The man pointed in the direction where the thick forest thinned out and dissolved into a clearing. The clearing was bathed in the light of the early morning sunrise.

"Across this little hill down on the other side you have to cross a field. After a mile you are in the West, and behind the horizon, where the sky is lighting up a bit, those are the lights of the city of Kassel."

Emmi pulled a crumpled wad of paper from her coat pocket and pulled a few wrinkled monetary notes, and pressed them into the hands of the man. "This is all I have left." The man grabbed the money and without a sound disappeared like a fox back into the thickets. Emmi and the children walked slowly in the direction of the lights on the horizon, until they reached a clearing and looked across the broad expanse of a stubbly cornfield. They continued to drudge and stumble as the bristles and stubbles scratched their legs through layers of stockings and pant legs, keeping their eyes focused on the faint lights on the horizon as their gauge.

Suddenly, bright floodlights swept across the field. A man with a commanding voice called out. "Halt! Stop! Raise your hands high above your heads. Do not take another step closer!" The boys dropped into a ditch and pressed themselves flat against the ground. Emmi instinctively pushed her youngest child down into the rutted groove and threw herself over her child's small body.

The weight of the sewing machine bore down on her emaciated body. Emmi clutched the child's small frame close to her own to protect her against the cold ground, and in a vain attempt shield her from the expected salvo of bullets. She murmured to herself. "It's over now…it's over, this is the end for us. They are going to shoot us."

The floodlights swayed back and forth across their trembling bodies, seemingly without end. The voice continued to holler, breaking into the stillness of the early morning with a threatening boom. "Get up! Get up with your hands up high. Get out of the ditch, now. Get out of the ditch immediately." But nobody moved. Emmi's voice quivered in terror as she prayed. "Hail Mary, full of grace… pray for us in the hour of our death."

Suddenly the lights were turned off. A strong male voice boomed across the field through a bullhorn in an almost friendly tone. "Fear not! Good woman! You are on West-German soil. You can come out. We are the West-German border patrol. We are here to help you."

At that moment, Emmi burst into tears, and sobbed uncontrollably. The sobs racked her worn-out body, she kissed the snow-covered ground and gathered the children in her arms, as they struggled to comprehend that the ordeal was over.

The early morning traffic noise echoed across a nearby highway. To Emmi it sounded like a Ninth-Symphony. She felt rhapsodized, as if surrounded by heavenly music that swelled her breast, and a delirious ode to joy swept over her. She raised her tear-streaked face and looked relieved as she watched her sons run with great enthusiasm toward the sound of the voice as the floodlights dimmed and they climbed aboard the truck. The border patrolmen rushed to help Emmi and her child back on their feet.

The uniformed men supported her across the rough stubbles, and hoisted mother and child aboard the truck, and asked. "Where to?" Emmi replied. "City of Kassel! My husband found work there. Here is a map. She pulled the crumpled paper from her coat pocket, and showed it to the men, as the little girl asked. "Where is Papi?" The border patrolmen smiled. "We will drive you to the train station, but first you get some chicken soup to eat at the police station, so you can warm up your hands and feet. An American colonel will ask you a few questions. After that you are free to go." He leaned down to the child. "You will see your Papi soon."

A stone of paralyzing fear had been lifted. It had weighed them down for so long, and now their hearts were set on fire, as joy took hold of their feeble spirits, the spirits that had lain dormant and buried deep within their soul. The children unleashed a delirious inhibition and all its inherent joys. For once they felt the freedom to express themselves, to talk freely and ask questions without fear. They were free to let spirits bubble to the surface in their chatter flowing free, and a little girl would never again hear upon her childish questions the dreaded sound of "Hush! The walls have ears."

At the train station they were ushered into an office. They were ushered into a room and asked to sit down across the desk of an American colonel. Bowls of chicken soup were sat down before their hungry eyes. The chicken aroma wafted deliciously around their nostrils. Hesitantly the children slurped the hot liquid, while Emmi listened to the unfamiliar nasal sound of the officer's questions.

"Can you tell us how many Russians are stationed along the border?" Emmi shook her head resolutely. "Do you know in what area they are concentrated and in which direction they are moving?" Emmi shrugged her shoulders again, and replied.

"I really know nothing." She leaned exhausted against the knapsack. As soon as the soup bowls were emptied, the little girl closed her eyes, and was instantly sound asleep on Emmi's lap. In her dream a dog was chasing her. Just as he was about to pounce on her she tried to scream, but she could not make a sound. Her mother shook her and she heard again the calm voice of the officer. "Okay. Thank you for your time!"

He pointed to the door to let them know they were free to go. "Have a good trip, ma'am."

Emmi understood nothing of what he had said, but it sounded pleasant to her ear. She realized she need no longer fear anything. She looked forward to be reunited with Josef, and pushed her children toward the door. She could hear their stomachs growl on the walk to the train station, especially after eating the hot soup. It was as if the hot liquid had awakened their stomachs to new life. Their stomachs quickened with hunger pangs as they passed storefronts laden with food, which seemed to spill out into the streets. The first impressions of their new world were overwhelming. They felt like new-born babies, peering into a new world for the first time. A fantastic world of cobblestone streets had opened up, lined with neat and colorful stucco and crossbeam buildings that had survived a thousand years and many wars. The wood beams were decorated with carvings of fanciful nostalgic farmer's wisdoms. The children marveled at flowers bursting forth in brilliant colors even in the depth of winter.

Inside the store windows, they spied beautiful nativities and animated Christmas displays. Mountains of oranges were bidding them a glowing welcome into a world of glitter and glitz. Wonderland had opened its doors for them, and it felt good just to look inside, and inhale deeply the rich aromas of their new world in the 'Golden West.'

The town had awakened to its labored existence with people going to work on foot, on bicycles and trams. The broad daylight revealed to the children that nothing of any consequence would happen. Everyone seemed to move about serenely, almost complacently surrounded by such abundance. They had no urgent need for satisfying a hunger, nor clamoring for possessions, or grabbing of anything as soon as an opportunity arose.

Pepi quipped. "Welcome to Shangri-la."

Totally awed the children ran from one side of the street to the other. They had never seen such an abundance, nor were any lines forming in front of a store. The children saw that nobody was rushing at sales counters. No one was pushing or shoving other customers for all the plenty in store. The children felt as if they had spent a lifetime in a dark tunnel and finally had reached daylight. The time of miracles was over, and the children expected none. Even Emmi stopped reminding them to pray for the miracle of a return home to their beloved home in the heart of the mountains of their beloved Sudetenland.

Over the last few years Emmi's prayers had grown shorter. She prayed for the children's good health, our daily bread, forgiveness of sins and for reunification with her beloved husband, her sister Anninka and sister-in law Marie, and their children, her many aunts and uncles, the multitude of cousins, nieces and nephews, yes, she even prayed for Josef's mother, Anna Kudronovsky.

She wondered what fate had befallen them all and would she ever see any of them again. She shook her head in remembrance of the woman who once had been the richest woman of the region and the first person and only woman in Mastig who owned a Dusenberg. Despite her wealth, Josef's mother had worked hard alongside field hands, pitching hay, planting and harvesting potatoes, as if she were one of the hired helpers. Anna had never known vanity, just hard work, and a love for children and God. At every opportunity Emmi told her children of events from an unlimited reservoir of stories from another time and place, until the events of the past rolled like a movie screen in front of those, who were too young to remember. Emmi lovingly focused her stories on the home Josef had built, and where he had planted every tree. His favorite was a cherry tree Josef had planted right in front of the dining room alcove.

Emmi remembered with a smile on her lips his reasoning. "I want to reach out my hand and pluck the cherries right from the window. He never got the chance to enjoy even one cherry." For years he had meticulously pruned the delicate branches, checking the tree for blossoms in the spring and watching the ripening fruit until at last they were ripe for picking, before the birds could eat them.

Lest the children might forget, she described the house to the children in smallest details, down to the intricate patterns of the wallpaper, carpets and her beloved gold and rose-patterned Rosenthal dinner ware, which she had received as a wedding present from one of her wealthy uncles and the oval oak dining room table with six padded chairs.

She absentmindedly told her daughter a motherly secret. "Papi always wanted a girl like Margit, your cousin. We only had boys, but after Horsti died we had room for one more child. It was good that you came along when you did or you would not be here.

Emmi could not bear to close the chapter on all she had lost, without mourning that loss. The child looked up at her mother. "I want a sister! I don't like brothers because they won't play with me." Emmi shook her head and ignored the child's plea closing the chapter on any further discussion.

Emmi reflected on a time when life began like a fairy tale. Once upon a time not long ago, we had it all, we had love, we had dreams, and a lot of pain. Now we have nothing left except each other. But to others we were the refuse of the world. Emmi felt as though in crossing the Iron Curtain border, she had nailed the coffin shut on all she once had cherished, and all her dreams would remain shuttered for eternity. Although, she now felt safe in body and free in spirit, her heart and soul remained bound forever to the home she and Josef had built with love and filled with children.

All her hopes, and all she had shared with her husband were for her children's future. All would remain unfulfilled. Within the confines of that home on a hilly landscape, she hoped to live in harmony and die in peace, now her dreams lay forever buried. She was disconsolate.

All was lost. Gone was her home of distinction, her heritage and dignity. Gone were family ties, cherished relatives, friends and neighbors who had been scattered like dandelion seeds into all directions across the globe, blown apart by the gusting winds of socialism that had raged across Europe. She knew not if any of her relatives had survived or perished in the raging tidal wave of hatred. If they had survived, how would they ever find each other. Emmi prayed that they were not lost to her forever; else she would mourn them for the rest of her life. She had to face the new reality, in which any home would forever be any place where she could lay her head.

The boys ran ahead and found an empty table with a red and white checkered tablecloth in the waiting room of the train station. A waiter stepped up to the table and Emmi ordered five glasses of water from the faucet. The children looked around the dining area in wonder while they had to wait before the train's departure. Their hungry eyes burnt in the smoke filled and dingy waiting room. They could do no more than meekly sip the water Emmi had ordered. The tantalizing aromas wafting through the smoke-filled room teased them brutally.

Their sensory perception were being pushed to the edge. Pepi murmured. "I feel like Lazarus under a banquet table waiting for the crumbs to drop, as the rich men are feasting." Pepi mumbled in his delirium, but the bubble had to burst, and it did, when Emmi calmly murmured. "It's a feast, alright, but we are Lazarus under the rich man's table."

The bitter irony of that statement would haunt her children for the rest of their lives. Their empty stomachs churned at the sight of travelers sinking their lips against frothy beer steins, and alternately biting into sizzling, tantalizing aromatic and steamy juicy knackwursts on crispy golden bread rolls. The intensity of the pain in the pit of their bellies intensified as they watched others eat. The little girl skipped over to the food counter and pressed her nose against the glass encased enticing display that looked so inviting.

She finally squeezed her eyes shut, as tears welled up deep inside her, brought on by agonizing hunger pangs. She came back to the table and glumly traced the pattern of the red and white checkered table cloth, to avoid watching others eat. The comparison to the biblical Lazarus, which Mama had often told her, flashed through her mind.

She remembered the story of Lazarus, laying under the rich man's table waiting for crumbs to fall to the floor, while the rich man's dogs ate better than Lazarus. It was no comfort to this child, that Lazarus was exalted in heaven, and the rich man suffered eternal damnation in hell. Somehow, she could not find comfort in the conclusion of this story, as she watched those fat faces stuff delicacies into the caverns of their bulging bellies, paying no heed to the huddling, penniless, and shabby looking refugees. She looked around the room, and realized that she, her brothers and mother, were representing a shabby bundle of nameless humanity, who had been tossed about like a bag of refuse. She had always thought of her mother as a beautiful woman, who presented herself with a noble poise and dignity, even under demeaning and grueling conditions.

She always insisted on a properly set table covered with a white linen tablecloth. She made even the simplest meal a festive event. She maintained a sense of decorum, and propriety, and instilled it in her children, insisting that cleanliness had no price tag.

Her mother always made sure her long blond hair was neatly braided before she was allowing her daughter to leave the house to go to school. She scrutinized fingernails and the hollow spot behind the ears even though they had nothing more than a washbowl full of cold water.

Shoes had to be polished the night before and set beside the door. Torn clothes were mended. She viewed a hole in a sock as scornfully as a mortal sin, and took great pains to darn, patch, and mend every broken stitch before she let her children leave the house to face the world.

Compared to these neatly dressed Westerners, the child saw herself and her mother looking shabby in their darned and patched heels, knees, and elbows that were the calling cards of their heritage.

She recalled her mother's spiritual words of wisdom that now gave little comfort to a little girl who started to compare herself to those who looked well dressed, when her mother reminded her that earthly goods measured little compared to matters of the heart, and that a man's abiding faith in God and his God given health were his true net worth.

Her family was comprised of only six people among the armies of people who carried the memoires of their lives in a few boxes and bundles—-those, who, with bags and baggage as their only possessions, were a ghastly sight. Although not openly scorned, they were not easily welcomed. There were no open arms waiting for them, and no champagne was flowing to baptize their new birth as rootless tumbleweeds in the edifice of time.

They were like the millions who had fled before them, and the millions yet to come, given a new class distinction—-Refugees.

A strange looking young man wearing a green uniform, with yellow stripes on his arms and US insignias on his collar, stopped by their table. He politely removed his little boat shaped cap. "Excuse me, lady!" He smiled and spoke in a strange language with a nasal accent, like the one they had heard earlier at the police station. "Would you mind, if I bought your little girl some chocolates?"

Rudi nudged Otto and whispered. "She always gets everything." The young man added.

"Can I buy you a malted beer and a Cola for the boys?" Emmi looked stunned and fought back the tears that seemed to well up in her tear ducts constantly now and stammered. "Oh, thank you. I would love a malted beer." She was embarrassed to be a recipient of charity. But she was grateful to the young man for his friendly gesture. Emmi's eyes looked misty, as she stammered. "This is so kind of you!"

She pressed the handkerchief over her eyes and wept again.

The soldier motioned for the waiter to take an order and prodded the little girl. "Go to the counter and pick out some chocolate candy and pick something out for your brothers, too." Her eyes lit up as she skipped to the counter in a flash, ogling the bright red foil-wrapped lady bugs, symbol of good luck. She was thrilled, and thought what fun it was to be able to choose anything her heart desired; and not having to share it with her brothers.

She looked back at her mother and noticed that the worn and haggard look of a few moments ago, had miraculously dissipated. Emmi was smiling and a warm glow settled over her. She slowly sipped the beer relishing every sip, and the children nibbled the chocolates, deliberately slow, to make the little squares last the few hours until their train arrived. Emmi smiled at the young man. "May I ask your name? I want to remember you in my prayers." He responded politely. "My name is Joe. Short for Josef."

Emmi smiled like she had not smiled in years. Her gloom was lifted. The children were delirious to see their mother smile again, as she tried to pronounce the young man's accented name. "Tschow! Tschow!" She repeated it over and over, as if to emboss it in her memory. "There are still good and kind people in this world, one of whom is named "Tschow!"

Pepi laughed. "From now on Tschow is my name. Don't call me Pepi again." He resolutely hoisted the knapsack over his back. "My Czech grandmothers named me Pepi, and I hated it."

I'm done with everything having to do with Czechoslovakia. Socialism be damned. We live in the Golden West now and we will live our lives by Western standards." He headed for the train platform and Emmi and the children followed. The thought of being home soon with her husband filled Emmi and the children with high hopes and good spirits.

The children had counted the hours by the minutes until they would be home with Papa again, and all their homeless trekking would finally come to an end. They stepped off the train in the city of Kassel, Germany, believing that this big city would become their new home on a hill. They walked through the train station full of high hopes and good spirits, and were greeted by a sun hanging like a fireball over the city, suspended over the black ruins, the likes of which they had not seen in their lives thus far.

The House My Father Built

Having lived in a small village, which was left unscathed by the ravages of war, they stared in utter disbelief at mountains and mountains of twisted steel beams and shattered concrete blocks, amid cavernous bomb craters. A jungle of ruins greeted them with gaping jaws everywhere they looked. There was not a brick atop a brick as far as their eyes could see.

In the distance a spire pointed into the sky, like an angry finger of warning, and foretelling of impending doom. Emmi looked pained and speechless, she slowly lowered her knapsack to the ground, sank on top of the step and stared ahead speechless.

Suddenly, she threw her hands over her face and wept bitterly, muttering intermittently. "My God! Josef, why did you bring us to this hell?" Her gangly boys shuffled around in awkward silence. The little girl nestled against her mother and dropped her head in her mother's lap. She cried along with her mother, unable to grasp the horror that caused her mother to break down in tears. She was unable to understand what hell had raged here and burnt living flesh? What hell had created this giant death camp, where in a single October night in 1943 in a hail of bombs, fire and brimstone had poured down in an endless, merciless air bombardment, in which most of the city was destroyed.

The child wrapped her arms around her mother for comfort, as the brothers helplessly watched their mother disintegrate before their eyes. "Jessesmarren, Josef! Why did you bring us to this hell, Josef, why?" She shook her head in disbelief.

"Damn this world for all its Godlessness." For the first time, the children heard their mother curse. Emmi had been so full of high hopes and good spirits during the train ride.

Before the war had taken its toll, she had always found a boundless energy and strength in the little miracles of life, and her abiding faith in God, who, she insisted, always had an angel waiting in the wings, to help people cross life's bottomless abyss.

At last, she raised her eyes and wiped them dry with her kerchief. The cards had been dealt, and they had received a bad hand. Emmi was determined to make the best of a fateful existence, if not for her and Josef then maybe for the sake of her children.

She whispered to herself. "My children have been robbed of their childhood. I want to make sure they have a chance for a life worth living." She again took out the wad of crumpled paper and studied it a moment. Her eyes scanned dejectedly across the expanse of the rubble looking for a spire she had seen a moment ago.

Then in the blink of an eye, she focused on something in the distance. "I believe this is the church steeple." She read some instructions again, and meticulously studied the sketchy map which showed a spire as a landmark. Yet, despite the drawing, the heaps of rubble allowed no recognition of road markings and street names.

Signs were either non-existent or burnt beyond recognition. A single spire provided a point of orientation on the distant horizon, it was a church. "Where I find a church, I find hope." Without uttering another word, she hoisted the knapsack over her shoulders, and with a deep sigh of resignation, strode ahead.

The children followed meekly dragging their feet, with sagging shoulders, as each hauled a heavy bundle reluctantly. They walked past mountains of rubble, craters, and twisted steel beams. A million words could never describe the vastness of devastation they were passing by.

Emmi walked briskly, her eyes fixed on the steeple, straight toward the burned-out skeleton of a church atop a grass-covered knoll, which appeared like a peaceful oasis in the middle of this vast devastation. The outside walls were charred, but standing tall and seemingly intact, the stained-glass windows were blown out, looking like charred holes of a blackened hulk of a shipwreck. The only part that remained untouched and untarnished was the steeple with a golden and shiny crucifix on top. Emmi walked up the steps and strained to open the church portals. She spotted an inscription on a commemorative plaque and read out loud.

"On the night of October 22, 1943, over 600 people who had sought shelter during an air raid over the city, were killed when a bomb dropped dead center in this church." The church had become a mass grave. For time and all eternity, this church would be preserved as a gruesome war memorial to remind future generations of the horrors and insanity of war.

As Emmi stood reading the inscription, the child looked up and wondered about a wrathful God who had allowed firebombs to rain on his house. As pious as Emmi had always been, she told her children that a church was a peaceful sanctuary and a house of God. But this sanctuary had become a house of horror for six-hundred souls. Emmi had seen in the steeple with the untarnished crucifix

The House My Father Built

an omen and a symbol of hope. She hastened with new determination to pull on the heavy brass rings to open the portal.

Slowly the doors creaked open with a heavy moan. Emmi cautiously stepped inside and the children gingerly poked their heads through the door, unsure of whether they were even allowed to go inside. They expected to find a bomb crater, and a giant mass grave before their feet. To their utter amazement, they saw that God was present here.

A makeshift altar had been erected, covered with a simple white linen cloth. A huge golden crucifix brilliantly illuminated the back wall. White linens draped the charred walls, and, where once had been the roof the linens formed a tent. A blue banner dangled from the top of the tent, and a white peace dove hovered just above the altar, extolling mankind to "Worship the Lord in the beauty of holiness and give Praise unto the Lord for He is good." The ground above the bomb crater was covered by rough wood planks. Emmi dropped to her knees, crossed herself, and bowed her head low before the cross. She knelt there in silent prayer as the children watched in awkward silence.

She rose slowly, crossed herself again and briskly walked out with the children in tow. Emmi looked refreshed and determined to get home, wherever that place might be. In the aftermath of the calamity of war, she had glimpsed a rainbow of hope in the tiny flickers of life, the newness of creation all around, and the untarnished golden cross atop a steeple. The children found it hard to maintain their mother's pace as she seemed to walk faster and faster.

As they walked amid the rubble and tonnage of devastation, they noted the frenzied activities suddenly emerging everywhere. They saw men, women and children, young and old swing pickaxes, shovels, and plows. They pounded with sledge hammers against charred cinder blocks and crumbled brick walls, filled handcarts and wagons with the cleaned bricks and hauled them to new building sites.

The once picturesque cultural city that had enjoyed great renown among European royals, known as the plush playground of Hessian nobility, dotted with great summer palaces, parks and mineral spas. This splendid city from centuries of glory had once been the summer residence of the likes of the German Emperor Wilhelm I, Napoleons brother Jerome Bonaparte. It had hosted a European summit meeting reigned over by Queen Victoria and forty European heads of state, which looked more like a family reunion of royal aunts, uncles and cousins.

Now, this beautiful city was nothing but a heap of rubble. It lay mortally wounded where nothing remained but twisted steel girders, burned timber and piles of bricks. Emmi and the children walked along the narrow winding torn up and rutted cobblestone streets to the city's outskirts until they reached a Garden area, where plots of land had been set aside for city dwellers so they could grow their own fruits and vegetables. Havens, wherein they could find a place of respite from the daily grind.

Behind tall hedges lay a patch of heaven wherein weary souls could find a sense of normalcy, privacy and peace, however fragile, after years of turmoil—-and amid the mortal wounds of war.

A single file pathway led them to a tiny bit of paradise, where garden sheds looked like they had been freshly painted. Although it was winter, certain flowers bloomed. Emmi pointed one out. "This is the Christ Rose. You see these pinkish petals looking like a face, surrounded by dark fringes in the center looking like a crown of thorns, which gives the name "Christrose" a heavenly credence, because it blooms in the winter under the snow."

There between the city limits and the gardens, they knew that a time of resurrection had begun.

At the end of the pathway, in the farthest corner of the garden area, nestled behind trees and bushes, and surrounded by a picket fence, they noticed a man leaning against a fence post and shielding his eyes against the rays of the setting sun. He looked as if he had been waiting for a long time. A smile flickered across Emmi's face, and she quickened her pace when the man waved them on, and she waved back, and then he just stood there with his arms outstretched, and the little girl screamed. "Papi!"

The little girl ran as fast as her legs could carry her despite a heavy bundle on her back. Her braids flapped about her head. The man crouched down to catch her in his arms. Her arms fell around his neck and she held on tight. He murmured softly, as he stroked her hair. "All is well, little one, all is well." The family was reunited after all these lost years of war and separation. Josef and Emmi fell into each other's arms, glad that their odyssey had come to an end. Hidden from view behind a row of Hawthorne trees Emmi spotted a tiny stone shack, next to a barren strip of land, and winter barren fruit trees. Josef saw her hopeful look.

"There is enough room where we can plant a large garden here, with lots of vegetables and the trees bear tasty green summer apples the kind you like." Emmi listened to him, just too glad to be reunited with her husband again, and glad he had found a roof over their heads however tiny, with a large garden around it. Any roof would do, as long as they were free of fear. Free to fall asleep and not fear a knock on the door at night with the ominous foreboding of what new terror the morning would bring, or where they could lay down their heads to sleep. The boys brought up the rear, glad the long drag with knapsacks on their backs was behind them. Josef forced open the creaky door to the shack, made of rough-hewn boards. Emmi and the children squeezed inside.

She tried not to look shocked at the appalling condition and size of the shack while Josef apologized. "It is not a villa, but for now it is the best I could find."

Emmi somberly replied after taking a sober assessment, not daring to look Josef in the eyes, lest he might see her shock and horror. "It is a shack with a leaky roof and broken hinges. But what is most important, our family is intact. Nothing matters after that. Everything else is secondary. We have each other, that is all that matters." Josef chuckled. "Actually, it is worse than a shack for human habitation. It is actually a dog house." Josef responded with a sarcastic chuckle. "This hut belongs to a man named Bergmann, a brother of the man from across the school house, where we once lived. He leased this property from the city, built this shack for his garden supplies, and kept his dog here to guard his garden. During the day he works at the Electric Company behind those Hawthorne Trees. There is another piece of garden plot next door."

Josef pointed to the little knoll in back of the shack. Emmi could see that the shack had been built for a large dog. It was a solid cinder block building with one tiny vent to allow air circulation, and cement floors and one pot belly stove. Josef tried to explain. "The city has no apartments available for our size family. New ones are being built for the local population, for small families but not for large families like ours. Those who owned a house before the war, could get government mortgages to rebuild over the ruins of their old house. There is a long waiting list for housing. As refugees we don't fit into the city planners' scheme. As soon as I told them how many children we have, they tore up the application. I checked out a refugee camp outside the city. It is another lice and flea infested tent city, where one has to sleep beside total strangers." Emmi winced and stroked his face, knowing how it pained him that he had not found better housing.

He had hoped to start anew in the Golden West, when all he could find was not fit for human habitation with a proper stove and a real toilet. "All is well, my beloved Josef, we have each other. After all we have been through, it is a miracle that we have survived this odyssey. Our children are alive and healthy. Our family is intact, that's all that matters to me. I do not want to spend another day in another lice-infested refugee camp made of wooden shacks or tents where the wind howls through the cracks, and strangers sleep side by side on field cots."

Josef explained his plans for the future. "All these garden lots belong to the Electric Company behind the fence. I have secured a lease for the adjoining property from the city where we can plant vegetables this coming spring. I have tried to get a permit to build a real house here, but the city has refused my request because they want to build the autobahn extension through the area, that's why we cannot hook up to the utility company. We have no electricity, no sewer or septic. The lot next to this one is vacant I can build a new house there. It will be a small house because city planners allow nothing bigger than a garden shed here. We have to be able to hide our little house behind these Hawthorne trees and bushes. The well water is not palatable and the boys will have to carry buckets of water for cooking every day from the electricity company. But we have apple and plum trees on the lot. When we have to answer natures' call, we have to hide our indignities in the bushes. I am trying to buy out Bergman's lease and pay him something for this doghouse. Down the road is a public indoor swimming pool and bathhouse, which miraculously survived the war."

Emmi nodded as Josef tried to explain his ideas, listening to his well thought out plans and imagining that there would be a light at the end of the tunnel maybe, someday. She unpacked the knapsacks, rationed out a few slices of bread with the rancid margarine, while Josef turned to the boys and told them to get straw from a farmer in Sandershausen.

When they were gone, Emmi took a closer look around and shook her head, wondering about the irony of their fate. "We have to sleep in a dog shed and sleep on straw? Now I know how Mary and Josef in the stable of Bethlehem must have felt, because there was no place for them in the Inn." After Josef and the boys returned with bundles of straw, they spread them evenly across the floor, and covered the straw with field blankets. Emmi ordered the children to lay down on the blankets side by side. She kept her youngest child closest to her and covered her up with blankets and tucked the ends under her. "We have to lie close together for warmth."

Wake-up calls came during the night as bladders roused the meek. One after the other they crawled out from under the covers, and learned to hide their indignities in the bushes beneath the scrubby Hawthorne trees. After those necessities were taken care of, they used this opportunity to sneak around in the dark looking for something to eat. Maybe a stale piece of bread which their mother had not hidden well enough? Emmi guarded the few provisions like a Rottweiler, to make sure that no one could stuff his belly full, while others went without.

The next evening a motorcyclist wearing a black leather jacket rushed into the yard with a tremendous noise. Josef took a few steps toward him. "Good evening, Mr. Bergmann, my wife and children have arrived from the East Zone last night." The man rudely ignored the friendly greeting unwilling to hear any lengthy chit-chat and gruffly demanded. "Do you have my money?" the man wasted no words on civility. "I am just here to collect the rent!" He grunted threateningly.

Josef tried to mask his embarrassment with an explanation. "Last night my wife and children escaped across the border and are dead tired. I just started working and won't get paid until the end of the month. You must be patient till the end of the month."

Bergman's reply was a sharp. "I don't give a damn. You'll be damn sorry if I don't get paid by tomorrow, or you are out of here." He cursed loudly, stepped on the gas and sped away at high speed. The mud from the spinning tires splattered about him and smacked in Josef's face. Emmi took her apron and wiped Josef's face as he said. "I already gave him a lot of money, now he wants another 500 Marks rent for this doghouse. I don't know from whom I should get that much money. I have just started working at the Pondorf Iron Factory, stoking an iron smelter. The pay is lousy. It is hardly enough for food on the table." Emmi put her arms around him to comfort him and replied. "Maybe my brother Leopold can help us. You remember the one with the grenade splinter in his head. He married a wealthy woman named Martha from this area. I might locate him through the Red Cross. He will help us again."

After work, late one afternoon, Emmi noticed an old, tall and skinny man with a bent back, as he struggled to ride along the muddy garden paths with an even older rusty rickety wreck of a bike. He went to his little garden shack across the path where he kept a coop full of pigeons. He never looked at anyone, paying no attention to anyone or anything. Nothing mattered to him, only his pigeons mattered. He was oblivious even to the fact that his nose was running like a leaky water hose. Emmi noticed also that the pigeon keeper was dressed every day in the same black clothes, looking more like a scarecrow. The children had noticed the strange man and were discussing his disgusting mannerisms and imitating his eccentricities. Emmi determined, despite the man's frightful sight, he was harmless and she would greet and treat him with dignity and respect, in spite of his demonic look, and dreadful habits, whereas, the children made fun of him and his ill begotten exterior. The children had found cause for endless laughter and ridicule, for as the man rode his bike through the mud, instead of wiping his nose with his kerchief; he caught the drips with his tongue with ease. He could reach the tip of his nose with his tongue.

For lack of better things to do, the children demonstrated what they had observed. It brought moments of comic relief in their miserable living condition. With the children's silly antics, hilarious laugher ensued, and Josef was alerted to this strange man, whose lack of propriety gave ample reason for raw humor. Ever suspicious of people's motives, Josef never sought out friendships with acquaintances. For all he had heard about this man, Josef planned to check the old man out in the hope of learning more about the demographics of the area from a local.

Maybe the old man knew something about better living arrangements, maybe a better shack to rent? One Sunday, he watched and waited for the old man to finish cleaning the coop. He ventured over to the man's yard, and introduced himself as Josef Staffa. The old man withheld his hand and ignored Josef's outstretched hand. The man continued to shovel bird shit, and glumly said without looking at Josef. "I am Wenzel Hucke, what do you want?" Josef had waited all Sunday to speak to this man, he was not going to be intimidated by such an unwelcoming response. "Mister Hucke, I need to find another place for my family, another garden shack or apartment to rent, maybe you know of a place?" The man shook his head and kept shoveling manure and Josef continued.

"I have paid Mister Bergmann already 100 Marks, and now he is asking for another 500 Marks for the shack we live in. It's too much rent to pay for a dog house."

Mister Hucke stopped working, pulled a dirty rag from his pant pockets and blew loudly into it, then he spat out a slimy substance beside the tip of his boot as Josef looked away in disgust. Mister Hucke leaned on the shovel and looked at Josef askance.

"That's extortion. I hope you didn't give that guy any money? Bergmann had built the shack without permission from the city. It sits on that lot illegally. He knows, the city can come any day and tear it down. The miserable bastard wants to exploit your misfortune." Josef looked stunned as the enormity of the man's words registered. "The rotten bastard!" escaped Josef's lips and thanked the old man profusely for his honesty. As revolting as the manners of this old man were, at least he was an honest man. Then the old man showed Josef a picture of his daughter, and Josef was stunned at sight of a beautiful girl.

Wenzel Hucke, did not only have a beautiful daughter he showed Josef a picture of a beautiful wife. He wondered how the two ever got together? "Maybe it was a miracle? But thank God, the young woman smiling back at him had not inherited any of her father's repulsive looks. The young woman looked like a young Liz Taylor. She had married an American and now lives in Texas."

The fact, that Wenzel Hucke fathered a beautiful girl, earned him a bit more respect. Josef told Emmi about the conversation with Wenzel Hucke and Emmi replied in amazement. "It's no wonder an American spotted her and whisked her off to Texas." Josef replied with a snicker. "Well, maybe Missus Hucke planted a cuckoo's egg in Mister Huckes nest. However these two got together in the first place, is the first miracle, that they have a beautiful daughter that is the second miracle. If this is really his biological daughter, I can only say, hats off to Mister Hucke. But what do we do about Bergmann?

He told me if he didn't get his money on the first of the month, he would take a sledgehammer and tear down the roof of the dog house." Josef replied. "He is extorting or blackmailing us. He knows our situation and uses it, to put the squeeze on us. He knows we have no chance of getting an apartment. We have no option but to string him along. As long as we don't let him know, what we know now, and as long as he thinks that we will pay him some day, he won't throw us out, we have to play along."

When the spring rays warmed the garden and the sun shone late in the afternoons, Mister Hucke's wife came on Sundays. One could not help but notice the sharp contrast between husband and wife, particularly after Mrs. Hucke was gradually developing into a Hollywood diva wearing fancy clothes and perfumes sent by her daughter from America. One day the whole family arrived from America and organized a Texas barbeque, and Mister Hucke stood suddenly tall in everyone's eyes, as one of his new in-law relations plopped a Stetson on his head.

Emmi still wondered about the miracle theory and quipped. After all these events everyone talked about Mister Hucke with a quiet, but distant respect. Josef had learned a lot from the old geezer, whom the children quickly had dubbed Hucke Wanzel, as if they were talking about a maggot, in disrespectful conversations, due his ever-present repulsiveness.

Emmi was now the one who waited for Mister Bergmann every evening, to deal with the man herself. She was afraid Josef would lose his cool in a delicate situation that required her more eloquent diplomacy.

As soon as she heard the sound of his motor bike, she walked to the garden gate and greeted him as if overjoyed to see the man, with the skills of an actress to convince him, that she was working hard to save up the money, and pleaded for more time. But, one day he made his ultimatum known.

"You have one month, or I will rip the roof off over your heads." Every evening after the sun went down, the sound of a motorbike could be heard and Emmi shivered for fright each time she heard it from some distance away. Josef mumbled. "Bergmann is here! Emmi did you know he was the brother of that communist from across the street of the "old school house."

Emmi pretended to look stunned. "Why am I not surprised? Karen's brutal father is the brother of this despicable man." Josef nodded and it all was crystal clear why the word "mister" had long been dropped, and Josef went outside to meet the swarthy biker, who repeatedly gunned the engine with impatience. He wasted no time on civility, instead he bluntly demanded.

"I demand to be paid my money by the end of the month or I will tear off the roof from over your head." Just then Hucke Wanzel appeared and said. "Don't pay that crook another penny, the property does not belong to him. He has no right to be paid rent. This doghouse is not worth a plug nickel. He is a crook." Josef ran toward Bergmann and screamed at the man. "Get lost! Don't come back here for one month." Josef went into town and signed a lease agreement with the city and obtained a building permit for a small "weekend garden shed." Once the ground had softened, Josef worked feverishly digging out the foundation. He came home late every night after his day job with a handcart full of bricks and beams, which he had dug out of the ruins of a devastated country. Then he worked until midnight behind the bushes and out of view from prying and spying eyes. The boys chiseled the old mortar off the bricks, which Josef had dug out of city ruins.

He rummaged through junkyards and climbed into bomb craters that once were homesteads looking for items that could be repaired or mended. He searched in buildings that were being demolished. He hauled everything of minutest value to the garden plot with his little handcart. Brick by brick, and layer by layer, the walls went up until a cute white washed building had a weather tight roof added. He loaded a broken sink and toilet to the new building site, framed out windows and doors, pounded posts in the corners of the property and put-up fences to separate the vegetable garden from the children's play yard.

One day Josef walked with a great sense of satisfaction around the property, on the day the shack was ready for limited occupancy. Nobody, outside the family knew Josef had put a new roof over the family's heads. A small vestibule jutted out of the bushes, but the main building remained tucked behind the trees and bushes, which were still used to piss into. Bundle after bundle, and arm load after armload, the children moved what little they owned, including field cots and an old wrought iron sewing machine, from the dog house into the new shack on the day on which the ultimatum was up.

It was a day of jubilation and triumph as the shack filled with a euphoria, in anticipation of Bergmann's arrival, whom Josef was pleased to insist, on greeting himself this last time. Such triumph the family had not experienced in years. The children stood straight and tall in the door frame to welcome their father home with applause and shouts of joy and jubilation. Inside the shack was still a dirt floor and no kitchen and no toilettes, the windows were covered with wooden boards, and the doorframe was covered with a blanket. Inside the misery was bathed in soft candle light.

As anticipated Bergmann rode into the yard with a roar. Josef walked toward him and showed him the lease to the property and the permit to build a house on the adjoining property.

Bergmann's face turned crimson with fury. He spewed animosities when he saw the children standing in the doorway, laughing and mocking him. A blanket was draped over the doorway on one side. Bergmann screamed at Josef. "Where is my money, are you trying to make an ass of me." Josef calmly replied.

"You made an ass of yourself. You tried to extort money from me for a doghouse that does not belong to you. You had no right to demand payment for it." Now, I have leased the property from the city myself, so don't set foot on my property again. You go to hell, if the devil will have you, you miserable creature!" Bergmann flew into a rage. He took a pickaxe and sledgehammer and pounded the walls of the concrete dog house down to the cement foundation and left the pile of concrete in a heap. He took off at high speed and roaring noise, never to be seen again. Few people knew, a little dog house had been turned into a little doll house in the garden area, complete with mother nature's own toilettes. Had the city planners known that a complete house had been built they would have put a quick end to this Garden of Eden. The few visitors labeled it a dollhouse surrounded by a little paradise. The children called it a shack, but Emmi referred to it as her castle. Emmi embraced her husband, as he apologized. "Finally, we got rid of the Bergmann plague. It's not much of a house or villa, but it's a start." Emmi reached up and gently stroked his face. "My dear man, it is not a villa, but it is our home."

On a fateful night in October 1943, the area surrounding the city center of Kassel had suffered intense bombing raids during the war especially hard hit was the area surrounding the utility company, whose fields were pockmarked with deep bomb craters like Swiss cheese. The main targets of the air raids over Kassel were the Henschel locomotive factory and Spinfaser, which made tents and a munitions factory nearby.

The utility company manager graciously gave the family permission to tap water from the faucet in the guardhouse. Every morning, before school the boys walked quite a distance around the compound to the front gate, where they had to dodge a multitude of bomb craters along the way which looked like holes in a Swiss cheese, they schlepped buckets of water to the little shack so Emmi could cook another pot of soup. Sometimes she went with them and discovered that the wife of the director of the utility company, Madame Luschinski was looking for a housekeeper.

The Luschinski family was from Poland. They had a little girl named Gabriele, who was the same age as her little girl. The lady of the house invited Emmi to bring her child along to play with Gabriele. She even allowed the little girl to take a bath there and gave her clothes that her child had outgrown. Sometimes she even gave her a fresh hard roll as a treat. Emmi earned a little money cleaning houses for wealthy people, and thankfully brought home leftovers and hand me downs. One day on her way to the directors' villa she was horrified to see her boys digging in bomb craters looking for scrap metals and wiring of bomb fragments. She stood on the rim of the bomb crater and shouted at her boys. "Get out of those bomb craters. I heard a little girl got blown up when she picked up a grenade."

The boys waved her off. "We are careful. Don't worry about us. Just keep the little one away from here. She follows us around everywhere we go. We always tell her to go home. But she doesn't listen to us. We don't want her here." The boys waved off Emmis fears, knowing they had found a goldmine.

Emmi worried nonetheless knowing her boys had thrown caution to the wind. She helplessly shook her head and prayed that nothing would happen to them while the boys gleefully hauled the metal fragments to a nearby scrap metal yard and were paid handsomely for copper and brass.

In a short time, Otto had earned enough money for a fancy bike and a small accordion which he learned to play by ear and without any music lessons. He played the accordion every night and added a joyful mood to the stillness of the gardens. Eventually he landed a gig at an Army night club and saved his earnings for a boat ticket to America upon his eighteenth birthday.

Emmi stoked the fire in the pot belly stove and left the door open to warm up the shack. There was room for only one pot in which she cooked a pot of beef broth, added a few noodles, turnips, potatoes and anything she could find on her scavenger hunts. She made sure there was something hot to eat when Josef and the boys came home from work.

It was spring and the fields became muddy with slick clay, the gardens and meadows began to bloom. Otto built a rock garden with a little goldfish pond in the center. Josef added room after room, built into back of the yard and hidden behind bushes. Josef added a chicken coop. A few of the young chicks had started to lay small eggs. Josef pruned the fruit trees. On her days off, Emmi planted potatoes and vegetables while Otto provided a little night music, which aroused the curiosity of neighbors who came to chat in the evenings while replanting their plot of land for the new season.

The oldest son had changed his name to an American sounding, Joe and found work as a bookkeeper at Bertelsmann bookstore. He added his pay to Emmis' newly installed piggybank, and with her keen sense for frugality, she put everything to good use.

After the turbulent years as homeless refugees the family had settled into comfortable routines. The worse of the after-war-years was over. Life was not perfect, but orderly in a most rudimentary way. Everyone had chores to accomplish. Emmi told the children, they had to be enrolled in a new school and said to her young daughter. "Your braids have to be cut into a little Bubi hairdo, because we have no shampoo and no water for washing your hair."

Mother and daughter went outside and Emmi grabbed her daughter's braids. With a few snips, the beautiful blond braids were cut into a bob and Emmi marched the children off for their first day of school. Her youngest clung to her mother's hand as she was introduced to her new class.

She looked around, and saw that her new class mates were wearing similar duds to those her mother had sewn from bags filled with tattered hand-me-downs and noticed that she did not look any different from the rest of her new classmates. Some looked better dressed in better hand me-downs, some looked worse. Her mother just had a knack for making the best of the worst.

Some kids wore shoes that looked too big on tiny feet. Some shoes were stuffed out with cotton balls, because the shoes were ill-fitting hand-me-downs. Nobody made bones of the fact, that there was no fashion trend or uniformity of design and color requirements.

Unlike what the children had experienced in the East German schools, where the color red was ever present, here in the West girls wore pink and blue, green and purple and skirts and jeans and blouses pulled from clothes bins in Catholic charities used clothing shops. There were no red bows or red kerchiefs adorning every child's head. The children realized, that the others looked a lot alike, in that they all looked hungry.

At noon the children lined up for US Care packages of chocolate milk and bags of dried fruits and nuts, which the children dubbed "bird food."

During recess the girls in the schoolyard looked each other up and down, silently comparing themselves to one another. One pretty girl named Monica stood out in the crowd because of her non-stop chatter. Wiser than most her mouth was in perpetual motion. Whenever she entered the classroom, she caused a great commotion, and all the prepubescent boys rallied around her, not only because she looked and talked as if she were filled with earthly wisdom and charm, but because she had started to fill out so that her blouses stretched tightly across the first signs of perky little bosom sprouting beneath thin cotton shirts, which put the rest of the girls at a great disadvantage.

The children welcomed the "newcomer" who found Monica especially appealing, because Monica smiled broadly whenever she made eye contact with her. Her laughter rang throughout the classroom and hallways, and everyone around her broke out in hysterical laughter, even if they had no clue as to what she had said. She had such an indomitable spirit, even the sternest of teachers could not resist that girl's effervescent spirit.

The pretty girl ogled the newcomer from the side with such frank curiosity.

"My name is Monica, Monica Blum. Like a flower. What's your name?"

The new girl giggled. "I'll call you Blümchen. I am Jenna." She wanted to be just like Blümchen, who dressed like a life-sized doll every day. Her hair was piled high about her head like a crown, which gave her a regal look in complement to her wide swinging knee length skirts, under which she wore full petticoats, tight fitting metal belts, and skin-tight jeans. She explained to the wide-eyed girls how she shrinks her pants to skin tightness. "I lie down in a tub of water, jeans and all, and shrink the fabric until it clings to my body."

One day it appeared that "Blümchen" had gone a bit too far. Her hair was bleached blond, as if a bottle of peroxide had spilled all over her head. She wore bright red lipstick like Marlene Dietrich, and stalked into the classroom wearing high stilettos, she looked as if she stalked on wobbly stilts. She was wearing her mothers' ill-fitting stilettos, which Bluemchen had stuffed out with cotton balls. The heels flopped up and down with every step. The clickety-click of the high heels caught the teacher's attention.

When the teacher entered the class room, he looked as if he had been struck by lightning. The very prim and proper teacher, Gottlieb Helbig, stood a few minutes ramrod straight, surveyed his class from the door before he called it to order. He always looked dignified and evoked awe and respect from even the most-unruly students. His eyes surveyed the riff-raff flock, until the hype and hoopla over "Blümchen's" latest escapade had petered out.

This very noble teacher, who never lost his cool, was left speechless. His black horn-rimmed glasses slid down his nose. He struggled to maintain his composure after doing a double take, he adjusted his glasses, shook his head in disbelief, then his thumb jutted out signaling Blümchen to follow as he walked toward the door and hissed. "Monica! Out!"

Monica obediently followed him on wobbly legs, looking proud as a peacock as she strutted outside and the door closed shut behind her. For some reason, Blumchen was always accorded special privileges, which peaked the other children's curiosity. They pressed their ears to the door and listened to what Mister Helbig had to say.

"Monica, what were you thinking? You go straight home and change your clothes. Don't come back again to school with such a get-up."

In the summer the fruitful gardens had become a healing oasis. Now in his mid-teens, Otto invited friends with whom he had formed a band, who brought their guitars, drums and wind instruments, and their girlfriends. All danced on the slab of concrete of the erstwhile doghouse to a new happy, carefree and exciting rhythm of their youth.

Emmi had worked all day until her feet were tired but she and Josef enjoyed the merriment of their children.

To please his parents, Otto played some of the favorite Viennese Waltzes and Josef prodded Emmi to dance with him, but she begged off. "Not now, teach Jenna, how to Waltz." Josef prodded his daughter to stand on his shoes and carefully showed her how to place her feet on top of his shoes so they would not slide off as he moved to a three-quarter beat.

But as soon as the music changed back to Swing and Boogie, her brother Joe grabbed his little sister to practice with her and danced to the rhythmic beat of rock n' roll. She learned to dance from her brothers, who already harbored visions of America with the shining city on a hill. Every evening the garden oasis was filled with a euphoric sound of Rhythm and Blues and Swing and Boogie until late into fall.

One day, Emmi noticed that a new family had moved into the garden shack next door, a woman and two men. For Josef any good neighborliness had always been for naught, ever suspicious of strangers, he tried to avoid all contact with unsavory characters. His main worry was for food on the table and the soundness of the roof over his family's head. He minded his own business and concentrated on his own turf. He was setting glass panes into window frames for which Emmi made curtains.

Doors were added with locks and handles, no one slept on the bare floor anymore, everybody had their own field cot. Emmi finally had a real kitchen with a real oven. Few people knew that a real doll house had been stamped out of the ground, hidden behind thick trees and shrubs. Emmi was finally able to use her cooking skills to produce magic in her kitchen, thanks to the fruitfulness of the garden and the canned goods that would feed them well through the winter. But at night, they still had to run out of the warm shack and into the bushes, to relieve a full bladder in the comfort zone of thick shrubbery.

Whoever was not awakened by the bladder in the middle of the night, was awakened by an acrid smoke and stink that took everyone's breath away.

For several days the strange smell was coming through the bushes, from behind the hill of the utility company. Josef whispered to Emmi. "It smells like burning rubber."

In the morning the acrid smell mixed with the morning dew, and hovered as smog over the scorched earth around the pockmarked bomb craters area like holes on a Swiss cheese. The black smoke was getting thicker and blacker night after night and became a cause for concern and sleepless nights. Josef cautioned the children to step carefully in the dark, because he was afraid that a lot of bombs or grenades might still be around. Whomever nature awakened at night, knew their designated little corner in the dark, and knew that any misstep into the underbrush might be their last.

Clad only in her nightgown the child climbed upon the knoll. The twigs breaking under her feet made crunching noises, and the nightgown got caught on the prickling Hawthornebushes. Her favorite spot was up on top, away from the poison ivy bushes, where the moss and shrubs were thick and she could lower her little behind, so her brothers could not see her.

Suddenly she heard male whispered voices and laughter and the sound of beer bottles being popped. She looked cautiously through the bushes and watched as four men sat around a bomb crater and made a fire inside a crater pit. As they continued laughing; and sipping from bottles of beer, she thought at first the men were having a barbeque, like Hucke Wanzel had for his guests from America.

She expected the men to hold a shish-kebob over the fire. She raised her head, but instead, what she saw was not a campfire grilling hotdogs. It was an inferno. The two men dragged huge coils of wire into the flames and in moments, the fire melted the rubber and what was left was pure copper wiring.

By the light of the fire, she recognized the men as her next-door neighbors. She almost defecated into her pants, knowing instantly her life was in grave danger, remembering the word papa had whispered to mama. He had called them gangsters.

She could feel her heart pulsing in her neck, and she could feel the tremors in her legs as she quietly crawled back inside the house and slipped back unto her cot, pulling the covers over her head trembling, from head to toe. She never said a word to anyone, lest all might become alarmed, and break the illusion of a safe and wholesome world.

In November Emmi started to prepare for Christmas, which would still be measured in austerity. She baked batch after batch of delicious cookies, spent the evenings knitting scarves, hats and mittens, which she festively wrapped and stowed away until the glorious feast. Although cookies, chocolates and oranges were now the standard treats for Christmas, no one had to cut a chocolate bar into pieces and share it with the rest of the family ever again.

But that was all that Saint Nicholas had in store for them since their defection from the Soviet controlled Socialist Democrat sector, and for a little girl, the Christmas of the prior year remained a childish mirage, which would never be repeated.

Always afraid of being made fun off by her teasing brothers, she cautiously wondered. "Maybe Saint Nicholas doesn't know where we live now?" Rudi poked fun at her for asking such a dumb question. Josef tried to comfort his little "Gitchen," as he still liked to call his little daughter in memory of his beloved niece, whom he had not seen in years and probably would never see again. He often wondered what might have happened to the Gernert family. His beloved sister Marie, sweet Margit, clever Kurt, the children who were dearest to him, next to his own.

He went out into his work shed and installed a swing for Gitchen, under the roof behind the chicken coop. His daughter could steer clear of her brothers and play contentedly until sundown. She was delighted to be able to swing her legs until dark in the shed from where she could watch Papa working in the yard at the same time. She was filled with admiration as she watched how he fixed things with his talented hands in a house that was still a work in progress.

Gone were her memories of nagging hunger pangs that could never be satisfied with flour soups. In her gratitude, Emmi felt it her duty, to share the bounty with which they were blessed. She sent food packages to Karin's mother in the east zone, those same people who had once labeled them "Christian Bums."

Joe attempted to remind his mother as she packaged oranges and chocolates, and such rare delicacies as canned pineapples for people living behind the Iron Curtain. He grumbled. "Our own living standards are still at the bottom of the barrel. Why are you sending all those goodies to people who called us Christian Bums? Who knows if these people even receive it? Maybe the customs officers stash the best of the stuff into their own pockets. Besides we are not swimming in riches. I can't remember you ever buying pineapples for us? Why do you send them pineapples? "

Emmi believed in the basic goodness of people and sharing the blessings with those less fortunate. She looked sad and replied nonplussed. "Because we are Christians, I feel sorry for the children. I don't do it for the parents. I do it for the children. They have nothing. At least we have something."

One year later that following spring, progress in the standard of living was measured in little steps forward when the chicken coop was turned into a bedroom for Jenna. Another chicken roost was added deeper in the woods.

Josef plowed the ground for the new season. While spreading fertilizer, he pointedly tried to ignore the people next door as best he could, but he could not ignore the stench emanating from the neighbors' yard.

At first, he thought it was emanating from their fertilized fields. Emmi had been cooped up during the winter and was eager to get to know the new neighbors, since now her home looked more respectable, she would have liked to chat with a friendly neighbor lady once in a while. She waved a friendly hello to what she thought might be a mother, father and son. Emmi looked nonplussed when nobody waved back. Emmi wondered why the trio had pointedly snubbed her as they left for work early every morning and returned late at night.

After the men had left, the woman sat totally listless and slovenly in front of the hut smoking one cigarette after another all day, as if she had nothing else to do. Emmi guessed the woman to be in her mid-thirties. Her face was deeply lined and her complexion was chalky white. Her bleach blond hair glistened orange in the sun, like a piled high, windblown heap of straw. By her feet lay a German shepherd seemingly asleep, but as soon as Emmi walked toward the fence, the dog leaped up against the fence. The chickens fluttered and quaked with fright, as the dog paced back and forth with a furious bark. Emmi was glad that the chain link fence held tight and warned the children not to go near the fence. Emmi never again tried to initiate a friendly greeting.

Every Monday was laundry day. Emmi scrubbed the clothes in the yard in a big washtub on a scrub board and hung them on the line to dry. She moved the line away to the other side of the yard across the play yard, because of the enormous stench coming from across their yard. She noticed that the source of the smell was a pile of rotting horsemeat these neighbors had thrown out for their dog right in front of their daughter's new bedroom window. The meat was left to rot causing a great stink and a swarm of flies. The stink from next door was becoming more and more nauseating, and allowed for no sleep at night.

Josef thought it was time to have a little chat with these neighbors. He tried to solve the problem diplomatically by telling the woman politely that the stink of the rotting meat was unbearable for the whole family, and that the windows could not be opened because of the thick swarm of horse flies. His pleas seemed not only to fall on deaf, ears but caused the neighbors to become more obstinate. There seemed to be no reasonable means to solve the problem. The neighbors built the dog kennel right beneath their daughter's window, and they threw more meat into the kennel than what the beast could consume.

They never bothered to clean the kennel of rotting meat, garbage and excrements. Josef tried to avoid an escalation of the nauseating problem with polite explanations, to no avail.

Josef was becoming more readily agitated lately. The obstinate behavior of his neighbors peaked Josef's curiosity. He was determined to find out what these people were up to at night. He paced across the room like a caged tiger up and down in front of the window watching what was going on outside. One night he learned the truth and told Emmi his concern and she replied.

"We have to report them to the police, to put an end to this terrifying situation." But Josef cautioned. "We can't go to the police, because then the city will find out that I didn't just build a weekend garden shed, but a real house that we live in year-round. These gangsters are a threat to our existence here. When the police come and search for these criminals, they will also find our house. We can't chance that"

Emmi looked at her husband with round eyes and he knew she was as scared as he was, as she asked. "What can we do?" Josef shook his head adamantly. "We can't do anything. We cannot go to the police."

Emmi replied. "We have to do something! I wonder how much copper they have already stolen?" Josef shook his head and replied. "We have to pretend that we know nothing. If these gangsters knew, that we know what they are doing, they might kill us. We have to stay out of this mess. What if the police think, we are in cahoots with these people, or that we knew, what they have been doing, and didn't report it. We have had enough problems with bureaucrats in the past. I never could deal with bureaucrats. They'll question us, as to what we know? We'll have to go to court, and testify against them. and what if they get off the hook, then our own lives will be in danger."

Emmi tried to reason with her husband and replied. "That would be awful! But we cannot sit here and let them steal tons of copper from the electric company. They burn rubber off the copper rolls by the tons, right out from under the nose of the company, while our boys dig for hours in bomb craters for every gram of copper scraps. We are scared to death when we have to go into the bushes at night, what would they do to us and to our children, if they got wind of the fact that we know what they are doing?"

Josef cautioned. "Emmi think about what it would mean for us if we turned them in. We'll live on the street again. We only have permission to use this place as a weekend retreat, not a year-round dwelling. I cannot start all over again. I have had enough!"

He shook his head in dismay, his head dropped on his chest, and he looked out the window, beaten. "God, I thought at least we could live in peace here, unafraid of our government. I have tried to be a decent human being all my life; and all I got is a kick in the ass every time."

Emmi kept her thoughts to herself, wondering if there wasn't another way to help turn these criminals in without notifying the police. Maybe a night watchman ought to come around here at three in the morning, and then they would catch these men red handed. She knew they had reached an insurmountable, ever more miserable impasse, with not only an unreasonable neighbor, but a gang of criminals.

Josef could not contain his disgust at sight of the men next door. He spat on the ground when he saw them walk in the yard. He talked loudly, about the trashy people, when he saw them throw meat to the dog. The neighbors responded in kind, hurling insults and accusations along with various expletives across the fence, along with a few stones. Josef threw one back and one of the stones hit the neighbor on the leg.

The next morning Josef was charged with assault, fined more money than he could earn in six months and was fired from his job. Josef was too embarrassed to confront Emmi with these facts. He dared not go home and tell her, he had lost his job, instead, he wiled the time away in a nearby bar. Instead of going to work in the morning, he went to the labor department in the hope of finding another job before Emmi would find out.

But when he left again empty handed, he had nowhere to go every day, but back to the bar, to drown his misery in alcohol, before he staggered home late at night.

One night, the dog next door was roused and jumped up and down inside his kennel. The dog started barking furiously. Suddenly, floodlights swayed across the yard, police cars blocked the garden path, and minutes later policemen surrounded the house next door.

The barking of the dog awoke Emmi and Josef. They jumped out of bed, and carefully pushed the curtains to the side. Moments later the two men were led away with handcuffs. The neighbor lady stood motionless in the doorframe and blew smoke rings into the night, while her orange-colored hair shone like a burning bale of straw.

Emmi whispered to Josef. "It's over! It all happened so fast, we are home free." The terror of the mysterious neighbors was history, but Emmi wondered. "How can this woman sleep at night, after her son and husband have been arrested? I don't understand people like these."

Josef shrugged his shoulder and snickered nervously. "I am glad, they are gone, they were a stone in our shoe, but I wonder how long it will take before the city officials find us."

A few days later, there was a knock on the door. Just as Josef had predicted, city officials walked around the area, and were surprised that the little shack behind the bushes was a cozy hide-away. Emmi bade the men inside. They were astounded at the welcoming ambience and cozy comfort of the little shack. The walls were covered in floral wallpaper. The rooms were filled with easy chairs and a wide sleeper sofa. Cabinets were stuffed to the brim with freshly washed linens. The steam from pots and pans filled the kitchen with succulent aromas.

To the officials, it was clear, this was not a weekend hovel for rakes and shovels, but a year-round home. The officials looked nonplussed and made their position clear. "Well, this is no longer a weekend cottage, this is a complete house. You cannot stay here. You must move out." For the first time in her life, Emmi looked defiant and equally nonplussed replied. "Then you find us a suitable home for our family. Where should we go with four children?

The communists robbed us of the house my husband built in Czechoslovakia and now you socialist democrats want to tear down our little abode. You are all one and the same. We have nowhere else to go, so we stay." Emmi looked frustrated and pleaded for more time with government officials, to no avail. "You cannot stay here, because we are planning the extension to the Autobahn through this area."

Emmi looked round-eyed, but defiantly replied. "You cannot build an Autobahn from one day to the next, until then we stay right here! The day you pull up with heavy equipment, cranes and backhoes and shovels, we'll move but first you have to find us a suitable place to live!"

Just then Otto entered the room with an even bigger accordion. He opened the case of the beautiful black Hohner, and played "Muss i denn…muss i denn." He cynically announced. "If we have to move out of here, I am going to America."

"A few of my friends have gone across the pond and others are planning on going as soon as they have the visa, and I am going with them." Emmi looked horrified. "You just stay home! What will you do in America? You have just finished an apprentice ship as a tool maker. You haven't had time to hone your skills. How will you survive in America?"

Otto replied confidently. "If someone like Hucke Wanzels daughter, without an ounce of social graces and education can make it in America, then so will I. I'll play my new accordion in nightclubs and bars!" Emmi laughed hysterically, and then in anguish cried. "Where will you earn a living, on the street corners of America? Americans don't listen to accordion music.

They only listen to belly-ache music that sounds more like cat's howling under my window at night. Do you really think you can earn your daily bread there? You will wind up in a gutter." Emmi was reeling from the arguments and every word ruminated and replayed in her head.

It had rained all day, turning the clay into a slippery mess. Emmi went outside to feed the chickens, suddenly her feet slid out from under her and she fell down into the mud. She lay there helplessly unable to raise herself up. She screamed for help incessantly until her boys came running to help. They could not lift their helpless mother up. Otto ran to the main road to find a place from where he could call an ambulance. Before an ambulance could transport Emmi to the Catholic Saint Maria hospital, an hour had past.

The boys went with her and the doctor told them, that their mother had suffered a broken leg in two places and she would have to stay in the hospital for six weeks.

When Josef came home that night the boys told him, what had happened to their mother. Why the city planners wanted the family to move out, because of plans of an Autobahn extension coming through this area. Josef looked devastated at the prospect of forcefully being moved out again, of the house he had built.

The boys explained to their father, how angry their mother had become, when these bureaucrats ordered the family to vacate the place. Where would they go to sleep at night? How could he put another roof over his family's head, food on the table and clothes on their back. With Emmi in the hospital, how could he feed his children now? Now he was without a job and Emmi would be unable to work. There won't be any money for food. They would again lose the home he just built. The prospect of Emmi being hospitalized for several weeks, caused Josef to fall into a deep depression.

He silently left the room, looking totally defeated. Out in the chicken coop, he found solace again, as he emptied one bottle after another, which he had secretly stashed away, so Emmi could not find them. She was not here to cheer him up, and calm him down, to reassure him that all would be well again. His anger built in remembering all that he had to endure over the years.

He started to curse Hitler, Stalin, Benes and the devil in one breath. In desperation he swore at those self-important bureaucrats and crooked politicians, who thus far had brought him nothing but one hell after another, in a world that seemed to have gotten the better of him. He was tired of fighting and wanted it all to end. He had lost his will to live. He smashed the empty bottles against the wall of the chicken coop, pounded the walls with his fist, until the chickens fluttered around in wild confusion from their perches.

He grabbed the big sledge hammer from his work bench and entered their little shack swinging it over his head, screaming and cursing.

He screamed at his frightened children, who were huddled together in a corner of the room, and stared in horror at a father who had never so much as raised a hand in anger, a father who had never given them a reason to be fearful of him.

"These bastards have pulled the rug out from under my feet, my life and my existence. There is no room for us in this world not here or in Czechoslovakia, there is no room for us anywhere. I am going to put an end to this hellish existence."

He screamed and ranted as he swung the hammer. The oldest son raised himself up in full height from the cot, and stood strong and tall, towering over his father, he planted himself firmly between the menacing sledgehammer and his younger siblings. Joe was in full control of his senses, and knew what he would have to do, in order to save his younger brothers and little sister and himself. He knew his father was too drunk to comprehend what he was doing.

His father was a broken man in body and spirit, and out of his mind. Joe lunged for the swinging arm and pushed his father to the wall. "Papa, if you want to kill us all, than you have to start with me, but then you will have to explain to our mother, why she has to visit her children in a cemetery." At that moment Josef, dropped the hammer and left the room sobbing. The thought of Emmi, and what she would have to deal with was all he needed to be reminded of, even in a drunken stupor.

The bones did not heal and had to rebroken but after six long weeks, Emmi was released from the hospital. Nobody said a word to their mother about the moment of their father's madness. Joe only cautioned his mother to check out the chicken coop for bottles of booze. Emmi was shocked what she found there, and dumped out the liquid poison. Emmi had noticed the change in her husband. At night she heard him cry, or scream in a nightmare, in the daytime, he would sit listless and say over and over. "I have lost it all."

Emmi found out soon enough that he had lost his job, when he didn't bring any money home, instead, he sheepishly asked her for money so he could buy a beer or two. She knew he was looking for another job, even tried to start his own little business. She read the license applications and the subsequent rejections from licensing bureaucrats.

She had stopped praying for miracles, instead, she secured herself more cleaning jobs. Rather than confronting and humiliating her husband about his drinking problem and his inability to put a legal roof over their heads, food on the table and clothes on their backs she bought a bottle or two to be shared and enjoyed during their evening meal. She quietly poured a glass of beer, and told him. "Josef, we have been together for thirty years. I remember the man you were in your youth, before Hitler came to power. You have not lost everything. You have me and we have our children together. They will always remember, that you saved our lives, when you dragged us out of the Russian labor camp. You gave us hope when you helped us escape across the Iron Curtain border."

Every night they sat in peaceful contentment side by side like two turtle doves, in love as they had always been. Emmi was convinced she could keep his drinking problem under control, and the children out of harms' way. But Emmi also noticed the change in her children, since her release from the hospital. She noticed the pin-drop silence engulfing the room, as soon as their father entered the shack. The boys threw suspicious glances at him from the side, watching his every move for signs of drunkenness. The teenaged daughter no longer ran up to her father to hug and kiss him on the cheek, instead she steered clear of him, as best she could, even at the dinner table. Emmi convinced herself, that it was due to her daughters age of puberty, that she was afraid of her father, and avoided being alone with him. She avoided him, and treated him dismissively like a stranger, eyeing him with great mistrust.

To a growing teenager, her Papa was no longer the man she had loved, more than anyone in the world. Emmi feared the time of the empty nest in an empty shack, alone with a man, who in his sorrow over all he had lost, rarely ventured out of the house, had in fact become a recluse and slept his life away in a drunken stupor. He had become an alcoholic in his own bed.

Emmi did not blame him, and reminded her children how tormented a man he had become, having lost his name of renown, his pride in workmanship, and his dignity as he was forced to live like the dregs of this world, who had to live off the crumbs and generosity of others. She tried to comfort him as he bemoaned his wasted youthful and productive years in the trenches of the Russian tundra. Having been born between two chairs and being shoved from one political camp to another.

"For what?" The children often heard him mutter to himself. He had become a shadow of the man he used to be. He was a man with a broken spirit who wondered. "For what? Everything was for nothing."

Emmi prodded Otto to play the kind of country music even her husband liked to sing, the music that brought smiles across Josef's face. But even in a rare moment of cheer, the overall mood in the shack remained gloomy and tense. The only lively chatter was all about America. Emmi was sick of hearing about America and finally told her children.

"I will never let any of you go. I will not sign any consent form, and sign off on your doom, because you will all wind up in the gutters of America." Undaunted Otto practiced with his band, but instead of playing homeland and country music, they practiced the music of their young and exuberant generation. It was the time of Rock 'n' Roll, and a time, when Elvis was stationed near Frankfurt as a GI.

From an early age, Joe always was a self-assured man. An utterly handsome man of the world, who was always impeccably dressed like Frank Sinatra.

Otto had grown into a very handsome young man, who resembled and dressed in Elvis Presley fashions, wearing black shirts and white ties, black and white shoes. He allowed his sideburns to grow and piled his hair slicked back with pomade with swirls falling over his forehead. He could swing his hips provocatively, as he played with his musicians at the American officer's club on an army base nearby.

When Josef was told that Rudi planned to work as a waiter, he scoffed. "What, a waiter? You'll break all the glasses?" Josef was convinced that clumsy Rudi would never amount to much because when Rudi picked up a hammer the handle broke off. His father never let Rudi forget that clumsy incident. Boy was he wrong. Tall and lanky Rudi landed first class waiter jobs in five-star hotels in Switzerland, Paris and Montreal wearing tuxedos and white ties. He was a class act, who as a clumsy boy who looked like George Hamilton could not hold a hammer. He had learned to balance trays filled with wine glasses without spilling a drop of expensive fermentation.

One by one without further ado the boys packed their bags, embraced and kissed their mother, shook a father's hand and said good bye, before they left for brighter shores. America and the world beckoned them to adventure. Josef sat staring at the pictures of his sons as a mournful Freddy Quinn melody echoed through the empty room. "My boy, come back, come back home soon." While tears rolled down his cheek. But the boys did not come back. Instead, they sent home pictures and postcards from somewhere USA, along their travels across America, France and Canada, where Otto played his accordion to raucous applause and money tossed in a hat.

Letters arrived from Otto, the quiet musician, who painted a more realistic picture, tainted with sarcasm. "If you think we lived in a shack, you should see the shacks in America. All you see in America are shacks nailed together with linear boards and covered with aluminum. When the wind blows, the houses fall apart. Then they have to hammer the boards back together. Americans would love to have a garden shack like we had. In America they call the type of house, our father had built a bungalow. Fancy that! Our shack would be called a bungalow here!?"

But other letters were stuffed with green backs, which counteracted the negative impressions of the earlier letters after Otto found real employment. His eye for precision and painstaking accuracy had earned Otto the respect of his company's superiors which manufactured nuclear reactors that were shipped around the world. As foreman his job required precision accuracy in the transfer of blue print measurements to sheet metal that would be welded into cylindrical steam kettles the length of several train cars.

He no longer played an accordion on street corners. For amusement or a special occasion, he could be persuaded to play his beloved accordion, which had taken him on trips around the world.

Emmi was not saving for a rainy day. She was saving for a proper house with rental units, so she and Josef could live out their lives in dignity and without the constant fear of old age ailments. Emmi was convinced that her sons' emigration to America had given them all hope and limitless opportunities. Every letter from them, was more reassuring than the last and added to their parents' blessings.

It had become clear to Emmi that her sons had found their place in this world within a few years, which in the end made a difference for the entire family.

In retrospect she was glad that she had not been able to stop her sons from emigrating. She no longer had to worry about her sons. But now she had to worry about her daughter. Despite her sons' obvious successes, she was determined to stop her daughter from developing "American pipe dreams." Never mind, that despite some bumps and bruises along the way they had reached a substantial amount of success.

Even with the money sent from America, Emmi continued working as a cleaning lady to put her daughter through business school. She didn't want to lose her daughter to what she feared might happen to her on the streets of heartbreak hotels.

Her self-conscious daughter was growing up faster than Emmi liked. She spent too much time in the American library, reading too many books like Gone with the Wind. She spent weekends babysitting for American families. As her daughter put it, to improve her English, and for the extra fifty-cents to pay for a ticket to a Doris Day movie. Emmi sewed her dresses she had seen these divas wear in movies. She dressed in high heels like Doris Day and wore her hair like Sandra Dee, and Emmi reminded her daily. "Knock these ideas out of your head…you are not going to America. You can find work in Frankfurt or Munich, that's far enough."

The daughter paid scant attention to her mother's ranting about the frustrations, other mothers experienced, whose sons and daughter had emigrated. "If you go to America, I'll have nothing left. Young girls like you wind up in a brothel or in a gutter somewhere." She heard her mother cry in agony. "You should hear the stories I have heard from other mothers, whose daughters went to America. The books you read depict America as a utopian dream. It is not a Shangri-La and you are not Doris Day.

"Okay, okay that's what you said to the boys" She was tired of her mother's endless litany and Emmi snapped at her in outrage. "Here you speak German. You spend too much time in the American library. You read too many books about America. You don't need to read "Gone with the Wind."

Our own ancestral history is also gone with the wind. We were blown away like dandelion seeds in the turbulence of time. You better learn to bake Plum Cake. If you learn to cook you can make a man happy right here. You need to learn to cook because love travels through a man's stomach. Stay here and get married."

Her daughter laughed at her mother's old-fashioned views of a woman's role in the world, and replied with a hint of sarcasm. "I think it takes more than a plum cake to make a man happy.

I want to do more with my life than cook and bake for a man, unless of course he is Rock Hudson or Cary Grant." Emmi countered nonplussed. "You are so delusional, with no idea of the real world. Why don't you come and help me clean one day, and see what I do all day."

One afternoon the 16-year-old visited her mother at the factory, to give her mother a helping hand. For years she had wondered what her mother was doing in a factory, while she was in school. Emmi showed her around and gave her the dust cloth and cleaners. Emmi showed her the offices and desks of the head honchos. Then she climbed down the steel grid stairs to the factory floor and showed her the latrines she was to clean next. The daughter grimaced in disgust. "How can you clean these every day?" Emmi looked at her daughter somberly. "I do this…so that you will never have to!"

But no amount of lecturing about the real world convinced an obstinate teenager to spend more time practicing more practical skills, such as cooking and cleaning, to be a proper housewife someday. Instead, the girl spent little time in the kitchen, but ever more time on a sewing machine, fashioning clothes she had seen on a movie star. She lightened her hair, shaved her legs, and spent more time with friends like "Blümchen," who dressed like Sandra Dee and looked around for boys who looked like Troy Donahue.

In her daughter's eyes, Emmi was as ever stingy about everything other than what was absolutely necessary for survival, saving every dime out of a looming fear, that someday they might go hungry again. It was her weekly dilemma, wondering how she could scrape enough money together for a Rock Hudson movie. What little money she earned working as a finance intern and baby sitting on weekends for children of an American officer, she had to fork over every last penny. But the greatest bonus from the weekend job was having access to plenty of study material, magazines and American literature. The kind family allowed her to take the books home to read.

She had nothing else to do at home but read, since they had no television. She read late into the night, until her father turned off the breaker switch which he had installed by his bedside. One day she was given a magazine and her eyes fell on an article about Nazi atrocities. As she read the captions beneath the pictures, she looked thunderstruck at the most horrific pictures she had ever seen in her life. She yelled at her startled parents, and showed them the magazine with the pictures before their wide eyes.

Her father looked out the window and Emmi's eyes filled with tears. "Where were you when this was going on? What did you do during this time?" Emmi's eyes became round and mysteriously clouded over in horror. She snatched the magazine from her daughter's hand, as Josef said. "We had the misfortune of living in Hitler's time. How can a child like you understand anything like this?" He lamely mumbled, and slowly walked with a stooped back out the door and into his shed. He slammed the door shut and his daughter knew that her father would get drunk in the chicken coop. He never drank in front of the family. He only drank in the company of chickens. As soon as he felt the dizzying numbness of alcohol, he went to bed to sleep away his immense grief.

At this moment the daughter bemoaned having been born at all into this terrible world with a high pitched voice. "Why did you bring me into this world? My father stays in bed drunk out of his mind, and you have to work two jobs cleaning toilets, why do you stay with him? All my life you taught me patriotism and that I should be proud of my heritage and my ancestral accomplishments, with a quest for perfection like a Porsche. What a dichotomy? How can I be proud of my family? Who is my family? I have no family, no cousins, aunts, uncles, grandmothers. Now what am I to be proud of? What should Beethoven's alleluia mean to me? That's all I have heard you sing for years. What legacy has your generation left my generation? I can't stand this hypocrisy. My mind is made up, I am going to America!"

She filled out the forms for a visa application, and pointed an accusing finger at her mother, who looked numb, stung by her daughter's fierce accusations, Emmi stared into space and slowly and mechanically as if by remote control, she began slowly. "Let me tell you some things. We were both only seventeen when we fell in love. Her narration opened with stories of their youth and how the politics of the time changed the blue prints of their life. How communism and socialism had squashed their plans and destroyed their life on the razors edge and how he had saved their life from starvation in a disease infested Soviet labor camp. How they had lived in constant fear, terrified of the knock on the door, terrified of the spy among "friends and relatives," terrified of one's own shadow, as evil dripped into veins like ether so slowly nobody noticed it until it was too late.

"We are Germans and a thousand years of proud heritage cannot overcome the thirteen years of Hitlers' reign of terror. But we suffered too! That is what the world wants to forget.

We watched history unfold before our eyes like a film reel, viewed through the curtains in our living room. We were dust beneath Hitler's feet, and blown away by the shifting winds of our time. We trembled like mice, before the venomous fangs of a viper. We lived in a remote area and kept quiet, hoping nobody would notice us.

At every moment in those years, we feared being dragged before a firing squad. So, we never stepped a toe out of line."

Nothing her mother said and tried to explain, seemed to register or provoke any sympathy from a quick-tempered adolescent, who pompously declared. "I can't believe that there was nothing anyone could do. I would have done something." Emmi grimaced in remembrance, as her thumb came down hard on the table and she twisted it. "Hitler squashed everything in his path, like a gnat on his arm. But so did Stalin. That's what I remember, as if it were yesterday, July 20, 1944 when Hitler walked out of the bunker like the devil himself, merely dusting himself off, while others around him were killed. Nothing ever touched him. That's what irks me. The brave assassins along with thousands of conspirators were shot or strung up on meat hooks. Sometimes I pause to wonder, why God did not help these brave men. But we knew nothing about concentration camps, I had ominous feelings. We were told that the Jews were being deported to Palestine. I just prayed for the hate and madness to end. Her daughter replied still in a state of shock. "How could such hell be allowed to exist in a civilized country?"

Emmi spat out the words. "Hell, what do you know about hell? We lived through hell, Hitler allowed no heroes, even the slightest criticism of whoever opened his mouth was lined up in front of a wall.

One didn't just fear losing one's own life, but the life of ones' entire family. Even heroes like Ernst Rommel or Claus Schenck von, 'what's his name? were labeled as traitors and never heard from again." She shrugged her shoulders and looked out in silent meditation.

"We cannot change our history." Her face looked bathed in sorrow and Emmi looked ten years older.

"Our lives are whole again. We have raised four healthy children in most difficult times. It took years of work to instill in our youth again the finer ideals of freedom of a New Germany. You too will find a young man just as handsome as your brothers right here in Germany."

Against all promises and bitter pleas, as soon as their daughter received her visa on her eighteenth birthday, she planned her trip across the big pond. She showed the stamped documents of a visa and a boat ticket jubilantly to her mother and started to pack. Her father watched as daughter sorted through her meager belongings, and said, you must have a good coat. I cannot let you arrive in America looking like a beggar."

He turned to Emmi, and instructed her to clean out the savings account, of whatever she had scraped together over the years. "I will take our daughter shopping and you stay home, because you will spend hours turning over every price tag. Then you will spend another hour turning over every coin ten times before parting with it."

Emmi looked surprised, because Josef had become a recluse over the last few years. He had not set foot in a store to buy a loaf of bread or a pair of socks. He had avoided all contact with the outside world for years, to the extent that when company was expected, he would go to bed, pull the blanket over his head and stay there, feigning sleep until the visitors had left. How would he even know where to find the women's clothing department or where to find a bargain?

But his insistence on taking his daughter shopping to the finest fashion house, came as a shock. In all her frugality, her husband's idea struck a blow against her carefully crafted budget. Emmi looked aghast over this unexpected departure from his usual behavior, but she dared not challenge him on his quest. Just by looking at him and hearing his firm, no ifs nor butts, determination, she knew there was no point in arguing with him. Emmi knew when to keep her mouth shut! Her protests would be in vain in any situation involving his 'Gitchen'.

With a wallet full of money, Josef prodded his daughter to go with him for a train ride into town. Without looking around, Josef steered his daughter straight to one of the finest couturiers of the city, and headed straight for the better coat section. He prodded the sales clerk to help his daughter find a good coat. He never looked at a single price tag and handled himself as though shopping for such extravagant finery was no more unusual than buying a loaf of bread.

When they arrived home Emmi's jaw dropped as her daughter walked through the door and twirled around like a model on a catwalk. Her reading glasses slid off her nose, revealing her disbelief. As her daughter pranced, proud as a peacock, around the room, Emmi stammered. "Oh, my God…you look like Zsa Zsa Gabor…but you're not married to Konrad Hilton." As if thwarting the expected criticism, Josef rendered his own reasons for what he had done. "I don't want my daughter to arrive in America as one of the huddled masses and look like a beggar."

Emmi quipped with marked annoyance. "Americans don't know any more about Russian sable, than they know about Beethoven. To an American this fur could be from a sewer rat."

On the day of her departure, Josef bade his daughter to kneel on a hassock before him. He had not prayed in years, but now he placed his hands on his "little girls" head and blessed her. She wept quietly into her handkerchief, in memory, how he merely shook her brother's hands in a final goodbye. She shook with emotions as her parents prayed for her safety and well-being in her life across an ocean. Her father had stopped going to church when he felt forsaken in the trenches around Stalingrad. He had given up on God and the world a long time ago.

Unlike her mother, whose faith in God had never wavered, and all the travails she had endured only seemed to have deepened her conviction that all things work together for good. She was convinced, a miracle had brought her husband home from the Russian front, as she remembered the names of countless young man, who had lost their lives there. Her mother hated to hear his cynical tirades against God, and why he had administered every kick personally to him?

Many nights Emmi found Josef curled up in a fetal position, as if he were ducking his head dodging invisible bullets. She knew her husband had lost his faith in the trenches at the Russian front. Josef never prayed and for that reason Emmi prayed twice. Now he felt compelled to pray for his favorite birthday present after all, knowing he had nowhere to go for solace, but his knees. He prayed for his lost child, for strength she would need, to survive the wild west of America.

Emmi escorted her daughter in mournful silence on her train ride to Bremerhaven, dreading the moment when the ship SS Berlin would embark for New York.

Mother and daughter never felt closer as in these last moments together, as they strolled arm-in-arm on the promenade deck an hour before departure, until the final request for guests to leave the ship, was announced. Despite her feverish excitement, the young girl felt an unexplainable urge not to let go of her mother's arm.

Her mother reached in her pocket and gave her a wad of paper. "I wrote you a poem and a diary. I hope you will find time to read it someday. Promise me that you will never forget your homeland, your father's land." With these words her mother tore herself away from their last embrace and quickly walked down the ramp, as tears rolled down her cheeks uncontrolled.

The girl dressed in a fabulous coat watched from the promenade deck, as her mother slowly receded into the mass of humanity, as tears slowly rolled down her cheeks while her mother's form melted into the crowd. The girl pressed a handkerchief over her mouth to keep from screaming. 'Wait! I changed my mind. I don't want to go.' She found herself yearning to be that little girl again, to crawl back on her mother's lap, and be rocked to sleep with lullabies. What bliss it had been to feel so protected, despite the hardships of the times, which her mother and father had endured. If only her mother would turn around one more time, so she could see her loving face once more, she thought. But if she did, she would run after her and cry. "Mom, I'm sorry. I want to stay home. Mom, turn around just one more time, please." She whispered into the windy night. Maybe it was a crazy idea to leave a sheltered home, for an uncertain life in America after all, which now, without her parent's protection seemed strangely wild and dangerous.

As the anchor and tow of the boat were loosened from the pier, she felt as if the umbilical cord had been cut at that moment. When the last boat whistle echoed across the harbor, she burst into tears. Her childhood had ended at that moment, and she would be on her own to chart the course of the rest of her life.

No sooner had Emmi turned her back on her youngest child, the tears flowed in torrents down her cheek.

Emmi knew she could not turn around to take one more look at her little girl, standing alone and small on the deck, because if she did, the sight of her child would surely break her heart. She knew she would spend the rest of her life in sleepless nights wondering about the welfare of her child. Did she have a sound roof over her head? Was she healthy or sick? Was she warm or cold? Did she have enough to eat?

She walked faster, unable to watch the boat leave the harbor into the dark unknown. She knew that their miserable poverty and the success of their sons, had prompted their only daughter to search out her own destiny. If they had never been forced to leave Czechoslovakia, there never would have been a need for her children to venture so far away. "But why so far?" She sighed deeply. "I didn't expect them to live next door or around the block, but why did they have to go to America? Why to a land where everyone is an alien, one man to another, where cowboys have no manners, and gangsters have no morals. Such was Emmi's sober assessment of America. Why couldn't her children have moved to Munich or Frankfurt, so I could at least see them for Christmas and birthdays?"

For years she had looked forward to a time when children and grandchildren would surround her, like it used to be in the multitude of her and Josef's cousins, aunts, uncles, and grandmothers, even though little harmony existed between them. She still missed her brothers and sister, and Josef's sister Marie. Not a day went by, in which she didn't think about them, and reminisced about the wonderful times they had spent with Marie and Gustav. She wondered what had happened to them all. "Now, I have nothing left. " She muttered to herself. "The Czechs robbed me of my home and America robbed me of my children."

Emmi arrived at home and stepped into the bedroom to check on her husband. She found Josef weeping, inconsolably. The pillow was soaking wet with tears. She knew, he had wept unabated from the moment their daughter closed the door behind her. She recognized her husband had suffered a nervous breakdown. His nonstop sobs were gut wrenching as he cried in screams.

"Where have all my children gone?"

As Josef was hoisted into the ambulance, Emmi stared into the empty space around her as her eyes filled with tears. She had no answer for her husband's tormented questions. Instead, she murmured.

"Now I have nothing left."

A Staffa Family Union

After more than twenty-five years I had returned to Germany to spend precious time and one last Christmas with my mother and father. My mother planned one muted and emotional Christmas in reflection of childhood years. It was November and my mother started her usual Christmas preparations, baking a Stollen and my favorite butter almond cookies. She decorated the living room with pine branches, dusted off old ornaments and bought a small pine tree. She admitted that she had not decorated a Christmas tree, since I had left home almost twenty-five years ago.

Over the years she had located many of the relatives through the Red Cross, most of whom seemed to have gotten stuck behind the Iron Curtain. Emmi was able to reconnect with many of them, and kept in touch with them through birthday, Christmas and Easter cards. My mother found out, that the Gernert family had been deported from Czechoslovakia and had been resettled near East Berlin. No one knew what happened to their children, Margit, Kurt and Christa. She had received one photo of Gustav and Marie with three adorable grandchildren. Later she received notices that Gustav and Marie had passed away.

Other than an occasional postcard, nothing was heard from Kurt, Margit and Christa. One person seemed to be lost for good, Kurt. Not a word was ever heard from him and no one ever talked about Josef's favorite nephew. The Gernert Family had not communicated with any relatives in the west in over twenty years. All inquiries to the Red Cross fell on deaf ears and with deadpan faces everyone just shook their heads. They seemed to have fallen off the face of the earth. Decades had past, in which the fate of those who had been deported into East Germany, was sealed like an iron armor had been wrapped around them. It would take a miracle to tear down this armor.

The cracks in the armor had been visible for decades. It took only one more nudge to shove communist ideology in the east-bloc countries over the cliff. It was the Ninth of November 1989 when a political earthquake rocked the world and Christmas cookies were forgotten. The phones were ringing non-stop. As soon as the news focused on the 'Wall' in Berlin, my brother Joe and his wife Lucia came to watch in total fascination as the events were rapidly unfolding. My brothers Rudi in LA and Otto in Toronto, called to say, they had dropped what they were doing, booked flights and rushed to airports.

Earlier, on a visit to Berlin, President Ronald Reagan had said, "Mister Gorbachov, tear down this wall." People heeded the call to arms. The Russian Premier realized, nothing made sense anymore. He let go of the people, who pressed to live in freedom. They shook the cudgel of communist oppression. Communism was defeated by three men named Ronald regan, Pope John Paul II and William Casey. The people of the East bloc countries stormed the Wall, the eyesore of the twentieth century, which had kept people apart for nearly forty years. Country after country fell like dominos, as people rose up against an oppressive regime and said "Enough! is Enough!" The people flocked to the wall in droves, swinging hammers and chisels, hacksaws and chainsaws. Cries for freedom blended with the music of Beethoven's Ninth symphony, performed in every concert hall around the world, in celebration of the unity of humanity.

While my father was totally oblivious to what was happening, fireworks were going off around the world. He dozed through the most historic event of his life. Once in a while, he lifted his head wondering if we were watching a crazy Hollywood movie and were acting like a bunch of idiots, while we were all crazed on this day of jubilation.

My poor father had no cognitive sense of the significance of the moment. Emmi pulled out the old cigar box and passed out the photos of people I had never seen in the flesh. I had heard their names and the stories attached to them so many times. I had seen their smiling faces on old black and white communion photos, I had their visual image burned in my brain. The phone rang again and a commanding male voice said. "Aunt, Emmi, we are coming! We are on our way." My mother listened for a moment and screeched into the phone. "Kurt? Is that you?" Nobody wanted to go to sleep after that phone call. We stayed up all night celebrating. We did not want to miss a moment, not an hour or a minute of this historical event.

Hours later, the doorbell rang. My mother buzzed, whoever it might be, coming up the steps. I heard laughter and the footsteps coming up the three flights of stairs and moments later I heard my mother screech with delight.

"Oh, my God! It's Margit and Christa. Oh, my God it's Kurt! Jessesmarren!" My father tried to leap from his wheelchair, but slumped back when he realized he had no legs. He pounded the table in frustration screaming as Kurt stepped into the living room. Josef stared at the imposing man, who took all the oxygen out of the room. My father cried. "Kurti, this is the miracle I have prayed for."

Kurt was impressively decked out in the uniform of a high-ranking East German army officer. His chest was covered with Stalin tank medals, a Russian dinner-plate size hat, accorded to high-ranking officers revealed his noble face. I knew instantly, who he was, as I stood in the vestibule watching the euphoric greetings of those hugging and shrieking as they pressed themselves into the small living room to shake hands and hugs that never ended.

I knew this man was Kurt. He was making the rounds greeting everyone. When he saw my father sobbing unabashedly, he walked over to the wheel-chair. Kurt crouched beside him and reached for his frail hands. They looked at each other, as tears flowed from both their eyes and Kurt merely said. "Uncle Josef, how have you been?" My father waved off his question and replied.

"You can see, what they have done to me. But what have they done to you?" Kurt patted his hand and simply said. "I know, uncle Sef. They made a military man out of me." My father screamed. "No, they made a Communist out of you." Kurt looked embarrassed and simply replied. "No, uncle Sef, they made a radish out of me. We were forced to be Red on the outside, but we were white as radishes on the inside. We had to adjust to survive, and made the best of a bad situation." Josef stared ahead in silence, as Kurt turned his attention to the guests from east and west. With military precision and great personal aplomb he greeted everyone with a snappy salute. He slapped my brother, Joe on his back then hugged him with the accustomed greeting. "My cousin Pepi looks good and well fed." My brother winced at the sound of the old Czech nickname, he had not heard in forty years. He chuckled good naturedly and replied. "My name is Joe now!" Kurt heard the twang of his cousins' Americanized new name and with a snappy salute said. "Aye, Aye sir!"

He grabbed Joe with his powerful arms in a bear hug and with military comradery said. "Nastroviet, Joe!"

To lighten the mood, Kurt pulled out a balalaika and danced a few steps as if he were about to entertain them with a Cossack dance. Kurt had always been the life of the party, any party. He brimmed with life and luster with a dazzling tantalizing and quick-witted charm. I stood quietly in the corner watching the merriment as my mother, ever the pragmatic problem solver, who had become accustomed to the American answer of feeding unexpected company, called out to me. "Order Pizzas!"

That's when Kurt noticed me and crossed the room with quick strides, and stood in front of me. His forget-me-not blue eyes twinkled from underneath the Russian dinnerplate size hat. He held out his arms to hug me. "Let me take a look at my American princess," and held his hands a few inches apart and chuckled. "You were this big the last time I saw you." I smiled at this utterly gorgeous man and queried. "So how do we address you, Colonel or Comrade?" He gave me a bear hug, swept me off my feet, and twirled me around in a dizzying spin. "My American princess can call me any name she likes." He replied in perfect English.

We settled into comfortable chairs around the coffee table and told stories of our lives and Kurt told stories of his life. His striking blue eyes surveyed the family, as they gathered spellbound around him. He took off his hat and a full head of blond curly hair spilled over his forehead. With a sheepish grin, he put on the fur lined cap with the Soviet red star affixed in front. My mother looked shaken and asked him, why he had never responded to any of her letters and he replied.

"Ever since I was forced to join the army, I, and the rest of the family, were not allowed any contact with relatives in the west.

I was not even allowed to attend my mothers' funeral, because the Stasi thought, I might come in contact with relatives from the West." My mother shook her head and looked at his impressive uniform and attire and she asked with grave concerns. "Kurt, I have one question. It is obvious you rose to a high rank. We always knew you were someone special, who would rise to the top anywhere. We love you! But how could you go along with this Communist regime? Kurt stared at the floor for a moment in silence and replied unapologetically. "Aunt Emmi, what was I to do with my life, count raindrops? I had no choice. I was indoctrinated as a youth into the Socialist regime and I knew no better. But it was during the Prague Spring in 1968, when my eyes were opened. As everyone held their breath, along with the rest of the world. I remember how the unrest in Czechoslovakia had the world wondering, if the Soviets would loosen their stranglehold on the East-bloc countries.

The House My Father Built

I was summoned to Moscow, where I was offered a promotion to General. But, what I had witnessed in Prague, shook me to the core and I turned down their offer. I no longer wanted to play along. After we were driven from our homes, we always hoped and prayed for changes, hoping and praying that real freedom might return to our beloved Czechoslovakia, if only the country could shake off the Soviet shackles and rule the country by democratic principles but that was a utopian dream. I was a colonel then and the tank commander of the Warsaw pact troops that rolled from East Germany across the Sudeten mountains. We rolled south along the Elbe River and as commander I used the opportunity to swing with my tanks slowly into Mastig, the tiny village we thought nobody could find on a map, but I knew the way there. I stopped my caravan at my parents' old garden cafe and bought my men a beer and told them to stretch their legs a while.

I drove my tank to the old factory gate, of what once had been the old Mandl textile factory. I hunkered on the turret with my field glasses, scanning every face coming and going out of the gates. I waited until the end of the work day just watching and scanning every worker's face as they passed by. Then I saw Rudi Kostial, the guy who had said to me when they had arrested my father and dragged him away. "Now you will never see your father again." I jumped from the turret and grabbed that scoundrel by the collar. He was shaking in his boots and scared to death. I wanted him to shake in his boots and let him know I had come back as his nightmare. I pushed the wimp against the chain link fence and said.

"Hey, Rudi, Rudi Kostial. Remember me?" The trembling little man was quaking.

"Rudi Kostial, I stopped here before moving on to Prague just to tell you, I did see my father again and I will be back to settle a score."

I gave the man another shove against the chain link fence, climbed on my tank and gave the command to move on to Prague. I made one more stop at Oma Staffas old house. Pavel Koczian, and his wife were allowed, to live out their lives there. Since that day we maintained our friendship. I bring him sausages and Pavel serves me Vodka. He has visited me often in Berlin and I spend every vacation in Mastig. I was glad, he was allowed to live out his life in our grandmothers' house. Then I went across the street to take a look at villa Staffa. Nothing had changed inside since your mother last saw it in 1945.

Borufka was the name of the man, who kicked you out. Emmi, one of the many relatives of Franziska Borufka, your own mother. He was a policeman and turned the house into a police station into which he moved with his wife and two children. Their two children are still living in the villa Staffa today, and all of aunt Emmis' personal belongings from that time are still there."

As he told that part of the story, I saw how my mother was shaking, and shivers were running down her spine. "Then, after witnessing the carnage in Prague, nothing made sense to me anymore. I was ordered to come to Moscow. I turned down the Russians offer. I no longer wanted to participate in such barbaric destruction to keep a country under the yoke of Socialism." For a short time there seemed to be a moment of reprieve. But the full weight of communist oppression bore down on Prague and hopes of freedom for Czechoslovakia's people were dashed. Kurt went on telling stories from his endless reservoir.

"I did accept another offer, and became the translator for the Warsaw Pact generals, being fluent in Czech, Russian, Polish, German and some English, I gladly accepted the new role as interpreter. I stood beside Mikhail Gorbachev, I translated for him as he said. "Nothing makes sense anymore." As the family continued to chat amiably, I felt like an outsider looking in among all these strangers who had known each other since childhood. They brushed aside the years, and the lines in their faces seeped away like sand from bare feet. They recognized each other from years gone by. Kurt and his sisters had booked a room at a local hotel for the overnight visit. The next day, Rudi and Otto arrived and the celebrations continued.

As the family gathered and plans were hatched, it was decided that we could not just meet this one time, we would have to organize more visits every year. We planned to get together in the Spring of 1990 in Czechoslovakia.

Soviet troops were leaving the East bloc countries, as country after country they had oppressed for forty-five years threw off the shackles of Socialism. For many years, I believed that only a miracle could reunite East and West Germany and unless a miracle happened, I would never meet my cousins, while aunts and uncles were most likely deceased. The long prayed for miracle had happened after forty-five years of separation, East and West-Germany were reuniting. The Wall that had divided the German people was chiseled away. The coils of barbed wire, the world knew as the Iron Curtain, which had stretched from the Balkan countries to the Baltic Sea were rolled up and away. A narrow concrete hiking trail across which the border patrol once rode their mopeds, to keep their populace enslaved behind the barbed wire and minefields. The guards who rode with binoculars to ensure that nobody could defect from the stranglehold of Socialism. This concrete hiking trail became a favorite tourist spot.

It was the German year in which Germany celebrated its unity and freedom but even won the World Soccer/Football Championship. My mother had phoned Karen and told her. "Your little friend from across the street is coming for a little visit."

In the six months before our planned trip to Czechoslovakia I visited the East German town from where we had defected in the middle of the night on cat feet and angel wings when I was seven. A few days after Christmas I took the train back to the places I could remember, which without a border was only an hour away by car. The Iron Curtain fence was no more. The roads were being reconnected. Karen and her husband drove me around in the Russian Supercar, the Moskwitch. It rumbled through the narrow streets, where I could feel every bump in my spine. Karen warned me not to speak negatively about Socialism, because her brother and his wife were convinced of socialist righteousness. Karen's husband laughed cynically. "What socialist righteousness do we have here? Socialist righteousness is a joke and we were the biggest joke here for years. We even made jokes of the system ourselves.

Here is a joke for you, of the work ethics of socialism. "All are kept busy, but nobody is working. Although nobody is working, our socialist plans are fulfilled. Even as our plans are fulfilled, the stores shelves are empty. Even though the stores shelves are empty, everyone has something. Even though everyone has something, all are griping. Even as all are griping, everyone is happy to live in the utopian wonderland of Socialism.

That is the truth of the Socialism we had to live with. We didn't want to open our eyes to the lies, the bureaucrats have been feeding us. So, we lived like radishes, red on the outside only." We arrived at the home of Karen's brother Hans-Otto who greeted me with open arms and admired my fur coat. "It looks like life has been good for you." I smiled and said. "I gave up other things to own it." Hans Otto replied. "No matter what I give up...my wife will never own a coat like yours."

As we chatted amicably, I remembered that Hans-Otto was the boy who had thrown a stone at my forehead. He was the boy who had called me a Christian Bum. I did not mention, that I remembered this incident from a time, when we were children. This was the childhood home of Karen, which Hans-Otto now lived in with his wife and son. The old neighborhood with the cobblestone streets and houses that had not been painted since before the war looked dismally grey. The same neighbors still occupied the houses, they grew up in.

The old neighbors remembered the Staffa family, who had lived in the old school house for five years. They told me that Gerber, my father's arch nemesis, who had vainly tried to indoctrinate my father into the arms of Socialism, had fled to the west, when he realized himself, all was for naught in a world where nothing made sense.

One question that had plagued me during my early childhood, was the memory of a last Christmas here. Was it a figment of my imagination? I remember playing with dolls, a doll stroller and a dollhouse for only one day and then all was gone. I remembered the details, down to blue and white curtains and forget me not wallpaper, built with hinges on the back, so, it could be folded up like a box. I was left wondering, if that magical Christmas had ever happened at all. I remember that my mother took my toys across the street as a gift to her children.

As the children in the neighborhood were told that an American woman had come to find memorabilia of her childhood, they all gathered. I asked the children if anyone had ever seen a dollhouse. They shook their heads, and said that they remembered many toys that had been left behind. The toys had been passed around from one family and generation to the next. A red lacquered doll stroller had made the rounds for years, but none had ever seen a dollhouse. I wondered what might have happened to it. My German side told me that the doll house had to be here somewhere. Germans don't throw anything away. They repair, restore, recycle, mend and darn or give it to someone, more needy than themselves. As I described the dollhouse my father had built to these wide-eyed children, they ran excitedly on a scavenger hunt of the old school house that now had been restored to the Evangelical Church. They searched the attic of the school house under every rafter. I had just resigned myself that the dollhouse would never be found, and told the kids. "Let's just forget it, it makes no sense anymore." Just then one of the children screamed. "Here it is! I think I found it." Tucked deep underneath the rafters and despite the thick layers of dust it looked just as I remembered it.

The dollhouse my father had handcrafted for me, and had brought across the Iron Curtain at grave risk so that I would have a Christmas to remember and I did. In the years that followed our defection from East-Germany I often had a dream of a magical Christmas, in which I had a visit from Saint Nicholas, not knowing it was my father

We planned a family trip to Czechoslovaka for June. I had prepared for the seven-hour trip, packing comfortable clothes, t-shirts and jeans, hiking boots, walking shoes, and one dress for a gala dinner Kurt had arranged at the old Hample pub, the pub for riff and raff. I bought a lot of fruit to munch on and noticed that cherries were especially expensive that year. I settled for apples, grapes and bananas. My brothers' wives declined the invitation for the ride into the past, saying, "This is a journey for the Staffa clan to enjoy together as a family." I was glad because I would have had to sit in the back seat of the beautiful Mercedes, my brother had just bought and still smelled new. I felt bright-eyed and bushy-tailed, eager to discover my history and heritage, and write about it for my children's sake.

Before we left, Joe asked my eighty-year-old mother one more time. "Are you sure you don't want to come along. It is a seven-hour ride. We all want to see the house my father built, and what they have done with the wealth the Czechs stole from us."

My mother looked at Joe with sad eyes and somberly said. "No! This is my home now. It would break my heart to see what they have done to the house my husband built over a period of two years, solid enough to last for generations. He never got to enjoy the fruits of his labour. Four years later he was drafted into the Czech military. What the Nazis did not steal, the Socialists did. They took the machinery and hauled it off to Russia. After they kicked us out, they allowed four gypsy families to move in. No thank you!"

Otto and Rudi had rented a van for the trip. Joe and I followed them to Berlin, where we met up with Kurt, Margit and Christa. Like a caravan we followed them across the border into Czechoslovakia.

As we neared Mastig, from a great distance, I could see the house my father had built. It towered still prominently over this hamlet just as it had almost sixty years ago.

We rode down the main street of Mastig, and Joe pointed out the places where the stories, which I had heard around the dinner table for years, had actually taken place and I could imagine the footprints of his childhood that where still visible today. Joe pointed out the Elementary School, he had attended for six years. The sports field behind the school. The Mandl factory and adjacent Mandl villa. Marie Gernert Garden Cafe. We drove past the buildings where once my father's lumber business had been buzzing with activities.

We drove past the pond where four children had drowned. A natural spring which had been turned into a public swimming pool. We drove to the Holy Family Church, where my parents had married and we were baptized.

Kurt had arranged for crude accommodations that looked more like shacks for the seven dwarfs. It was the best available in this remote area and for this large a group. We unloaded our belongings and freshened up in what looked more like a campground toilet.

I kiddingly whispered to my brother. "What this place needs, is a little Hilton." Joe nodded and snickered. "Yeah! Just a little Hilton would be nice."

Kurt, Margit and Christa had a standing rental agreement for a cottage, in which they had spent their vacations every summer. It was the same cottage in which the British agents had once lived. Kurt explained that ever since the Prague Spring he and his family spent every vacation here.

He had ordered a dinner table for twenty at the old Hample pub, and invited the man named Borufka and his sister Mila to dine with us. Mila was a school teacher and declined the invitation. She feared for her job and any repercussions for consorting with Germans. The two had grown up in what once had been the villa Staffa. I looked puzzled and whispered. "Borufka?" Joe whispered back.

"Yeah, this guy Mika Borufka, and his siter Mila are the children of the policeman who had kicked us out of our home." Joe continued. "They came in three waves and three groups, the Czech military, the Narodny Vybor (Czech Nationalists) and local militia. Borufka was one of them, and the worst of the ilk.

First; they ordered all weapons to be turned in, a month later they searched every home suspected of hiding weapons, and anyone who resisted the search, or was found with a weapon, was shot on the spot. Finally, we were given one hour to pack our belongings, but no more than 50 kilos. At gunpoint they ordered everyone, who did not have a Czech passport out of their house. Anyone who resisted was shot. After they kicked us out, Borufka moved his wife and two children into our home in July 1945. Joe shuddered as he reflected on the past.

"I remember every horrific moment like it was yesterday.

The House My Father Built

That man, Borufka was the worst of the Narodny Vibor. Under the guise of socialist justice, he advocated wealth distribution. He claimed the house he wanted as his own and declared it as the new "police station." There was nothing anyone could do. We were glad to get away with our lives. For a month the Russian General restored some semblance of law and order, but as soon as the Russians left, all hell broke loose." I looked stunned. "Our grandmothers' maiden name was Borufka." Joe nodded and explained.

"Two Borufka sisters married German men because old age was creeping up on them and they were afraid of being labeled old spinsters. Our mother's mother, our grandmother, was kin of the Borufkas. But that clan held so much hatred for Germans. Our grandmother did not attend her own daughter's wedding to a German even though she herself had married a German. She rarely came to visit us. The parents of Mila and brother, Mika are the people, who kicked us out. Mila and her brother are his children."

Milas brother had accepted Kurt's invitation and came for dinner, but Mila declined, saying that she feared for her job as a school teacher if she associated with Germans. We shrugged our shoulders, saying. "Oh, well. That's too bad. The ancient animosity never died." I put my arms around Mila to let her know, we understood. I surmised she was embarrassed to be reminded that we were the same people who had been kicked out of our house by their father and his ilk.

We rode around in a brand new metallic blue Mercedes and pulled up in front of The Hample pub, where the Innkeeper welcomed us like royalty. Kurt and his sisters were waiting there and our host handed us the menu, written especially for us in perfect German, with a choice of Wiener Schnitzel or Fried Chicken Dinner, which he had especially prepared for us.

While local patrons sitting on barstools stared at our sumptuous banquet table, I strolled past a group of men on the way to the ladies room and heard a man say. "As soon as we have Democracy the Staffa's are back. We were back, and did not mind making a show of the fact, that we had survived a carnage their parents had inflicted on us. It was a moment of sweet vindication. Living well was sweet revenge, for what their idea of social justice and wealth distribution had done to us. After dinner, we strolled around this peaceful hamlet that had seen such horror forty-five years ago.

Rudi and Otto linked arms with me, as I struggled to walk across cobblestones wearing Italian stiletto shoes. My bold floral printed dress, with a wide swinging skirt, made for quite a show, as we strolled three abreast through the main street of Mastig. Where the only car on the road was my brother's Mercedes. Joe just let his car roll slowly ahead of us all the way to the house my father had built.

A house that still looked impressive almost fifty years later. As I looked closer, I noticed that the pale green paint was in dire need of a fresh coat. Nothing had been done to maintain the house not even a coat of paint.

Mila was not home, but her brother and his wife bade us all to enter the house. I felt, as if I had stepped inside a church. It was such an amazing experience. With every step I felt as if I was walking on hallowed ground. The man allowed us to look inside every room, even the room that had been my parents' bedroom. I stepped out on the balcony and imagined my father standing here, enjoying the view of the valley below, where the rooftops of his mother and brothers' houses were visible, and the lumber yard once bristled with activity. The factory was now used for hay storage. We climbed up into the attic and I saw my brothers' sleds and skis still tied under the rafters. It was, as if my parents had just left the house. I stepped into the kitchen and imagined my mother cooking here. I saw the cherry tree laden with fruit and I told Mika Borufka why my father had planted the tree so close to the dining room window. We settled down to chat on the garden bench and enjoyed the flowers that surrounded us. The silver and purple irises, magenta peonies, bright blue delphiniums were in bloom.

I knew these were from the roots my mother had planted. The man's wife came out with a tray of powidl pastries. She poured the coffee and passed the pastries around, which we gladly devoured, but pretended to take sips of the coffee, with a thick layer of grounds on top.

We thanked the man and his wife and left through the garden gate and I wondered if my fathers' BMW bike had ever been found underneath it. Everything inside the house was as my mother had left it forty-five years ago. Even the portraits on the walls and the flowers in the garden that were bursting forth in a profusion of the colors my mother loved. Our next stop was across the street where Kurt and his sisters were waiting for us at what had been my grandmother's old house, the house my father had grown up in.

Here was Koczian, limping toward us, greeting us warmly and offered homebrewed vodka. His wife cut up slabs of lard and chunks of bread. It was obvious that Koczian and his wife were dirt poor, but they offered us the best they had. Kurt unloaded his car and gave Pavel bottles of Schnaps and sausages to defray the cost of hospitality. I could not understand anything that was said because the men spoke a mixture of Czech and German. But it was obvious that Kurt and Pavel enjoyed a long history of solid friendship as they cajoled and drank just as heartily.

I finally asked Pavel. "I want to ask one thing. What kind of a man was my father?" Pavel looked solemn into my eyes as tears welled in his. He formed a circle with his thumb and finger and thrusting them in the air. "Your father was first class". Then he added. "Life was good when the Staffas' were here. Now we live in abject poverty. Their greed destroyed a perfect infrastructure. They squandered the wealth the German people were forced to leave behind. Once the wealth was pissed away nothing was left no industries, no jobs, no food production except what we scrape from the earth. We have nothing left and no hope. They dug a deep pit before our eyes into which they have fallen themselves." I wanted to jump up and hug him, but instead, I looked around the large kitchen with tears in my eyes as I imagined my grandmother and grandfather. My aunts and uncles and how they had lived here long ago. I noticed a picture in an adjoining room. It was an oil portrait of Pavel as a young man, holding the reins of a horse. What a handsome young man Pavel had been in his youth. "That was you? Wow, you were very handsome." His wife smiled a toothless smile and nodded. "That's the horse that kicked him!"

We hugged and wished each other well, and said good-bye, knowing we would never meet again. We drove over to Saint Anna's church, which my grandfather had built and for which my father had donated the lumber for the steeple tower. I saw the small funeral chapel with the painting of the Risen Christ and the inscription "I am the resurrection and the Life."

Kurt pointed out the spot, where four children had been buried in one mass grave. Next to it was the empty grave, where a British agent had been laid to rest. Thanks to Kurt the British were able to bring a gentlemen home to England after the war. Kurt was still proud as he proclaimed.

"I was responsible for that. I made sure the man had a proper burial."

We walked through the overgrown weeds to my grandfathers' grave and stood around the rusty broken-down wrought iron railing. Kurt and Joe set the railings upright around the grave, where once had been a marble grave plate. In its place was a cement slab. We knew, it was the spot where our grandfather Josef

Staffa, baby brother Horsti, and beautiful Hildegard had been laid to rest. We found the marble grave cover on the grave of one of my parent's tormentors, whereon the gold inscription of the name Staffa, was still visible on the side of the stolen marble plate, stolen from my grandfathers' grave. We picked forget-me-nots, and laid the sprigs on the grave and held hands, forming a circle around the crypt. We prayed the Lords' Prayer, wiped our eyes and said our final goodbyes.

The next morning, we wanted to take just one more look at the house my father had built and noticed the cherry tree was bare. Not a single cherry was left. The man came out of the house dragging a huge bag behind him. He waved for us to wait a moment. He hoisted the bag over the fence. "Here, these are for you." The bag was full of cherries, and so big the bag barely fit behind the backseat. Joe whispered. "That man must have picked cherries all night. He put a lot of work into that present. I wonder why he did this?" I wondered that myself. What had prompted the man to do this?

"You know why? Guilt. The man felt guilty for what his father had done to our father and mother. The cherries were a small repayment and the only thing he could give us in repentance." Joe nodded and concurred. "The Socialists who sought to spread our wealth and live off what riches they had confiscated, had squandered it instead. Now they live in abject poverty.

There are no jobs in this area for the younger generation. There is no one, who can rebuild the infra-structure they had destroyed.

When we arrived at my parents' house, we dragged the bag of cherries up the stairs and explained to our astonished mother, how we had been gifted with this huge bag of cherries. My mother just said. "Jessesmarren! I will be very busy making a lot of cherry perogies."

My father glanced at the bag. "Papa, these are the cherries from the tree you planted in front of the house you built." He just smiled meekly, gave me a puzzled look. I knew he had not comprehended a word I had said. He murmured softly as his eyes fixed on a large porcelain crucifix hanging above the foot of his bed. "Jesus, take me home. Only in my dream can I be where I belong.

I want to be in my beloved home in Czechoslovakia. Only in Czechoslovakia can I be at home." He drifted off to sleep, and went home to his sacred soil in Czechoslovakia.

Printed in the USA
CPSIA information can be obtained
at www.ICGtesting.com
LVHW052256050524
779270LV00005B/4